McNaughten

McNaughten

A NOVEL BY
SIÂN BUSBY

This paperback edition published in 2010

First published in 2009 by

Short Books
3A Exmouth House
Pine Street
EC1R 0JH

10 9 8 7 6 5 4 3 2 1

Copyright © Siân Busby 2009

A CIP catalogue record for this book is available from the British Library.

ISBN 978-1-906021-88-7
Every effort has been made to obtain permission
for material in this book. If any errors have unwittingly occurred,
we will be happy to correct them in future editions.

For Robert, who knows why...

"We have it in our power to begin the world over again."
Thomas Paine

"There are strings in the human heart that had better not be vibrated."
from *Barnaby Rudge* by Charles Dickens (1841)

Note on Historical Background

THE EVENTS recorded here occurred during the terrible winter of 1842-3, described so memorably by Charles Dickens in *A Christmas Carol*. 1842 had been one of the worst years of the century: the mass movement for parliamentary democracy (Chartism) had prompted a national wave of strikes and violent demonstrations, and was met with swift and harsh retribution; two assassination attempts were made on Queen Victoria; there was war in China and Afghanistan, failed harvests, high unemployment and a massive trade deficit. There was also dissent among the middle classes.

At the end of the Napoleonic Wars, a system of duties called the "Corn Laws" had been introduced in order to protect the domestic corn market from foreign competition. Operating in the interest of the landowning aristocracy and agriculture, the Laws kept the price of bread high – at a time of unprecedented unemployment and famine. To supporters of the Anti-Corn Law League, the Corn Laws were a hated symbol of class division and a threat to the future prosperity of the nation.

Sir Robert Peel, the Tory Prime Minister, recognised the economic and humanitarian necessity to end protectionism; but his was the party of the landed interest to whom reform of the Corn Laws was anathema. As the argument for and against Free Trade raged, the cries of distress grew ever louder. By January 1843 they had reached a crescendo, and threatened to roll out in a terrible thunder across the whole land.

Dramatis Personae

Daniel McNaughten......................................A Scotch Wood-turner

Samuel Warren, L.L.D..Barrister-at-Law

Edward Drummond, Esq..............Secretary to the Prime Minister

Inspector Samuel Hughes ("A" Division)..An Inspector of Police

Alexander "Cockie" Cockburn, Q.C.............The Buck of the Bar

Miss Drummond.......................................A Devoted Sister

Mr. Renton Nicholson..............................A Print-seller and Rogue

Mr. Bransby Cooper

Mr. Guthrie senior   } ....A trio of Society Doctors

Mr. Guthrie junior

James Parrott..A Footman

Inspector John Massey Tierney

    of the Active Duty.....................................A Plainclothesman

"Carlo"..A Villain

Mrs. Eliza Dutton...A Madwoman

Abram Duncan (the "Gray Goose").............................A Chartist

P.C. James Silver (A63)....................................A Police Constable

(maknaw'ten) n. ~ rules (Eng. Law) rules dating from Regina v. McNaughten (1843), under which mental abnormality relieves from criminal responsibility only if the person did not know what he was doing or did not know that what he was doing was wrong.

CHARING-CROSS,
SHORTLY BEFORE FOUR O'CLOCK P.M.

It was the Season of Distress; it was the Age of Famine and Over-populousness; it was the Time of Smoking Chimneys and Railroads; of Slums and Brickbats, Monster Charters and Bread Riots; of New Model Prisons and Poor Law Bastilles. The world was coming to an end, but a thin young man of shabby genteel appearance, Scotch, a wood-turner by trade, had an idea how to save it and make it whole again. An ellipse; a geometric eccentricity; something intricate and beautiful: a new law for a new world. First, though, he had to plane the surface of the old: for one cannot, you see, do good work on a poor surface.

He was standing on a freezing corner at the Centre of the Empire waiting for the portly gentleman to leave the counting-house: ready to do his duty, ready, finally, to be happy. His name was Daniel McNaughten and he was dressed in worn-out Blücher boots, threadbare trowsers and a thin dark overcoat. He looked like one more mechanic out of a situation (which, in a way, he was) – unremarkable in every regard, save for the fact that he was hatless and held the dead-weight of a brace of pistols against his breast.

Charing-cross was freezing: a keen north wind bringing sleet from the river; the light like dirty ice. It was the last business hour of the day, and in the rich warm glow of the counting-house he marked the comings and goings of the gentlemen in their thick-heeled boots; the hiss of their cigar-ends dropped casually by the entrance for the old cigar-end-finder to retrieve. And he marked the people going on – just as they always did – resigned as the steam of horses' breath, oblivious to the raw imploring palms of the tract-sellers and the sledge-beggars huddled about King Charles's statue, slumped against the icy palings around the Nelson Column.

He reached into his pocket and brought out a wee token, tossing it up in the air. Heads; tails: he didn't mind how it came down; it was all the same to him. He no longer believed in fate. He believed in infallible things: the laws of nature, physical, intellectual, moral. He tossed the coin to fill the time, that was all – the time spent waiting.

"Fusee for your cigar, sir?"

A raggit urchin was tugging on his coat-sleeve: just like all the others, barefoot, niddered, pinched blue by cold. McNaughten reached into his weskit pocket and dropped a whole shilling into the wee shivering hand, but he did not take the fusees – he had no need of them. The child blinked up at him in stupefaction, but he was not moved by gratitude. He went back to waiting, waiting for the portly gentleman to leave the counting house. Heads up; tails down.

We can judge the heart of a man, he was thinking, by his treatment of others.

He hunched his shoulders now, cupping his hands in front of his mouth. He was pacing to keep warm, his teeth chattering. He was wishing that he had not lost his hat. He was wishing that he had flitted off – taken the railway to Greenock, slipped on board a barque bound for New York, Jamaica, Shanghai.

Is this, he thought, is this how we might make ourselves happy?

And behind him the steeple of St. Martin in the Field expelled a tell-tale creaking, a hint of rust. Soon it would be four o'clock, and yet no sign of Mr. Drummond. The portly gentleman was a creature of habit: it was not like him to be untimely. A metallic rasp from the bell-tower; an oily grinding: a few minutes more and the peeler would be rounding Scotland-yard and the whole plot fankit. He was thinking how his father was right: how everything he attempted was doomed to end in failure. He was thinking: I am not worthy of happiness.

What might he have done? What could he have hoped for? Now that he knew there was no just God looking down, now that he knew this was all there was, he wished, he wished more than ever that there was a way to plane the surface of the mind so's ye could start over. He wished, o he wished that he could cease the chug of his thoughts. If only, if only, he thought, he could have stayed the same, and the world made different. On the frozen corner everything was crystallising, hard and cold, frost-bright: so clear it hurt. He clutched the wee token in his fist and wished that he could stop himself from seeing, feeling.

When he looked up, there was the portly gentleman, standing in the doorway of the counting-house, bulbous, red, smoothing his jabot as he looked about him; a crafty wee smile on his chops.

"Fusee for your cigar, sir?"

The portly gentleman scowled, muttered, waved the wean aside. He set his old-fashioned wide-brimmed hat upon his bald pate, and with a complicit nod began to walk down Charing-cross towards Downing-street.

You can judge the heart of a man. *You can judge the heart...*

McNaughten tossed up the token one last time, and set off after him. To be is to do, he told himself as he wrapped his long, delicate fingers about the first pistol.

A brilliant flash knocking him back a step or two, resolving into a broken star of sparks; a crack clear and flat, hanging in the brief silence before the noise of the traffic cascaded once more: the cries, the whin-nying, the peeler shouting from the other side of the carriage track. The portly gentleman spun in surprise at a flame licking at his coat-tails. He put one hand to his side and a small curl of smoke, rising like a feather on a breath, slipped from beneath his palm.

And as McNaughten reached for the second pistol it was as though one precise line was gradually declining into another right before his eyes. The graceful ascent of the curves, the subtle eccentricity: the manufacture of a new order. And in that moment he truly believed that he was witnessing, in the intricate beauty of a new beginning, the un-fathomable architecture of belonging.

WHITEHALL,
A LITTLE EARLIER IN THE DAY

In which we meet Mr. Warren, the author, and discover the true price of Corn.

Eight years had elapsed since the destruction by fire of the old Palace of

Westminster, and yet those ancient, noble precincts of public life were still nothing more than a ramshackle affair of burnt ruins and tipsy scaffoldings: a fitting symbol, as it were, for the Condition of England in January 1843. Certainly it seemed so to Samuel Warren, L.L.D., (Barrister-at-law, Inner Temple) as he passed them by on his way to dine with the Prime Minister's Private Secretary at Bellamy's chop-house.

He was at that time a handsome and ambitious man of five-and-thirty, who had long since recovered from the inebriation of the Conservative triumph of '41. He had waited so long for the Toryism to which he cleaved to be a term of reproach no longer, sitting out those wearisome years of Whig jobbery and Utilitarianism. But now that Tory government had been a hard fact for a full nineteen months, Mr. Warren had discovered how laced with bitterness were triumph's libations.

The country was in a mess, but it was *our* mess now, not *theirs*. It was not possible to turn back the clock and pretend that Parliamentary Reform and all the wretchedness that had ensued from it had never happened. The Whigs had enfranchised a quarter of the nation's householders, who were not all like us. Of course Mr Warren understood that nobody now in government wished to return to the rancour, the tedium, the sheer despondency of the Opposition Benches; this was why popular necessities – *bread and butter matters*, if you will – had become the order of the day. Whether you called yourself Whig, Tory, Liberal, Ultra, or Radical, the futility of your promises, the insincerity of your opinions, were all that was true and certain – *that is*, so long as they satisfied the whims of the lowly ten-guinea voter and mollified the dangers of democracy.

Mr. Warren mulled upon this as he walked on, marking with disapproval the skeletal figures raking through the icy rubble, the workmen leaning on their shovels, idle, listless. The new St. Stephen's Tower had been so long under supposititious construction that it was by now more dilapidated than the structure it sought to displace. The quicksands kept claiming the foundations; the architects kept running out of money; the masons kept downing tools. Nothing progressed, ever. It was all so *dispiriting*. For a gentleman such as he, one who nursed ambitions in respect of public life, there was an objectionable whiff of hopelessness in wondering (as he always did whenever he found himself in the vicinity of Westminster) whether he should live long enough to see the new Palace from the vantage point of a seat in the Chamber.

He shuddered: breathing in that claggy gloom that perpetually cloaks old Thorney Island; regarding with dismay the drab hoardings with their fly-posted advertisements for Holloway's pills and Tussaud's wax-works shoring up the whole rackety enterprise. He sighed to see the crooked exhortations to ATTEND TO THE END OF THE WORLD and STICK NO BILLS, and he thought: *That's everything that's wrong with the country; that's the whole sordid mess right there*.

He was waiting to cross the carriage-way. It was snowing, as it always seemed to be. On a patch of frozen ground near to St. Margaret's Church, a tatterdemalion party were crowing against the "Bread Tax". One of them, a stunted grubby fellow in a decrepit shovel hat, such as an old-fashioned country parson might wear, was waving a blood-smeared loaf atop a sort of pike. He was so begrimed it was impossible to tell if he was a black or a white, yet he was not the worst of that feckless assembly that had somehow escaped transportation to Van Diemen's Land with all the others of that ilk. The best that could be said of them was that they did not look drunk, though they were certainly idle. They were meagre types: small tradesmen defeated by the numerous distresses of the times, a miscellany of moleskin and kerseymere, and nine-and-four-penny Wellington boots.

"Avenge the plundered poor!" cried one.

"The Bread Tax murders trade and hope," cried another.

"Why should the starving pay to the aristocracy a penny on every pound of bread?"

Mr. Warren sighed. The specious arguments put by the Anti-Corn Law League had wreaked havoc upon the public understanding of complex matters; playing up common fears and hazy assumptions to such a swell that, in truth, Mr. Warren rather pitied the ragged democratists. He considered engaging them in a purposeful debate. *Cheap Bread and Cheap Wages will be found together*! he would have proclaimed. But back then, on that fateful day, he was a young man in a hurry, and so he contented himself with raising a critical eyebrow at the crew as he crossed the road.

The events soon to be related occurred (it will be recollected) but a few months after the Holiday Insurrection of '42 – the so-called "*legal revolution*". Mr. Warren had written extensively, in *Blackwoods* and *The Times* &c., &c., of how this rascally contrariety had been contrived at by a coterie of rapacious Northern factory-owners – every one of whom was a subscriber to the Anti-Corn Law League – who had compelled their labourers by gross tyranny (with factory lock-outs and threats to reduce wages) to promote agitation in every town in the land. In an attempt to preserve the rule of law, the Office of Home Affairs under the command of the Home Secretary had caused to be established a secret police network, and spies – the agents of governmental vigilance – were now everywhere to be found. Or so it was rumoured, for no official notice was ever made of this retributive measure; and in the majority of instances, this rumoured existence was sufficient prohibition in itself.

Mr. Warren's considerable and considered reportage of all of the above – under the *alias* FIAT JUSTITIA – had attached something of a reputation to himself. He thundered against the plainclothesmen with the same strenuous argument he had previously mustered against the incompetencies of the Scotland-yard bobbies (who now assumed a more benign aspect than they had previously enjoyed). And he blazoned everywhere that the Anti-Corn Law League was not (as might popularly have been supposed) a kindly organisation dedicated to bringing cheap bread to the starving masses, but rather one of the greatest threats yet faced by a civilised nation. In truth there was scarce any man alive who knew more of the nefarious intentions of that devillish combination than did he. And Mr. Warren doubted not that it was this that had caused the invitation to dine with the Prime Minister's Private Secretary to be issued.

Yet, as he approached the shop-house steam of Bellamy's, that earnest and principled young man found his thoughts assuming a somewhat anxious cast. He had no doubt that his reputation preceded him, and yet he could not help but wonder what *true purpose* lay behind the request. He was not nearly worldly enough, but he knew enough of the world to understand that in the political sphere not so much as a pinch of snuff is ever given freely and unstintingly. What then, would be the due recompense of sharing a spot of dinner with one who sat at the very hub of power?

Having no family connections of which to speak and none of the advantages of an expensive education to draw upon, everything Mr. Warren had he had made for himself. At that time the tally was thus: letters after his name; a practice in a dismal attic chambers, honoured with but a very few briefs, and those only in cases slightly productive of fees; pupils, not many; and a clerk, neither smart nor particularly able. He had long been constrained, therefore, to nib his pen in the interests of economic survival at a level commensurate with getting on. But in the eyes of the benchers of the Inner Temple, writing was a trade and a damnable low one at that, and *noms de plume* a necessary precaution against debarment. FIAT JUSTITIA was his just-respectable-enough mask; and when it came to earning money, he depended upon his far less acceptable *alter ego*: "The Author of *Diary of a London Physician*", the recounter of bits of "flash" nonsense (murder, madness, hauntings, body-snatching) and creator of a popular periodical novel. It will be appreciated that such a man as Mr. Warren had little enough to do or say with the judgements which others formed of him and his usefulness to them; had even less to say or do with what they might ask of him, or what he might ask of them in return. In short, he was enslaved to the task of getting on as surely as any poor plantation nigger.

In his published musings upon the topic of Corn, Free Trade and Protectionism, Mr. Warren had been not one iota more tolerant of the government than he had been of the Anti-Corn Law League. This had seemed to him to be a necessary, not to say lucrative, stock-in-trade; but now he was wondering how sensible he had been. Was he, he wondered, about to be chastised for his disloyalty to the party of his choice? He considered the likelihood that the gentleman with whom he was about to dine – Mr. Drummond of the Treasury – might share his own low opinion of the Prime Minister whom he served as Private Secretary. Certainly, Mr. Warren was not alone amongst respectable Tories in regarding Sir Robert Peel as a Janus, a low ambidexter, who dined at the Carlton with a protectionist peer on a Tuesday only to take tea at the House with Mr. Cobden of the League and a party of northern millocrats on a Wednesday.

Mr. Warren had once considered the Prime Minister to be a great man – a very great man – even an honest one; but since his return to power, Sir Robert Peel had kept his political principles as finely balanced between Whig and Tory as the celebrated Indian Juggler balanced balls on his chin. The introduction of the Income Tax at 7d in the £ had come like the booming of a knell; but the unforgiveable tampering with the Sliding Scale on foreign corn imports had given rise to grave concerns that the Prime Minister was now poised to do the unimaginable, *to whit*: dispense with the Corn Laws altogether!

It was occurring to Mr. Warren that he had been summoned to Bellamy's in order that he might be persuaded to view the Corn Laws as an unjust monopoly &c., &c., the surrender of which would mitigate the sufferings of the masses at a pinch, and other such humbugs. He fancied that he understood the ways of Westminster – its laws and amenities the same as any other calling in which dirty work and back-stair influence must be paid in kind – and he wondered what inducement Mr. Drummond might offer to him in exchange for which he might assume a stance more acceptable to the Prime Minister. All men desire fame, power, wealth, and as he prepared to enter Bellamy's, Mr. Warren knew that he had never before been so close to those things – nor so far from them. A decisive hour awaited him. And crossing the threshold into the habanah-fugged domain of influence he felt a quickening in his breast.

Bellamy's was busy, but with the new Parliamentary session almost a fortnight off, and most of the Honourable Members still at their country retreats, it was nothing like the ruthless crush of rumour and gossip it would become in but a few days' time. No clusters of committee witnesses; no lawyers and their clients; no agents looking shifty; no Members lounging in reprehensible disarray as they waited for the division bell to summon them: just a few of the more incorrigible Westminster types partaking of a tender smoking steak and full-bodied Madeira.

Mr. Warren came upon the Secretary quite by accident: an unpresumptuous man of rather full figure, ensconced in a secluded corner and intent upon a large Nankin plate of saddle of mutton with a glass of sherry at his elbow. Mr. Drummond, for his part, had already spied out his guest. He had half-risen from his seat, wearing the same convivial half-smile he almost always wore in public; he smoothed his jabot and proffered a hand in greeting. He was dressed very old-fashioned, as was his custom: a little like a Quaker, in a suit of sober black knee-breeches, below which sat worsted stockings of the same colour, ending in a pair of wide-buckled shoes – all of which lent to him the faded, neglected appearance of something put away in an Exchequer cupboard thirty years before. He appeared quite mild of manner and was quite bald, apart from two surprising profusions of jet-black hair running either side of his round head and meeting at the back; an olive complexion, offset by ruddy smudges upon each cheek, mirrored in a queer symmetry by two thick dark rectangles that appeared to be have been stuck just so above his eyes; eyes that were dark and welcoming, even kindly at first, giving less and less away the longer one tried to engage them.

"How do you do," he said in the manner of one who wishes to come straight to business. "I'm delighted to meet you. *Delighted.*"

A deft, subtle raising of one jet-black eyebrow immediately summoned the waiter from the other side of the busy room: the only hint at the influence delitescent behind the amiable smile.

"No-one could accuse you of being a *latitudinous* thinker, Mr. Warren," the Secretary began in a perfect mildness of tone. He had taken his seat and was giving all of his benign attentions to his mutton. His guest made a little acquiescent bow, presuming this to be a compliment, and requested of the waiter one of Bellamy's excellent clarets and a bowl of mock-turtle. "It appears that when you speak in your essays of Tories, you mean those Honourable Members who will brook no further tampering with the price of corn – no matter what the cost to the nation."

Mr. Warren stroked his top lip circumspectly. "I suppose," he replied, "you could say that my concern is for the Old Party, sir." At which the Secretary pursed his smile. "I consider," continued Mr. Warren, "Toryism to be the only bulwark against the revolutionary effects of the Reform Bill."

"Eight years in the political wilderness," Mr. Drummond said, turning a piece of gristle over with his fork, "has had its effect upon the Old Party. I am not at all sure that things are precisely the same as they were – or will ever be so again."

"But protection of the Landed Interest by means of the Corn Laws, surely, that is still an article of faith among Tory gentlemen…"

"You are certainly very orthodox for such a young man," said Mr. Drummond. "Where were you at school?"

Mr. Warren ran a hand through his thick dark curls.

"Manchester," he confessed.

The Secretary glanced up from his plate. "The grammar school…!"

"My father had at the time the living at Ancoats."

Mr. Drummond pulled a little face. "Well, then you are to be commended."

The soup arrived, but not the claret, and the Secretary returned his attentions to the mutton, attacking it with relish now. After a few moments he said, "I presume you've heard about the Parliamentary Radicals... we learned just last week that they intend to commence the new session with a demand for nothing less than the free import of foreign corn."

Mr. Drummond, his bald head bent over his plate, spent some time chewing over a forkful of mutton, leaving Mr. Warren to consider his response. "Doubtless," he observed at last, "Lord John Russell and the Whigs shall side with Mr. Cobden and the Radical flank."

The Secretary did not look up. He dabbed at his mouth with his napkin.

"O, they will start baying for Repeal as soon as Her Majesty's Speech from the throne is over," he said, with no trace of irritation. "They will do everything they can to embarrass the government and put it in a tight spot. Everything they can to foster discord in our ranks." He looked up, his large dark eyes levelled with those of his guest. "Nothing," he said, "nothing is more divisive than corn."

Mr. Warren felt a slight prickling, as though he were being challenged. He took a desultory mouthful of the soup and wished the waiter would hurry up with the wine. "Is it true," he said, "that Sir Robert Peel has agreed to lead a coalition of interests with the liberal Tories and the Whigs?"

Mr. Drummond smiled at his mutton. "Is that what's being said? Tut tut: the utter nonsense that is put about the place! The Prime Minister is of the opinion that we must make this a cheap country in which to live, that is all. The People, you see, my dear *FIAT*

[22]

JUSTITIA, the People are starving."

It had become quite the fashion to affect sympathy for the poor: it was, for instance, regularly put about that Sir Robert Peel made donations from his own pocket to the relief of Paisley. Mr. Warren considered inquiring whether the Secretary gave to every beggar he passed on the streets.

"Three failed harvests," Mr. Drummond continued matter-of-factly, "industry in decline; a serious diminution of consumption in those articles which contribute to the public revenue; a falling off in the Excise equal to two millions and a half; a total deficiency of five millions and a half. A fourth part of the population of Carlisle dying of famine. The town of Paisley entirely bankrupt. In Stockport five thousand working men and their families in distress. In Leeds the pauper stone-heap standing at 150,000 tons. D'ye know, my dear sir, the guardians are giving the paupers six shillings per week for doing nothing, rather than seven shillings and sixpence for breaking any more stones? Imagine! In manufacturing centres all over the country the Poor Rate stands at upwards of fifty per cent, and every week tradesmen who might in better times have sustained it, must now resort to it in order to support themselves and their families. It is chaos," said Mr. Drummond, pronouncing the verdict with perfect equanimity of tone. "Chaos. And it occurs to me that something must be done – and done soon. Protectionism has had its day. Repeal is inevitable – a question of when, not if." He tapped with his knife the clean line he had created down the middle of his plate. "The Centre, you see, the Centre demands it."

"But Repeal of the Corn Laws will split the Party," said Mr. Warren.

"Poor Party," said Mr. Drummond with considerable feeling. "And how are we to save her?"

It was very fortunate that the wine arrived just at that moment. Mr. Warren took a long draft and the opportunity to think out his next move. He set his glass down with great purpose and said: "What, precisely, do you want of me?"

Mr. Drummond was smiling at the gravy. "We are gentleman," he said. "We understand each other. Yes?"

"But of course…"

"*Facta non verba*," said Mr. Drummond. "A precipitous occurrence – some discrediting event that will damage the reputation of the League – you follow my meaning, yes?"

Mr. Warren dabbed at his nose and brow with his napkin, and poured himself another glass of claret. He was feeling rather queasy.

"You mean – like the Holiday Insurrection?" he dared to venture.

"O dear me no! No, no," said Mr. Drummond, aghast, laying down his knife and fork. "No more Monster Mobs. Far too costly. Besides, it seems the Radicals may foment discontent all they wish by now: the People are having none of it." Mr. Drummond withdrew into his seat, smoothing his jabot. "The People want Free Trade," he continued benignly. "The People want cheap bread. The People want things to appear to be fair and decent. They do *not* wish to destroy society! Why, this isn't France! You see, my dear young fellow, in this country, political trouble is never truly alarming. Far from it: in general it is all rather good for government. Why, look at the unfortunate Spencer Perceval as a case in point: there never was a more despised Prime Minister until, that is, he was assassinated by that madman Bellingham in the lobby. I tell you, sir, when it comes to it, the vast majority of English people like to see the government deal harshly with madmen and rabble-rousers." Smiling, Mr. Drummond momentarily resumed his repast. "Economical discontent, however," he said, suddenly lowering his fork, "any trouble boiling out of taxes or bread or unemployment, ah now; *that* is a wholly different order of danger. What is required in such cases is a useful distraction: a straightforward outrage to common decency – something that will remind the People of England how much they love and respect the Law."

Mr. Warren ran a hand through his thick mop of dark curls. They were rather damp. It was stultifyingly warm in the close interior of the chop-house. He reached for the decanter and poured himself another glass of claret.

"What if I were to tell you," said Mr. Drummond, "that since the summer Sir Robert Peel goes in terror of his life?" Mr. Warren did not wish to appear obtuse. He mopped his brow with his napkin. It was an effort not to perspire. "Were you aware that at the League's convention last summer it was suggested that lots be drawn in order to see which of a hundred men might kill him?"

Mr. Warren said he was very shocked to hear it.

The Secretary continued, "And did you know that during the Queen's visit to Edinburgh in October, a Mob crying for cheap bread attacked the Prime Minister's carriage? O yes. I saw it with my own eyes. Why, perhaps you might care to write something of that. I can supply you with all the details. What is more, it is part of my official duty to open all of the Prime Minister's correspondence, and I can tell you, sir, he receives a good many vile threats of the blackest shade. As a matter of fact, I keep a file about me containing the most dreadful. Only this morning we received a choice example! Would you care to see it?"

Mr. Warren nodded mutely.

The Secretary smacked his lips and wiped his chin, then, discarding his napkin with a flourish, reached into his coat and withdrew a copy of Malthus's *Essay on Population*, bound in dark green hard grain. He placed it upon the table between them and patted the marbled sides.

"The security of anything contained within these pages is vouch-safed, my dear fellow," he said, "for the simple reason that nobody in his right mind would ever *think* of looking there!"

"It is certainly a very dreary volume," said Mr. Warren.

Mr. Drummond chuckled lightly as he took up the book by its spine and gave it a little shake. The uncut pages fell away in a sort of fan, revealing a series of little pockets into which a number of documents had been slipped. "Only economic scientists and Whigs could possibly see any merit in this worthless essay," he said. "Not to say build an entire system for managing the population on the basis of a fundamental error in calculation factors." He withdrew a thin, slippery sheet of writing paper from one of the pockets. "*Dominus providebit*, Mr. Warren," he was saying; "the one non-variable: *the Lord will Provide*. I wonder how the Reverend Dr. Malthus could possibly have overlooked *that*."

He passed the sheet across the table. In a crooked, spidery hand were written the words: *Let us kill him and we'll have corn at our own price*. Coriolanus, I i. Mr. Warren swallowed hard as Mr. Drummond slipped the letter back inside the uncut pages of the volume.

"Tut tut," he said, withdrawing his watch from his fob. He shook it vigorously a couple of times, and held it to his ear. "Is that the time?"

The waiter came and cleared the table. He set down the bill before Mr. Warren. It was rather large: the claret alone came to ten shillings. The Secretary was busy replacing his watch in his fob and fitting a pair of plain black woollen mittens, smiling benignly all the while. He made no protest as his guest, not wishing to be the cause of any embarrassment, reached into his pocket.

"I shall be late for my four o'clock cabinet with the Prime Minister," the Secretary said, rising from the table and reaching for his hat. "And I have still to call upon my brother at the bank. It was most interesting to meet with you, Mr. Warren. Most interesting." He shook Mr. Warren by the hand, and then smoothed his jabot. "Most interesting..."

Mr. Warren watched the portly figure in the old-fashioned hat pick his way almost daintily across the room. He observed how subtly he acknowledged the subtle acknowledgements of others: how assuredly he gave not a thing away.

Strange now to think that within the hour the gentleman would be done for.

GARDINER'S-LANE STATION-HOUSE, DEVIL'S ACRE,
APPROXIMATELY QUARTER-PAST FOUR O'CLOCK P.M.

In which we learn that "all things should be done honestly, and by order." 1 Corinthians 14:40

Inspector Hughes of the "A" Division (Whitehall) was tired long before the Constable appeared before him in the station-house with the pistols and the Scotch maniac. To begin with there was the weather. Ho! Nothing meagre about the weather! The weather replete with an abundance of bitterness, a thick tangle of sharp frosts, a heavy burden of deep snows, and all the signs that a long and dirty thaw was to follow. Everyone was in agreement that it was as bad a winter as they could ever remember. Everywhere you looked it was upon badness and misery; the rotten and dank, raw and broken, lean and hungry parts of life strewn all about like vitals in a shambles, and although there were still a few angry souls left over after the exertions of the summer – going about the place ranting and raving, refusing to lie down and wait for it to pass over – for the most part the general tone of life on the streets of the Metropolis was one of resignation. Of forces spent; of things ground down, coming to an end.

And so, like everyone else, he dared say, Inspector Hughes was feeling tired long before the prisoner was brought to stand before him in the little railed dock, his arms fastened behind his back in the iron grip of Police Constable Silver (A63). Tired of the mortal cold laying siege to the paving stones; tired of moving on the mendicants from the steps of the government buildings on Whitehall; tired of the clerks out of a situation, the tradesmen on their way to pop their tools; the screevers with their ominous chalked messages, and the poor old orange and apple women, and the little skinny children tugging on his sleeve. O, he was tired of the whole lot, struggling to live on the pennies tossed to 'em. O yes, the Inspector was tired of the prisoner and his gaunt famished features long before he heard what he had done.

Behind the little counter he turned up his toes inside the unrelenting leather of his regulation-issue Wellington boots and allowed his long skinny legs to sag at the knee. Leaning on a pile of seditious pamphlets, he took a moment or two, as he always did, to look hard at the prisoner. He set a great deal by first impressions, and after thirteen years in the Force his instincts for a person were as well honed as a welt-cutter's tools. He had heard a deal of moonshine talked about how bad men will never look you in the face, but he knew well enough, as did all of the better sort of police officer, how wickedness'd stare at you out of an honest-seeming countenance any day of the week.

He could draw his own inference from the prisoner's gaze, how it was fixed on some point in the middle distance; how it was neither especially resolute, nor hardened; but soft, soft as a drizzle of rain on a spring morning. He made a mental note of the youth's features, making a comparison between the gaunt figure before him now in the worn, close-buttoned coat, the air of quiet desperation, and them copious descriptions of incendiarists and deserters he pored over each week in the *Police Gazette*.

"He's a Scotchman and he ain't said nothing political," said Constable Silver, as if reading the Inspector's thoughts. "Fact he ain't said nothing much at all." Silver laid a pair of pocket pistols on the ledger desk and then stood to attention to make the formal announcement for the record. "The prisoner was taken in the act of firing a pistol at Mr. Edward Drummond of Lower Grosvenor-street, senior clerk to the Treasury, at five minutes before four o'clock outside the Salopian coffee-house, number 41, Charing-cross."

Inspector Hughes turned down the corners of his mouth.

"The Salopian, eh," he said. "The Superintendent shan't care to hear that."

The Salopian coffee-house stood at that time directly across the carriage-way from Scotland-yard – the headquarters of the Metropolitan Police Force. The Inspector knew the Salopian same as he knew every other doorway of Charing-cross, every inch of Whitehall's gleaming strip, every nook and cranny of those dismal streets that abutted and surrounded it. He knew them better than he did the rooms of his own home. When I die, he always said, I reckon they could use my feet to make a map of London from Trafalgar-square down to Westminster Bridge. How his children laughed at that! But that was the truth of it. He knew them streets so well that he had only to step past the mean rents of the Devil's Acre, wind his way down them crooked lanes that run from Westminster to the station-house, to *feel* trouble seep in at the welt of his Wellington-boots, spread up his legs and settle in his bones.

The Inspector had inklings: he always had inklings, but this – this, he thought, this I never had a whisper of.

Unable to deduce anyhing, for the moment, from the prisoner, Inspector Hughes turned his thoughts to the Salopian. He was pondering his knowledge of the place, the significances perhaps only a Whitehall man would grasp – which were a sight more 'n chess and glasses of salep. The Greenwich mail put down right outside and a lot of gentlemen up from the country liked to keep a room there, seeing as it was so convenient for Westminster. Whig Members had resorted there during the late election, whilst their new Pall Mall club-house was having the finishing touches put to it.

Now then – Whigs and country gentlemen, thought the Inspector, his mind running on, as was inevitable in a policeman, running on to suspicious circumstances, to corn, to controversy, to numerous agitations. O, it was easy enough to put the pieces together like a dissected map.

But something, he sensed, something was missing.

He peered harder at the woebegone spectacle in the dock before him.

The lad was as commonplace as cabbage. The Inspector passed daily a countless number just the same: poor and hungry, hungry enough to do anything. And that, he thought, was what was wrong with the world: too many hungry young men idling about Charing-cross. He chided himself, knowing all too well that this is what comes of passing by without a second thought.

"In the pursuance of my beat-route," the Constable was saying, "I had just rounded the Yard, and was about to cross the carriage-way in order to continue in a southerly direction along the west-side of Charing-cross towards Whitehall, when I heard the report of a pistol on the other side of the road. I immediately looked in the direction of the commotion and saw a cloud of black smoke and a gentleman reeling on the pavement outside the Salopian coffee-house. His coat-tails were on fire and I saw what looked like a piece of paper burning on the pavement at his feet. The gentleman was pointing at the prisoner here, whom I could plainly see was drawing a second pistol from inside his coat. I dashed across the carriage-way and was on him quicker than an electric spark running down a telegraph wire."

Inspector Hughes knew nothing about telegraphs; nor electric sparks neither, come to that. He opened the Police Report Sheet Ledger and wrote the date and time upon a clean page, glancing up to gauge the prisoner's height from the measure on the wall behind the dock. The glimmer of a queer sort of smile was playing about the prisoner's thin lips and, spying it, the Inspector rocked back on his thick heels to take in the whole fellow once more.

"I make that five foot and eight inches," he said when he had seen enough. Then he reached across and dipped his pen in the inkwell.

"When cautioned," the Constable was saying, "the prisoner responded: 'Now he' – or it might have been she – 'now he shall not break my peace of mind any longer.'"

"He or she," said the Inspector, his pen hovering above the ledger, a black bead of ink poised expectantly at the tip of the nib. "Well, Constable, which is it to be?"

He was well aware that he was irritable. It was Friday. He'd been in his boots too long. He'd been looking forward to sitting down on the high stool, resting his feet on his topper for a couple of hours while he made out an inventory of some inflammatory anti-bread tax publications seized from a scabrescent print-shop on Holywell-street. He'd hoped to occupy himself in this manner until six o'clock at the very latest, ensuring he was well away before the first dismal troop of night-charges appeared in an untidy line at the station-house door. He'd hoped to go home early for a change, listen to the children say their prayers, enjoy a spot of dinner with the missus; lend a hand with the mangling (for she was very near her time).

Well, Sam, he thought, you can forget about all of that: there ain't no chance of this finishing early.

P.C. Silver's youthful features were a crease of perplexity. He had taken off his stove-pipe hat to scratch his head.

"Well, now," he was saying, "I thought at first that he said 'she' –"

He glanced at the prisoner, who was keeping cank.

"I dare say I must have misheard him," said Silver with a telling uncertainty.

"All the same, Constable," the Inspector said sternly, as the bead of ink dripped impatient onto the ledger page, "I must write down exactly what you heard – or thought you heard. That's the proper procedure, see." And with a lob lolly like this 'un, he thought, it will be even more necessary than usual to be mindful of the proper procedure; for it always goes big where the Quality's concerned, and you don't get more Quality – leastways not out of Season you don't – than Mr. Drummond of the Treasury.

He recorded the Constable's recollections on the line beneath the ink blot, then he picked up the pistols and inspected each of them in turn. They were a mismatched pair of poor-quality duellers; smooth-bore, not rifled. The one that had been fired at Mr. Drummond, the smaller of the pair, was an old flintlock that had been modified to take a percussion cap over the priming hole. Inspector Hughes didn't approve of percussion caps: if the flintlock was good enough for the British Army then it oughter be good enough for a common street ruffian.

"How far was the prisoner from Mr. Drummond?"

Silver considered. "About fifteen paces – give or take."

Inspector Hughes looked over at the prisoner. "He must be a good shot," he said, taking loose aim with the smaller of the pair. "These ain't made for accuracy unless they're fired off at a very short range." He made the observation for the benefit of the young Constable, for he liked to impart knowledge whenever he could, and knew that Silver had no experience of firearms having never been in the army – unlike Inspector Hughes who had had the misfortune to serve out seven years as a hunger conscript. "See," he explained, "it ain't considered gentlemanly to take a rifled pistol to a duel. Rifled balls are more accurate, and as such give an unfair advantage."

He brought the hammer of the first pistol to half-cock and removed the shreds of percussion cap, then he stuck the end of his quill in the barrel and rattled it around. He did the same with the second pistol, each time tapping the barrels gently against the ledger desk until dottlings of soot and ashes fell into a little pile.

"Where's the ball?" he asked, keeping his eye on the prisoner all the time.

"The ball?" said Silver.

"Yes, Constable – *the ball.*"

"Well now, I should think it lodged in Mr. Drummond's behind," said Silver.

"This ain't no pantomime," said the Inspector, turning down the corners of his mouth. "Mr. Drummond is a very important gentleman, and he shan't take kindly to being shot at."

Silver, to his credit, coloured slightly.

"It appears that both pistols have been fired," said the Inspector. "The ball from the first is quite possibly, as you say, Constable, still stuck in Mr. Drummond – but the question remains: where is the second?"

"Well, who's to say there was a ball," said the Constable, casting a meaningful eye upon the pile of ashes on the ledger desk. "I mean to say, when Bean fired at Her Majesty in the summer he only had a thimbleful of powder and 'bacco pipes in his pistol, didn't he? And as I told you, sir, I saw plain as day a piece of paper burning on the pavement whiles Mr. Drummond was beating out the fire in his coat-tails."

Inspector Hughes ran his hand down the long, grave lines of his long, handsome face. "The pistols ain't rifled," he said, thinking his patience sorely taxed, "they're smooth-bore, which means you has to wrap a bit o' rag or paper round the ball before you ram it down the barrel else it won't fire. It's called a patch. I should say that's most likely what you saw – leastways, the presence of a piece of paper burning on the pavement don't mean there weren't no ball."

Which was quite true; but then again, nor did it mean that there was.

"Well," said the Constable, a mite defensively, "it weren't as if Mr. Drummond was badly wounded or nothing."

"I see," said the Inspector with a weary sigh.

"As a matter of fact, he was right as rain last I saw of him. You can ask the pot-boy from the Salopian – I had him walk Mr. Drummond back to the counting-house, which went quite against the gentleman's wishes; he was most insistent that he was right as a trivet and there weren't no need for a fuss." Constable Silver paused to follow the Inspector's line of sight across the front office to where the prisoner stood, seemingly oblivious to either of them. He dropped his voice to a more confidential tone. "I looked about for one of Tierney's spies to escort the gentleman," he continued. "There's usually a whole gang of 'em hanging around King Charles's statue, but them rogues has a habit of disappearing at the first sign of trouble. I mean to say, it's no wonder I overlooked the balls now, is it sir? There was I holding onto a desperate shootist, on a busy thoroughfare, with a gentleman what's just been shot – and with no help from anyone, least of all the blessed Active Duty."

"That's *Inspector* Tierney to you, Constable. And I'm still waiting to hear what came of the ball from the second pistol."

Silver looked down at the floor, turning the brim of his stove-pipe hat in his hands. "It discharged on the pavement during the struggle as I was apprehending the prisoner," he mumbled, "and in all the excitement I never thought to gather it up."

Inspector Hughes set his hands flat on the edge of the desk. "When you're finished here, Constable Silver," he said, "you had better get yourself along to that stretch of pavement outside the Salopian. I dare say you shall know it better than you know your own mind before the day is over." Then with a telling sigh, he moved out slowly from behind the ledger desk, stretching his thin frame to its full height: that is six foot and seven-eighths of an inch in his stocking feet, which made him the tallest man in the whole Division by at least one seven-eighth of an inch, and when he had on his stove-pipe hat, one of the tallest men in the whole Metropolis. He stooped before the little station-house hearth and rattled the poker in the smoky embers, looking for all the world like a benign story-book giant.

"Cold ain't it?" he said not unkindly to the prisoner. "Want to come and warm yourself?"

The young man, pale as a ghost, may have glanced at the fire, but he made no move towards it. The Inspector reminded him that he was still under caution and asked him for his name. He blinked once and said nothing.

"Now, now, if you won't tell us your name, son, the Constable will have to search you for proof of identity. That's the way of it, see. And if you resist, well, we're entitled to use reasonable force. You with me?"

The prisoner looked straight ahead.

"Do you understand what it is I am telling you?" said Inspector Hughes more forcefully.

He paused for a moment or two to give the prisoner time to respond, before exchanging a knowing look with Silver.

"We got a right Captain Queer-nabs here, ain't we sir?" said the Constable, as in response to the Inspector's curt nod he set about the prisoner's pockets with the zeal of an absolved soul, extracting from the hindermost part ten pistol percussion caps, a penknife, a key, an admission ticket to the Adelaide Gallery of Practical Science, and a strange-looking token. The prisoner all the while remained quite still.

"Been to see Mr. Perkins's steam gun, have you?" said the Inspector as he turned the ticket towards him. "The Superintendent and Commissioners of the Metropolitan Police Force take a dim view of the steam gun. They don't think it's right that such an heinous instrument should be on public display no more 'n a stone's throw from Whitehall. They take the view that such a thing'll give certain people certain ideas."

"And after a year of Monster Mobs and Charters," piped up Silver, "I'm inclined to agree with 'em. Lor'! The Palace Guard called out to restore order, and riotous assemblies tearing up the palings around the Nelson Column and smashing the lamps in front of Buckingham Palace, and forcing a baton-charge all the way back to Scotland-yard.... Not forgettin' 'er Majesty fired at *twice* whilst out on her Sunday drive... I mean to say, who'd be the least bit surprised if the Chartists stole the steam gun and set it atop the Marble Arch? Not me! After the past year I should say just about anything could happen..."

Inspector Hughes did not trouble to respond. He was watching the prisoner closely. "Worth a visit is it – the steam gun?" he said. "Only my boy is very keen to be taken."

The prisoner shifted a little.

"O, it provides quite a thrill, sir," said Silver, intent upon the prisoner's trowser pockets, "rattles off a thousand shots per minute, and makes a righteous din an' all!"

The Inspector carefully put aside the ticket and turned his attention to the strange token. It was the size of a half-penny, and at first glance, resembled the sort of thing the Anti-Corn Law League handed out at meetings. On one side was the impression of a cloud with a rainbow breaking through it; on the other was inscribed the text: GENESIS IX *xiii*. Religious. Not political, then: a communion token, most likely. He reached under the ledger desk for the station-house Bible, but Silver gasping in surprise caused him to halt.

From the prisoner's trowser pocket the Constable had withdrawn a great pile of rag: three Bank of England notes carrying the value of £5, four sovereigns, four half-crowns, and one shilling and fourpence in coppers. He set it all in a heap upon the desk.

"He must be a clerk at the Drummonds' counting-house who's been caught bilking," exclaimed the Constable, regarding the prisoner with amazement.

"Where'd you come by all this then," asked the Inspector, setting his large brown, knowing eyes upon the prisoner's weird, watery gaze. It was like trying to focus on a mist. "It don't matter to me, son," he said, "you're entitled to keep your peace until you're set before the magistrate tomorrow morning; but I tell you what – Mr. Drummond'll be giving me his version by and by, that's for sure."

With a deep sigh he returned to the other side of the desk and began to enter a list of the prisoner's property. He was interrupted by P.C. Silver letting out a low whistle and laying a piece of paper on the desk in front of him.

No. 7959   2nd June, 1842

THE GLASGOW AND SHIP BANK

Received from Mr. Daniel McNaughten, 90 Clyde-street,
Anderston's frontland, Top flat,
seven hundred and fifty pounds sterling
which is placed to the credit of his Deposit Account with the
Glasgow and Ship Bank, Trongate.
                                            Jas. WATSON Cashier

Entd. MJB

INDORSED
Received of Messrs Glyn & Co., this 29th day of November, 1842
Twenty Pounds
                                            Daniel McNaughten.

"*Daniel McNaughten...* I take it that's you, son?" the Inspector asked. He took in once more the pale, hatless young man in the dock: half-starved, the stale and crumpled linen, the fraying stock, the cheap cloth coat, worn shiny in places – and hardly adequate against the terrible cold. "Lor'!" he exclaimed in a jovial tone. "What trade do you follow? Only I'd like to know! It'd take a Police Inspector the best part of a decade to put by that amount of money, always supposing he had no wife and children to spend it for him in the meantime, that is!"

The prisoner closed his eyes, as if he was tired of all of this.

"I see you withdrew twenty pounds back in November," continued the Inspector. He took in the pile of cash on the desk, making the calculation in his head. "You must live very carefully..."

The prisoner swayed slightly in the dock.

"What's it mean, Inspector?" whispered Silver.

Inspector Hughes frowned. "Get this lot down to Scotland-yard straight away," he said. "And if I was you, Constable, I wouldn't count on doing anything else this evening. This'll ramify, you mark my words."

When he looked at the prisoner again it seemed to him that there was a smile on the face of the pale thin young man; and, though he couldn't be sure, it seemed to be mocking him.

HIGH BEECH, WALTHAM CROSS, ESSEX
LATER THAT EVENING

In which we meet a very clever barrister; and show the consequences of sticking to one's principles.

Alexander "Good Old Cockie" Cockburn Q.C. ("the Buck of the Bar") was "in" up to the tan strip of his top-boots. He had been "in" long before he broke the wax seal and read the dark precipitations hastily scribbled on the sheet of Reform Club notepaper. He was "in" too far for a forensic consideration of whatever mazy purpose lay behind the interest of the Chief Whipper-in of the Parliamentary Whigs in the seemingly random shooting of a Tory civil servant on Charing-cross. Damn it, he was "in" so far he had no choice but to acquiesce – no matter how much he might try to persuade himself to the contrary that he was a free man and master of his own actions.

He was brooding before the library fire of his beloved uncle, the Rear-Admiral Sir George Cockburn, who was at that very moment lying gravely ill in his bedchamber – the result of some ill-considered remark, instantly regretted, that the ungrateful nephew had let fall from his lips earlier that evening. He was toying precariously with a miniature sword (the gift of Lord Nelson to the Rear-Admiral) which he had used to open the Chief Whipper-in's letter, torn between waiting for the doctor to confirm his worst suspicions and running away like the coward he was. The missive from London complicated matters greatly: it did nothing whatever to lift the frightful depression of spirits into which Sandy had descended.

"No go, I'm afraid, sir," announced his confidential valet returning from the village. The fellow exuded a gust of freezing air as he crossed from the door to the fire to warm himself. "Every room taken. Perhaps Lady Cockburn might be persuaded to let us stay until the London railway train leaves in the morning?"

Sandy waved the sheet of Reform Club letter-paper in a desultory fashion. "Hatchett, old man," he said, "it would appear that my aunt is not alone in wishing me gone from here."

Hatchett took the missive and read aloud.

"'*Drummond of the Treasury was shot this afternoon outside the Salopian coffee-house at Charing-cross. Lord John Russell is most anxious that you attend the hearing at Bow-street Police Court tomorrow at 10½ in the morning in order to take a view. Meet me at the Club for supper in order that we might discuss the implications of the matter. 7 o'clock sharp.*'"

The loyal servant was smiling when he looked up.

"I say, sir, you really do have the luck of the devil! A brief! Not to say a fee!"

Cockie scowled at him.

"Well," said Hatchett, not to be deterred, "at least there's the offer of a capital supper. Surely that ain't to be sniffed at!"

"Supper!" groaned the master, "at the Club!"

Hatchett drew a long and considered breath. "This offer of a brief," he continued, "together with the fifty pounds you had of your uncle –"

"– you mean the share of it he hasn't won back –"

Hatchett looked at the fire. "Well, sir, all I'm saying is you ought now to be able to satisfy a few of your pursuers before they bring the duns in."

"You know how I hate to be compromised, old man," said Cockie with an elegant sigh.

They listened to the sound of urgent footsteps coming and going on the stair and on the landing, subdued murmurings, the tell-tale sloshings and gurglings of sick-room paraphernalia.

"How is the Rear-Admiral, by the way?" inquired Hatchett.

Sandy took a draft of the brandy that rested at his elbow.

"The quack's with him," he said, and he closed his eyes as if in prayer.

"O dear, I am sorry to hear that, sir."

"The physician says it is a broken blood vessel in that venerable neck – the same around which I have so often thrown my arms in gratitude," said Cockie.

"I had no idea it was so serious, sir," replied Hatchett, joining his master in morose contemplation of the fire. "Perhaps the Rear-Admiral had some underlying difficulty, a complaint that has nothing to do with the circumstances…"

"The likely cause is *apoplexy*," said Sandy gulping down another brandy, "occasioned by too vigorous debate."

The Rear-Admiral had a daughter but no son, and so was very fond of Sandy – by whom, he often said, he was reminded very much of himself when younger. They had the same red hair, clear blue eyes, and striking features – although the Rear-Admiral was altogether a larger, burlier, and far less elegant man than his nephew – and the fond belief that they were as close as father and son could ever hope to be had been fostered by them both since Sandy was a boy. Over the years the nephew had listened indulgently, time and again, to the old salt's tales of setting fire to Washington in '14, or carrying Napoleon to St. Helena; and for his part the uncle had come to eagerly anticipate – not to say provoke – those frequent debates on the contentions of the day which had become yet one more bond between the pair of them.

As a result of all these kind attentions – and despite the reservations of Sir George's good Lady (who was that wholly unusual creature, a woman utterly impervious to the seductive charms of the *soigné* little silk) – Sandy had always found sanctuary in his uncle's home. Whenever he sought solace from the desolations of London out of Season; whenever the effort of feigning knowledge in affairs of state and the relentless pursuit of thwarted ambition proved too much for his constitution; whenever he had exhausted the patience and good-will of his father and associates; whenever he found himself hunted about by bailiffs or jealous husbands; in short, whenever it seemed as if all of London had found him out, and from every lip he passed dropped the name of cheat, card-sharper, swindler, scoundrel, adulterer, &c., &c., High Beech had been there for him.

It was less than two hours before that uncle and nephew had sat in a glow of geniality over a hand of cards and a decanter of brandy, discussing the nation on the brink of bankruptcy, the social fabric about to crumble to pieces.

"This is the most corrupt parliament that ever sat since the reign of Charles II!" his uncle had gambitted with typical gusto. "Damn Peel – he is nothing but a political hoaxer who changed notes as soon as he arrived in Downing-street! And why? I'll tell you for why: because there are one hundred and forty members sitting on the benches behind him whose votes are the precise opposite to the principles they all professed to advocate on the hustings a year ago!"

Sandy, slumped careless in his chair with his legs stretched out under the table, frowned at his cards. He had a poor hand, but that was not the only reason for his disaffection. The flagrant untruths of the last election had become a plague to him. He had spent too long as a Parliamentary Counsel. Each and every day of the past long session he had sweltered in the harness of the committee rooms, picking over the numerous despicable deceptions adopted during the canvas and upon the hustings, arguing charges of corruption brought by Whig petitioners against Tory sitting members and defending charges of corruption brought by Tory petitioners against Whig members. He was sick of the noisy frothiness of those who thought nothing of buying their fellowmen as beasts in the market-place; and who were troubled not at having found their reward in the sycophancy of a degraded constituency – men of whatever colour to whom principle, patriotism, are as nothing to *Party*.

"The Tories might have succeeded in juggling themselves into office," he said, "but only a fool would deny that there is a thing to choose between one aristocratic click and another."

His uncle drew heavily on his cigar, beaming his expectation of a rollicking debate, but Sandy merely sighed content to let the matter drop. A gentleman must make alliances, and as a consequence of certain factors of heredity, patronage and club membership, Sandy found himself hitched to a buff and blue wagon.

"The Reform Bill of '32," his uncle was saying with an adventitious gleam in his eye, "has proved efficacious in nothing – nothing – save in the promotion of bribery."

Sandy winced. He was of that generation of Whig idealists who had expressed such fervent hopes in the extension of the franchise a decade ago.

He exchanged one card for another.

"Every man has his price," he remarked sourly.

In those halcyon days – a mere eighteen-month ago – before his so-called elevation to Queen's Counsel (following the successful defence of another of his father's brothers, the dean of York, on a charge of simony) and the corresponding diminution in his fortunes – Sandy would have said that *his* price was a thousand pounds a year in fees for Railway Petitions. It could not be denied that at the conclusion of each successful railway bid he had found himself wondering what the likely fate would be of those wretched hordes cleared out to make way for yet another length of railroad; but at least railroads were progress. The calumniation of Democracy, however, in which Sandy now found himself enmired, was a betrayal of everything in which he had ever assumed belief: an act of murderous treachery committed against the shimmer of his own youthful ideals.

"You know, sir," Sandy said, "I really think that I would do almost anything, anything at all, to avoid another six-month suffocating in the mouldy charnel house of government, up to my knees in the quicksand twaddle of the Election Committees. Why, I would rather rot in the debtors' gaol along with all the other Regent-street *trottoirs*; fight a dozen duels with jealous cuckolds; I fancy I would almost rather go on Circuit, even though I can ill afford to meet my mess-room obligations, and am surely too old by now to be caught clambering from a Devizes hotel window in the dead of night. At least when one is on Circuit it is possible to seek redemption in the defence of a poor girl taken in infanticide, or a pea-picker caught stealing a mutchkin of milk for her children; at least when on Circuit a gentleman of Radical proclivity might persuade himself that he is doing some *good* in, as Bentham would have it, ensuring that some of the poor, at least, might have justice."

Sandy reorganised his hand, but it was still wanting.

His uncle puffed away on his cigar. "The Tories care not what they promise," he said, stubbornly, "so long as it wins them a few tradesman votes, and serves their insidious ambitions."

Sandy laid his indifferent cards against his chest and contemplated the middle-distance. "I had a visit a few weeks ago from a discreet coterie of Temple gentleman," he said, "all *Tories*, of course – come to inform me of the Queen's alarm on learning that a notorious Liberal swell had somehow contrived to take silk. It would seem that Her Majesty wished me to know how the temper of the times is far more for meddlesomely moralising now than it might once have been, and more particularly that it is no longer acceptable for a bachelor gentleman to occupy his Wednesday afternoons over in Clapham with the pretty wife of a brother barrister – nor I assume the early hours of his mornings with the numerous delights of the *poses plastiques* girls. Now, what do you think of that, sir?"

"Damned impertinence!" exclaimed Uncle George throwing in his hand. "You will defy them, of course!"

"The blasted imposition really put me upon my mettle, I must say!" said Sandy, unexpectedly pocketing the winnings, "although if I am to be honest, I had been looking for a convenient way out of the entanglement for some time by now. The thing had rather run its course – well, I dare say *you* know how it is – but the lady was clinging on, rather. She had grown careless."

His uncle divined at once his meaning. "You may have to answer a challenge," he said, "as a matter of honour. I shall act as your second, of course."

Sandy laid down his cards upon the arm of his chair and took up a bumper of brandy. "How I *loathe* this current fashion for interfering in a man's private life," he said.

"We never had any interference in my day," exclaimed the Rear-Admiral. "Why a man could get up to whatever he wished – as long as he paid his gambling debts, of course. Mind you, the pox took a good many." His uncle paused to relight his cigar. "I say, dear boy," he resumed between puffs, "you don't suppose that this coterie will uncover that unfortunate business in Cambridge with the grocer's wife?"

Sandy took another sip of the brandy, let it infuse his heart. Among all the numerous indiscretions of Sandy's life, his uncle had hit upon the one that was a source of the *intensest* anxiety.

"Pah!" he said. "That was almost twenty years ago!"

His uncle was winking thoughtfully at the lit end of his cigar. "The college vice-master was all for having you sent down."

"I was rusticated for a term."

"You came here, to High Beech."

Sandy had not forgotten. He had not wanted to go to his father's house with the ignominy of his misdemeanour so stark before him. He had been too, too *heart-broken*. He was keen to move along the conversation, but the Rear-Admiral deftly plucked the topic from his maudlin grasp.

"You see," he blustered, "that is what comes of giving the vote to a rabble of ten-pound householders. One must buy their morals along with their support. Your father had the devil of a job paying off the grocer, as I recall. That episode ought to have shewn you, dear boy, how shop-keepers are not like us: they do not share our *joie de vivre!*"

Sandy did not raise an objection, allowing it all instead to confound: the failure, the vacuity, the traitorous missing of so much *good*; his own guilt, and acute sense of having failed...

"Forgive me, sir," he snapped, when this line of thinking had all but depleted him, "but the extension of the franchise hasn't a thing to do with it."

His uncle's eyes gleamed with delight at the prospect of the bait having been taken.

"O pray don't begin again with all your Radical clap-trap! We all know what your answer to the sordid mess is – a further extension! Let in one hundred thousand working men to swamp the system!" The Rear-Admiral thumped the card table with his fist, setting the cards and brandy things jumping as if in fright. "Let things slide even deeper into the miserable abyss."

"You are quite wrong, sir," cried Sandy. "The wretched imposition to which I have been subjected is but the corollary of setting a short and not well-proportioned *hausfrau* upon the throne! And as for that opinionated, stooping dunce of a consort! Pah! If he were to be stripped of his title I doubt he'd even find a partner at a country dance!"

Uncle George clamped his teeth hard about his cigar and grew quite red in the face, billows of smoke issuing forth like steam from a locomotive. It occurred to Sandy that he had not seen the Rear-Admiral look so roiled since the occasion, on a previous visit, when he had declared Boney to be a much greater man than Wellington.

"And consider the cost to the nation!" he continued unabashed. "Innumerable working men starving on the streets of our cities, the national debt standing at above eight hundred million pounds – and yet Her Majesty receives *daily* – daily, mind you! – one hundred and sixty-four pounds seventeen shillings and tenpence for her daily use, and her dim-witted consort one hundred and four pounds – at a time when many thousands of labourers' families must subsist on no more than threepence! I tell you, sir, I did not hear more sense spoken in the whole of the last session than in that alleged utterance of the Chartist fellow who fired pistols at the royal carriage at the start of the summer. 'Damn the Queen', say I with him, 'why should she be such an expense to the nation!'"

The insult to Her Majesty, it seemed, proved too much for the old salt. As Sandy looked on with dismay, the Rear-Admiral puffed unrelievedly, helplessly, on his cigar, stuttering in vexation for several pendulous moments, before clutching at his throat and promptly falling into a dead faint.

"The *apoplexy* you say?" said Hatchett, as his master finished recounting the events of the evening. "Well now, that certainly can be very serious."

"It's looking bad, old man," said Sandy. He had a rather strained, seared look to his face.

"Why, it will take more than the apoplexy to see off that gallant old tar!" said the valet. "He'll be as right as a trivet, don't you fret, sir! I was never more certain of a thing!"

Hatchett was frowning and chewing upon his lip. "Do you have any of the money you had of him?" he said.

Sandy dug into his pocket and handed over the winnings. Hatchett counted them out. "I should say there's just enough here to arrange a pair of horses," he said.

Sandy groaned. "I arrived here with not a sou in my pockets," he cried. "Even darling *Maman* refused me the loan of a paltry five pounds. And now this has to happen! I'm a busted flush, I tell you. It's all over with me. I'm finished!"

"Now, sir," chided the manservant, "this ain't the time to capitulate to them old Blue Devils! And as for being finished!" He brandished the Chief Whipper-in's letter. "Why, I should hardly say that of a man whose opinion is sought out by the highest in the land!"

"Face the truth, old man," said the master, bitterly. "I am on the losing side."

Hatchett turned upon him an expression of the gravest concern, the sort of look no gentleman ever wishes to see upon the face of his manservant; and seeing it, Sandy revised thoughts of abandoning the wig and gown altogether and disappearing across the Channel.

"You might as well paste bills about town," he said, "advertising an Auction of Effects of a Man of Fashion Gone to the Continent. I shall end my days in a gloriously shabby Paris atelier, with a good cigar in one hand, a jug of brandy in the other, and a couple of opera-dancers tucked in at either side." But even as he indulged the scenario for the dozenth time, Sandy knew that this was not how it would go for him.

"You're forgetting, sir," the valet said, "people have short memories. Now everything that's wrong in the country is all the fault of Sir Robert Peel and the Tories, and it won't be long before the Whigs are once more in favour. A man like you, sir, a clever man, a young man, vigorous, impetuous, I should say, you still have a great deal to offer. The Party needs you, sir; they need you, else they would not have sent for you."

Sandy despondently tossed Lord Nelson's dagger to one side and at his manservant's urging, took the Chief Whipper-in's letter into his own hands, drawing his top lip in to a sneer as he reconsidered its contents. He drank down the last of the brandy and laid the glass aside. It was scarcely sufficient for him to know that vanity, interest, imminent ruin, and every other consideration urged him to look with favour upon the Chief Whipper-in's proposal; and yet, and yet even though all other inducements were wanting, the habitual carelessness of his disposition stepped in and weighed down the scale on the other side. He knew this, felt it; but he also knew that come the morrow he would return to the metropolis. He had quite possibly murdered his only disinterested benefactor; he was too tired to resist; he was too broke; and, finally, he was too easily flattered.

O God, he thought, how I hate this life – a thought of such immensity that there was no room in his overworked and anxious conscience for any other consideration. Which was, perhaps, why it never occurred to him to ask why, *why* was the Chief Whipper-in of the Parliamentary Whigs expressing such a keen interest in the shooting of a Tory civil servant?

No. 19, Lower Grosvenor-street, Mayfair,
at about the same time

Showing a sister's love, a brother's secrets, a doctor's mistake, and the likely penalty of interposing oneself in a matter of honour.

Poor dear Neddie had been going along quite well until he succumbed to the attentions of the surgeon. Why, he had even asked for a soft-boiled egg and some port; but Mr. Bransby Cooper soon put paid to that, as to so much else. He said it was *probably* ill-advised, and *perhaps* they had better put her brother to bed straight away. Then he laid his spectacles on top of his head and spent a long time with his long drab face inches from Neddie's behind, peering mournfully at the small livid burn on the left flank, the only imperfection on a rump which turned out not to be horny-thick, as she had always imagined it to be, but white as marble with delicate blue veins rippling through it; and soft, as soft as a goose-feather bed.

"The ball appears to have struck from behind," Mr. Bransby Cooper said, finally, exhaling sadness over Neddie's prone figure.

[45]

"I could have told you that if you had but troubled to ask," snapped Neddie. He was lying face down in the pillow. "Now perhaps I might be permitted to dress and have a glass of sherry and a little pudding?"

Mr. Bransby Cooper's Self-esteem, she could plainly see at the top back of his head, was exceptionally flat and unimpressive, which meant that, unusually for a surgeon, he had next to none. She wondered why her brothers had sent for him and not his far more distinguished uncle, and then she remembered that Sir Astley Cooper had been dead for over a year by then, bequeathing all his business to his nephew. Naturally, it did not occur to her to question in any other respect the necessity of a visit from the Duke of Wellington's own physician: it was an essential precaution where reputations were at stake. It was just such a pity that the nephew did not appear to have inherited one iota of his uncle's skill.

Plumped up by the side of the bed, safe and snug beneath her little lace cap, softened by the warm glow of the Argand lamp, she could hear on the other side of the box-bed drapes the pillow-muffled objections of one being worked upon inexpertly with implements. Poor dear Neddie! She sighed and shook her little round head until her tightly packed curls rustled against her mob-cap.

Poor dear Neddie!

Miss Drummond was no stranger to the sick-bed and the death-bed; she took solace in the inevitability of physical suffering and demise. The thick velvet curtains were secured fast against the nasty rain-gashed street; her small, black velvet-slippered feet reclined upon the footstool, her sewing settled on her lap like a snoozing cat. She was feeling dozy, well fired as a Mrs. Toby, round and shiny and cherry-nosed and dimpled. Neddie on the other side of the curtains gasped once more in pain, and hearing it she smiled to herself in a satisfied way and tried to slip into a little sleep.

She had hopes of resuming her dream of the Duke of Wellington. Considering what had happened to her brother – the remarkable *coincidence* – it might be considered prescient that she should have been dreaming of the Duke of Wellington when the news of the calamity was broken to her. But the fact was this: Miss Drummond often dreamed of the Duke of Wellington; indeed she had been dreaming of him ever since that evening, long ago – long before Catholick Emancipation and Parliamentary Reform had hastened the end – when the beau accompanied her to the vestibule after a *soirée* at Lord Sidmouth's in Richmond, and waited with her while her brother went to fetch the carriage. In the dream she was always far more adept in the artifices of fashionable intrigue than ever she had been in waking life. The Duke, however, was gallant as he ever was. He sought her opinion on the condition of England, and listened attentively as she gave it.

How irritated she had been to be awakened from such a delicious flight by Parrott the footman stirring the recumbent ashes back to life with the poker. It was only a quarter to five, but she must have dozed off over her sewing – aided, no doubt, by her customary drops of Rowland's Aqua d'Oro taken in a cup of warm water shortly before four. Coming to, she might have mumbled something to him about how the time moves so slowly when the winter draws on, some such commonplace or other; she had certainly thought it.

Beyond the parlour drapes, the wind loitered on the street, rattling the front door. Something flapped helpless against the railings, and it crossed her mind that there was an ominousness to that gust; and, yes, something *human*.

"Forgive me, Miss Drummond," Parrott had said in his soft, low voice, "I didn't mean to startle you."

She noticed at once how his smooth brow was creased a little in perturbation.

"O, I was far away," she said, "somewhere else altogether."

The footman rattled the poker against the guard before laying it gently in the fire dogs, and watching him, it occurred to her that no matter how many shovels of cold ashes might be heaped upon it, hope would never be entirely extinguished.

Parrott sat back on his heels, watching the fire speculatively. "I– I trust it was somewhere pleasant, ma'am," he said.

"O yes, very much so."

Parrott had not been long in her service, but Miss Drummond was gifted with certain *insights*. She had Large Concentrativeness, and a talent, therefore, for pursuing abstracts and metaphysical questions. She divined at once that something had obtruded itself upon her footman's mind; something troubling. Or was it, she was thinking now, that she had already by then received an intimation that *something was about to happen*? If so, how curious that impression was, and yes, how *certain*.

"Miss Drummond," Parrott was saying hesitantly, "a messenger has just been from the bank."

There was nothing surprising about that. Neddie was supposed to call there that afternoon and collect from the vault the incriminatory scrolls he had obtained from the King's Remembrancer, in order that the wretched things might be burned.

"Did he bring a portmanteau?" she asked.

"No – no, I'm afraid not," Parrott said. "He came to inform us that there's been an accident."

"An accident? What sort of accident?"

"Mr. Drummond is on his way home in a carriage. They were waiting for an apothecary to attend to him. I expect he will be here very soon."

The morbid fancy crossed her mind that some desperate ruffian must have followed her brother as he left the bank with the scrolls; and perhaps taking them to be something of value, he had attempted to rob Neddie at the point of a knife.

"It appears he's been shot at by a madman," said Parrott with admirable clarity.

"How perfectly frightful," said Miss Drummond. "The Duke of Wellington is quite correct. Since Reform things have got by so much worse! The streets are now full of danger. This is why I have eschewed the mazy and perilous paths of the world, and am quite contented to stay at home."

And then, just at that moment, from beyond the drapes came the chinking of a bridle, the clip-clop of hooves, the horses snorting against the cold air.

She felt a little faint, distant, as if in a dream: mournful fancies crowding in her mind as she found her way to the front door. Pulling her spencer about her pillowy shoulders, she stood at the top of the steps, not daring to venture further towards the bitter cold, the vicious hiss of the gas-lamp, and all the hazards of encounter. The crooked stack of chimneys on one of the opposite roofs seemed to be a row of ugly faces frowning at her; and looking along the street, she thought she saw the man coming with the coffin on his back – just as he had come when the time came to take away Mama and Papa and her dear sister Matilda. The apparition made her shiver and give way to a new train of fears and speculations.

Parrott was at the carriage door even before the driver had the opportunity to dismount, inquiring in his low tones, applying thick blankets and assurances. When she looked back along the street, she could see nothing: nothing save, emerging bedraggled and forlorn from the spirals of sleet, the dingy drooping figure of Mr. Bransby Cooper; as dingy and drooping as it had appeared that other night, a dozen or more years ago, trudging in the brash, unfaltering steps of his illustrious uncle: physician to three monarchs, doctor to the Duke of Wellington, twice President of the Royal College of Surgeons.

When she looked back her dear brother Neddie was stepping from the carriage: his face ghastly and white, like something once glimpsed long ago in the corners of the nursery at the fleeting moment between day and night.

"But the end is not yet!" she heard herself exclaim, and regarding Neddie's shocked, ashen features as he passed her in the vestibule, the curious thought occurred to her that perhaps this was all some sort of test – of faith, perhaps; of loyalty.

"Did you get to the bank this afternoon, dear?" she whispered to him. Their older brother Charles had been so insistent that the scrolls be removed at the first instance.

Neddie scowled and handed her his broad-brimmed hat.

"Take this," he hissed, "and, for God's sake, keep it well-hidden!"

Inside the crown of his hat she glimpsed lurking an inconspicuous modest volume, bound in dark green hard grain, with marbled sides: *An Essay on the Principle of Population*. Miss Drummond was surprised that the Reverend Malthus's essay on the vexatious topic should be the object of such conspiracy on the part of her brother. She had often heard Neddie dismiss its "dreary" and "dismal" controversies as "worthless"; how he considered it a work that offered no hope of salvation in this world or the next, beloved of nobody save "Whig lawyers" and "political economists" – for whom her brother held equal stores of contempt in reserve. It was not at all what she had been expecting him to bring from the bank, but she contrived at once to conceal it in the folds of her leg o' mutton sleeve and vowed to keep it there until she could safely transfer the volume to the intimacy of her boudoir.

It was Mr. Bransby Cooper who halted her solipsistic meanderings. He was wiping his hands on a napkin that Parrott was holding up to him; they were blood-sticky as far as the elbow, where his shirt sleeves were crammed into a pair of leather guards.

"I really do think that, perhaps, we ought to send for Mr. Guthrie," he said. "It is just that, you see, he is far more expert than I in the matter of gunshot wounds." He closed his instrument case, smiling weakly, his features long like a face in a spoon. "I'm afraid I only ever performed the duties of an assistant surgeon in the Wars. My duties for the most part consisted of the disposal of amputated limbs."

Neddie, from the pillow, expressed a most earnest wish that Mr. Bransby Cooper's skill in that quarter would not be required.

Everybody laughed.

His naked behind was now concealed beneath a bit of muslin cloth. She thought he sounded more tired than he had before.

Mr. Bransby Cooper freely admitted that he had not, as yet, been able to find the shot, and the prevailing medical wisdom altercated on the question of how expedient it was to go "fishing" for such in any case. What he could say with some exactitude was that the wound on Mr. Drummond's hip appeared to agree with the holes in his breeches, shirt and flannel waistcoat. Parrott held them all up to Miss Drummond's scrutiny. She saw a sequence of holes about the size of a pea, and only slightly less perfect; edged by a jagged ring of scorch-marks. To look at it one might have thought it made by nothing more dangerous than a Trichinopoli cheroot.

"Fancy!" she exclaimed, resisting the urge to ease her pudgy finger into the opening. "It really is quite astonishing, is it not, Neddie dear, the way the lower orders seem to have formed such a dislike of you of late? Did you know," she said turning to Mr. Bransby Cooper, "that Mr. Drummond was the unfortunate object of violent attentions of a Mob of Combinationists when he accompanied the Queen and Sir Robert Peel on their visit to Scotland in October? They overturned the carriage in which he was riding, and treated him very ill. They might have done worse, but fortunately he was saved just in time."

Her brother grunted something into his pillow. It sounded like an admonition. She regarded him coolly and clutched her sewing, in which was concealed the tell-tale volume, to her bosom. Her little peridot eyes came to rest upon her brother's wounded left side, and at that very moment the jarring memory of something returned to her with such vibrancy it was as if her very breath could sound it – indeed she could not stop herself from issuing a little gasp. For a moment everything around her seemed to stop; when it resumed motion again it was as if she found herself in a different place altogether.

"But if we send for Mr. Guthrie," she said in a measured tone, "what are we to tell him about that – that other matter? The matter concerning the Duke of Wellington and the opprobrious insult he suffered and for which he demanded satisfaction?" The surgeon blinked uncomprehendingly: the very model of a booby. "The duel!" she cried in exasperation. "The duel in which my brother so recklessly interposed himself...!"

Mr. Bransby Cooper's face darkened with perplexity.

"The thing is," he said, "I am unable to find the shot, and, ah, I am not at all sure that I have been looking in the right place, or if I am in the right place, then how much further I ought to – ah – *probe*. I am concerned lest, lest – that is to say – well – surely if we confine Mr. Guthrie's expert eye to the *posterior* then he need have no suspicions of – of – ah – *anything else*. That wound was *anterior*, do you see? Mr. Guthrie is sure to find the ball, that is to say – ahem – the – the *present* ball – not the – er – not the *other* of which you speak. He is *very* practised."

"So you say," said Miss Drummond. "However, what if Mr. Guthrie were to turn my brother over onto his back and discover the piece of shot that was left there by the Duke of Wellington – inadvertently – at the time of his duel with the Earl of Winchilsea? What then? He might start to draw certain conclusions, and a great man's reputation, so long safeguarded, would be threatened." She crumpled her face into a little crease of distaste. A fester the size of a crown piece was seeping through the bit of muslin draped across her brother's hind-quarters.

She applied a fat little hand to her hair, smoothing it, delicately patting it into place at the nape and the temple and ran her eyes up Neddie's body to where the swell of his Secretiveness could be glimpsed behind the swatches of jet-black hair he still had either side of his head, just above his ears.

"Better keep Guthrie out of it," her brother decreed hoarsely from the pillow.

Miss Drummond smiled. She had known that he would say so.

"But I really – I really think that it would be better –" said Mr. Bransby Cooper, forlornly, "that is to say, in my opinion..."

"Just mend the damage you have done," said Neddie in a weary voice, "and we shall say no more about any of this."

There have always been secrets in this house, thought Miss Drummond, settling back contentedly in the chair with her sewing. Her brother's ample girth had, for fourteen years by now, supplied a hiding place – a bulwark against possible scandal and the ruination of a great reputation. Few men in history had done more in the service of their country!

Back in '29 the Duke had been quite within his rights to challenge the slur upon his honour issued by the Earl of Winchilsea; but he had been ill-supported by the physician charged with delivering the weapons – who, not being a gentleman, could not have appreciated the degree to which supplying a duelling pistol with a rifled barrel would be considered *unsporting*, were the oversight ever to come to light. Neddie was, at the time, the Duke's Private Secretary, and had formed the opinion that it was unconstitutional, or some such nonsense, for the Prime Minister to fight a duel. Neddie was quite wrong about that, of course, as so much else, but had taken it upon himself to race to Battersea Fields – the location of the duel – with the intention of halting the *affaire d'honneur*. He arrived just as the Duke – very properly – was preparing to aim wide of the Earl, emerging from behind a tree waving his hands about and shouting "Desist!"

From the bed came a queer little squelching sound, followed immediately by a low moan and a soft sigh. Mr. Bransby Cooper had evidently decided to go against the prevailing medical wisdom, and do a little more "fishing". The noises gave rise to some association in her mind from which she instinctively shrank; something disgusting, nauseating.

"O! O! Let it go!" cried Neddie, and hearing him, Parrott hastened to his master's side, or as close as Mr. Bransby Cooper would suffer him to come. The surgeon had scooped out a gorget of Neddie's flesh, and was peering at it, one eyebrow raised in surprise.

"Is everything alright, Mr. Drummond, sir?" the footman asked. "Perhaps – perhaps we ought to send for the other physician after all."

She marked with disdain the concern in Parrott's smooth, dark features, suppressing the strong desire to mimic him.

"Why not leave it?" gasped Neddie, his voice thin with pain. "I pray you. Leave it. If the – er – *shot* is so small that it cannot be found, what harm, I wonder, what harm can it possibly do one?"

"It is my belief," said the physician with a well-meaning smile, "– and I am sure it would be the belief of Mr. Guthrie were he here – that these things are in almost all cases better out than in."

"That was not the view of your uncle fourteen years ago," exclaimed Neddie. "Leave it where it is, he said – and it has remained there ever since!"

Mr. Guthrie pulled at a piece of Neddie's vein or muscle with what looked to her like a pair of sugar-tongs.

"O! O! I pray you," cried Neddie, "I beg you, let it be!"

Miss Drummond was accustomed to armchairs at the sides of sick-beds. She scarcely gave a thought to how long she would remain there. She just kept her head bowed over her sewing all the while, succumbing every now and then to a sudden tinge of melancholy, a powerful weariness at the necessity of inhaling the bad air of this disappointing world. A good many people are never fired at once, she thought, peeping sideways at her groaning brother from beneath her lowered lashes.

"Ow o wow owowowo!"

"Poor, dear Neddie! Do try to bear it!" she encouraged. She was sure that his thoughts were of the Duke of Wellington, too: that immense reputation, that distinction, and how to safeguard it for posterity! Such a great man: one could never permit any besmirchment to such *honour*.

And so gallant! she thought with a blush of approval, as Neddie implored the physician once more to put an end to his agonies; yet not, perhaps, as good a shot as one would have imagined.

On the Surrey-side,
a little before eight o'clock p.m.

In which Inspector Hughes comes face to face with a Prophetess of the Scotch persuasion.

Inspector Hughes had left Westminster for the time being. He was crossing the river by Waterloo Bridge with Constable Silver at his side, deftly avoiding the icy yellow puddles trickling from the dirty snow-heaps, averting his eyes from the couples in the recesses. The pair of them strode on against the concoctions from the white lead works, in time to the measured plashings of the lightermen's oars; past the fancy-men taking noisy leave of their women, through the clouds of Prescot-street habanahs.The Inspector had crossed over, as he always did, in a spirit of resignation leavened only by a dim satisfaction that so far the inquiry into the shooting of Mr. Drummond at Charing-cross appeared to be *progressing*. At least, it seemed, they had discovered an address for the prisoner.

A Recruiting Sergeant of the 10th Huzzars, the usual confection of flash talk and dazzling braid, had witnessed the shooting as he was plying his trade up on Charing-cross, and recognised the prisoner as one he had spied out as a likely recruit a few days before. Inspector Hughes regarded Recruiting Sergeants as among the very worst of all the parasites of the street. It disgusted him the way they preyed upon poor hungry boys – the sort to whom the offer of a shilling comes as a blessed miracle. To Sergeant George Jones the prisoner in his broken boots and thin drab overcoat was as likely-seeming a recruit as it was possible to be. He had taken McNaughten to the Carpenter wine-vaults on King-street and tried to treat him to a crock or two of Old Tom. It weren't done out of pity, of that you could be sure.

"Turns out he was a teetotalist," recounted the Recruiting Sergeant, with a dismissive gesture, "so I bought him coffee and a hot potato instead. Well, he fell on it like a starving man!"

This immediately struck the Inspector as queer. With a small fortune sitting in his trowser pocket the prisoner certainly had no reason to beg a dinner. He wondered if the Scotchman was just miserly, as a good many are. Certainly, going by the evidence of the rag found on his person, McNaughten had stretched the twenty pounds withdrawn from his bank in November like it was a piece of india-rubber – apparently succeeding in living on no more than thirteen or fourteen bob a week: out of which, it must be supposed, he had paid for a pair of pistols. Of course, it was perfectly possible to live on so little – there were plenty at the present time constrained to live on a good deal less; most weavers, poor sots, were bringing a family along on no more than eight shillings – but it weren't to be recommended. And there was something undeniably curious about such frugality when one was in possession of seven hundred and fifty pounds.

"Was he interested in joining the Army?" asked the Inspector.

"O bless you, no!" exclaimed the bluffer. "Hardly nobody is – not when you first puts it to 'em. My line of work is all about persuasion, see. Most men don't know they has it in 'em, but I always say anyone can be encouraged to do his duty by Queen and country."

"Yes, I dares say you can prove very persuading," said the Inspector. He was thinking, though he did not say it, that the Recruiting Sergeant's boast weren't up to much – not when within a hair's breadth of Charing-cross on every hour of every day there were a hundred boys who had come to the conclusion, as Inspector Hughes himself had done once upon a time, that a quick death somewhere else is preferable to a slow one at home.

"So how come this Dan is in my cells and not your barracks then?" he asked, turning his steady gaze upon the sergeant.

"Well, I could tell he weren't the right material, see. O, you gets to know in my line of business. There are certain *signals*, you know..."

Inspector Hughes grasped his meaning at once.

"You mean there ain't no guinea in it for you if you brings a recruit to the army surgeon and he turns out to have the consumption on him."

The Recruiting Sergeant sniffed. "He took a coughing fit in the Vaults, didn't he? I saw the blood on his kerchief – though mind you he tried his best to hide it from me. Lacking in moral character, I should say. That's a sure sign."

"Poor sod," said the Inspector.

"O, he was mighty pleased to be taken out of the cold, I can tell you," the Recruiting Sergeant was saying, "and though I says it as shouldn't, I can be a jolly companion to blow a cloud with!"

"I don't doubt that," said the Inspector, "so long as it suits your purpose." With a sigh he opened the ledger on a clean page and wrote the date and time at the top.

The Recruiting Sergeant leaned in confidentially.

"Well," he said, "he told me that his name was Dan, and that he was a wood-turner lately down from Glasgow. He said he'd given up his business and was looking for another line to go in to."

"Another line, eh?" said the Inspector.

"That's what he said."

"Did he happen to mention how long he'd been in the metropolis?"

The Recruiting Sergeant considered. "I had the impression it had been some time," he said. "He told me he'd been round all the turning yards in the metropolis looking for an occasion."

"Did he now..."

"Yes. Said they were a decade behind what he was used to."

The Inspector duly recorded the statement upon the ledger, then he took the sergeant down to the cells, where a positive identity of the prisoner was made: the prisoner, for his part, hardly troubling to look up.

It was a stroke of luck, the Inspector was thinking as he walked along, that he'd only had to go to two turners' shops before arriving at information. Mr. Hedges's was over in the Devil's Acre – a large and well-established business; and the proprietor a very respectable man, well known to the Inspector for a number of years by now. He told the Inspector that a fellow by the name of Dan McNaughten, and fitting the prisoner's description, had called by with another Scotchman a fortnight or so before Christmas in search of work. The encounter had not been of any length, but McNaughten had made an impression on Mr. Hedges.

"It struck me," he told the Inspector, "that he was *different* in some way."

"How d'you mean – *different*?"

The turner knocked back his cap as if to give his thoughts more air in which to assemble themselves. "The fellow with him, Gordon, he was the usual hungry type. But that McNaughten – well, I hardly know how to put it, Inspector. There was something... something *gentlemanly* about him, I should say. O, he was as poorly dressed as any of 'em, but he didn't seem to me to have that *desperation* about him."

"You mean it was as though he didn't really want a situation?" prompted the Inspector.

"Yes, yes, now you put it like that. I accounted it to him being a respectable sort, you know, embarrassed to find himself so reduced. But then the most peculiar thing occurred."

"Go on," urged Inspector Hughes.

"I told them I needed a man who could operate that lathe over there. It's very, very fine, Inspector – a Holtzapffel rose engine. Worth hundreds of pounds, I should say, of anyone's money – though I came by it rather cheaper than the market price owing to the demise of a wealthy gentleman out near Ware who liked to turn things for pleasure, as it were. Any turner worthy of the trade would relish the chance to work a Holzapffel, but those with the skill are far and few between since not many yards are fortunate to own one."

The Inspector cast his eye over the machine.

"Well," continued Mr. Hedges, "the two of them fell into a discussion. Gordon was saying he couldn't drive the machine as well as McNaughten, so he couldn't take on the work; and McNaughten was saying Gordon had more need of the work than he did. After a few minutes of arguing back and forth like this, McNaughten asked if I'd be agreeable to him demonstrating to Gordon there and then the more intricate workings of the machine. He said he was so expert he could teach a monkey to turn watch-backs, if it came to it; and then he rolled up his sleeves and set to work. Well, let me tell you, Inspector – that Scotch fellow knew the workings of the Holzapffel better than any man I have ever come across in thirty years of engine turning. I reckon he could've turned brass watch-backs out of the air – or anything else he fancied, come to that. A rare affinity, that's how I'd express it – as if he and that fine machine were one. I tell you what, he must have worked for some very good yards indeed."

"How much," asked the Inspector, who had kept his eye on the machine all this while, "did you say it could fetch?"

"Hundreds," said the master turner.

The Inspector rubbed his chin. "As much as, say, seven hundreds?"

Mr. Hedges whistled and knocked his cap even further onto the back of his head. "Well, it's certainly a rare thing, Inspector," he concurred, "and in the right market I dare say you could ask any price. The difficulty in the present time would lay in finding a yard with enough capital to purchase it."

"Yet," said the Inspector slowly, "this Scotchman had somehow come by such a one and learned to drive it…"

"Indeed he had. And very well at that."

The Inspector and Mr. Hedges regarded the machine thoughtfully, the former trying to picture the famished, apathetic young man of his recent acquaintance driving it with zeal and skill. It put him in mind of his old pa, who was never happier than when a visitor chanced by the attic and he could show off his skills: working a treadle with his foot, setting the mill spinning while he juggled five-and-thirty bobbins; picking up the cross-thread with his long, bony fingers…

"Pride in his trade," Mr. Hedges was saying, "is an excellent quality in a man."

"Indeed it is," said the Inspector, "indeed it is. Tell me, is Gordon about the place? Only I should like to talk with him."

Mr. Hedges shook his head. "He worked for two full days – and proved to be more than satisfactory – but come the third day, he never appeared. And from that day to this I have never clapped eyes on him again. What's more, he never even called by to collect his wages."

"That's queer," said the Inspector. It was also a sight concerning: the Superintendent would not care to learn how there was a Scotch associate of the prisoner at large in the metropolis. This Gordon would have to be found: which would be like searching for a grain of sand at low tide.

"I don't suppose he left an address?" he asked, hopeful.

"Not a word," said Mr. Hedges, "else I'd have sent round the wages. Though now that I think of it, he did give me McNaughten's lodgings – I asked for them having it in mind that I would send for him if another situation arose."

The Inspector permitted himself a little smile of satisfaction while Mr. Hedges went to the small office at the back of the shop. He returned a few moments later with the day book, which he set before the Inspector. There it was writ, plain as day:

> *Daniel McNaughten c/o Mrs. E. Dutton, 7 Poplar-row,*
> *Newington Butts.*

And so it was, the back of their throats stinging with the sour air coming off the vinegar manufactory, that Inspector Hughes and his Constable came to be walking in measured strides across Waterloo Bridge and into a very seedy district over on the Surrey-side, not far from Horsemonger-lane gaol and, as Constable Silver, fresh and jocular from a congratulatory meeting with the Superintendent, pointed out: "Very 'andy for the Bedlam, an' all!"

The Inspector didn't ever care to be so far off his beat. He found no comfort in the knowledge that the same dingy blanket of sky sat above them here as over Whitehall. The street-lamps occurred at far less frequent intervals. They seemed weaker too; wavering uncertainly in the biting wind, as if the gas itself were shivering with the cold.

We won't find no answers here, he thought. And for a moment the questions, ramifying thick and fast about the matter, threatened to overwhelm him and he found himself giving way to gloomy presentiments.

"The Superintendent reckons it's all down to Glasgow thuggery," said Silver. "He reckons every Scotchman in the metropolis oughter be regarded with suspicion."

You could be forgiven for deducing that P.C. Silver was the only man in the whole Division party to the Superintendent's views on the matter in hand. In fact, every single constable had been summoned to Scotland-yard, and told they were on the brink of a national emergency. It might have seemed that way to those of a less phlegmatic cast than the Inspector. Why, just half an hour after Mr. Drummond had been shot, the Duke of Wellington had been knocked flying as he crossed the park on his way to Horse Guards. And it weren't just Scotchmen they had to look out for, neither. Haranguers, ranters, nigger tract-sellers, dollymops, drunken tars, fusee-sellers, organ-grinders and their blessed monkeys, vagrants of every class and description: every doorway along the Parliament-street, from King Charles's statue down to the Westminster Bridge, had to be kept clear of the whole lot until further notice.

"Invoke just cause, men," said the Superintendent. "Just cause." The merest glimmer of suspicion on the part of a policeman: enough to sweep away anyone found between sunset and the hour of eight in the morning, lying or loitering in any highway, yard or other place, and not able to give a satisfactory account of themselves.

The Inspector had committed the 1839 Metropolitan Police Act to memory. He understood the meaning of *just cause*.

"The Superintendent's sent one of the New Detectives up to Scotland on the railroad," Silver was saying.

His round face was glowing with a pride dazzling enough to warm your hands before it; and as he caught a glimpse of it passing beneath a street-lamp, the Inspector couldn't find it in his heart to tell the young Constable that it was high time he stowed it. O, let him have his moment, he thought, for life was harsh enough, wasn't it? And it could not be denied that it took guts to charge across Charing-cross at four o'clock in the afternoon in order to wrest pistols from the grasp of a maniac shootist. He supposed he ought to tell the young Constable that he had made a fine job of his first proper arrest – even if he had overlooked that second bit of shot – but when it come to it he lacked the heart, and he couldn't ever bear to pass an insincere remark, always preferring to say nothing at all.

He took a good lungful of the bitter night air.

After a time Silver said, "The Superintendent should have sent you up to Scotland, sir. You're the best detectivist in the whole Division; everyone says so. It's a crime you weren't made up to one of them New Detectives."

"I prefers to wear the uniform, Constable. I'm not at all suited to disguises and the like: to my mind there's something unprofessional about policemen skulking about, jobbing and trading in mystery and generally making the most of 'emselves. It ain't why I joined Sir Robert

Peel's force back in '29. Besides, Glasgow's a bit far off my beat. It's better to stick to what you know. You'll find that out in due course."

"The New Detectives might be plainclothesmen," rejoindered Silver, "but at least they're proper police, ain't they?" The Inspector pulled a face. It dismayed him this fascination the young constables all had for the Detective force which the Home Secretary had introduced in the summer. Where, he wondered, where was the pride in uniform? "Proper police," repeated Silver, "not like the busted Active Duty – a bunch of paid informers swaggering about the place, spying on people – gives us bobbies a bad name, does that."

The Inspector's left leg was giving him a spot of trouble, all stiff and painful. He grumbled softly to himself, accounting it to all the walking about in them blessed regulation-issue boots. In thirteen years he had never had a pair that fitted. They were either too big, in which case your heels were rubbed raw as your feet slopped around all day inside a casing of solid leather that had to be a good sixteenth of an inch thick; or they were too small, in which case your toes were nipped and pinched until they looked like a string of uncooked sausages.

"Odds on that scranning cove Tierney wishes he'd been sent to Glasgow," piped Silver. "He shan't care to be done out of his reward! I heard that the Active Duty took more 'n a hundred pounds during the disturbances. It's a nice line is that: touring about the country taking money off magistrates in exchange for rounding up a few starving rebels – especially when there's no shortage of informants prepared to sell their own mothers for a few goes of gin!"

Inspector Hughes frowned. "*Inspector* Tierney, Constable. *Scranning* cove, indeed."

Silver shrugged. "It's what everyone calls him. The way he's always wheedling and busting for cash; him and his blasted informers with their secret signals and nods and winks always making things out to be worse than they are. Lor'! As if they ain't bad enough!"

"First of all," said the Inspector, "there ain't no reward money in this instance. Second, it seems to me that there ain't a thing about this case that cannot be drawn out by straightforward policing. And thirdly, the Glasgow force happens to be very well organised and has no need of Inspector Tierney and the Active Duty. The Scotch have their own ways of dealing with insurrectionists."

"They oughter – they has enough practice!" Silver rubbed his hands together in the cold air. "And if you ask me, the Superintendent oughter ask where the Active Duty was when I was there on me tod trying to keep the peace on the Queen's Highway!"

"Yes, well, Constable, nobody is likely to ask you," said the Inspector, although he was thinking that what the boy had to say was quite true, even if it were a sight disrespectful.

Not that the *scranning cove* ever displayed the slightest regard for anyone other than himself.

Inspector Tierney had arrived too late for the meeting that evening at Scotland-yard to receive most of the Superintendent's instructions. He was wearing a pair of top-boots, Inspector Hughes recollected, soft as butter and fitting his calves as snug as did a footman's silk stockings, and he was sure to let them all know how he'd come direct from an audience with the Permanent Under-Secretary to the Home Office. It was the opinion of that gentleman, Tierney had assured them, that this *present calamity* would doubtless be proved the work of the Anti-Corn Law League.

The Superintendent had pulled a face, and informed Inspector Tierney that the suspicious nature of the deposit receipt found upon the prisoner's person had not gone unnoticed, and you didn't need a lot of paid informers to help you to a poor conclusion. It was well known that the Anti-Corn Law League had a great deal of money in its coffers, and they were prepared to pay highly to have their arguments put to the industrious classes.

"I have heard," the Superintendent said, "of these so-called 'lecturers' being paid as much as two hundred pounds a time." He had paused tellingly. "Now ask yourself," he said, "how long would it take a Scotch turner to come by seven hundred and fifty pounds on that reckoning?"

The Inspector sighed. It was beginning to snow again. He could think of a good many ways in which a wood-turner, Scotch or otherwise, could come by a large sum of money. And he didn't never care to see a case being made before the evidences was in.

"I looked up that queer token in the station-house Bible," he said, thinking it high time for a gentle lesson in the proper procedures.

"Genesis nine thirteen. It has to do with Noah and the flood. *I do set my bow in the cloud, and it shall be for a token of a covenant between me and the earth.*"

"What's that mean then?" said Silver.

"I don't know exactly," said the Inspector, watching the sky, "but it might turn out to be significant. The Superintendent reckons that '*covenants*' has a particular meaning to the Scotch – a meaning synonymous with trouble." But the Inspector knew nothing of that, and even if he did, he weren't one to go jumping to conclusions. "It looks like a communion token to me," he said, "and I had wondered if it might have something to do with the Scotch Church up on Regent-square. I reckon it might be worth a visit there at some point."

"You think the prisoner might be one of them religious ranters?"

"I ain't in possession of all the strands, Silver," said the Inspector. "All I know is what I see. The prisoner appears to me to be a respectable person who has been brought down: shabby, perhaps not quite right in the head."

"Coo – how d'you reason all that then?"

"Well, he ain't much of a drinker – not even when a Recruiting Sergeant's buying the grog. Going by Mr. Hedges's opinion of him, he's industrious, skilful, and takes a pride in his work.What's more, it seems he's very frugal. When you take it all together, it wouldn't be surprising to discover that he was a church-goer an' all."

"Yes, by gum," said Silver, "the Scotch Church could be full of mad cank Scotchmen wi' murder in mind, couldn't it! Why, it might turn out to be the very place where they do all of their plotting!"

The Inspector frowned. It weren't an easy job, this policing the biggest metropolis in the whole world, while dressed in a swallow-tailed coat and a stove-pipe hat and armed with nothing more offensive than a rattle and a short wooden stave: nobody could say it was. But at that moment it seemed as if it was just about the most difficult job a man can do: getting at the truth in a matter, when everyone else was just looking for a convenient explanation.

They crossed the New Kent-road, the Inspector marking with disapproval the very bunched-together nature of the newly thrown up housefronts.

"The Superintendent says I've proved meself worthy of the uniform," said Silver, for the dozenth time since leaving the station-house.

"Yes well, Constable," said Inspector Hughes," and so you have. But then again, a man oughtn't to say what he has done."

In the weak light spilling from a nearby window, he caught sight of the disappointment in the boy's face and, briefly, he wanted to lay his hand upon his shoulder. Instead he said, "It's too bad that second bit o' shot ain't turned up," and then was instantly sorry to see the boy's head droop.

"They have the first bit," Silver said quietly.

"Always supposing Mr. Drummond surrenders it. A good many people in his position would be content to leave it where it is. No, a second bit of shot would be material evidence, see: proof that the Scotchman intended to do for his victim no matter what. If it don't turn up he might get away with nothing more than a flogging."

"You mean like what was dealt to that dwarf-boy, Bean, who fired at the Queen?" said Silver, full of thought.

"Yes, well, it was proved beyond doubt that his pistol was charged with nothing more 'n a few bits o' paper and some pieces of pipe-clay. But you recollect, I dare say, the fuss that was got up all the same?"

"The Superintendent," said Silver, "said it would all be taken care of one way or another."

"Did he now...?"

Silver stuck out his chin. "Yes, he did. And, what's more, he said I might even make Inspector some day. Besides, it weren't as if Mr. Drummond was badly hurt..."

"Let's hope not, for all our sakes."

"O no. He weren't at all injured. His nephew had a good sight of the wound at the counting-house, and his impression was of a modest burn."

"Hem. Most likely caused by the patch a-catching fire of the gentleman's trowsers," mused the Inspector.

"Exactly," affirmed Silver. "Why, for all we know there *weren't* no second bit of shot – and you can't prove something that wasn't, now can you...?"

They were entering an even darker section of the newly built-up area around the Elephant: no lamp-light, and the streets as yet all unpaved, abandoned; as if someone had tried to put it right and then thought better of it. Inspector Hughes side-stepped a slick of icy mud and thought it best to say nothing further on the matter.

"This is it," said the Constable, coming to a sudden halt before a dingy opening in the terrace, "Poplar-row." The slanting beam of his bull's eye illuminated a narrow tottering alley-way, an ancient remainder amidst the red-brick entrenchments stretching far as the eye can see.

Silver ran the ray of light along a set of lean-tos in various stages of decay, from which emanated the feeble signs of habitation – weak orange candle-glows, thin wisps of chimney smoke – until finally bringing the light to rest upon a ramshackle wooden building isolated from the rest and cast in total darkness. "And that's number seven," pronounced the Constable.

It was hard to imagine anyone living there. There was a faded sign hanging in the unlit window. It read: *Room to let reasonable rates inquire within*, and seeing it, the Inspector felt his heart sink.

That's that, then, he thought: the end of that line of inquiry.

No sooner had the dispiriting thought come to him than a raucous cry of "Bloody Bluebottles!" came from the other side of the street, immediately followed by the heavy thud and splat of a rotten apple against the front door – narrowly missing his collar badge. Inspector Hughes had been clobbered more times than he cared to number, by bricks, bottles, fists, cans, stones, handfuls of mud (and worse), potatoes, tin mugs, fish heads, dead cats, pieces of china, and, most particularly, by that favourite missile of the street wit, orange *peel*. He had been threatened with chains, with knives, with axes and with pistols; and he had not passed a single day in thirteen years in which he had not heard someone cry out "Bloody Bluebottle!", usually along with a stream of oaths bad enough to make a Drill Sergeant blush. A couple of mouldy costards certainly weren't enough to put him off his stride; but the thud of them against the door had alerted the occupant of the lodging-house. From the other side of the door came a woman's voice, low and breathy, and of a surprising resonance.

"Is that you, Dan?" she said.

"Did you hear that," whispered Silver, and his eyes stretched in amazement. "She said Dan! You're a blessed marvel, Inspector! I don't know how you do it!"

Inspector Hughes tipped himself forward onto his smarting toes, and winced.

"What d'ye think on that then, eh wean?" said the voice on the other side of the door. "Dan's come back to us! D'ye see how the Lord is merciful. Hallelujah! He hears all our prayers!"

"Open up," said the Constable, "open up in the name o' the law!"

"Dan?" said the voice. There was a hesitation. "Huv ye no' got yer latchkey?"

Silver and the Inspector exchanged a look as from the other side of the door came the sound of someone fumbling in the dark, followed by the crackle and hiss of a struck Lucifer. "Wisht wean, wisht," came the voice again, this time more urgent. "D'ye want them to take ye? No? Well then, ye maun stop all that awfu' greetin' and gowlin'. If ye're efter lodgings," the voice said, more stridently, "I've nay rooms. If it's payment ye're wanting ye'll need to come back, God bless ye!"

"Begging pardon, missus," said Inspector Hughes, tipping his stove-pipe hat respectfully at the door, "it's the police."

A forlorn mustiness caught in the back of their throats as slowly the door opened to reveal a little lady holding up a thin, smouldering candle.

"We're from Scotland-yard," said the Inspector, looking down at a birdlike person so tiny she scarce reached up to the middle of his brass buttons. "We want to ask you a few questions about Daniel McNaughten."

There was a chill settled all about the little lady and her ill-lit abode, cold enough to make you shiver. It was quite plain that there was not one fire set there, and not one candle flickering, other than the queer glim which she was holding up to his face.

She put her head to one side and peered hard at the Inspector.

"D'ye come in search," she said at last, "d'ye come in search of the new moral world?"

***In which Mr. Warren discovers that not all the ways
are ways of Truth.***

"As far as I know he ain't breathed a word to no-one, an' he's left orf his supper of cold tinned mutton an' all – though he took the bread and the can of coffee readily enough." Sergeant Shew's breath was illuminated in the uncertain lantern ray. It rose valiantly against the dark atmosphere for an instant before succumbing to the brick that lined the steps leading down to the stone-cold station-house cells. "He ain't moved much above an inch in more 'n an hour, I should say. He's a deep 'un, that's for sure. So, you're a mad-house doctor, are you? Inspector Hughes reckoned they'd send for one of you lot sooner or later."

Mr. Warren smiled and made a little bow. It was a slight deception, bringing immense convenience. Two years of medical studies in Edinburgh, and a decade as "the Author of *Diary of a London Physician*" – producing countless blood-chilling tales of insanity – had given him, or so he reasoned, as much claim to being a mad-house doctor as anyone else. It certainly put him at an advantage over the press of newspapermen clamouring for scraps of information at the station-house front desk.

He had hastened to the station-house as soon as he had learned that Mr. Drummond had been shot at. Such a calamitous assault on a gentleman of Mr. Drummond's calibre – occurring as it had done in the open street at broad face of day, as he made his way to Downing-street from his family's counting-house on the corner of Charing-cross – would have always seized the attention; but the fact that it had occurred less than an hour after Mr. Warren and Mr. Drummond had parted company added measure to the incident. Such an extraordinary confluence of events – particularly when one considered its propinquity to the conversation at Bellamy's.

Mr. Warren had already made inquiries at Mr. Drummond's house

[67]

in Grosvenor-street (where he had failed to gain admittance), and se-cured an appointment with Mr. Drummond's deputy at the gentleman's office in Downing-street for later that day. Now he had come to see for himself the would-be assassin.

"Inspector Tierney's in there with a witness at the minute," the pock-marked sergeant was saying, "so you shall have to wait for him to finish." They had come to a halt in the mid-point of a long, damp corri-dor with a row of heavy iron doors set in either side, each with no more than a few inches between the other. "For a sixpence I could show you the boy what winded the Duke of Wellington, while you wait – though he don't seem to be at all mad as far as I can tell."

"Madness is not always obvious to the untrained eye," said Mr. Warren. He gave brief consideration to the sergeant's offer before ar-riving at the conclusion that the wretch who had collided with the hero of Waterloo was grist, as it were, rather than the pie-crust of the matter. "I came here to see the rogue who shot at Mr. Drummond," he said, "and that is my sole interest."

His attention was taken by voices coming from a little further along the corridor.

"I'm afraid I really couldn't swear to it, Inspector Tierney," one of them was saying, as they emerged from a cell. "The fellow I spoke to was much shorter to my recollection – and darker of complexion – *dirtier* somehow. And he was wearing a hat. A very curious, close-brushed affair it was – it could have been a very battered old shovel hat, like an old-fashioned clergyman might wear – only very dirty – broad at the top and curled up at the sides. I should know it at once were I to see it again."

"Come, come, sir," said his interlocutor. He spoke in a mazy, insinu-ating tone that Mr. Warren could not quite put his finger to. "You cannot infer a thing from a hat. Hats are misplaced. Hats are stolen. Hats are replaced with other hats."

"Well, yes, that is certainly so," said the first voice. "He was most definitely *Scotch* – of that I am certain."

The first voice was familiar to Mr. Warren: indeed, he had recog-nised it almost at once as belonging to a gentleman office-keeper at the Board of Trade with whom he had a passing acquaintance. The office-keeper was in conversation with a somewhat elegant fellow, dressed in a quality frac and very fine top-boots, who Mr. Warren deduced at once to be one of the new-fashioned plainclothes detectivists.

"How do you do," he said, hailing the office-keeper.

The pair looked up at once, although it seemed to Mr. Warren that the smart fellow withdrew ever so slightly into the shadows.

"Mr. Warren! How d'ye do! Well, well, 'pon my soul," said the office-keeper, "and what brings you here?"

"I was about to ask the same of you."

"Now that really is the most curious thing," said the office-keeper. "Would you believe that I'm here on account of Drummond of the Treasury? You've heard the dreadful news, of course? Well, what do you think of this, Mr. Warren – a few days ago I myself had an alarming encounter on the steps of the Board of Trade."

"No!"

"O, but yes! I can assure you, sir. I was just telling the Inspector here. I came as soon as I heard what had happened. Indeed, Lord Ripon was most insistent. He said I was to leave my desk and come at once. He and Mr. Drummond are very close, of course."

"Of course," said Mr. Warren with a slight bow. Lord Ripon had received the Presidency of the Board of Trade from Peel in '41 at the suggestion of Mr. Drummond – or so it was said. Certainly the two had known each other for many years.

"I'd seen the rascal lurking there on the steps for a few days before – and once, though I cannot swear to it, outside the Privy Council office. I didn't like the look of him, Mr. Warren. Nasty, brutish. I wondered if he was a plainclothes police agent, and attempted to ascertain his credentials. 'You are a police agent, are you not?', I asked him. And what do you know, Mr. Warren, he looked straight back at me and said that he was!"

Sergeant Shew had come to stand in the corridor behind Mr. Warren, and muttered some disparagement of the plainclothesmen. Hearing him, the elegant fellow in the top-boots, who had hitherto been inspecting his nails in a nonchalant fashion, looked up sharply.

"Well," said the office-keeper, "there are so many of those dratted fellows hanging about the place I dare say it was only a matter of time

[69]

before some confoundment of the sort occurred. But you haven't said, Mr. Warren – might I ask what brings you here?"

A nascent perturbation had assailed Mr. Warren's senses. He did not wish to find himself drawn into the glare of an investigation, but nor did he wish to deprive himself of a possible source of information.

"Well, as a matter of fact," he replied, "I dined with Mr. Drummond this very afternoon."

"What an extraordinary coincidence!" exclaimed the office-keeper.

"Yes," continued Mr. Warren, "and on my way to meet him I came across a crew of Anti-Corn Law League rabble-rousers, dangerously close to the Palace of Westminster – or what remains of it – and one of them was wearing a hat exactly like the one I have just heard you describe."

"Indeed," said the detectivist. His lips parted slowly in a thin, vulpine smile.

Mr. Warren nodded circumspectly. "I wonder – perhaps I too ought to examine the prisoner in order to make an identification?"

"A crew you say?" said Inspector Tierney, thoughtfully. "The Anti-Corn Law League, eh?" He appeared to be weighing up the evidences he had just received.

"Quite so! And I should definitely know were I to see any of them again."

"I say, this will make a capital subject for one of your stories, Warren!" said the office-keeper, putting on his silk hat and preparing to leave the gloomy cellars.

"Stories? What stories?" said Sergeant Shew, his piggy features pink with indignation. "You never said you was a newspaperman!"

"You never asked," said Mr. Warren.

He was quickening with anticipation as he approached the cell door in front of which the top-booted fellow was standing, so that he was forced to crane his neck in order to see in. It was a very small, bare cell, with no window or fire; nothing at all, in fact, but cold, damp stone joined to cold, damp stone.

The prisoner was sitting bolt upright and quite motionless in one corner, upon the only piece of furniture there: a solitary bench suspended from two thick ropes of chain linked to two solid rings. His gaze seemed transfixed, focused upon the shadows cast by a solitary candle ensconced in the wall behind him. He did not appear to mark their intrusion at all.

"On your feet," barked Shew.

The prisoner obeyed immediately, scooped up in the swaying beam of light from the bull's eye, without a word or a look in their direction. The sergeant came to stand hard by him and held up the lantern to his face. The glare was considerable in the gloomy cell, yet the prisoner did nothing more than blink once or twice at the dead wall.

"Is this one of those you saw this afternoon?" Inspector Tierney asked Mr. Warren.

Mr. Warren peered hard, scrutinising the prisoner; he was taking note of every detail of his appearance, skilfully measuring out the distance between the eyes, the depth of the brow, the thickness of the skull at the back of his head. He could determine no trace whatever of the degradations of demeanour that characterise the true villain. Far from it: the prisoner had a somewhat gentlemanly appearance. He was mild of manner and his features were regular, handsome – even *delicate*. In short, there were none of the usual ciphers for criminality, imbecility, or insanity.

"No," he said at last. "It's not him."

"You are quite sure, sir?" said Inspector Tierney. There was a menacing edge to his voice. "Look again. You may take your time."

Mr. Warren took a step back and stroked his top lip. He was struck by the utter composure in the features which confronted him.

He had no idea how a mesmerised person might look, never having seen one, although he had once written a very successful story under his pen-name of "the Author of *Diary of a London Physician*", in which an evil hypnologist places an innocent young clerk under magnetic influences, constraining him to carry out the bloody murder of a rich old gentleman. The story, cleverly constructed and very well researched, had but a loose basis on true events; but that was not to say that something of the sort could not happen. Certainly, "The Look" had caused a sensation when published in *Blackwood's Magazine*, and was even credited with having started the current craze for all things psychical.

What was more, Mr. Warren's acute understanding of the law had led him to the startling conclusion that if such a thing were to occur in reality, then the jury would be compelled to return a verdict of death by misadventure: the perfect crime!

Mr. Warren waved his hand in front of the prisoner's eyes, up and down and then from side to side. The prisoner blinked a couple of times. There was the trace of a smile. Whether he was under the influence of animal magnetism or not, the prisoner was evidently of high intelligence.

"No, I am quite sure," said Mr Warren at length, "that the fellow I saw was a good deal older, and thinner. He had long gray hair and a long straggling beard. And he was dressed in filthy rags." He took a step back. "How very alarming," he mused, "that someone of such calibre as this fellow appears to be would have attempted to murder a civil servant in broad day on the open street – and a short distance across the carriage-way from Scotland-yard."

"If, that is, we can assume that Mr. Drummond was the intended victim," said Inspector Tierney.

"Whatever can you mean?" said Mr. Warren, feeling the stirrings of something.

The plainclothesman had come to lean upon the door-frame, running an appraising thumb over the nails of one hand. He said, "These days all the strength of the terrible threat we face lies in its *invisibility*." He was looking at Mr. Warren through half-closed eyes. "The unshorn fellows in their fustian and battered slouch hats are not the only ones we must guard against. We must also watch those with a veneer of respectability – manufactors, tradesmen, mechanics – anyone with a grudge against corn..."

"Quite so," said Mr. Warren.

The Inspector coolly removed his frac and handed it to the sergeant. Then he rolled up his shirt-sleeves. There was something in the manner in which he performed these simple actions that made Mr. Warren feel uneasy.

"I'm afraid you shall have to leave, sir," said the sergeant. He held up the lantern, showing the way out of the cell. "Inspector Tierney has some police business to attend to."

The top-booted Inspector was circling the prisoner, grinning wolf-ishly. Mr. Warren could not have exaggerated the disquiet into which the spectacle threw him, and he glanced concernedly at the prisoner. The expression that he read upon those spectral features was an alto-gether curious one: one to which he could not easily put a name. Certainly it was not a fearful look, much to Mr. Warren's relief; nor was it a defiant one.

He was headed towards Downing-street when it struck him: the look the prisoner had given the police inspector was unmistakably a look of *pity*.

No. 7 Poplar-row, Newington Butts,
at approximately the same time

In which we discover certain Revelations concerning the prisoner McNaughten and the End of the World.

The little bird-like lady was, the Inspector reckoned, above eight-and-thirty – perhaps as much as five-and-forty – and might once have been very pert and handsome. She was dressed in a plain black widow's bombazine, grown quite rusty with age along the line of the sleeves and the bodice, a threadbare Paisley shawl, and a squeezed and pinched widow's cap that struggled to contain a luxuriant thatch of gleaming black hair that was entirely at odds with the exiguity of everything else in that place.

"The new moral world?" repeated the Inspector. He was thinking: that sounds like trouble. "And what might that be, then?"

She placed her head to one side, her large blue eyes flickering alarm-ingly.

"O! It has begun," she said in a surprisingly low and vibratory tim-bre. "Behold, the Lord maketh the earth empty, and maketh it waste, and turneth it upside down!"

The tiny lady was evidently in a somewhat unfortunate situation. In short, she was as mad as Bedlam.

"Religious fervour," murmured the Inspector as they followed the woman into the room.

Silver nodded shrewdly.

"The commonest cause of mental affliction in women of a certain age," said the Inspector knowingly.

"Drink, too," said Silver. "Drink takes the reason of a good many – and the pox."

The Inspector winced.

"She seems perfectly respectable to me, Constable," he replied in a hoarse whisper.

The room into which Mrs. Dutton – for that was the landlady's name – had led them occupied the whole of the ground floor. It was quite bare, save for a rocking chair, a grate of cold ashes, and an upturned portmanteau set in the middle of the floor with a worn shawl draped over it. On top of the portmanteau lay an ancient Bible, a marker resting on an open page. The Inspector crossed over to it. Book of Revelation. Chapter XXI. The pages were damp, and in the groove where they met, tiny insects writhed.

"Dinnae touch the altar," commanded Mrs. Dutton. Silver had lifted up a corner of the shawl which he let drop straightaway. "Only myself and the Reverend Duncan are permitted tae touch the altar." She busied herself straightening the shawl, muttering beneath her breath as she did so. "Some folk huvnae a drap o' respect! Am ah right wean? Am ah right?" She turned back to the two policemen. "It's just as well The End is comin'," she said.

Inspector Hughes shot an admonitory glance at Silver, who was grinning in a wholly unsuitable way.

"Aye, that it is!" She had assumed a somewhat fierce, rapt countenance. "It will a' be done awa' wi' Thursday week." She handed the Inspector a handbill from a pile on the rocking chair. He took it with a respectful bow and began to read with enormous care.

Set beneath a crooked, primitive representation of a boat floating on three jagged waves was a piece of text,

And he shewed me that great citie, that holie Hierusalem,
descending out of Heauen from God. Revelation. XXI:ii

The End will come Thursday 2nd February!!!
Attend the Ark of the Covenant – Democratic Chapel – Poplar-row,
Newington Butts. Midnight Wednesday 1st February 1843 anno dom.
Witness the Judgement Visited Upon the Citadel!
Utter Ruin to the Wicked! The People Freed From Bondage!
Admission 1d

"Covenant, eh," said the Inspector. He was thinking of the queer token found on the prisoner.

"Look at the date, sir!" gasped Silver. "Thursday second of February – why, that's Queen's Speech Day!"

The Constable was quite right.

Inspector Hughes frowned. "Hum, I think that we oughter take a look at the rest of the house, if we may, missus," he said.

Mrs. Dutton peered at him.

"Whit's that wean?" she said. "We've unbelievers in our midst? Aye. That we huv!"

"Sorry for the inconvenience," said the Inspector, "but might we see the room where Mr. McNaughten lodges?"

She scowled and grumbled to herself, but prepared to show them the way in any case.

The rest of the house comprised two small rooms to each of two landings: every one as chill and fusty as a sepulchre. Indeed, the whole building was permeated with a morbidity which set the very marrow of one's bones on edge; and as he was led up the stairs to McNaughten's room in the attic part, the Inspector was aware of a great heaviness in his legs and on his chest: a doominess, as enervating as anything he could ever recall since his childhood.

"What sort of lodger is Mr. McNaughten?" he asked.

"A righteous man," she said. "Quiet and verra clean in his habits. He nivver goes out wi'oot polishing his boots in the room there. He nivver misses his half-crown rent, and he nivver takes a meal at hame. He leaves the house each day at nine o' the morning, an' he disnae come back 'til nine o' the evening."

"He sounds like a very agreeable lodger, indeed," observed the Inspector. "Tell me, does he work at all, as far as you know?"

"He's in search of a sitty-ation. He wants to read the law."

"Does he now..."

"Aye, he's a scholar. Most respectable. He's lookin' fer a position where he can carry oan wi' his studies an' improve hisself. Och but this world is awfu' hard."

"Isn't it though," said the Inspector.

"Aye. Mind it's no' long tae run."

The Inspector sighed. "Has Mr. McNaughten been out of an occasion for a good while, do you know?"

"Aye. Since giving up his business. Above a year."

"And is that how long he's been in the metropolis?"

The landlady sniffed. "Aye. All told. He was here for a wee while a year ago before this last time."

"And when did he return?"

She shrugged, her shawl slipping down to reveal the prominent bones of her shoulders.

"He studied medicine, d'ye ken that?" she said. "But no' the anatomy. He wouldna go into the bodies of the poor. Och, it's awfu' cruel, is that, denyin' folk a Christian burial. The body is the temple o' the Holy Ghost. Whit's that wean? O aye, I'd forgotten that. The wean says Dan was aye after some position in the government."

"Was he now – which branch?"

The landlady listened to the emptiness of the landing for a few moments.

"East India office," she said at last.

"You never heard him mention the Treasury?"

She listened a while longer.

"The wean says it was something to do wi' patents," she said decisively. "And if that dinna come to him then he was off to Amerikay, to be a cutlery salesman."

"I see. But he came here instead."

She was far away, as if trying to catch the thread of a conversation taking place in another part of the house. She sighed wearily. In the smoky wavering light of the candle the Inspector could see the fine lines gathered about her eyes and mouth; the very paleness of her skin; the slight smattering of freckles. It put him in mind of his own poor

[76]

mother – lost a good many years ago, when he was still too young to let her know how much he'd have liked her to stay.

"It would've been October," said Mrs. Dutton, her dark eyes glinting at the recollection. "I was takin' the jugs tae the pump, and I opened the door and there he was. I see you have a bill in your window, he says, is it for ma old room? Aye, says I. You see, he says, ah told you I'd be back."

"Is that so," said the Inspector gently.

"I'd an awfu' shock to see him so clarty and puir-lookin'," she said. "His trowsers all patched and nay hat tae his name."

"He seemed much reduced in circumstances, did he?"

"O aye, that he did, yer honour. Why, only the other mornin' he comes to me asking if ah've an auld pair o' boots to use since his own were that broken! Imagine! A gentleman such as him, beggin' a pair o' boots aff a puir widder woman! Whit's the world runnin' tae? Mr. Carlo said he could get him a pair as guid as are your own there, sir," she said. "Och, but Dan wouldnae huv any o' *that*."

"Who's Mr. Carlo?" asked the Inspector, making a note of the name. "Is he an associate of Mr. McNaughten?" The landlady either did not hear or affected not to hear, so the Inspector asked the question again in a different form. "Does Mr. McNaughten have any associates, as far as you know? Have you ever heard him talk of a man by the name of *Gordon*?"

"Och, he's nae time fer any o' that clishmaclaver! He's devoted to his studies an' getting on. Mind, ah've telt him: there's nae need o' that! The End is comin'! Study nothin' but your Bible, son, ah telt him. Och, he's a guid young man, so I should say – even though he disnae believe in the Prophecy. Selfish, the Reverend Duncan calls him – an' he's known him since he was a wee lad. But ah think he's jist a bit lost. Isn't that right, wean? Aye. The wean agrees. Wisht," she hissed, "haud yer tongue, ye gyte carle!"

Inspector Hughes was a little astonished. He understood that the unfortunate lady was cracked, but he had nevertheless taken her to be the sort around whom an air of withered gentility hung, like ivy on a church-yard monument.

"Wisht, I say," she cried with more force than before. "O, aye, I heard what ye said ye fouter!"

It appeared that Mrs. Dutton was directing her fury towards one of the closed doors on the landing behind him. The Inspector cocked an ear and listened, but could hear nothing save the dense rustle of the landlady's bombazine skirt brushing against the banister, and Silver breathing in the dark behind him.

"Away wit' ye!" she shrieked, "and dinna come back here!" She shuddered in disgust, before crumpling against the banisters as though exhausted by the confrontation.

"Would you like the Constable to enter there, missus?" asked the Inspector, indicating the closed door. A curious expression had settled upon the landlady's features, and her luminous eyes still flickered in that alarming way, as though tracing the carriage of a moth about the gloomy landing – although there was nothing living there but the three of them.

"Och, they willna be caught out," she said, "they're awfu' cunning. Naebody ever catches them at their vile plotting!"

Inspector Hughes caught Silver's eye, and a knowing look passed between them.

"Very sorry for the inconvenience, missus," he said gently, turning the brim of his stove-pipe hat in his long fingers, "but if we might progress to Mr. McNaughten's lodging, I'd be much obliged."

Her wild eyes gradually came to rest upon his gaze, like a swirling murmuration of starlings swooping at dusk to settle on the branches of a tree.

"You'll find no fault in him," she said in her low resonating voice. "And not a bone o' him shall be broken. For whatever it is they say he's done, these things were done that the scripture be fulfilled!"

Then she turned her head sharply, the candle-light catching the sheen of her hair in a flash of something like triumph.

"Go on in," she said nodding towards one of the doors, "it's never locked."

The First Meeting

I had heard that McNaughten was a man of so retiring a disposition and so averse to conversation or notice of any kind that it was very difficult, even for those in whose care he had been placed, to glean from him any information as to his state of mind or the character of his supposed delusions. It has been commonly supposed that he imagined himself to be the subject of annoyance from some real or fanciful being or beings – *the Tories of his native land*, as he had once averred in public; but more than that was not known, for he studiously avoided entering into the subject with anyone. If any stranger were to come near, he would at once withdraw into the water closet or some darkish corner where he would read or knit until they had gone away again. And nor was he in the habit of engaging much with the others who shared his fate, preferring to sit alone in a covered shed that stood in the centre of the yard while they played at fives or other sport.

I must confess to being not at all surprised to learn of these tendencies. I have had an amplitude of occasions upon which to observe how the victim of real delusions will plunge, with a celerity it is almost impossible to imitate, into his insane notions whenever conversation tends near them; and so the observation that McNaughten would not be drawn whatever upon the subject aroused in me, almost at once, a well-founded suspicion that his was (as I had long suspected) nothing more than a "sham" insanity. It is, I believe, invariably a matter for circumspection when a subject avoids answering questions, or pleads inability to answer questions put to him on the grounds that he cannot remember; for the real lunatic, when accosted, will in almost every case attempt to summon his wits together and repudiate any suggestion of his insanity by answering as fully as he may.

So closely did the descriptions I received of McNaughten's reluctance to speak of his alleged torments tally with my own understanding of "pretend insanity", that I might almost have concluded the matter of my investigation there and then – had not my considerable experience in the subject strengthened in me a belief that madness is the most complicated of matters in which virtually nothing may be taken for granted. In particular, there are few undertakings, I believe, more difficult than the attempt to uncover the counterfeiting of insanity – as must surely be evinced by the fact that McNaughten had been pronounced mad by a clutch of (we must assume) competent scientific observers.

It was with some trepidation, therefore, that I made my first encounter with him, determined to prove my suspicions concerning the veracity of his alleged delusions beyond all doubt, yet wary of arriving all too swiftly at an *impasse*. Certainly, there was nothing in those first impressions, as he entered the room set aside for our interview, suggestive of any abnormal conformations of the head; nor did he possess the unhealthy complexion and aspect frequently observed of the insane person. On the contrary, I was greeted by a man of apparently perfect health (I had already learned that there was no indication of the deficient circulation, accelerated pulse, or morbidity of secretions, &c., &c., which typically betoken the afflicted brain). His features were regular and their expression mild and prepossessing, and as I laid out my pens and papers upon the table, he took his seat opposite mine, where he sat quite placid and contented.

I had already decided that I would commence my examination by putting the question that had most vexed me down through the years. I had been given assurances by all those in whose charge McNaughten resided that he would not give me any sort of reply, but it has long been my experience that there is much to be deduced from the manner in which a question is *not* answered – indeed, I have often observed how much *more* may be evinced from a silence than is ever to be obtained from any number of lengthy and eloquent disquisitions.

And so I set it out at once.

"Before we proceed," I ventured, "I must ask you whether you believe that you were, at that time, *out of your mind*? And, if so, are you so now?"

I observed a slight, imbecilic smile resting upon his lips, but no indication that he intended to make any sort of a response. I was expecting this, of course, and had already decided that I would simply wait, without further prompting: wait and *observe*. The advocates of what is nowadays somewhat fashionably termed the "moral treatment" of the deluded would have it that those afflicted are uncommonly sensitive to the humours of others, and that it is therefore always advisable to temper one's own behaviour lest it be the cause of disturbance or agitation in the subject. I followed the prescription, reasoning that there could be no harm or difficulty in doing so, even in a case of "pretended insanity".

For a while our breathing was the only noise or motion in the room. McNaughten's eyes were heavy-lidded and appeared to be directed at some indeterminate point or object in the middle-distance. He did not stir a muscle. Then:

"Such was the verdict," he said at last.

I confess to having been taken aback: the peace and solitude for so long of the setting had caused me to drift into contemplation. "I beg your pardon?" I said.

"Such was the verdict," he repeated, "the opinion of the jury after hearing the evidence."

He settled back in his chair with the same slight smile that I had observed upon his lips – perhaps, I could not be sure, tinged now with something of the *ironical*.

"And is that your opinion too?" I asked.

He folded his arms across his chest. "Are you able to help me?" he said. "Only, I should like to get away from this place. It really is too bad! I have spoken about it many, many times, but it is quite useless."

"I see." I confess to a fluttering of excitement at finding myself brought into his confidence.

"If I could go back to Glasgow," he continued, "my native place, I should be quite well there."

"*Glasgow*?" I repeated.

McNaughten reached across the desk and took hold of my hand; the grasp, though gentle as a woman's, was not to be resisted.

"You will help me?" he said. "Yes?" His eyes were open and looking towards my own, but very difficult to read.

"Very well," I said. "I will see what can be done. And in return, suppose – suppose you begin by telling me – tell me about Glasgow..."

And after a moment's consideration, in which his gaze moved passively about my face as if taking in the details of my expression for later contemplation, McNaughten began to talk. His words unschooled: a stream of thoughts and sensations, no more, unkempt and unruly. At first such volubility took me by surprise, but as I began to transcribe, my nib ran faster and faster across the page, and I found to my immense interest that I was taking down in stenographic sound-hand a life – unpatterned and unset. Material to be worked upon – like clay: like wood.

The lathe, he said; *the lathe takes full advantage of the available light, which is not, in any case, over much.* It stood before the wee barred window in the space he shared with it for more than half of his young life. It was the centre of his existence, the progenitor of all shape and sense. For many years – this long, long after he had left that place – whenever he shut his eyes he would taste at once the bitter rust rising from the cast-iron poppets, the acrid friction sharpening the soft saw-dusty air. And he would see his father's silhouette hunched over the rounding plane, moving up and down at one with the workings of the foot-treadle; the lines of the window bars dissecting, the light from the spaces in between pouring from him, seeping back into him, until it was aye impossible to tell for sure where that big black mound of a man began and the dirty rectangles of Glasgow sky left off.

And always, always the buzz of the plane, the rattle of the driving wheel, the throb of the belt, and the swirling clouds of sawdust, the slivers of wood spat out in all directions around about.

His salvation.

You might say that his whole life had been the iteration of a weakness so pervading: a wicked impulse, an abomination shaping him from the moment of his illicit making. He had been saved, this much he knew; but saved *from* what; *for* what? Salvation began with the blank indifference of his father's saw-dusted coat-sleeve. It began with his own small hand slipping inside the loose and calloused grip leading him away from the quayside with the Heritors and members of the Kirk Session of the Parish and the Presbytery glaring at their backs. It began with being led from the place where she had left him sitting on a wee pine kist with the note pinned to him:

This boy is the natural son of Daniel McNaughten, Esq.,
turner of Stockwell-street.

He could read well for a wee tyke – even upside down.

There was a life before, but it was ebbing from him with the leaving tide; destroyed utterly, dead upon the curst, curst earth.

"Stand there and watch," his father had instructed him on the second day. He watched the wood spin back and forth in his father's grasp; marking the application of the chisel bit with different degrees of pressure; the relaxing or speeding-up of the treadle, barely perceptible to all but the practised observer, how it seemed to make a difference. He was, he was told, fortunate to be learning a trade. He witnessed in silence the miracle of the flat-angled pieces of wood gradually transforming into spindles, porridge spurtles; perfectly rounded chair legs.

"Green wood is softer to work with... Ash is best for chair seats."

"Aye, guid. Why do we re-turn the ends of the spindles?"

"Because they oval as they dry out."

"Aye, guid."

The screwit Clyde loitered dangerously in the corner of the shop where he slept on a wee feather bed set in a hiddle amongst the sawdust sweepings. The river caught in the back of his throat, filling him up with the taste of death. O but it was easy to blame the waff of the Clyde for the course of his life. The board with the steamers chalked upon it stood at the brig-end of the street, tantalising him with Greenock, Batavia, Montreal, Valparaiso, and other salvations.

But that was all to come when he had grown from a tongue-tackit spindle-shankt wean to an awkward gowk: after years of standing, keeping still, staying quiet, watching and learning; poking corners of pie-crust and clumps of caller-herring into his mouth as he sat in silence with his pa, side by side on their cuttie-stools; mashing down draibles of sour, crumbly cheese on thick bannock-cakes with dusty fingers. Eyes always cast down lest he was being watched: fearing he was not.

"Dinnae blether, dinnae fu' my ears wi' a' that clishmaclaver..."

"I'll nyse ye, so ah will..."

At night, alone with the river, he cried himself to sleep with the blanket pulled up around him while outside the world went on well enough without him: the passing shadows clipped by the window bars; the girnings of a distant wean; the barking of a dog some way off; a drunk channering to himself as he stumbled down the close to take a piss. And somewhere on the other side, the tidy home in Gorbals village refulgent in the orange-glow of candle-light, hearth-light, where his father sat reading the *Herald* wi' a full pipe beside him on the firestone: pianoforte, Sunday best; the infusions of warm steam pouring off Mrs. McNaughten's rich puddings and sturdy broths; and the wee brothers and sisters sitting about the dinner table in their clean pinafores.

And when he was tired of picturing it, he would console himself in the dark by turning patterns, trying to discern the precise point at which he ceased to be and all the rest came into being; fading in and out at will; occasionally uttering aloud some words, so as to shatter the emptiness and leave his mark upon the surface.

He was about fourteen, fifteen when he had begun to realise that he would never belong. Naebody was like him. Naebody knew the things he knew. Naebody understood the way he felt, saw, heard. At first light on Argyle-street the housemaids standing their turn at the well would nudge one another as he filled his stoup, twisting their curls in their fingers and smiling in ways he did not understand. On fine afternoons he'd wander past the Horse Brae by the bridge, ignoring the calls of the 'prentices taking noisy dips in the Clyde waters. He saw how they smirtled at one another when they saw him coming along: as if there was a want about him, as if he wasnae a' there.

"Hech! Thinks he's too guid for the likes o' us."

"Barmpot! He's nocht but a foundling."

"Wee bastard!"

Still, he was makin' something o' himself. He bought a waistcoat of brown figured velvet, and he read books: philosophy, history, poetry, and other things too – not just the Bible. He taught himself a word a day. Gubernatorial. Numismatic. Avocation. Eleemosynary. He bought a wee volume of the *Maxims* of La Rochefoucauld and a notebook and a lead pencil and copied out the parts that appealed most to him.

"In order to succeed in the world people do all they might to appear successful."

"We are often as different from ourselves as we are from other people."

"We all have strength enough to endure the troubles of others."

That summer – it must have been that of '31 – the railroad came to Glasgow, and everywhere the talk was of Progress and Reform. Business was good on Stockwell-street and his father took on a journeyman bodger to help with the orders. Abram Duncan was a tall thin man, gaunt – careful and precise, but none too slow. When he spoke it was always in tones of the utmost mildness, yet one felt compelled to listen. His gray eyes were always full of thought and understanding.

"Yon lad o' yours works like a champion," said Duncan, looking up from the pole-lathe to smile at the boy.

"Aye," said Mr. McNaughten senior, "and he's nae dummy – despite appearances."

His father was a contrary man. An appearance before the fornication polis at Duncow sessions in his youth – three bouts o' penance for himself and the dyke-louper whom Dan had once called *mother*– had strengthened in him an inclination to the cross-grained where religion was concerned. The rest soon followed. He left the Kirk behind him at once and went over to the Episcopalians: the Piskies were Tory to a man when most o' Glesga' was Whig. Not that it ever did him a jot o' harm in business, by the way. He was in wi' a click o' independent-minded men who were not affeart to give full-swing to character: men reamin' sure of how it went in this world and how it would go in the next; who studied the marts like other men might study philosophy; who read the *Glasgow Constitutional* from cover to cover, gathering in the lunting air of a howff to discuss its contents over a hot toddy. Monday nights at the Lodge; Wednesdays doing business with the farmers in the Temperance Hotel up on Argyle-street: a proud tradesman in the days when that counted for something.

Mind, he had his enemies. He was cauldriffe and miserly, and he treated his labourers very ill – as a matter of fact, Duncan, always so mild of manner, was one of the few able to tolerate his moods and his tempers for longer than a week.

"Piskie!" the Rads would hiss behind old man McNaughten's back.

"Tory loon!" they'd shout through the open door of the shop.

"Fuckin' Nob shite!"

"Youse want to watch that rabble," customers would say. "It'll be a jar of vitriol being flung at ye next!"

But his father wouldnae give the time o' day to such fearsome thoughts. He'd hurl chunks of wood after the rabble, and those who called wi' inflammatory pamphlets and talk of Combinationism and the extension of the franchise.

"Whit's the city comin tae?" he would wonder, slackening the treadle to muse. "The Tories are done fer and the Whig click'll own Glesga' noo! Twelve times the number of voters!" He spat upon the mound of sawdust at his feet. "Havers! How will they keep control o' that Mob – for all their jobbing?"

Duncan nodded slowly. He was refining a chair leg with his draw knife, the gray eyes never wavering. "The great quarrel," he said without looking up, "isnae between Whig and Tory." His voice was soft and untempered. "That's fer gentlemen – an' a gentleman shall aye win the day. The Great Quarrel is the same as it's always been: between property an' nae property. These are bitter times, Mr. McNaughten. Mad and incendiary. There is a disease raging in the system."

"Aye, well, ye're no' wrang there, Mr. Duncan. The whole lot should be strung up on Glesga' Green as a warning tae the rest!"

"Or the majority o' men must be gi'en a say in the way the country's run."

Mr. McNaughten senior snorted, grim, humourless. "Och, I dare say there are countries whaur the labouring classes can be intrusted wi' the vote," he said, over the rattle and buzz of the lathe, "but no' here! No' in Glesga'! Havers! The whole country'd be a republic inside a week! And that, Abram, wouldnae be guid for business!"

Outside the shop there was a savage rise to the air, and everywhere a hungering. One afternoon down by the Trongate, Dan found himself on the edge of a thumming crowd that was listening to a fellow tell of how the working men of Britain were as oppressed as any negro slave. The crowd was made up of men who had no work to go to – idle slaipers, his father would have said; but not all of them were Irish or teuchter exiles just stept off the steamers frae the Highlands. Here and there were to be found citizens of Glasgow: weavers, shoemakers, tailors, dyers, cotton-spinners, even turners, watching him with a slinking menace in their downcast eyes. One of them, a miserable wretch, not much older than him, begged a portion of the meat-pie he was munching, and not feeling he could safely refuse, Dan handed him over the whole of it. They fell to talking. It was the first time he had had a conversation with a lad of his own age, which must have been why he found himself standing the fellow a wee dram in a nearby howff – something he had never done in his life before.

In the beer-washed, tobacco-riven tavern he had a better view of his companion, matted hair sprouting from beneath a greasy slouch hat, obscuring a face that was niddered and pinched by long nights in the cold. Still, something in his black eyes sparked and gleamed, and the skeigh certainly had a guid conceit of hisself. Carlo was – or so he said – a wood-wright, too. That is to say, he'd worked the last Fair Week, earning a few shillings by constructing booths and platforms for the penny geggies. He had since been reduced to begging, he said, by a click o' employers. "Nobs. Tories," he spat, "wha had him down as nocht but a troublemaker, and wouldnae gie him the time o' day."

"Well, an' they're right in that," he laughed as they stood together in the press of unwashed bodies and pipe fumes, while all around them the talk picked up on worldly things. "Ah tell ye, Dan, ah'm aye efter trouble and ah know where to find it, too: in every nook o' the city!"

It was, Dan decided, something to do with being a man. He drank a finger of whisky, feeling the world rush towards him, dim and un-steady as the light off a bad Lucifer; afterwards, a certain satisfaction: a warm glow in the shadow of the old, old yearning. His new pal, Carlo, clapped him on the shoulders and asked if he'd somewhere he might stay for the remainder of the night.

"Ach, it's awfu' cold out there on the street, Dan," he said, suddenly sober.

Dan did not feel he could refuse. He had never had a friend before, and though there was something in the wild and clarty nature of Carlo that made him uncertain, it was also true that this same uncertainty guarded him against causing offence.

Carlo shouted, swore, and ran very fast along the quayside,

punching the gloomy air with his fist. Dan followed close behind, the Clyde's black waters drifting by. The whisky had left him feeling cold and empty and a wee bit sick. "Mind youse'll huv to leave before ma pa comes in the mornin" he said. "He disnae care for strangers in the shop."

He was never sure that Carlo had heard him. Or if he had, that he cared a damn.

CHARING-CROSS,
ABOUT TEN O'CLOCK P.M.

Introduces the Reader to one who takes great delight in punching holes in the fabric of Society.

The Brobdingnagian Peeler had made a good effort. He had found the witnesses; he had asked all the pertinent questions; he had made the rounds of the turners' yards; he had found the lodging. It was a good night's work by anyone's reckonings, and the more so when measured against the customary standards of the "A" Division. Or so ran the opinion of Renton Nicholson, Esq., book and print-seller, rag-grubber and bone-picker extraordinaire, author of *The Swell's Night Guide*, or a *Peep Through the Great Metropolis Under the Dominion of Nox* (with numerous spicy engravings) – *alias* Old Peeping Tom of London Town, *alias* the Lord Chief Baron – the flashest of flash habitués of gambling dens and boozing kens; the arbiter elegantiarum of fashion and folly; blabber, screever, moocher, scrivener, and prick up the arse of society.

Mr. Nicholson could arrive at more truth in an hour's consideration of a matter than an honest peeler could in a week, so when he reckoned that Inspector Hughes – so ponderous, so diligent, so mindful of his blessed Nine Points of Policing – weren't so far behind him in the pursuit of this knotted string of rascality, then that was to be counted as an observation very much in the favour of the Bene Old Cove – even though it would doubtless make not one jot of difference in respect of the likely outcome. Ah dear me no...

[88]

Old Peeping Tom could sniff out a conspiracy quicker than a starving man sniffed out baking day, and conspiracy had left its smell all over the matter of the shooting of Mr. Drummond of the Treasury. It was a fact of life that truth, diligence, ponderousness, even the Nine Points of Policing themselves were all as ill-matched against conspiracy as was a workhouse washerwoman finding herself pitched in a pugilistical against the iron fists of Dutch Sam. Not that any of this mattered much to Mr. Nicholson, to whom the whole business was nothing more than a spree. He picked up his spirits, and casting off any melancholy reflections that might have otherwise threatened his customary good humour, he returned to the task in hand: the thing he did best in this life, a bit of poking about. On this occasion he was poking about in the doorway of Cock and Biddulph's, a spit away from the scene of the incident up on Charing-cross. He was looking for something which (he had learned by dint of the other skill at which he excelled: that is, overhearing the conversations of others) the bobbies was as eager in their determination to find as is any groom on his wedding night.

He was a square, beefy fellow purposely got up to look like he had spent a week lying in his own filth in a necessary. It was a particular favourite of his numerous disguises, and an especially good one for following peelers about the place as they conducted their h'investigations. Transforming oneself into yet one more open palm projecting from the corners of this great metropolis rendered even the infamous Mr. Nicholson invisible. For he had long been of the opinion that with every highway crowded with their stink, every doorway rank with their piss, the desperate poor were the real owners of the city: those lone sentinels moving very slow in the great charge of humanity, seeing and hearing all – and utterly overlooked.

He had recovered from the profound disappointment of learning that the choicest bit of stam-fish to have been wafted under his nose in a long time was nothing more than a half-truth twisted and wracked out of shape. He ought to have known that you can't ever take the word of the street mob, for bent rumour runs on faster than a barrow with a greased wheel, and in London it don't take much for the firing of a pistol at a fat Tory to be transfigured into the assassination of the Prime Minister.

Earlier that day he had been revelling in the dust and gloom of his print-shop that stood upon old Holywell-street, that squalid ditch that used to run along the wrong side of the Strand, straightening a pile of O'Connor's *Remedy for National Poverty and the Impending Ruin (or The Only Safe Way of Repealing the Corn Law)*, when the sprightly boy who helped the Jew old-clothes man in the next-door premises had come bursting in at the rotten door.

"Wot d'yer fink to this, Mr. Nicholson, sir!" the boy had cried delightedly against the weary jangling of the cracked door bell. "Someone's only gone and shot the Prime Minister!"

"Good heavens!" said Mr. Nicholson, feeling a sudden little elation, "Where?"

"In the arse!" said the boy quick as a flash, and seeing something so exquisitely ludicrous in the jest, he had burst out laughing.

Mr. Nicholson had wasted no time. He had been intending to spend the evening placing a gross of Presbyterian Society Tracts in plain brown wrappers so that they might go under cover as copies of *Bigenio the Hermaphrodite* and *the Dreadful Disclosures of Maria Monk* – but that lucrative line in trade could wait. He had run back into the shop to collect a greasy knapsack and a muffler and went straightway to Charing-cross. There were rags to be be grubbed, bones to be picked over; and the light was already failing and the snow beginning to fall in thick obliterations.

It did not take him long to determine that Sir Robert Peel was yet alive and kicking, and that it was his Secretary, Mr. Drummond of the Treasury, who'd been done for. He supposed that when all was said and done, it didn't really matter much: 'twas all business, after all. The kimbau was being got up as the biggest sensation since Arthur Thistlewood and the rest plotted at Cato-street to blow up the cabinet twenty year ago; the greatest shock since Bellingham shot dead Prime Minister Spencer Perceval in the lobby of the House of Commons thirty year ago – and though, to Mr. Nicholson's mind (and he knew more than a thing or two about plots), the firing of a pistol into the backside of an official weren't nowhere near as grand a grape-seed as either of those occurrences, times being so werry, werry 'ard, it would do; it would have to do.

No doubt there was more to the matter than met the eye. Mr. Nicholson wiped his nose on the back of his hand. But whatever it was, he mused it weren't political. To begin with, whoever heard of a Radical firing a pistol at a Tory without shouting out some slogan or other? No, my pippins, when it came down to it, that was the part that had him proper mystified. Poor bastard, he thought with a shudder; for there weren't a scraping of the prisoner's worthless marrow that Inspector Tierney and his masters at the Office of Home Affairs wouldn't hold up as evidence against: of that he was certain. There had been *too much of this sort of thing* of late: examples would have to be made. Which was why the deed was being painted blacker than any since Judas Iscariot buffed himself to Old King Herod.

Which is the one problem with being a nobody: anything can be made of you. And Mr. Drummond's would-be assassin had materialised out of nowhere. He was a bit of Scotch mist with no ties, no baggage; no nothing, save an abundance of money – which at a time of great scarcity was bound to be a thing of wonder and suspicion. Mr. Nicholson scratched his whiskery old chin and considered. Mistaken identity never did play long with such a master of disguises, and so he had discounted almost at once the notion that McNaughten had intended to do for the Prime Minister. To begin with, the Secretary was a short man of very full habit, whereas the Prime Minister was tall and only moderately well-built in proportion. The Secretary was a bald man of a dark, florid appearance: the Prime Minister fair and trichoid. The Secretary's eyes were chocolate brown and very twinkly: the Prime Minister's pale blue-gray and cold... O, he could go on, my pippins, but you probably see the full picture.

"Move along!"

The bobby currently making his way back down that side of Charing-cross had already been past a dozen or more times. He was riled to spy the crafty old grubber still scratching at the pavement like a starving rat. The bobby, or so Mr. Nicholson had earlier gathered from an overheard exchange or two, was engaged upon "looking for the second bit o' shot", and would "'ave no peace from Inspector Hughes" until he had done his level best to find it. This was all Mr. Nicholson needed to hear, and despite the very frozeness of the night, he had wholeheartedly enjoined to the untangling of this particular clew.

The bobby was holding up his bull's eye, its thin uncertain strips of light giving to the road a precarious shape; their points, extending all the way to Horse Guards, picking out Mr. Nicholson's rootling form in the doorway.

"You can't stay there," the bobby said. "You shall have to find somewhere else to bed down."

"Where do you suggest?" responded Mr. Nicholson, with a vulgar gesture. "Morley's fuckin' 'otel?"

"I don't care where you go. I 'as orders. There's been an incident."

Mr. Nicholson withdrew from the shadows of the doorway and turned with a theatrical flourish towards the spot of Mr. Drummond's felling.

"Is that where the old gloak got shot in the bum?" he said in a dramatic whisper, his eyes shining in the lantern light.

"Move along," said the bobby, sticking out his roundly decent chin in a laudable show of bravery, "or I'm afraid I shall have to arrest you."

"Arrest me? On what charge?"

"Why, vagrancy of course, what d'you think...?"

"Wagrancy? Wagrancy? I ain't no fuckin' wagrant! I'm a screever, I am. 'Ere, see me fuckin' chalks if you don't believe me." He started fumbling in his rags, "Only it ain't no good in the fuckin' snow, is it?"

"What's the problem, Jim?" inquired a second bobby who had appeared in a pool of dirty yellow gas-light.

"He won't move on," said the first. "I'd arrest him only he don't look too clean. You can get the cholera off the likes of 'im."

"We 'as just cause, you know," said the second bobby, every bit as shallow-pated a blab as was his mate.

"Just cause? Just fuckin' cause?" Mr. Nicholson chuckled richly. "Ha ha ha! That's good, that is. Ho ho! You shall have to do better 'n that if you want to lock me up. Though, mind you, it'll be a fuckin' sight warmer in the station-house than it is out here, that's for sure"

He shooed the bobbies away with his arm, the stink coming off him making them step back, gagging, eyes watering. Just as he knew it would.

"'Ere," he said, "you let me be and I'll give you some information."

The bobbies exchanged a glance.

"The Tory who got shot in the bum – he's a dirty ole bugger, 'e is."

"What d'you mean?"

"He's one of them gentlemen what likes to touch a bit of scarlet – only he's too fuckin' mean to pay for a proper huzzar, ain't he? Scotch blood, see. Besides, he likes 'em pure, 'e does. Likes to take 'em 'ome wiv 'im fer a spot of *Bible-readin'*."

He inwardly smirked at the tale, variations of which were always going around the streets because there was more than a grain of truth in it.

He was advancing on the policemen, backing them into the doorway of Tatham's gun-shop until they had nowhere else to go and he was stood so close to them that the brim of his filthy hat was almost touching the nose of the second bobby. The poor lob was straining hard to get away from the smell.

"Likes to save their fuckin' souls, 'e does. Well, I dares say it's a better fate than being stirred into a workhouse stew – or ending up on a 'natomist's table with your vitals sold to make sausages."

"How do you know all this?" asked the first bobby.

Mr. Nicholson winked.

"How do I know all this?" he parroted.

He started to walk away from them, briskly, the sway of their lantern following him warily, picking out a small patch of black, brazen against the snow. Mr. Nicholson stopped and kicked the patch over. It was a scorch – gunpowder – and beneath it, he could plainly see, was a hard, round plug of something interesting. He stooped and skilfully nudged it out of the ground with a piece of bent nail he kept for grubbing.

"What's that you've got there?" cried the first bobby. "'Ere, leave that – that's evidences, that is!"

"You buffoons," snarled Mr. Nicholson, as he dug. "Ain't you figured it out yet, then?"

"Spring your rattle, Jim!" urged the second bobby.

"Spring yer rattle! Dam'me! I shouldn't bother with that," cried Mr. Nicholson over his shoulder. "I'm fuckin' Active Duty, I am! Check with Inspector Tierney if you don't believe me!"

A good dodge that, he thought, noting how the two bobbies recoiled at once: I shall be sure to use it again. It seemed that not even officers of the "A" Division could tell a common rag-gatherer from one of their own.

Chuckling darkly, Mr. Nicholson walked off in the direction of the river with the second bit o' shot carefully screwed into his palm. He did not look at it until he was safely out of sight of the bobbies and alone with the streets: the lovely gloomy streets, which, he had often found to be the case, would always reveal their secrets to one of their own.

No.19, Lower Grosvenor-street, Mayfair,
AT ABOUT THE SAME TIME

In which we learn how closely doctors must stick together.

Mr. Bransby Cooper was explaining to Mr. Guthrie senior – who had come as soon as he could – how he had thus far been unable to deter-mine the course of the ball through the wound. For over an hour he had been boring into the hole he had made in Neddie's hip, skewering flesh and tissue and lymph upon an array of implements and, latterly, the point of his index finger. He wiped it now upon the pillow slip: great coppery smears of blood.

"I enlarged the opening," he said dismally.

"Did you, by Jove," said Mr. Guthrie senior, frowning at Neddie's supine form.

"Doubtless the shot is very small," said Mr. Bransby Cooper.

"Doubtless," said Mr. Guthrie senior. He was taking Neddie' pulse and looking fiercely at the scarlet and blancmange gash in his behind.

"It must have gone in very deep," said Mr. Bransby Cooper, holding up his finger. "I say, might yours be a little longer?"

"I wonder – what did you hope to find?" said Mr. Guthrie.

Mr. Bransby Cooper looked crestfallen. "Well, you're the gunshot expert," he said, forlornly.

The pair of them fell into a sort of conference, which they conducted *sotto voce*, their heads bent intently over Neddie's bare behind. She strained to listen, trying to suppress the indecent pink of her brother's spongiform nakedness, the sudden shock of the thick black hair sprouting from the middle of his buttocks. She had not acquiesced to Mr. Bransby Cooper's plaintive requests that Mr. Guthrie senior be sent for; it had been done in spite of her. Neddie, his reason skewed by pain, had demanded a more proficient attendant: she trusted he would not have cause to regret the decision. There was nothing whatever to suppose that Mr. Bransby Cooper would not make certain revelations to Mr. Guthrie senior; after all, doctors, it was well known, had a habit of sticking together.

Miss Drummond paused in her stitch-making.

She supposed that, seeing as it was the Duke of Wellington's own doctor who had provided the unfortunate pistols for the duel all those years ago, the hugger-mugger instincts of the medical profession might work in an advantageous manner to preserve them all from scandal, should Mr. Bransby Cooper reveal all to his colleague. She strained to listen to the murmured conversation taking place on the other side of the bed, and picking up on nothing to suggest that any mention of the Duke of Wellington, duels, and misplaced rifled shot had passed between the medical gentlemen in the course of their conference, she unpicked then remade her little stitch.

She was beginning to weary of subterfuge, and so, leaving her brother to the mercies of the surgeons, she decided to withdraw to her toilet table where she settled to an inspection of Malthus's *Essay on the Principle of Population* – the volume that her brother had handed to her on his return, urging her to secrete it somewhere safe. The book was uncut and she discovered that when held by its spine, it opened up into a series of thrilling little pockets, wherein were placed scraps of Turkey Mill, oddments of blotting, pages of thin, slippery writing paper: each containing an immense, dark secret. She had sat for above an hour in reading. What she had discovered appeared to be a sort of sub-Treasury: a repository – but not of the familiar secrets of books and papers such as might be locked up in chests or safes in banking-houses, in strong-rooms, in church vaults, to be revealed at the turn of a key.

What she had here were secrets barely whispered and glimpsed at; the inscribed intimations of winks and nods and coded handshakes: matters thought and never voiced. As she read through the missives gathered there, certain phrases caught her eye, imparting a heaviness to the air: their shadow thickening and thickening all about her as she read.

"...*I got him pretty lushey and with a bit of coaxing he began to talk of the particulars of the plot, the pistols, the slogan, the agreed signal, &c., &c...*"

"...*I heard him with my own ears address the assembly with a text from Kings, urging them to do away with the present government by whatever means they could determine...*"

"...*I was alarmed that they might uncover my true purpose and give me a smugging, and so I left and returned to my hotel...*"

"...*On account of some long-held animosity or other, he is prepared to swear that he heard them explain how gunpowder may be put in a bottle with a percussive cap upon it, and that one of them said it would be a fine thing to make sure it had some nails in it...*"

Miss Drummond felt the blood run cold in her veins with the horrid suggestions that sprang from these writings, and yet – and yet, she could not stop herself from reading on. Here were many examples to justify even the darkest fears and suspicions: her brother's secret realm, the seat of all his power – and now it was hers, too. Having read enough, she was replacing with great care the pieces of paper just as she had found them, when, towards the back of the volume her eye fell upon a few scraps of paper covered in Neddie's own hand. Or more truthfully, the scraps appeared to be the product of several attempts on the part of her brother to disguise his own hand by the writing-out of some lines of Shakespeare, over and again, as if in a schoolboy's copybook, with here a different slope, and there a more emphatic loop.

Whatever deception Neddie was attempting, it did not fool his sister. She withdrew the scraps – a dozen in all – and spread them out upon her toilet table.

The text was: "*Let us kill him, and we'll have corn at our own price.*"

What could it mean? She was certain it must mean something, else why would Neddie have taken the trouble to conceal it? Indeed, Miss

Drummond thought, as she hid the volume and all its contents in the drawer wherein she kept her linen, why ever had Neddie chosen to keep so many nasty secrets intact? In all his years at the Treasury she was quite certain that her brother had never once left a pertinent missive unburned... She returned to his bedside still brooding, and feeling a trifle despondent, to discover Mr. Guthrie senior prodding the wound in her brother's behind.

"O – O dear God!" groaned Neddie. He looked a little yellow, she thought.

"Poor gentleman," said Parrott. "Might not a cold dash help? Perhaps a drop or two of barley-water?"

Miss Drummond made a stitch and then unpicked it, casting a sly glance towards her brother. She was seeking out his Secretiveness, and was momentarily cheered to see that it was still rather large. She had recollected a fragment of conversation from about a year ago, that had drifted from the downstairs dining-room where Neddie held his petits cabinets. He did not know how she was in the habit of retiring to the little room that communicated with the dining-room, dropping the curtain which sealed off the closed doorway. How often she had retreated there! Entire afternoons spent waiting for all the commotion when Nursie or Mama realised that she had not been seen for above an hour. So cosy! She had fallen asleep there many times, only to awake to the dispiriting awareness that she had not been missed. No Argand lamp: once the candles had burned themselves out one must succumb to darkness. And darkness concentrated her powers of acuity. O, she was contented to sit and listen, unobserved, undisturbed – except for those occasions when a gentleman Member unknowingly intruded on the space, in search of the convenience that was kept there in the sideboard.

"Leave him be," Mr. Guthrie senior was barking at the footman.

"Now, now, good fellow, your master is in excellent hands," said Mr. Bransby Cooper kindly. "It is but a flesh wound and will mend soon enough. You see, Mr. Drummond is quite alright, are you not, sir?"

Mr. Drummond was biting the bolster; his Secretiveness bulging in plain sight above his ears, and pressing down upon it, Cautiousness.

Secretiveness tempered by Cautiousness, she thought. Ah yes! Her brother was compelled to conceal, but bounded by circumspection, by the need to act prudently. And being ever the eximious servant, he was above all bound to obey. She remembered the conversation quite clearly now: Sir Robert Peel's insistence that no man in public life ought to succumb to the burning of papers. In all her years of listening at doors Miss Drummond had never heard anything more ridiculous! Surely, she had thought, it is an unpleasant fact of life that Prime Ministers must burn things, just as Home Secretaries must, from time to time, read other people's letters, and Foreign Secretaries spread untruths about foreign heads of state. Even Neddie – for all his studied obeisance and obsequiousness – had been barely able to contain his indignation at such a foolish notion.

Ah yes, she nodded to herself: Sir Robert Peel! He was undoubtedly the reason behind the continued existence of the nasty volume and all its wretched secrets.

"Can you not apply a little opium or bark at the very least?" Parrott was saying. "Poor gentleman, the pain must be very great. I believe Miss Drummond has some drops."

She had made disapproving note before now of the watchful tenderness with which her footman regarded her brother, but was never more sickened by it than at that very moment. "I'm afraid the drops are all gone," she lied, fixing Parrott with her most malefic look.

"Are you a doctor or a footman?" demanded Mr. Guthrie senior. He had been intent upon the ooze of scarlet from the wound, but his eyes blazed with fury as he lifted them to meet Parrott's own dark trusting ones. "I have seen many years' service as an army doctor and I dare say have tended more gunshot wounds than you've cleaned boots. Now, make yourself useful, you confounded fellow! Turn your master on his back in order that the anterior part of his body might be inspected for this dratted bit o' shot!"

"I wonder, is that *really* necessary?" said Mr. Bransby Cooper. His face had elongated with dismay until it resembled a cheese left upon the range and melted.

"Yes, it is necessary," said Mr. Guthrie senior. "It is necessary that I salvage some part of the mess that has been perpetrated here today."

"I pray you, leave it, leave it, sir, for I can bear no more," said Neddie weakly from the pillow.

[98]

But nobody heeded him.

"Turn your master on his back as I bade you," directed Mr. Guthrie senior.

She was aware that Parrott was watching her, beseeching her with his eyes; as was Mr. Bransby Cooper, chewing on his nails and emitting short, hurried breaths.

This was not the first time in her life that she had had intimations of things unnatural and dark: being cursed with great powers of Observation, she could not but see and understand. On those all-too-frequent nights when sleep did not come, she was given to wandering through the rooms of the house in placation of the dear-departed; and nor was she so steeped in dainty delicacy that she was ignorant of the odious inclinations of the world. Poor Miss Drummond could not stop her sensitive nostrils against the miasma foul with impurities poisonous to mind as well as body. She had nursed two parents and a sister, for goodness' sake – breathing in the fetid air of the dying day upon day, night upon night. O, she had never known the touch of man, but she had endured the numerous indignities of the death-bed.

What was more, she had listened at doors. She smiled a thin, satisfied smile.

"I do not think we should disturb Mr. Drummond," said Parrott, his anxiety for his master writ plain upon his face. "Surely, he has suffered enough."

She might have interceded, but it was just at that moment that Lizzie the housemaid came to the door of the bedchamber announcing the arrival of Mr. Guthrie junior. He had been sent for by his father, and was immediately ordered to roll up his shirt-sleeves and lend assistance.

"But – but is it safe...?" Parrott was persistent. He stood by helpless as the three doctors heaved Mr. Drummond onto his back. "What of the exertions upon the wound in Mr. Drummond's rump?"

"O! O! O!" cried Neddie, like a little stuck pig, squealing all the way home.

"O, my poor master!" cried the footman. "For pity's sake! What has he done to be used so ill?"

Mr. Bransby Cooper cast to her a look of purest astonishment which she did not connect with; her thoughts were elsewhere and she had momentarily forgotten the danger inherent in an inspection of Neddie's front. Such easy effrontery! Miss Drummond was thinking with a little shudder in respect of the footman. It had been just this sort of unseemly display, the liberties permitted and tolerated, that had led her to dismiss Parrott's predecessor, the unscrupulous Tutton, who had left her service last summer under a dark cloud and with Papa's second-best gold watch and two pairs of silk stockings. What was it, she wondered, what failing of character caused her brother to invite such degradedness on the part of the male servants?

And so she marked, without the merest trace of pity, Neddie's anguished cries as he was finally laid upon his back: the great mound undulating before him, the veiny rivers running through it, the little hillock of white flesh lying snug in the disgusting forest of ashen hair.

"The doctors know best, dear," she said airily, in spite of Neddie's weakening protestations. "As to everything else, pray, do not worry." She leaned in confidentially towards the bed, dropping her voice a little. "*That* is all taken care of!" she said. "*Everything* is taken care of!"

"What the devil is this?" said Mr. Guthrie senior. He was peering fiercely at a distinct blue-black lump on Neddie's lower quadrant.

It was only then that Miss Drummond remembered – too late! – the Duke of Wellington and the ill-fated duel, and the consequences of Neddie's hapless attempt at intervention. Why, she thought, taking a restorative sip of Rowland's Aqua d'Oro, why did her brother always have to spoil everything?

WHITEHALL,
AT ABOUT THE SAME TIME

In which Mr. Warren heareth not the sighs of the People.
Proverbs 29:2

The more he thought about it the more it seemed to Mr. Warren that, at their encounter that afternoon at Bellamy's, Mr. Drummond had exercised a prescience of almost uncanny dimension in mooting the necessity of a "precipitous occurrence", only to be shot at an hour later. This was a remarkably fortuitous combination of seemingly random events, in the coalescence of which, Mr. Warren felt sure, must lay the most capital opportunity to come his way in a long time. It being in his nature always to try and kill two birds with one stone, it had occurred to him that he ought to graft onto the shooting of the Secretary all of the dark intimations which that gentleman had lately given in respect of alleged threats to the Prime Minister made by members of the Anti-Corn Law League. In this way he might hope not only to advance his own career as the acknowledged opponent of the League, but also make of the calamity the desired outrage by which the Treasury gentleman appeared to have set so much store in the interest of the Party.

The only difficulty was this: despite several hours of inquiry, Mr. Warren had yet to obtain the degree of clarification required before he felt *confident* enough to introduce the notion into the public domain. He did not care to consider the possibility of any sort of *skulduggery*. He was at that time (is still) an honourable and remarkably straightforward gentleman. What was more, he worried a good deal that he might cause offence – especially to those to whose patronage he aspired and *depended* upon; he worried that he might be exposed and debarred; he worried that he might be laughed at. And every singular presentiment, impulse and vagary of thought which occurred to him as he tossed over the matter caused him to hesitate considerably before he would own to it.

He could do not more, he supposed, as he mulled all of this over for the dozenth time that evening, than trust that some *modus operandi* would ensue shortly from the understanding that in law, as in life, a circumstance, such as the shooting of Mr. Drummond, was a *fact*: from out of which any number of *plausible* presumptions and inferences might rightly be drawn. He had high expectations of his legal training, but he thought it prudent, nevertheless, to discuss the matter with Mr. Drummond before finally constructing his argument. However, Mr. Drummond was not receiving visitors. Three separate trips to Mayfair in the course of the evening had elicited nothing but the footman's assurances that the poor gentleman was "going along as well as can be expected". Upon leaving Grosvenor-square for the third time, Mr.

Warren decided to surrender all hope of a conference for the time being, and repaired instead to Downing-street where he had arranged to depose Mr. Drummond's deputy, Mr. Stephenson.

The deputy quite properly affected to know nothing of Mr. Drummond's secret volume when quizzed, but, tellingly, did not appear the least bit surprised to learn of its existence. And nor had he any understanding of especial instructions from either Mr. Drummond or the Prime Minister in respect of communications received from the Anti-Corn Law League. *Let us kill him and we shall have corn at our own price*, was, he wryly observed, a sight more literary than most of the threats they received; but then he supposed that a good many people of all complexions, including a good many educated and respectable people, desired the death of Sir Robert Peel – and not just on account of the Corn Laws: the Income Tax, the war in Afghan, the New Poor Law, the Charter – all these, and a host of other so-called wrongs against the People, were sufficient.

Doubtless a good proportion of complainants would, he added, turn out to be Scotch.

Mr. Stephenson said all of this as if it were a thing of no great consequence. "A hundred threatening letters," he remarked, "do not in themselves lead inexorably to a pistol being raised against the Prime Minister any more than a simile constitutes an argument."

Mr. Warren had to agree with him that this was indubitably so.

What was more, the deputy reminded Mr. Warren, despite the copious threats delivered daily to Downing-street – and not counting a few duels here and there – only once had a Prime Minister ever been fired at. And that was when a madman named Bellingham had shot and killed Spencer Perceval in the lobby of the House of Commons more than thirty years ago.

But Mr. Warren was not easily deterred.

"All of what you say is very true, Mr. Stephenson," he demurred, "but surely it is even less likely that someone should wish to shoot at a Treasury Secretary!"

Mr. Stephenson sighed in a melancholy fashion.

"Mr. Drummond is a most amiable gentleman," he said with a considerable degree of feeling for a civil servant. "Nobody – neither Whig nor Tory – had ever anything bad to say of him. Indeed, I would go so far as to say that it is quite impossible to countenance him having any enemies whatever."

Mr. Warren noted with his keen novelist's eye, how the gentleman paused reflectively for a moment, before continuing in an altogether more business-like tone.

"An astounding achievement after thirty-five years in the Treasury."

Upon leaving Downing-street, Mr. Warren resolved to go straight-way to the station-house in Gardiner's-lane, having it in mind to entice some more police informations from the obliging Sergeant Shew; however, a very earnest Inspector had placed himself at the desk and was refusing admission to anyone unless they had evidenc-es which they wished to set before the magistrate. This was a great pity, for it was well-known that the entire contents of a police buff box might be had for the price of a meat-pie and a glass of hot grog. Momentarily thwarted, he left Gardiner's-lane and walked through the snow along a curiously abandoned Whitehall back to Scotland-yard where every one of the requests for information he sent up to the Su-perintendent and the Commissioners, submitted on the back of his card, were rebuffed.

A lesser man might have given up at this point, returning home to his wife and a consolatory dish of mock-turtle and forcemeat balls; but Mr. Warren would not have achieved half so much as he had in his life if he were so easily put off. He left his card one last time marked with the observation that the Superintendent would do well to consider who paid his salary, and returned to the snowy streets.

He looked towards the Salopian coffee-house, wondering if he ought to repair once more to the scene of the crime in order to eaves-drop upon the police patrols, but it was by then grown quite cold and the prospect of the Ship hotel a little further along was altogether more enticing. I could always talk some more with the pot-boy who witnessed the shooting, he thought; and was just about to sally forth when it came to him that what he really ought to do was way-lay Mr. March Phillipps, at the Office of Home Affairs. The Home Sec-retary, Sir James Graham, was still out of town, but would have had few anxieties about leaving his Permanent Under-Secretary in charge of the division – even at a time of crisis. Mr. March Phillipps was a zealous defender of the *status quo*, who had garnered considerable renown unto himself by intervening in person against the Welsh Chartists a few years previously.

Mr. Warren crossed Whitehall with a great eagerness, and having determined that the Under-Secretary was still at his desk, set up on the steps of the gentleman's offices and waited for him with all the philosophy and fortitude he could muster. By nine o'clock he was just beginning to doubt that even such a conscientious gentleman as Mr. March Phillipps would have eventually to quit his business and go home for his supper, when – mercifully – he appeared. The Permanent Under-Secretary made no secret of his irritation at having been thus importuned, but accepted the shelter of Mr. Warren's umbrella and suffered him to walk him to his cab.

Mr. Warren renewed their acquaintanceship through the network of Temple allegiances and obligations, and let it be known that he, too, was a writer of a successful legal text-book (he did not admit to any other writing practices).

"I can scarce compare my rather paltry endeavours," he fawned, "to your *seminal* work on the law of evidence. Why, how long ago did it first appear? 1815? And yet I believe it is still – deservedly so – in print, and continues to be very widely read: nothing having come along in a score and more years to equal it."

Mr. March Phillipps proved very susceptible to flattery and thawed a little.

"I dare say you will have been kept very busy today, sir," said Mr. Warren, "with this terrible calamity involving Mr. Drummond of the Treasury."

"We are kept busy every day, engaged in service to the rule of law," sniffed the Permanent Under-Secretary. "There are many who seek to destroy the way in which we live, Mr. Warren; the principles of civilisation that govern us are under constant threat. In that regard today was no different to any other."

"I do not doubt it for a minute," said Mr. Warren. "We live in precipitous times – even so, it is not every day that a civil servant is made a target of. I wonder that you are prepared to walk to your cab without police protection."

"I have received my share of abuse. At the time we were engaged upon putting down the Welsh Chartists I was personally vilified and made the target of ruffians and destructionists everywhere I went. But I can assure you I have never been afraid. Those of us who love the law must be prepared to do everything we can in order to defend it."

"Absolutely, sir! The law *must* be defended! O, I could not agree more. As a matter of fact, I made the very same observation to poor Mr. Drummond when we had lunch today at Bellamy's."

"You had lunch with Drummond?"

"Why, just a friendly engagement, you know. We talked a great deal about the disorderly habits of the lower orders, and the precarious condition in which the present distress has placed the nation."

"Did you, by Jove..."

"Indeed we did. Mr. Drummond seemed to be of the opinion that there are secret evidences suggestive that the Anti-Corn Law League is *particeps criminis* in intent with regard to threats made against the Prime Minister." Mr. Warren observed how the Under-Secretary kept his head bowed in contemplation of the icy paving stones and gave nothing away. "To my mind there is a certain irony in that observation. I have been considering it ever since I heard the dreadful news. I wonder, sir, do you suppose that there is a *connexion*?"

"The would-be assassin was a Scotchman," said the gentleman.

"So I had heard..."

"It certainly seems possible that he mistook Mr. Drummond for the Prime Minister."

"I had wondered if that was the case..."

"There is a great deal of discontent among the lower orders in Scotland."

"Indeed there is..."

"In Glasgow..."

"...a dreadful place, to be sure..."

"...in Glasgow at the present time there are legions of lazy, unreasonable, *reckless* men, given over utterly to those rabid notions which proselytise the destruction of everything we hold dear."

"Were you aware that the Anti-Corn Law League convened a large meeting in Glasgow a little above a week ago?" rejoined Mr. Warren.

The Permanent Under-Secretary looked somewhat alarmed. "And did Drummond see something significant in that?" he asked.

Mr. Warren inclined his head in a non-committal way, as if to imply that he was not at liberty to divulge such intimacies.

The Permanent Under-Secretary had arrived at his cab and was mounting the foot-plate. He turned, tipping his hat at Mr. Warren.

"I am assured that reason will be given at Bow-street tomorrow morning," he said, pulling shut the carriage door. "I thank you for your kind words in respect of my *Treatise*. When I wrote that I was a much younger man – much like you; I believed then that the principles by which we live, governed by the manners and habits of society, are good. I believe it still. They are good, Mr. Warren, because our society is good. Better than any yet devised. It is a great pity that more people may not benefit by them. I pray you, recollect that in the coming days and weeks." He settled back into his seat and signalled to the coachman by tapping on the ceiling with his cane.

"Kindly extend my sympathies to Drummond," he said as the cab moved off at a slow trot. "I trust he will soon mend."

GARDINER'S-LANE STATION-HOUSE,
SHORTLY BEFORE MIDNIGHT

In which Inspector Hughes considers certain contents of the prisoner McNaughten's lodgings, and is told something grave and disturbing.

Inspector Hughes had settled on the high-stool behind the ledger desk with his feet resting on his topper, and was applying all of his attention to composing a route-paper description of Gordon. The Scotchman who, it will be remembered, had accompanied the prisoner to Mr. Hedges's turner's yard in search of work just before Christmas, had apparently vanished off the face of the earth – that is to say, he was nowhere to be found in the metropolis. Certainly, those constables tasked with making inquiries about the vicinity of the fellow's late lodgings had failed to lay hold of a single clew.

It was, of course, possible that the fellow had returned to his native Scotland; but what troubled the Inspector – the reason he could not bring himself to let the matter lie – was why, in these uncertain times, a Scotchman would leave off a good position in order to return to squalor and starvation. Perhaps, he reasoned, the sudden illness or worse of a loved one had prompted the departure; but then why had Gordon left without first collecting the wages he was owed? To the Inspector's mind, this behaviour went beyond everything that he understood of human nature; and having considered all of the innocent motives, he felt inclined to let his thoughts run to the possibility of something troubling and altogether less honest as lying behind the Scotchman's sudden departure. Having satisfied himself that no body matching Gordon's description had been fished from the river, or uncovered in a back alley with its throat cut, he tasked a few of the constables with consulting past editions of the *Police Gazette* for informations involving Scotchmen taken in the act or actively sought. There were a good many of those, as can be imagined, but none of them being Gordon, the Inspector decided to make the fellow the subject of a route-paper of his own – to be read to every man in every division of the Metropolitan Police Force. *Find Gordon*! became the watchword of the day. It was imperative, the Inspector reckoned, that this fellow be found. He was a known associate of McNaughten, and it followed therefore that whatever he was, or knew, or had done, or was considering doing, had a potential bearing on the perplexing question of the prisoner's own motivation.

The route-paper was the last task he had set himself in pursuance of the matter for the day. He had written his report for the Superintendent, and made everything ready for the magistrate's hearing at Bow-street the next morning. He had carefully transcribed the witness statements, given all the evidences a number, and placed the whole lot in a regulation-issue buff box. He had written a description of the pistols to be taken around the pawn-shops. He had compiled a list of coffee-shops and cheap eating-houses in the vicinity of the prisoner's lodgings for the men of "L" Division (Lambeth) to investigate. He had prepared a bill of inquiry to be delivered to all the counting-houses in the metropolis with full details therein of the bank deposit receipt found on the prisoner's person. He had rid the station-house of a score or more badgering and cadging newspapermen. He had tested the pistols.

And all was now as wound down as the station-house fire glowing weakly in the grate: at least for the time being. Beneath him the cells were groaning with all them poor souls cleared off the gleaming strip; and this being Friday, he had still to contend with the usual endless stream of night charges sidling, creeping, swaggering up to the dock rail to be measured by him in degrees of height and villainy. One by one, hour after hour: the all-too-familiar faces. He would while away the remainder of this long, this very long day, his book open before him, giving his judgement of them all. Who would be punished and who let go; writing down for all time all that they had done: their censure and entreaties, their quarrels and their threats, their weeping, their slurring, their excuses: the horrors, the lies.

He hoped always to get at the truth: the truth was all he cared about. Truth and justice.

He sighed. If only it were as simple as all that.

The route-paper completed, he carefully blotted it and placed it to one side to be copied and distributed, and opened the buff box of evidences to insert a note of its existence. The witness statement supplied by Mr. Harvey Drummond, elder son to Mr. Drummond's brother, was lying on the top of the pile of papers. The Inspector frowned at it, and all those doubts he had been nursing in respect of the busted shot began to churn and curdle in the pit of his stomach; for young Mister Harvey was of the decided opinion that the hole in his uncle's coat had not been made by a ball at all, but, rather, was the product of nothing more dangerous than a burning patch.

"See," Silver had retorted upon learning the same, "didn't I say it was a waste of time sending me so many times to look for that second bit o' shot?" The boy's face shone with an unbecoming flame of indignation and glee. "I *told* you I saw a burning piece of paper on the pavement and nothing more!"

The Inspector had cautioned the Constable, of course, and made quite clear his own anxiety concerning the considerable doubt that was proliferating around the question of whether or not the prisoner had taken the trouble to load up his pistols before firing 'em at Mr. Drummond.

"If we ain't careful," he had observed to Silver, "we shall have another Francis and Bean on our hands." For without the evidence of the guns having been loaded with lead shot, there was no proof of intent, and without proof of intent there was a good chance that the prisoner would escape with nothing more than a good thrashing. And it followed that there'd be an outcry about how it was all a licence for bullies to commit crimes without fear of punishment, and it went without saying that it'd be the police what bore the brunt of the public's opprobrium.

Following this very glum line of reasoning, there was but a glimmer of good fortune in the fact that Silver had succeeded in turning up a powder flask and a pile of shot during the course of their investigation of the prisoner's lodgings, earlier that evening – at least the news of the timely discovery was received with immense satisfaction by every one at Scotland-yard. However, it was incumbent on a cautious man, such as the Inspector, to point out that finding the shot weren't the same thing at all as proving that the prisoner actually used any of it.

"Which is why," he couldn't help but remark to Silver, "it would've been a sensible precaution on your part to have kept sight of that second bit o' shot."

"The Superintendent says finding shot is as good as proof of intent that the prisoner was determined to do for Mr. Drummond," Silver had objected.

"Does he now..."

"And besides, we shall soon have the piece that was fired at Mr. Drummond, shan't we?"

"Ho, I wouldn't pin me hopes on that," said the Inspector. "I wouldn't be surprised if Mr. Drummond decides to leave it where it is. Little good comes of having doctors go digging about in you, and it's not as if a little bit of shot in the rump ever did anyone a speck of harm. Why, when I was in the army I knew plenty of fellows who were walking around with bits o' ammunition in 'em, without it ever giving rise to the slightest concern. No, you see all of this is *specula-*

tive, Silver, whereas the evidence of that second piece – well – that's *incontrovertible,* is that. *Beyond all reasonable doubt.*" Silver had fallen instantly in to a protracted sulk which lasted the rest of the evening, but the Inspector felt obliged to persist, nevertheless, in ramming home the lesson. "You see, boy, without that dratted bit o' shot," he said, "there's no knowing what a clever barrister'll make of it all."

Constable Silver had found the powder flask and five leaden balls in an unlocked drawer, and Inspector Hughes had since tried the whole lot, together with the pistols and percussion caps found on the prisoner's person, in the station-house yard. The balls, once patched with a wad of paper, fitted the pistols snug, and he'd fired off two rounds for each pistol and retrieved them entire from the target. They were smooth-bore, that is to say, *unrifled*: just as he had expected them to be. He had packed away the powder flask and the five leaden balls in the buff box together with the other evidences gathered from the prisoner's lodging earlier that evening, and drawn up an inventory in his careful way. He withdrew it now from the box and checked it over, thinking how he had rarely seen a dwelling so bereft of any signs of habitation as was McNaughten's attic. He ran his eye along the tally, wondering what it meant. One bed, neatly made; one simple chair with volume lying upon the seat; one cupboard, empty, save for a pair of worn and tattered moleskin trowsers; one desk with three drawers, all unlocked and empty of content (save for the one containing the powder flask and shot). There were no coals, nor ashes neither, in the grate, and just one poor greasy stump of a candle sitting in an old tin holder on the mantel shelf, and close by a small pile of ashes and a long clay-pipe balanced across two cans. When the Inspector had rubbed the ashes between his finger and thumb, they smelled powerfully of Indian hemp.

The only other object of the slightest interest was the slim volume which the Inspector had discovered lying on the seat of the chair. Mrs. Dutton had been very distressed by the sight of the munitions, and had sworn to Kingdom Come that they had not been there when she had tidied the room earlier that day; but it was the book which had caused her the greatest consternation. *The Holy Scriptures Analyzed, or, Extracts from the Bible: shewing its contradictions, absurdities and immorali-*

ties, by Robert Cooper. Upon hearing the shocking title, she denounced it at once as a filthy object. If she had known it was in her house, she said, she would have burned the whole lot down. The wean agreed with her.

"We'll have nay mair o' yourn donsie tricks, ye splutin' falsifier, ye!" she had declaimed against someone or something that appeared to be lurking beneath the eaves.

The Inspector had turned over a few pages. Quotations from the Bible were organised under headings that could only be described as inflammatory: *Passages Contradictory*; *Passages Absurd and Unnatural*; *Passages Immoral and Obscene*. And as if this wasn't bad enough a quick scrutiny of the title-page had shewed that the book had been published in Manchester. The Inspector felt the corners of his mouth turn down. Nothing good ever came out of Manchester. He skimmed the text of the author's Vindication. "*At a time like the present,*" it ran, "*when the voice of reason and free enquiry is rousing the intellectual faculties of the people from their dormancy and enslavement...*" He had seen enough. Snapping shut the volume, he observed softly, "It's blasphemy, is this, and freethinking to boot."

"They've done this!" the landlady had cried. "They've done it to condemn him!" She had tried unsuccessfully to wrest the book from the Inspector's hand, her eyes wild and staring, screaming all the while. "But you will find no fault in him! No fault! No fault!" Beneath the Inspector's mild and steady gaze she was gradually restored to reason, smoothing her apron and gathering what was left of her wits.

The Inspector's mind had now begun to run towards political fanaticism in respect of the prisoner, yet he could not dismiss entirely his earlier suspicions of *religious* fanaticism. He had taken out his notebook and turned to the page whereupon he had made a little rubbing of the queer token found on the prisoner's person.

"Was Mr. McNaughten in the habit of attending any church?" he had asked, turning the page towards her.

Mrs. Dutton had held up her little greasy candle and peered at the image for a long time, her eyes growing large and glittering all the while. "O, it will be foul weather today," she said at length in a low, rasping voice that thrummed disquietingly against the cold air.

"If you recognise the token, missus, you oughter apprize us of its significance."

"He will blot out man from the face of the earth," she had said, "and bird and beast and creeping things. For He is sorry that he made them," and then she had thrown back her little head and burst into a wild laugh, that had scarcely the remotest trace of anything human, let alone feminine, to it.

"Does it have anything to do with the Scotch Church?" persisted the Inspector.

Mrs. Dutton stopped laughing in an instant. In the silence that ensued there came a low, low groan, a despairing groan, which seemed to issue from the dark landing, and hearing it the Inspector instinctively looked towards the door, although he knew it was unlikely that anything living was beyond it. When he looked back at the landlady he saw that her face had frozen into a horrible rictus and that her eyes were stark, staring mad.

"Ye great gaupie!" she growled. "Dan wouldna have a thing to do wi' those fouters!"

"And why's that?" said the Inspector. The firmness of his own voice had surprised him, for his knees were knocking against his Wellington boots and his mouth was quite dry.

Mrs. Dutton's demonic grin spread wider and wider across her face. "Because," she had said at last, "he was raised Episcopalian!"

The Inspector started now, rousing himself with a little shudder at the dream-like recollection. The candle on the station-house ledger desk was expiring in its socket, guttering in the little sigh of steamy breath he issued. He leaned on his elbow, cradling his chin in his palm and allowed his eyes to close for just a minute or two. He could not claim any great knowledge of the vagaries of the Scotch churches, but he knew that, like all Celtic peoples, the Scotch took the matter of religion very seriously indeed. The landlady's avowal, he was thinking as he began to slip from conscious thought, might turn out to be a matter of singular importance; but it might just as easily turn out to be of no signification whatever. That was the difficulty with police work. You could never be sure in what direction the truth lay. You had to follow your nose and hope it didn't lead you into trouble, or up a dark alley with no way out...

His head fell forward, snapping his neck. He shifted, sighing, letting his thoughts drift to the end of the day, whenever it would come, picturing himself gingerly settling on the edge of the bed so as not to disturb Mrs. Hughes; removing his boots; peeling off his thick woollen stockings; resting each foot in turn upon its opposite knee; taking his toes in large firm hands, and gently flexing them back and forth a few times. Ah! There he would sit, as the numbness of the day slowly succumbed to the satisfying bruise of warm blood returning to his extremities.

He had almost passed to deep sleep when he became aware of someone entering the station-house and coming to stand in front of him. The candle had expired; the front office was hung in shadows and stone cold. "I'm afraid that no officer is at liberty to divulge any information whatever," he said, springing to at once, "until the Commissioners have completed their preliminary investigations of all the evidences." He had assumed it was yet another inky inquisitor come in expectation of a line of copy and was about to direct whomever it was to attend the Police Court at Bow-street, at ten the following morning. He quickly fumbled in the candle box; scraped a Lucifer. Light filled up the grim corners.

"Hullo," came the sneering response, "what's all this then?"

There was something suggestive in every word that scranning cove uttered, as if he couldn't bring himself to trust even the nose on his own face. Inspector Tierney of the Active Duty, bold as a game-cock, had come to lean against the ledger desk and was leafing through the blasphemous book with an idle curiosity. He turned it upside down and shook it hard.

"That's evidences, that is," said Inspector Hughes. "I just put all of that in order for the magistrate tomorrow morning."

"You and your wretched buff boxes," said Inspector Tierney.

"I've been put in charge of this investigation by the Superintendent himself, which means I has responsibility for the informations."

"And I have my authority direct from the Commissioners, by way of the Home Office."

"Which don't give you the right to tamper with evidences before the Commissioners have seen 'em."

"O, but I'm afraid it does."

"Says who?"

"Says Mr. March Phillipps, the Permanent Under-Secretary of the Home Office, if you please, on account of some troubling informations that have come to light – something the prisoner told me."

"I don't care to know that you somehow persuaded that poor cank sod to talk – or hear a word of what you claim he told you – I just hope you had the good sense to caution him. The Superintendent is most anxious that everything be done in accordance with the proper procedures."

Inspector Tierney snorted and continued nosing through the contents of the buff box.

"I see young Constable Silver found the shot and the powder flask," he said. "Excellent fellow! You know, I have certain expectations of that young man. It appears to me that if our villain had wanted to be caught he couldn't have chosen a better, keener officer."

Inspector Hughes bristled, not caring to mark the scranning cove's insinuating tone.

"Constable Silver still has a good deal to learn," he said, reaching across to move the buff box beyond Tierney's reach.

Inspector Tierney yawned and carelessly tossed the powder flask onto the desk. "You know what's wrong with you, Sam?" he said, "You need to use your imagination a little."

"And what do you know about that...?"

"You're too stodgy; too plain. Tu'penny meat-pie and gravy. Detectivists must be prime beefsteak. I mean take just now, for example: here am I trying to tell you something momentous, and all you can do is grumble about your blasted buff boxes." Inspector Tierney was inspecting his nails. "Sometimes," he said, "sometimes you have to look beyond the Magistrate; beyond Scotland-yard; beyond the proper procedures. Sometimes you need to take a step backwards in order to see the whole picture."

"The whole picture, eh. Is that what you call it...? Well, call it penny plain if you will but I prefer to stick close to getting at the truth."

"Really," said Inspector Tierney. His eyes lit upon a pile of *Police*

Gazettes sitting on the ledger desk. "Well you shan't find it in that rag, that's for sure."

Inspector Hughes should have said something about how the clutch of Active Duty men habitually to be found on Charing-cross never did a thing to stop the prisoner shooting Mr. Drummond, never lifted a finger to help Constable Silver, were all a crew of lazy sots who wouldn't take the trouble to piss on their own trowsers if they was on fire, not unless there was a half-crown in it for 'em. He should – he really should have said something about how in the end it had all come down to the courage and presence of mind of a *uniformed* officer – one who had been trained by none other than Inspector Hughes himself – who did not stint in the execution of his duty to Queen and country, no matter what the personal risk. Who was proud to wear his swallow-tailed coat – and who did it all for no gratuities, and nineteen-and-sixpence a week.

He should have said all this and more, but he didn't. It wouldn't have made no difference; and besides, he was tired, too tired.

"What if I was to tell you," said Inspector Tierney, "that we need to consider the possibility of the prisoner having shot the wrong man?"

Inspector Hughes laughed for the first time that long, long day: it was an abrupt laugh, devoid of any humour.

"Don't tell me," he said when he was done, "let me guess. The prisoner meant to assassinate Sir Robert Peel. Lor'! Is that the best you got? I've been listening to versions of that supposition half the blessed night. Which of your informers sold you that crock of flummery, then? I tell you what, they must see you coming down the street."

"O, my source," said Inspector Tierney, "my source is impeccable."

"Is it, by Jove? Well, it'll need to be an' all if you're to make a case out of that load of moonshine."

"My source is none other than the prisoner himself," said the scranning cove.

The corners of Inspector Hughes's mouth turned down as far as they would go. He picked up the powder flask and carefully returned it to the box with the other evidences. Tierney was whistling cheerfully, but the Inspector did not mark him. He was thinking how he saw it all now, everything: he knew how it would go and where it would most likely end. What a world, he thought.

The Second Meeting

I came across McNaughten standing in the courtyard. He was dressed in the pepper-and-salt jacket, corduroy trowsers, and battered hat that were the uniform of that place; a good-looking young man, in apparent good health with no indications of any physical disease such as was likely to impair mental power.

He affected not to see me at first, keeping his eyes steadfast upon the ground.

"Did not they tell you I was here?" I said. "I was waiting for you. I have set up upon the table in the usual place."

He sighed, but said not one word. I had observed before how careful he was to avoid the tendency of many acting insanity to betray himself by too many varieties of erratic conduct. On the contrary: his behaviour was always calm and controlled.

"It would be a shame to end our association so soon," I said, "for I feel that we discussed much of interest at our last encounter, and I should like the opportunity to do so again."

"Forgive me," he said, "but I am tired. You see, I dinnae sleep so well here. When I shut my eyes it is as if the room is spinning and everything buzzes. Indeed, I am very uncomfortable. There is somebody always using me ill here. Ah! If I could just get out of this place and go back to Glasgow – it is all I would ask for!"

A discernible weariness had indeed scudded across his features, such that one might almost have believed his claims to be ruined in health as a result of the torments which, as has been alleged, he had suffered at the hands of his "enemies".

"Yes, yes," I said, "and perhaps it might be possible for you to have your wish if the truth of your situation were more generally known..." I chose my words with considerable care.

"The truth?" he said.

"Yes – the truth..."

He sighed. "Truth," he said, "is the child of time," and he made a peremptory little laugh, the tone of which might easily have discomfited a less assured person than myself.

He lifted his head until the mistiness of his eyes was level with my own.

"Why?" he asked.

"Why...?"

For a moment it seemed that he might grow agitated. Indeed, I was just wondering whether I ought to alert the keeper by means of the agreed signal, when McNaughten turned suddenly away, shrugging his shoulders with an air of resignation.

"You may fetch your writing implements, sir," he said. "Perhaps if I assist you – even though I cannot pretend that there is any pleasure for me in doing so – perhaps you will make a good account of me; and perhaps then I shall be allowed to return home."

"Yes," I demurred, "that is indeed a *possibility*..."

"Though I prefer not to go indoors. I find that the fresh air and natural light lessens the effect of my affliction."

I agreed readily with the suggestion. It was a pleasant day, and I did not care for the strange, unwholesome smell of that place. I went at once to fetch my pens and papers.

"Tell me, sir," he asked as I passed him, "but is it your belief that I am mad?"

He was smiling at me, and now it appeared to me that the smile was marked with nothing so much as an absence of *intent*.

"I do not know," I said. "Are you?"

I awaited his reply with some interest, for it is well known that the genuine madman is in the habit of repudiating every suggestion of his insanity, whereas the pretender is quite willing to receive the diagnosis.

McNaughten frowned, appearing to give the question the deepest consideration of which he was capable.

"I hardly think, sir," he said at last, "that *that* is for me to say."

He was sixteen or seventeen years of age: turned out smart, in a brown dress coat of good quality, with a red neckerchief worn the same careless way that Carlo wore his. He had the remains of a bruise under his right eye. It wasnae the first time he'd been beaten by the 'prentices, and it wouldnae be the last. They waited for him in burly gangs on corners. It helped to be seen about the town with a well-renowned tough such as Carlo, but Carlo couldnae always watch his back. It didn't matter that he kept himself to himself: it was a fact that if youse didnae gie 'em one reason they'd find another. It was being different that marked him out.

He preferred reading to stooshies: books from the circulating library, mostly; anything that promised to take him away from himself and show him other ways of living and thinking. Captain Drinkwater's *Siege of Gibraltar*; Scott's *Life of Napoleon*; an account of Hegel's lectures on logic at the German University; Shakespeare; Keats; Shelley; lyrical ballads; a *History and Description of the Steam Engine*; Ritson's *Memoirs of the Celts*; Napier's *History of the War in the Peninsula*; John Gray's *A Lecture on Human Happiness*. His father wondered what he hoped to do with a heid chock-fu' o' nonsense, but it dinnae stop him reading. Sometimes Abram Duncan would bring him a volume or two: improving stuff, for the most part – religion and politics, for he was of the opinion that the two were inseparable and needed to be reconciled if society was to progress. Robert Owen; Frederick Denison Maurice; Saint-Simon's *Dialogues entre un conservateur et un novateur*. He taught himself to read French from an old grammar: he had no sense whatever of the sound of the words, but he came to a good understanding of their meaning. When he read it seemed to him that anything was possible. The ideas tumbled out of him dense and impenetrable, but somehow the books had a way of resolving the chaos; and when he read it was as though the future was more than a vague force tugging him towards death. He began to see how one might shape circumstances through ideas; though he had yet to develop an understanding of how to translate thoughts into actions.

He was impressionable, he supposed. At this time he was certainly keen for the attention that Abram Duncan gave to him, and he often kept the gentle journeyman in mind as he read, sharpening his arguments for the next opportunity to display them at one of the co-operationist meetings the pair of them often attended at the time. He supposed that he went along the more to annoy his father than to please Abram Duncan, and not from any genuine interest in the movement. At this point in his life, it seemed to him, his opinions were suspended between the two men, his life circumscribed by what was said and done by them within the confines of the shop.

When he was perhaps about eighteen or nineteen, his 'prenticeship fulfilled, his father had a new sign made and put up over the doorway of the shop: McNaughten & Son. He watched the sign go up and thought of the future stretching out before him. The shop was to be his life, but he had sensed another possibility – an airy vague sufficiency. One day he thought he might travel to Jamaica and teach the poor niggers to read and write so that they could be made free. Abram Duncan smiled at him and said it was a braw idea. Another day he thought that he might go to the university and study philosophy. His father said that he had first better go to some respectable teacher and learn writing and arithmetic.

He made calculations on the back of pieces of wood with his round stump of a pencil. He could go to China with the army – a dragoon. India. He could go to the Americas, if he wished, and make a fortune trading tobacco, sugar. How difficult could it be? He had saved a good portion of his wages in a tin he kept beside his mattress: the boats left from the quay at the top of the street every day; the passage advertised was within his reach. But all of this was in the future: for now there was the shop.

McNaughten & Son: for this he had been saved.

"Ach, the Whigs want tae mak' the poor seem like traitors," Carlo was telling him. The world was changing. There'd nivver been sic a slew o' folk. There were too many folk, and the government wanted rid o' them. Pack 'em off on boats tae Botany Bay. Lock 'em away in Poor Law Bastilles. Carlo couldnae read or write, but he'd had thrupence off o' Dan and asked him to read to him the pamphlet he'd bought with it.

"I could teach youse tae read it yerse'en. It's no' hard."

Carlo snorted. "Whit guid is readin' tae me?"

The pamphlet blamed it all upon the factory system. It said there was an underclass of women and children prepared to do the work of skilled men for a fraction of the price. It said this was the end of the honest tradesmen. They were doomed tae starve in their workshops, if they didnae go beggin' fer work at a lower rate frae the manufactors.

Carlo said, "In England they put the poor in prisons, and when they die they gie their bodies tae the Burkers." He said that he'd heard at a meeting how the Whigs were ay fer doin' the same in Glesga'. "Well, I'm no' gonnae stand fer it," he said.

They were walking by the quayside in the rain. It was gray like lead. The smell and taste of metal was in the air, and on Carlo's clothes; it was coming from their skin, from inside them.

His father told him: "Och, Dan, youse can aye stay on as a journeyman. Havers! Youse do the work o' three men: I'd be a loon tae let ye go."

McNaughten & Son.

His father said: "Hech! Did ye no' realise when ye saw the sign? It's Neil I maun think on, now he's of an age to learn the art and mystery."

Neil: his father's legitimate, no' *natural*, son. The shop was fer him – no' the wee bastard.

Dan packed his books in a pile and tied a belt around them.

Carlo said, "Hech! Youse a fool to stick to ol' man McNaughten so long. He's a Nob. He nivver cared fer youse. He's had it comin' a guid long while by now. It's only because youse're my pal that the 'prentices huvna seen tae him."

Dan found lodgings with a shoemaker and his family. He spent his time studying Playfair's Euclid. He learned the postulates off by heart, and lay on his bed all day drawing ellipsoids on the margins, thinking about symmetry.

After a week or two, Abram Duncan offered to take him round the turners' yards.

"It willna take long to find yourse'en a situation, Dan," he said. "Youse're the best turner ah ever worked alongside."

He spent his evenings listening to men talking to other men in howffs. In the afternoons he wandered down by the quayside and stood there, watching the ships. Sometimes he felt feverish with excitement, sometimes fear skirled inside his head. Sometimes he felt nothing: nothing at all.

Duncan took him to meet an ornamental turner over in Garnet Hill.

"D'ye think he can learn to drive a rose-engine lathe, Mr. Duncan?" the fellow asked.

"This boy is a born turner."

While Abram negotiated a wage for him, Dan inspected the machine carefully, intrigued by its operation and taken with the delicacy, the complexity of the mechanism. The cutting parts were kept in a mahogany box. He turned them over in his hand: pieces of metal; patterns waiting to be released.

And so his life went on. Every morning he woke with a start wondering where he was. Each night he fell asleep with the memory of his father's silhouette before him, grinding his teeth like the cogs of the lathe. He paid his lodgings and saved the rest in a tin that he kept beneath his bed. Not for him feckless nights wi' other lads, drinking himself intae a stupor, or dawdling wi' lassies. He considered himself to be unique in the way he hovered between the two parts of society. He was an eccentricity: not a circle with one point of focus; but an ellipse stretching between two points in space. He thought of his life going on into infinity, and tried to visualise the end point. With his compasses he drew complex patterns on the backs of handbills handed to him on the street by dismal men in ragged trowsers: circles rolling in circles; parabola rising and falling from convergences of straight lines.

The handbills spoke to him of *The Great Struggle which Cannot be Avoided*. And then one evening, returning from work to his lodgings, he found that the tailor had put out all of his belongings in the street. A gang of children had made off with his best waistcoat and the silk cravat the colour of a duck's egg. The tin with all his savings was quite safe, but his books were all upturned on the cobbles, their words melting in the rain.

"Infidel publications," said the tailor. "I canna have them in the house."

The tailor's wife had found them when she was sorting his room.

She had alerted the Presbytery at once. He had crossed a line he did not know was there.

The ornamental turner couldnae give work to a known troublemaker, nivver mind how skilful or how hard-working. He said: "I couldnae have the Kirk elders looking at me with sic glunches o' disdain."

It was a disappointment: that was all.

His father cursed the Kirk in ripe language. "Mind," he said when he was done, "ye've only yersel' tae blame. I told youse not tae wittle yer time readin' books, not to mention the terrible waste o' candles. Och but ye're a guid worker, I'll no deny that; an' I can ay use another journeyman."

That night, back in the wee hiddle, he fell asleep reading about the parallel postulate: two lines in the same plane extending through infinity with no point of convergence; no coincidence; no equality. But when he dreamed he saw patterns: complex, interlocking. He saw multiple lines of difference, precise and perfect, filling up the space between them with contiguity.

"Aye," he said, as he drew our interview to a close, "when I dreamed I dreamed of connexions." A dreamy cast had settled upon his features, and his smile, for this one time, was just *a smile*.

"O, and there is nothing more beautiful than *connexions*."

Bow-street Magistrates' Court,
about ten o'clock a.m.

Introducing the lay reader to the sublime mysteries of that
black art called Law.

Mr. Warren found himself standing in the heaving centre of a cramped and frowsty court-room, cheek by jowl with a bedraggled host, the indecorous sprawl of Fearon's gin across his nostrils. The carriage people being still largely out of town, there was scarce a single person of any note to be found among the usual idlers hanging about the place: a huddle of briefless barristers, a press of penny-a-liners, one or two clerks of the Treasury and Home Office. It was disagreeable, of course, to find oneself hemmed in on every side by sweat-grimed linen, unbarbered chins and ill-fitting frock-coats; though there is always an undeniable satisfaction to be derived from finding oneself the only gentleman in a room.

The air was thick with rumour and loose analogies; but Mr. Warren stood stroking his top lip circumspectly, and congratulated himself on his ability to keep his head above the gossip. He had no intention whatever of giving himself away, but several times, overhearing the nonsense that was being babbled, he had to struggle not to interpose. Wisely, he kept his counsel: withdrawing from his pocket a leather notebook and a lead pencil he made jottings of his thoughts in stenographic sound-hand. It was not long before he arrived at the content of the threatening letter that Mr. Drummond had shewn him at Bellamy's the previous afternoon.

Let us kill him, and we'll have corn at our own price!

The alarming intimation had hardly been out of his thoughts. He tapped the lead pencil against his teeth, feeling a flutter of unsteadiness about his heart, a familiar sinking sensation followed by a sudden acceleration of the pulse; gooseflesh. He thought he saw Mr. Charles Dickens in the crowd, but mercifully he was mistaken: it was not that over-rated hack after all, but a junior clerk in the Board of Trade who resembled him somewhat. Mr. Warren did not acknowledge the fellow's cheerful gesture. He was agitated, very, with speculation upon what Dickens, in his guise of wearied reporter for a Radical newspaper, would make of the matter of Mr. Drummond's shooting: a popular affair, no doubt, giving full vent to his 'liberal' opinions in vulgar Cockney colloquialisms. Another *Barnaby Rudge*, perchance, damn him!

The plainclothes inspector Mr. Warren had encountered in the prisoner's cell the night before entered and took his seat at the magistrate's desk. And seeing him, the court grew very noisy and exceedingly close, yeasty with a restless anticipation. A bead of sweat urged itself onto Mr. Warren's forehead, as robust, swaggering rumour, taunting, mocking rumour assailed his ears. Mr. Drummond had been shot by a man who had sought a post in the Treasury... Mr. Drummond had been shot by a discharged clerk of his family's counting-house... Mr. Drummond had been shot by a madman... Mr. Drummond had been taken for the Prime Minister... They were all so many humbugs – ill-considered, random jottings every one of them; yet he could have plucked each in turn and shaped it, breathed life into it, and set it walking about the streets of the Metropolis. And in so doing, he could have conjured into being a whole way of looking at the world.

Mr. Drummond has been shot at by an assassin hired by the Anti-Corn Law League... He could utter it now, here, in this very place. He could set spinning a whirligig of his own devising, and confound everyone. But his heart, you see, his heart wanted the truth: fleetingly apparent, touching but lightly on possibilities, opening up misty depths of meaning and sense. How unfortunate, thought Mr. Warren, that there was to be found more acceptance in a probable falsehood than in a singular truth. It was shocking to realise that he was such an innocent that he could not bring himself to light upon a postulation at will and argue it up: was this why he had never succeeded in the law? By thunder, whatever was the matter with him? People made up things every day with no ill effects. He was a barrister, for goodness' sake: how long, he wondered, did it ordinarily take for a ray of conscience to penetrate the dark heart of a barrister?

A tall, forlorn-looking policeman closed the doors to the court-room and stood before the entrance, looking about him with the solemn, proprietary air of a grocer on a slow hour. And soon everything was settling. There was a hush. There was the dais. There was the court-room clock.

Of course, Mr. Warren would have to talk with Mr. Drummond before proceeding: it was imperative. Only then, he felt, would the matter clarify; for who would gainsay the word of a decent man who had just been shot in the back as he went innocently about his business? Mr. Warren felt a little calmer now that he had settled upon it, but his equilibrium was soon disrupted by an elbow dug into his side.

"Perhaps we shall begin soon! What d'ye say?"

He looked down upon a square-jawed, beefy fellow, who was rubbing his hands with glee, and marking the policeman on the door with the practised eye of one well accustomed to the operations of the court.

Mr. Warren sniffed. A penny-a-liner with too much of the race-track about him, dressed in a trowser of exceedingly large check. The pair of them were pressed in very close, their movements hampered by a great urgency of bodies on all sides. Escape to another part of the room was not a possibility, and so Mr. Warren inclined to be absent, as though his thoughts were on higher things and persons than those around him, and most particularly the beefy fellow.

"Newspaperman?" said the checkered trowser, jauntily indicating Mr. Warren's little leather notebook. "Well now, there's a coincidence! Renton Nicholson, Legal Correspondent of *Old Peeping Tom of London Town*," he was proffering a large hand and, much to Mr. Warren's horror, appeared to be winking. "Pleased to make your acquaintance!" he said.

After a few moments of broad grinning and winking, the fellow shrugged good-naturedly and withdrew his untouched hand from the space between them.

"I say," he said, undaunted, "perhaps we can stick together."

Mr. Warren focused all of his attention upon the dais: the witness box in the centre, the dock to the left, the magistrate's desk, partitioned from the crowded room by a small screen to the right, with the plainclothesman just visible at the head of it. He kept his eye keenly upon the little stage, studiously ignoring the benign gaze of his companion, as the great lumbering minute hand of the ancient court-room clock heaved itself onto the VI.

"Jolly good! We're off!" said the beefy fellow, as the magistrate entered and took his seat upon the bench. He nudged Mr. Warren hard in the ribs once again with his elbow. "I say, we're off!" he repeated.

The Magistrate made a very mumbling, inauspicious announcement. "In view of the great interest displayed in the case which I am about to hear," he said at the culmination of it, "my colleague has agreed to dispose of the night charges in an adjoining room."

The tall, lugubrious police inspector duly swung open the doors, and there was a great deal of grumbling and ill-natured shoving as those who had come to give support to associates taken the night before in acts of drunkenness and violence agitated their way to the entrance.

"That's good. We shall have a bit more room," observed Mr. Nicholson; yet each time Mr. Warren was able to move more than an inch or two from the wretched fellow's side, he followed him, his impertinent gaze passing all the while between Mr. Warren's face and the little notebook.

A hush descended over the court-room, and everyone strained forward as the prisoner was brought to stand in the dock. Mr. Warren was taller than most people, and so he had a good view. He could see the gaoler leaning back against the dock rail, rolling the barrel of a large key between his thumb and forefinger; and just above his shoulder the thin young man of shabby-genteel appearance whom he had seen in the cell the night before. The prisoner had a rigid phlegmatic cast to his features; an expression of some little anxiety, perhaps indicative of a depression of spirits – well disguised beneath an external composure of manner.

The clerk gave the prisoner's details as Daniel McNaughten, a wood-turner, late of Glasgow, now residing at number seven Poplar-row, a lodgings in the vicinity of Newington Butts. Mr. Warren took down the address and resolved to pay a visit.

"Perhaps we ought to join forces," said the checkered trowsers, "and make an expedition to the Surrey-side? What d'ye say, Mr... Mr...?"

"I think not," said Mr. Warren. "I scarcely think there will be a great deal to be gleaned from the lodgings that the police haven't already discovered."

"Really?" exclaimed the Legal Correspondent of *Old Peeping Tom of London Town*. "O, I'm not at all sure that I agree with you there, chum. Landladies, or so I have often found, are privy to a great many intimate details pertaining to the hidden lives of their lodgers. They know which are the *clean* linen days and which the *foul*, if you follow my meaning."

"Pray be quiet," said Mr. Warren. "I should like to hear the evidences."

"Found upon his person," the clerk was declaring of the prisoner, "a penknife, a key, a token, three Bank of England notes carrying the value of £5, four sovereigns, four half-crowns, one shilling and fourpence in coppers, and a receipt from the Glasgow and Ship Bank for £750 to the credit of one Daniel McNaughten..."

A great gasp went up from the court-room, and Mr. Warren, who had successfully transcribed the whole in stenographic sound-hand, felt a rush of excitement.

"Dam'me!" said the beefy fellow in the checkered trowsers, "that was unexpected! I say, that was unexpected! Now to what do you account that, then, Mr... Mr...? I'd say it was plain as day what's gone on here. What about you? What's it say in that there notebook of yours?"

What it said was that seven hundred and fifty pounds was a magnificent sum; so magnificent, it was quite impossible that the prisoner had come by it legally.

The charge was read: that the prisoner had attempted to assassinate Mr. Edward Drummond on the previous afternoon.

"Not guilty," said the prisoner when prompted.

A few people laughed, as if he must be joking; but the prisoner said it with such an air of modest firmness, possibly even sadness, comporting himself all the while with an anxious attention.

The fellow also spoke – a point of fact surely not without relevance – in broad Scotch.

The square-jawed fellow nudged Mr. Warren in the side again, and indicated the notebook.

"Corn," he said. "That's what'll be made out of this."

Mr. Warren slammed the notebook shut.

"Do you recall," said the fellow, looking about him, "the testimony of that gentleman who had attended the League's Convention over the summer and heard a manufactor swear he would draw lots of a hundred men to see which of them should kill Sir Robert Peel?"

Mr. Warren set his jaw on edge.

"Makes you think, don't it," he continued.

"About what?" said Mr. Warren.

"Why, Corn, of course," said the wretched fellow. "Ah yes! That's what'll be made of this alright. Plain as day. *Corn...*"

"Will you stop saying that," hissed Mr. Warren. "Confound you!"

But it was too late. A few about them had already taken up the incantation. *Corn. Corn. Corn. Corn.* Mr. Warren heard it whispered all about him like the chugging of an impending locomotive.

"A stiff birching and eighteen months on the treadmill," opined Mr. Nicholson, who was not at all abashed. "That's all the dwarf-boy Bean got for shooting at Her Majesty – and you can't deal a worse punishment for firing at the sovereign than you deal for firing at a Tory. Or so I should say."

A few of the people standing about them began to murmur their agreement, and within moments the courtroom was a buzz of postulations. Mr. Nicholson folded his arms across his chest and nodded, laughing a little; as if none of it mattered. As if it was all a game.

"If they'd hung drawn and quartered Francis like the judge wanted, Bean would never have thought to copy him..."

"...Prince Albert wouldn't have it. He said hanging drawing and quartering don't do honour to the leading Society in the Civilised World..."

"...It was an abuse of justice was that..."

"...misguided mercy..."

"...Oxford told his keeper at Bethlem that if a proper example had been made of him when he fired at the Queen two years ago, there'd have been no Francis and Bean..."

"...Oxford said that...?"

"...It was in the newspapers..."

"…You can't make scaffold heroes out of these young ruffians…"

"…They should all be shut away in Bethlem with Oxford for the rest of their days…"

"…Shame 'em…"

"…Preposterous…!"

"…Think of the expense to the public…!"

"…Why should Francis, who fired at the Queen, live in luxury in Bethlem, when the poor what's done nothing 'cept honour Her Majesty must starve in the workhouses…?"

"Silence!" barked the plainclothesman, much to the relief of Mr. Warren.

The office-keeper had finished his testimony, and the prisoner had indicated that he might have something to say, turning up his gaze as if in wistful contemplation of the ceiling.

"Lor'! Look at him, now," hissed Mr. Nicholson, nudging Mr. Warren in the ribs. "Cool as you like! What d'ye make of that, then? He looks like he ain't all there to me. Ho ho! He'll be joining Oxford in Bethlem alright, or I'm a blue monkey…!"

No.19, Grosvenor-square, Mayfair,
THE PREVIOUS EVENING

In which Miss Drummond is troubled by no secret. Daniel 4:9

"Write down," Mr. Guthrie senior instructed Guthrie junior, "that a protuberance was discovered lying just under the skin, on the patient's left side, between the cartilages of the seventh and eighth ribs."

He prodded it with his lancet.

"Gad!" cried Neddie in a queer strangulated voice so unlike his customary one. "Leave it alone! I insist. Leave it be!"

"I should say that's the wretched bit of shot, alright," said Mr. Guthrie senior. "Well, well, well… How intriguing… I should like a better look at *that*…"

Mr. Bransby Cooper made a morose assessment of the lump at Mr.

Guthrie senior's insistence. He said, "I wonder, sir, what harm can possibly ensue from leaving it be?"

"Write down," said Mr. Guthrie senior, "that the ball passed through the great omentum, having entered at the back, just below the stomach."

"We have had enough of writing things down, have we not?" cried Neddie. "Am I to be writ up in some confounded journal, like a dinosaurus?"

He spoke in funny little gasps.

Miss Drummond unpicked the stitch she had just worked and then made it over again. Neddie was quite right, of course. What was it, after all, this intolerable desire to leave extenuations in the dumb and dwindling sands of time?

Mr. Guthrie senior said, "I shall operate immediately."

"Are my bones to be preserved in jars and gawped at by locals in a travelling fair?"

"You must not speak, sir," commanded Mr. Guthrie senior. He was flourishing a bloody lancet. "Not if you wish to mend."

"O dear God," cried Neddie. "Have pity. Pity!"

Which were the last words that she heard him speak out loud in this life.

The absence of any particular shock and alarm on Neddie's part during the first few hours following the shooting had given rise to the anxious hope that the shot had not passed so directly across and that death would not *necessarily* follow as a consequence. Miss Drummond had acknowledged these glad tidings politely, thinking all the while how Mr. Guthrie senior could not possibly know how it would go with her brother.

It was quite true that there were few things in life that are unknown to surgeons; but as for death... Well, despite being the cause of so many, they know no more of death than does any mortal being. It was very apparent to her that Neddie had not exhibited any of the ordinary symptoms for the simple expedient that his thoughts were occupied elsewhere. If, throughout that long and fateful evening her own

thoughts had frequently strayed to the volume and all its dark and troublous inferences, then the same, she was sure, must be true of her poor
dear brother. Something would have to be done with it, and done soon;
but she had not yet settled on the appropriate method of disposal. It had
occurred to her that the intimations contained in the volume were likely
to prove as damaging to Sir Robert Peel as they were to any man alive.
Perhaps, she considered, Neddie had come to the same conclusion, and
had felt a strong desire to bear witness – to leave behind a testimony,
as it were; so that those others who, may it please God, will come after
us, may *know*.

Whatever, one thing was certain: she could not keep the book concealed for ever. There was always the Bank, of course, in many ways the
obvious depository; but she could see no way of secreting the volume
there without arousing the interest of their elder brother Georgie – and
why should she share her precious knowledge with him, who had never
once shewed her any kindness or interest, had always condescended to
her, the baby of the family, as though she were an imbecilic nuisance.
She could not bear the thought of sharing anything with Georgie – least
of all the privileged divinations that Neddie had entrusted to her. Besides, it was certain in her mind that Georgie would do what he always
did: he would place the interests of the Bank and the family name first,
and doubtless failing to grasp the more profound significance of Neddie's cache of secrets, he would consign them to the flames at once.

She thought of confiding in their cousin Henry, the head of the
Bank and the only member of the family capable of gainsaying Georgie. Cousin Henry was certain to appreciate the importance of the volume. However, he was devout-hearted to the point of derangement – he
pursued a religion of his own devising – and this, she feared, might
well lead him towards an *interpretation* of the intelligences in keeping with his peculiar beliefs. Moreover, Cousin Henry would not be
able to confine their revelation to a closed and privileged circle; he
would seek to impart them to a good many of the thoroughly undeserv-
ing. O, he would understand as she did that the volume demonstrated
how perilously close to the End we are: only she knew that it did not
tell of the End that Cousin Henry so fondly imagined. There would be
no trumpets and angels, no Ancient of Days with his white beard

scooping up the Righteous in armfuls; no judicious measuring of souls; no golden palaces; no ethereal singing. This End, the real End, the End that was coming, would be far more dismal, far more commonplace, and far more terrifying.

Miss Drummond shuddered, as she always did, whenever her thoughts turned to what was coming.

She looked across at Neddie. He was as pale as the jelly on a plate of veal and gazing disconsolately at the bed-canopy. She smiled sweetly. "I understand everything, my dear," she said. "You are not to worry. You know how you can always depend upon me."

Neddie's eyes flickered, and he sighed deeply, almost a groan. The doctors had forbidden him to speak, but it was not clear whether he could any longer. She watched him for a few minutes until his eyelids drooped and he appeared to fall into a light slumber.

It must be such a relief to him, she thought, to know that I have matters so well in hand.

The usual thrashings that attended surgery had been prevented in this case by the use of a lancet box which Guthrie junior had held a few inches in front of what he called "the Subject", while his father and Mr. Bransby Cooper performed the operation to remove the piece of shot from Neddie's front. The junior Guthrie had been present at the Royal Medical and Chirurgical Society the previous November when an account was read of the amputation of the thigh during Mesmeric trance. It was he who had first mooted the application of the method in respect of Neddie. The lancet box was kept at such a position above the forehead as to produce the greatest possible strain upon the eyes and eyelids, whilst maintaining a fixed gaze for the entire duration of the operation. Almost thirty minutes, Miss Drummond reckoned: which was a good deal longer than was expected, according to Mr. Guthrie senior's frequent expostulations; and largely owing to the infernal fumblings of Mr. Bransby Cooper.

Miss Drummond felt a degree of sympathy for Mr. Bransby Cooper. She understood what he was trying to do, of course. It would be awkward were the piece of shot in Neddie's front to be given to the police as evidence. Mr. Bransby Cooper was only trying to preserve the reputation of the Duke of Wellington. It was perfectly laudable of him, she thought; just such a pity that subterfuge was another thing at which he did not appear to excel.

As for "the Subject", he remained in perfect repose all the while; his placid countenance never once abating. Poor dear Neddie certainly had *bottom*! He shewed it as never before, submitting with patient resignation to all the slicing and probing, in the course of which he never once flinched; which was, she supposed, just as well.

The thing of it was, Miss Drummond imagined, not to fear. It was fear that governed us, fear of the unknown portion of our lives. If only everyone could trust, as she did, that everything was *knowable*, inscribed in the bumps and protuberances; then there would be no need for fear. Neddie, she knew, was not afraid; at least he was not afraid of *them*. How could he be afraid of the surgeons and their instruments knowing what he knew of the real Terrors that were yet to come...? What was mere mortal agony to the destruction and disintegration of everything that a man of his loyalty and devotedness held most dear?

"You poor thing," she whispered to him now. "You shall be better off out of it all, really you will."

A look of mild approbation passed across his eyes, or so she fancied, just before he closed his lids and fell into a maundering, tremulous sleep.

After the procedure a violent discussion had ensued between the doctors. Mr. Bransby Cooper averred that the non-expression of pain in surgery was a common enough thing.

"Well, you would know," snorted Mr. Guthrie senior.

"Why must you doubt!" said the junior Guthrie. "We have all witnessed the future of surgery here today. I have a good mind to write it up in a paper!"

"Perhaps," said Mr. Guthrie senior, "the subject is imperceptible to pain. Certainly the complete absence of the reflex-action at the first incision was quite extraordinary. If I had not seen it with my own eyes, I would not have believed it."

It amused her that not one of them doubted for a moment that "the Subject" had felt no pain. If they had troubled to look upon his dear face, as she had done, they might have noticed a solitary tear roll down his ample cheek at the time of the first piercing. It was true that after this uncharacteristic lapse, Mr. Drummond had uttered no cry whatever.

Of course, the physicians could not be expected to appreciate, as she did, the subduing effect a lifetime in politics has upon the expression of all true feeling. Poor dear Neddie's whole life's pursuit had been in the perfection of the art and mystery of dissembling, she thought, regarding him fondly. He had so often to say one thing and mean another and think a third, always to appear insensible to any argument, however reasonable, yet at the same time sensitive to each *nuance* of argument, that it was a wonder he had any feelings left at all.

"After entering from behind it would appear that the shot passed upwards into the cavity of the chest, traversing the left side of the body," Guthrie senior dictated to his son, who was still writing things down, "slightly abrasing the left lung at the inferior edge."

Parrott poured water from a jug over the surgeon's hands, water that trickled in a thin scarlet stream into a waiting receptacle.

Mr. Bransby Cooper held aloft a candle in his left hand, and peered beneath a flap of Mr. Drummond's skin that he had peeled back on the edge of his lancet.

"I can see a thick coating of lymph," he reported, "though the lung itself sounds to be well enough."

"The ball," the senior Guthrie said, leaning with a fierce intensity over Neddie, "ought to have perforated the diaphragm to arrive at where it was; most likely grazing the fat of the left kidney."

"Damage to any vital organ?" inquired Guthrie junior, looking up from his notes.

"None that I can see. There appears to be a great effusion of blood at the site of the opening."

The blood, they all agreed, ought to be drawn off, to the amount of perhaps twelve ounces.

They turned away from Neddie in order to prepare for the letting, Parrott taking the opportunity to lean over him. Miss Drummond could see his face quite clearly from her side of the bed; the large dark eyes vibrant with feeling. And seeing, it she felt a pain behind her ribs.

"How are you master?" Parrott asked. "Are you comfortable?"

Neddie attempted to whisper something in his ear.

How well he had inveigled his way into poor dear Neddie's trust, she thought, feeling her colour rise. One must never underestimate the perseverance of a bad mind in pursuit of a bad action.

"Hush, sir, don't try to speak," said the footman in his molasses voice. "The doctors say you are not to speak. Might he have water, sirs? He seems parched. He moves his mouth as if in want of refreshment."

"He is to have no water," commanded Guthrie senior. He was wrapping a large bandage around Neddie's arm, just above the elbow. When that was done he removed his thumb lancet case from his waistcoat pocket.

"Stand here between me and your master with the basin," he commanded Parrott.

Neddie groaned softly.

Mr. Guthrie senior grasped the lancet between his thumb and forefinger and prepared to apply it to the vein in Neddie's arm.

She poured herself a cup of hot water and added a tincture of Rowland's Aqua d'Oro. She had already had more than her usual ration, but it had been a very long and wearisome day; she was in need of sustenance, and after all that she had done, well deserving a little serious consideration, which it would appear only the drops were able to extend to her.

Mr. Bransby Cooper had succeeded in laying hold of the shot. Miss Drummond watched in muted alarm from the other side of the bed as the surgeon stood dumbfounded, gazing at the bloody ball, rolling around aimlessly in his open palm, as if as amazed as was he at its discovery.

Mr. Guthrie senior snatched it away at once.

He said, "One of us will be required shortly at the police court. I think that as the senior physician here, that ought to be me. There will be a great deal of interest in this case; it is important that we represent ourselves as well as possible."

Mr. Bransby Cooper sighed, looking mournfully at the shot now in the possession of his colleague.

"And what, I wonder, does the esteemed author of *Gunshot Wounds* make of that?" he said resignedly.

Miss Drummond looked up from her sewing to see Mr. Guthrie senior inspecting the bullet closely. When her sharp admonitory eyes sought him out, Mr. Bransby Cooper smiled haplessly at the floor; as though none of this had a thing to do with him. She stood up, laying down her sewing upon the seat of her chair and held out her palm across the bed towards Mr. Guthrie senior.

"I think," she said, "that it would be best for all were I to take charge of that."

Mr. Guthrie senior's piercing look met hers, gem-sharp. He hesitated, glanced once at the shot, once at Mr. Drummond, and then, frowning darkly, at her once more.

"But the police may wish to see the shot," he said. "It is evidence."

"In that case," said Miss Drummond, "you may direct them to me." She extended her fat little hand, palm up, a little further and with more emphasis, over her brother's body.

The surgeon, keeping his stern eye upon hers all the while, proffered the ball betwixt a blood-stained thumb and forefinger.

She slipped it into the purse she kept about her ample waist, drawing the strings tightly. And then she settled back in her chair and returned to pretending to sew.

BOW-STREET MAGISTRATES' COURT,
IN CONTINUANCE OF THE ARRAIGNMENT OF THE
PRISONER MCNAUGHTEN

In which Mr. Warren is further irritated by a checkered trowser and a cocky brother barrister.

Cockburn's arrival at the police courts seemed calculated to cause a stir. At some ungodly hour, after a sleepless night, and against all his better judgement, he had clapped spurs to one of his uncle's horses and made a dash across a dispiriting landscape beset with heavy snows, only to arrive at Bow-street, half-frozen, jolted, dusty, and in a temper as filthy as his top-boots, to discover that the court had been in session for more than a half-an-hour and he had missed a good many of the evidences. Having only the slenderest grasp of the case, he was therefore no closer to forming an opinion as to why the Chief Whipper-in of the Parliamentary Whigs was evincing such a profound interest in the random assault on a Treasury factotum.

Doubtless, a good many men finding themselves in his vexatious position might well have given up, but not Sandy: he was in too deep. Muttering dark oaths to himself, he knew that he had little choice but to stay and glean what he could from the remainder of the hearing, and reasoned that he could always patch up his ignorance with intelligences from a couple of legal copy-takers whom he spied there in the crowd.

Mr. Cockburn – touching as he did on the average height – could see nothing of the dais from the back or the middle of the room, and so he began to thrust his way through the crowd to the front of the court-room, arriving there just as the surgeon, Mr. Guthrie senior, was preparing to take the oath. Mr. Warren watched Cockie cut this swath, and marked with a deep-felt resentment how easefully the preening, jobbing Sardinapalian made progress through all levels of society. What the blazes is he doing here? he wondered. Mr. Warren could not have been more dismayed if Mr. Charles Dickens himself had materialised in the courtroom before him, with a full confession from McNaughten in his hand. He had been formally introduced to the dwarf counsel only once – at a dinner hosted a few months ago by a well-connected fellow barrister – but Mr. Warren knew Cockburn Q.C. in the way that everyone at the Temple knew `the wretch, dividing equally between intense dislike and deep admiration.

"I say," said Mr. Nicholson, who was still breathing hard upon Mr. Warren's neck, "I wonder what the Buck of the Bar is doing here!" He said it in terms which led Mr. Warren to suppose the Legal Correspondent must be an admirer; but even so, it was certainly a very good question.

"Good old Cockie!" said the checkered trowsers. "He must've heard something that's tugged at his liberal heart-strings. O, *werry* Radical is Mr. Cockburn. If he's come here this morning, I should say there's a wrong to be righted."

"Pshaw!" scouted Mr. Warren as another little buzz of rumour flew about the room. "Obviously, Lord John Russell has despatched him here – the Whigs know full well that a sighting of Mr. Cockburn will be sufficient to make most ignorant people think that the matter is not as straightforward as it appears to be. It is a cynical ploy calculated to make things difficult for the government, and nothing more."

Mr. Warren watched, with a shameful despising, the manner in which the little red-headed fellow assumed a barristerly stance: hands linked behind his back, beneath his coat-tails, body propped forward, as if intent upon some point of extreme interest, with a sardonical expression set upon his handsome features. The dratted fellow's popularity, badinage, dandyism, and inexplicable attractiveness to the opposite sex (to the sexes in general, if all of the vile rumours were to be believed) – all, all perfectly sound reasons to hate "Good Old Cockie", as far as Mr. Warren was concerned.

"As a matter of fact," he said, suddenly adopting a tone of intimacy towards his companion, a tone which he had thus far strenuously avoided, "I had heard that Cockburn was in grave trouble with his Society… some scandal involving the wife of a brother barrister. It was the talk of the entire Temple before Christmas. Indeed, I believe that Cockie might well be under threat of debarment…"

"Ho ho!" laughed Mr. Nicholson delightedly, "the wife of a brother barrister, eh! Ho ho! And ain't he a proper gent!" And he nudged Mr. Warren in the ribs once more for good measure.

Mr. Warren had made up the part about debarment – at least he didn't know for sure if that penalty lay in store for the confounded Robin Redbreast. It was certainly true, however, that a coterie of Temple benchers had felt it necessary to pay a visit to Sandy's chambers. His behaviour was an effrontery to the good name of the legal profession, and as far as Mr. Warren was concerned, Sandy Cockburn would be no loss to the Law. Ever since bagging a silk gown, he had usefully confined himself to doing the Whigs' dirty work for them in practice before Parliamentary Committees. He lacked the scholarship necessary to build a successful line of business outside Westminster; he was an indifferent advocate, the sort who got up his law for the occasion. He had the connections, was all – and let us not forget the fashionably liberal instincts. Cockie was "in" with a crew of drawling, simpering Radical reformists (which included that worthless penny-a-liner Charles Dickens), whose indignation on all points of societal injustice (as they saw it) was indefatigable; and he was forever being complimented upon his concern for the poor, the nigger slaves, the Chartist prisoners, the so-called savagery of public hangings.

Damn it! fumed Mr. Warren. Cockburn could make as much of this matter as anyone in London, apart from himself, of course. Cockie was simply doing what he always did, which was to push himself forward in any matter calculated to earn popular approval.

Resentment boiled over into loathing as he observed a coterie forming itself about Cockie and giving off a great buzz of excitement. He strained to hear what the wretch had to say for himself, whilst at the same time affecting perfect appallment at such a blatant disregard of the magistracy.

The checkered trowser was beaming. "I should say he's on the trail of some miscarriage of justice or other!"

"What miscarriage can there possibly be in the case of a man taken in broad day firing pistols at another? *Corpus delicti*! As a legal correspondent you really ought to know better! Why, it was executed in front of a dozen witnesses, including a police constable."

"O, you'd be surprised," he countered, "the number of times in life things turn out to be not at all what they seem."

Mr. Warren heaved a great sigh of exasperation. "And to what great cause," he said, "do you attribute this sordid and lamentable matter?"

Mr. Nicholson rasped his chin. The moveable moustachios were proving a sight uncomfortable in the heat of the court-room. "O, I never said there might be a great cause in it," he said. "It's you who has made up his mind regarding the prisoner's guilty complicity in respect of something alarming and low-principled. It might turn out to be anything at all. Why, who's to say that the prisoner himself has any idea what he's about!"

"You mean he might be stark staring roaring mad! Just like Francis and Bean were found to be, perchance?" Mr. Warren snorted, as querulousness and dissent bubbled and frothed, filling up the court-room.

The checkered trowsers scratched his chin and smiled to himself. He kept his eye upon Mr. Cockburn, who was stood at the front of the courtroom listening intently to the evidence of the surgeon, entirely unaware of the brouhaha got up on his account.

"Silence there," barked the plainclothes inspector from the dais. But by then the soft wash of controversy had swelled to a great tide of forceful debate. A good many men were arguing vehemently with one another, but it was Mr. Warren who, above the heads of everyone else, met the stern admonishing eyes of the magistrate.

"Silence, I say, or I shall have you removed from the court."

Mr. Warren felt his colour rise above his wilted stock. He ran a hand through his damp dark curls and affected a careless air, as if to say he had seen and heard quite enough, and there was no need to remain in that place merely to be rounded upon. With as much wounded dignity as he could muster, he put away the leather-bound notebook and pencil and began to push his way through the crowd towards the door, the choice rebukes of the ignorant throng ringing in his ears.

He needed a drink. He would find a tavern and then make his way to Mr. Drummond's house in Mayfair, where he would endeavour to put a stop to all this nonsense once and for all.

THE SAME,
A FEW MOMENTS LATER

In which Mr. Nicholson gives us cause to consider the text: Thy knowledge is too wonderful for me (Psalms 139:6).

To tell the truth, Mr. Nicholson was mightily pleased to see FIAT JUSTITIA leave the court room. The bonhomie of the checkered trowsers required a surprising amount of effort, as did mentally transcribing Mr. Warren's rapid stenography. He fumbled in his pocket for a scrap of paper and a mean stub of pencil, and, sighing relievedly, prepared to unburden his memory of a few of the choicer items gleaned from the gentleman's leather notebook.

The second bit o' shot he'd discovered the night before upon the pavement where it had been discharged was nestling in his pocket beside the pencil. He retrieved it, rolling it around between his thumb and finger. Now that he had done as much as he might in pursuit of the truth in this *werry dark and twisted matter*, he permitted himself a rare moment of purest gloating. Ah me! The interposing of mischief could be a wearisome business and did not often afford as much delight as one would imagine. But this, he thought smiling at the little oily pellet, this made it all worthwhile. He sniggered as he looked over at Black Jack Tierney sitting up on the magistrate's dais, looking shiftier than a Pimlico *schneider*; and extended a modicum of sympathy to poor Cockie over there, plucking nervously at the primrose gloves.

He scratched his false whiskers. *Ah, life's a riddle, ain't it, my merry Andrews*, thought Mr. Nicholson, as he made his way through the frowsty crowd to where Mr. Cockburn was standing, listening to the saw-bones. He himself had decided not to listen too well to the description of what that pair of Burkers, Guthrie and Cooper, had inflicted on the fat Tory as they went fishing for the ball. Doubtless, my pippins, Secretary Drummond had had it coming; but even so, it weren't a nice way to be dealt with, and a man of Mr. Nicholson's predilection could not afford to permit any sentiment for the victim to occlude his senses.

"Far better to have left the shot where it was, if you ask me," he whispered sidling up beside the little silk.

Cockie gave an abrupt laugh of concordance.

"Still, must have been some advantage in all that rummaging," he continued. "Doctors are always thinking of their reputations, don't you agree?"

The barrister turned to regard him with a quizzical expression.

"Do I know you?" he said.

Mr. Nicholson peeled back one of the moveable moustachios and winked.

"M'Lud!" exclaimed Cockie, delightedly. All the gentleman barristers who attended Mr. Nicholson's notorious Judge and Jury Society on Wednesday evenings in the Strand addressed him thus. "Is it you beneath that disguise?"

The Lord Chief Baron raised a thick finger to his lips and winked again.

Mr. Guthrie senior was now telling the court how the ball had been removed not from the old masher's arse – as every one had hitherto been led to expect – but from his front.

"Seems an unlikely journey for a poor bit o' shot from a rusty dueller to have made, don't it?" whispered Mr. Nicholson. "Especially when one considers the size of the victim."

Cockie clasped his hands behind his back and leaned forward in an attitude of keen engagement.

"The shot was slightly marked," the doctor was saying, "and had the appearance of having been rifled."

Cockie and the Baron exchanged a look.

"But I thought the bobby said that the weapons were smooth bore," observed Mr. Nicholson.

Cockie peered inquisitively at the pistols laid out upon the magistrate's desk.

"What became of the shot that you removed?" asked the magistrate. "May the court see it?"

Mr. Guthrie senior frowned.

"I passed it to Miss Drummond for safe-keeping," he said, adopting the confidential tones of a society quack.

"They're duellers, ain't they, Mr. Cockburn?" said Mr. Nicholson.

"So it would seem, M'Lud," said Cockie.

"And duellers ought never to be rifled?"

"Only a blackguard would attend an affair of honour with rifled pistols," said Cockie looking from the pistols to the prisoner.

"You ought to know, sir," said Mr. Nicholson. Cockie had been slapped in the face with a white glove more times than a good many other men have tasted fried liver and onions.

"The improved accuracy of a rifled pistol gives an unfair advantage," the silk was saying. "I have heard that it is possible to obtain duelling pistols which appear to be smooth-bore from the muzzle, but are in fact rifled."

"Ah," said Mr Nicholson, "yet the testimony of the Constable was most clear. He told us to the point of tedium that any shot fired from those pistols would need a patch, and so, ergo, they could not possibly be rifled."

Mr. Nicholson turned the second bit o' shot over in his palm: it certainly weren't rifled; as a matter of fact, it weren't even lead, though it had been fired, for it was scorched, oily, and black with powder residue.

It was a tight, thick plug of paper, saved from immolation by the pavement snows.

Now then my merry Andrews, he thought; I wonder what's gone on here...

A CORRIDOR AT BOW-STREET,
AT THE SAME TIME

In which Inspector Hughes is troubled by the representations
of a witness.

Inspector Hughes had left the court-room on account of the night-charges. He had stayed just long enough to hear that the surgeons had successfully removed the ball from Mr. Drummond, and so he had missed the evidences pertaining to its rifled appearance. He made a mental note to collect the shot at some point for the buff boxes, assuming that the doctors must have it in their possession. He hoped that Inspector Tierney would not take charge of it before he did. As for the ball fired from the second pistol, that had still not turned up, and so there was precious little in the way of material evidence – nothing to prove intent. What was worse, he had spied Mr. Cockburn in the court room. Very clever was Mr. Cockburn. And a clever barrister, as he knew only too well, could easily overturn a police case with no material evidence.

The Inspector sighed. He'd already had more than enough of the rum-do, and it was still only Saturday morning. The final straw that had broken the camel's over-laden back had been the testimony of a gentleman office-keeper brought as a witness by Inspector Tierney.

"I have seen the prisoner," he'd said, "a good many times over the last seventeen or eighteen days walking up and down near the Council Office and the Treasury. I have observed him looking earnestly in the direction of Montague House, the residence of the Duke of Buccleuch, on Whitehall."

Now, the Inspector had no reason to suppose that the office-keeper was anything other than a respectable gentleman; but he knew very well that the Scotchman the fellow had seen was another one altogether: one quite different in appearance from the prisoner. And, yet, the gentleman had stood in the witness stand, bold as a tar's collar, buffing himself to the magistrate.

Inspector Hughes knew that the Scotchman that the office-keeper had actually seen was a short dirty-looking fellow in a queer slouch hat who was often to be found loitering on the steps of the Board of Trade. He had been taken by the office-keeper for a plainclothesman, which supposition, when challenged, the short, dirty-looking fellow in the queer hat slouch had indeed confirmed. The Inspector had been in the room when the Commissioners had decided that it was better not to give rise to any more public controversy in the matter of plainclothesmen, and had suggested to the office-keeper that it was better he did not include this sequence of events in his testimony.

The office-keeper, presuming that one Scotchman was very like another, and all of them being a bad lot, had concluded, with the encouragement of Inspector Tierney, that it didn't really matter one iota. He just wanted to do his public duty.

"I saw him there last Friday morning," the office-keeper told the magistrate. "I saw him on the steps leading to the Council-office. I asked him whether he was waiting for any person and he said he was waiting to see a gentleman. He spoke in a hurried manner and walked away down Whitehall towards the river. I saw him again a few days later at about half-past ten o'clock and I asked him if he had seen the gentleman yet, to which he hastily replied, 'No', and again walked away. I saw nothing more of him for about half an hour, and then I saw him standing near the entrance of Lady Dover's residence *eating a piece of bread*."

Upon hearing this, the scranning cove, Inspector Tierney, had leaned across the table and whispered something to the magistrate.

"And where, pray," the magistrate duly inquired, "is Lady Dover's residence?"

"Directly opposite Gwydyr House," said the office-keeper.

"And where, pray, is Gwydyr House?" asked the magistrate.

"It stands in front of the residence of Sir Robert Peel on Whitehall-gardens," said the office-keeper, as if this was sufficient to an understanding of everything.

Murmurings of alarm and disapprobation had rippled through the court room, enough to make Inspector Hughes turn down the corners of his mouth. He weren't at all surprised; it was just so very disappointing to have his worst suspicions confirmed so adroitly. Truth got snarled all the time: Justice well and truly snaffled. A short grubby fellow in peculiar head-gear had transmogrified into the tall, shabby-genteel and hatless prisoner – even though the pair of them shared not one point of similarity: apart, that is, from *Scotchness*.

What really bothered the Inspector, though, was the knowledge that this was all about protecting Inspector Tierney's busted Active Duty. The whole metropolis suspected that there were preventative men posted about the place overhearing conversations, reading private correspondence; gadding about the country making trouble where they found none and collecting the rewards. And if that subtle understanding was ever to be made a thing of open declaration – in a court of law, say – well, then that would make the task of policing the metropolis even harder than it already was.

It made the Inspector's feet smart just thinking about it.

He sighed and told himself that none of it mattered; that it was all just another scratch in the scheme, another great gnarled oak ramifying in the forest of difficulties. After all, the prisoner had been taken in the act of firing pistols at a gentleman, which made him, in the Inspector's book at least, a bad 'un. There was to be no getting away from that; and perhaps it really was the case that everything else pinned on him was, you might say, no more 'n a matter of convenience. Certainly, the way things stood now, the scranning cove could pin just about anything he wanted to upon McNaughten.

As for the prisoner, he had listened attentively to the office-keeper's cant deposition, and then signalled to the magistrate that he should like to say something on his own account. He had looked levelly at the witness, his pale eyes soft as drizzle. "Are you sure," he said, "that you ever had any conversation with me?"

"Certainly I am," said the office-keeper.

The prisoner watched him steadily for a moment or two. It was uncomfortable, the silence; but there was no anger, no reproach in that look, and no pleading. It was a rum look for the circumstances: the sort that passes between two people when one of them has failed the other, and when, instead of bearing spite or hurt, the one who has been failed has decided to forgive.

"Really," the prisoner said, mild as you like, "that is most strange. For you see, I have no recollection of anything of the sort."

Late edition

SHOOTING OF MR. EDWARD DRUMMOND OF THE TREASURY

ARRAIGNMENT OF SHOOTIST AT BOW-STREET

EXTRAORDINARY STATEMENT IN THE DOCK

The prisoner McNaughten declined the opportunity to question the surgeon. During the course of Mr. Guthrie senior's evidence, he had taken to contemplating the ceiling, sighing once or twice as if regretful of the pains that had been taken in respect of his victim's injuries. He did not bring his gaze down as the magistrate informed him that he was to be remanded for a fortnight. He exercised his right not to say anything, indicating that he understood that anything he did say would be taken down and used in evidence against him.

[146]

When the magistrate had done with the formalities, the prisoner thanked him, said that he was obliged to him, but that he had nothing else to say, whereupon Tyrell, the gaoler, removed him from the bar, and took him down to the holding cells. A few minutes later, as the witnesses were swearing to the written reports of their testimonies, it was intimated to the magistrate that the prisoner wished to say something, and the thin young man was brought back to the dock.

He then made the following extraordinary statement:

"I wish to say that it was the Tories of my native city who have driven me to this act. They follow and persecute me wherever I go, and have entirely destroyed my peace of mind. They follow me wherever I go. I cannot get no rest from them night or day. I cannot sleep at night in consequence of the course they pursue towards me. I believe they have driven me into a consumption. I am sure I shall never be the man I formerly was. I used to have good health and strength, but I have not now. They have accused me of crimes of which I am not guilty; they do everything in their power to harass and persecute me; in fact they wish to murder me. It can be proved by evidence. That's all I have to say."

The prisoner paused, and the magistrate asked him if he had anything more to say. He thought for a moment or two before proceeding.

"They have completely disordered my mind," he said. "I am quite a different man from what I used to be before they commenced their persecution."

The magistrate asked if he had anything else to add to his statement.

He did not.

The statement was handed to him at the dock, and he put his signature to it; but when Tyrell the gaoler moved towards him, the prisoner indicated that he did have something else to say, after all. Looking very earnest, he turned back towards the bench, pointing in the direction of the cells.

"Shall I be kept in that place for the whole fortnight?" he

said. "Because if I be, I'll not live."

The magistrate fixed him with a pitying look. "O no," he said kindly, "you will be taken to a prison, where proper care will be taken of you until you come here again."

There was a slight semblance of relief on the young man's face; the paleness in his complexion would almost have borne out his claim to be consumptive. At about six o'clock that evening he was removed from the cells attached to the court and conveyed in the prison van to the Westminster County bridewell at Tothill-fields. Beyond the usual number of idlers to be found looking about on every occasion on which the van makes its appearance, there was nothing to indicate that any prisoner of any importance was being removed.

CHESTERTON UNION WORKHOUSE
CHESTERTON, CAMBRIDGE

Alexander Cockburn, Esq.,
4 Elm Court
Temple

13th January, 1843

My own dear sir,
It has been a good long while since you last heard from me. My heart counts it to be above sixteen years since we parted. I pray you be assured – it is not my wish to importune you, or to cause you any distress or embarrassment.

Mr. Sherwood went to a better place, may it please God, above one week ago, but he did not pass from this cruel world without absolving of his conscience that one untruth he maintained for my sake – wretched sinner that I am – the matter of which you know all too well. The boy took the news very ill, and I fear having buried one father, he has taken it upon himself to find another. I pray you do not spurn him if he comes to you. He is a good boy. If there was ever but one portion of true feeling for me in your heart, recollect it now and do not dismiss me from your thoughts, for I have kept you in mine all these years and never asked you for a thing until now.

Yours and very truly,
Mrs. Mary Ann Sherwood
(Polly)

PALL MALL,
LATER THAT EVENING

In which Mr. Cockburn goes to dine at his club.

"*Ach, daß die Luft so ruhig!*
Ach, daß die Welt so licht!
Als noch die Stürme tobten,
War ich so elend nicht –."

Einsamkeit. Loneliness. The plangent song from Schubert's *Winterreise – Ah, the sky so calm! Ah, the world so light! When the storm was raging, I was not so sad –* had been imposing itself throughout the day upon the thoughts of Alexander Cockburn, Q.C. Good Old Cockie. The Buck of the Bar. An accomplished spielbariton, he was one of but a very few able to render lyrically the clustering flats and sharps: one who did not know the way, abandoned to the inhospitable road.

And everywhere it was winter-gloomy, snow-shrouded; quite the worst January he could ever recall. He had read poor Polly's letter, had it still upon his person; but – ah! miserable coward! – he found it better by far not to think of its wretched implications. It only imposed itself upon a bleakness of mood that he could barely tolerate. In the night just past not even the additional Lancaster Black Drops had been able to drown the painful anguish roaring in his heart. And now, the garish streets rolled by, the winter air crackling with banter, while Sandy was slumped in the back of the cab with the hood up and the curtains drawn, wrapped in a thick blanket of *taedium vitae*.

He was on his way to his club, to dine with the Chief Whipper-in of the Parliamentary Whigs, where hopefully inebriation awaited him as well as the snatching jaws of ambition. His uncle, the Rear-Admiral, when Sandy had bid him a fond farewell at break of day, beamed at the opportunity presenting itself to his nephew, at the marvellous boy's good fortune, talent; sheer pluck. He had asked to be remembered to the Chief Whipper-in, and warned Cockie against the ten-pound house-holders and their teetotal morals; urged him to be true to himself and his interests; counselled him that one cannot get through this world without force; and, as soon as Lady Cockburn was out of the line of sight, slipped him five pounds.

Yes, he was, he supposed, on his way: *again...*

How many more chances, he wondered? Perhaps he was a lucky dog, after all; certainly something appeared to be keeping him buoyant – and not through any effort, he had to admit, of his own. But that was not to say that he was not also thoroughly depressed. Disappointment was inevitable. It was part of the grinding pattern of life.

As it was such a very disagreeable evening he had decided not to walk the short distance to Pall Mall from the rooms he kept at a very good address just off Park Lane, and had sent his man Hatchett to fetch the cabriolet he had rented since taking silk a little above a year ago. It would not do for him to be seen sauntering along Piccadilly or the Haymarket. He could not, you see, run the risk of encounter on the open streets. He owed his tailor several guineas; he had dallied with the wife of a brother barrister. And even though the sum was trifling and the lady resigned to his indifference, he was unable to fulfil his obligations on either account. And pray, do not forget, he had been cautioned: he must do nothing to bring his Society into disrepute.

Ah me, he sighed, his lips pressing lightly against the silver tip of his cane; "*the desolations of London out of season*".

Upon leaving Bow-street that morning he had decided to brazen it out and paid a long-overdue visit to his chambers, where a slew of communications awaited his attention. Bills, for the most part, which his clerk Frayling had folded, docketed on the back and tied into a neat bundle; some letters of recommendation from one of the Parliamentary agents – all pursuant to cases too late by now to chase; and a small symmetrical pile marked private. Sandy was dismayed to see how wretched he had allowed his affairs to become, but nothing wearied him more than the thought of making amends. He set the bills to one side and riffled through the private correspondence, his heart sinking beneath the emanations of a familiar scent, redolent with dimly recollected arousal and regret. He tossed the letters unopened upon the desk for disposal, and told himself it was too late to go back. He had had enough of hating himself.

The only other communication in the pile marked private he had overlooked at first. It was entirely unexpected – although there was a point in most days when his thoughts strayed to fond reminiscences of the sender. He opened it in a vague, undirected way, then catching sight of the dismal address, the lettering so spare and black, and, apprehending at once the likely meaning, he folded it almost shiftily and tucked it away in his pocket, unread.

Hatchett and Frayling did not observe the subterfuge. They were busying over coffee and hot rolls.

"The case is sure to be a sensation!" Frayling was saying. "Why, I can't remember the last time there was such a buzz on the streets of the metropolis!"

"No, indeed," concurred the valet. "I should think there's been nothing like it since the assassination of Spencer Perceval! Tell us, sir, what did you make of it all?"

Sandy's capacity for excitement was obtunded: the Bow-street of that morning already vague, distant.

Frayling persisted. "Is the fellow a madman? Is he a fanatic for suffrage or cheap bread? A Glasgow thug? A spy of the King of Hanover? I tell you, sir – out there everyone has his own theorem!"

Cockie had no theorem. There was a dim pity for the prisoner, the ordinary measure of concern towards the victim – by all accounts a perfectly amiable fellow; but no single strand of clarity from which to build an opinion. He might have riled himself by considering how easily London was thrown into convulsions over the shooting of a gentleman on its streets, when every night plenty died in those same streets of the cold and hunger without a single cry of alarm being raised. He tried, but could only manage a slight indignation. If he had had any choice in the matter he would have chosen to say nothing about the dreadful business until it had all died down. He raised a finger to his chin and assumed an attitude of elegant rumination, while his confidential valet and his clerk stood in awed expectation of some *aperçu*, some point of jurisprudence.

"The shot which the surgeon claims to have recovered from Mr. Drummond," he heard himself say, "if he is correct in respect of its appearance, could not have been fired by either of the pistols produced in court."

What it meant, he had no idea. The peelers had made a mistake... The surgeons had made a mistake... Had Mr. Drummond been shot at by someone other than the prisoner...? Who knew? And what did it matter? It threw up a doubt, was all; a chink; and he had been trained to scrutinise the surface for weaknesses, inconsistencies, openings.

"Fancy that!" exclaimed Hatchett. "You'd expect it to be a simple enough matter, surely: a man taken *in flagrante* as it were, with the weapons still on him."

"Never go by first impressions," said Frayling, hooking his lapel with his thumbs. "The understanding of an act is formed from the accumulation of evidences, proofs pertaining to the antecedent circumstances. Intention must be discerned; without intention there can be no ground of conviction. Ain't that so, Mr. Cockburn, sir?"

"Are you saying the prisoner might be innocent?" said Hatchett, who had spent the morning poring over every inch of newsprint concerning the matter.

"We are all innocent," said Sandy, pouring himself a cup of coffee, "until it has been proven otherwise."

He was mulling over it, now, in the back of the cab. Before hearing the surgeon's evidence he might have supposed the shooting of Mr. Drummond to be an entirely random incident: the sort of sorry thing that occurred from time to time on the streets of the metropolis – and of no greater significance than a boy firing a fowling pistol at a street-lamp in order to earn himself some respite from the cold. But the vagaries of the pistols and the shot had made him reconsider that position. It was intriguing to him that so much inconsistency should have clustered about the matter. He was unsure whether this was enough to waive a conviction – not if everyone from the Prime Minister down was set on one – but there were sufficient grounds, nevertheless, for *reasonable doubt*.

In a perfect world it would never be acceptable to convict a man on suspicions alone, on presumptions without proof. But this was not a perfect world. The prisoner had not only allowed himself to be taken in the act, he had all but supplied a plausible motive with his recondite statement in respect of the Glasgow Tories. If a book were to be made, Sandy doubted that the given odds would be in McNaughten's favour. His mind ran quickly over the likely consequences of losing a sensational case at such a critical time; but a true gambler never lingers long upon the possibility of losing.

It came to him that he had grown accustomed over the course of the day to assuming that he was to represent the case for the defence, even though the Chief Whipper-in's communication had given him no such intimation. He yawned, and lifted the curtain. London streamed past in a blur of frozen gas-light and frost-sparkled glass. He pressed his face against the window, feeling estranged, remote.

He was dressed in a dark blue coat with velvet facings and cuffs, a swan-gray hat, a cloak with silver satin lining, and a pale yellow brocade waistcoat with matching stock (the ensemble for which his tailor still awaited payment). He was aware that, as his confidential valet had put it, he looked the very *dandy* of a fellow, and had he chosen to walk to the club instead of immuring himself in his little confessionary of *ennui*, he would undoubtedly have caught the eye of those seeking the appraisal of the casual smokers. As Haymarket slipped by, it seemed to Sandy that he had never before felt so lonely. His heart was suffused with tenderness at the memory of what it was to feel affection, and he found himself fumbling inside his coat for the letter, allowing his fingers to caress it. He was conscious of regret, as searing as a bullet wound. He let the feeling swell in his breast, and he let it subside; disgust, chill and sobering coming in its place.

This filthy web of mutual dependence that is the world, he thought, and he tried to shut out all that he had done, all that he had failed to do, just as he always did.

Do not imagine that it did not ever cross his mind that if he had paid his tailor on time it would not be necessary for the girl who sewed his shirt seams to supplement her meagre wages by pursuing degradation along the Haymarket or in one of the private rooms at Kate Hamilton's. He knew how it all hanged together. He was not one of that growing band which clung to the notion that poverty was all the fault of the poor. He looked about him; he saw how it was. The very notion that a large portion of humanity was dismissed as surplus to requirement sickened him to the very core: it was the most hard-hearted theory that ever existed and it wounded him to think how shabbily all those beautiful phrases about citizenship and fraternity and equality and loving thy neighbour had been treated.

He chided himself for his hypocrisy.

The world had destroyed his capacity for love, for passion. He was a coward who lacked the courage to defend that which was to him most precious against the patterns of – what? – bourgeois conformity, the reign of priggishness. No Danton, he; rather a mortal coward going cap in hand – even as he went now – to beg for crumbs from the tables of the Mighty.

When, he wondered, had he become that thing he most despised: a man given over to compromises, to petty offices and attainments? When had he become a sham?

"*Als noch die Stürme tobten.*" He sang to himself with a great force of sentiment, but not the headlong fall into the spangled sea of pure feeling for which he yearned. When the storm was raging. "*War ich so elend nicht.*" I was not so sad.

The cabriolet dashed up to the steps of the club, and Sandy braced himself for the cold air, and the bonhomie that awaited him within. He climbed the steps two at a time, head down, frowning, preparing mentally for assailment by cries of "Whoah! Sandy 'burn!" "Cockadoodle-doo!", and a good deal of other such nonsense from the members taking their coffee in the loggia. As he handed in his hat and cane, he practised the defences of smiling and nodding at one and all. Gad, he thought as he entered the lobby, how I hate the pristine quality of all this imposing grandeur. And everyone was quite right about the size of the windows: they really were much too small.

He was struck at once by the sheer number of button-holing, rib-nudging members thronging the hall; some in attitudes of alarm or excitement; others set against the pillars in thick clumps of conspiracy.

Over there he spied a shareholder in the Scottish Colonisation Company who had seen off a thousand or more Highlanders from their ancestral homes in order to satisfy the English fashion in Scottish estates (as a scion of a fine old Scotch family, he found the whole trend as bewildering as the spectacle of Prince Albert in a kiltie). By the library stood a noble gentleman who was of the opinion that only emigration on a great scale could save the country. He had heard in this very place the People described as so many "locusts"! He returned the noble gentleman's raised eyebrow salute with a wry upturn of his top lip, as to the fellow's left his eye was caught by another, a millocrat who had opposed the Ten Hour Bill last session, on the grounds that the little children he employed ought to be kept hard at the power-looms for twelve hours, six days of every week, lest they fall into idleness and wickedness.

Sandy was so given to invective against these hypocrites, so prickled by his own conscience, that he did not grasp at once that he might have been the cause of all the consternation. He assumed that there must have been some announcement concerning Peel and the Corn Laws; or a ballot: that either somebody of note had been black-balled, or somebody of no interest whatsoever had been admitted. And well, what of it, he thought as he pushed past head down, determined to avoid contact with any of the ludicrous, polluting crowd. Why, the mood he was in, he would have pilled Jesus Christ himself had that gentleman tried to gain admission.

As he crossed the entrance hall towards the dining-room, a buck of about five-and-thirty and darkly handsome appearance stepped out in front of him, hesitating as if considering whether to bow first or not, and smiling weakly, as if in expectation of being recognised. Sandy, who had not the faintest notion as to who this might be, bristled, unsure as to whether he had been cut or not, and looked past the interloper, at which sign the fellow duly used the hand he had begun to proffer in greeting to sweep back a limp curl from off his forehead. It was a gesture so deftly made, and so indicative of ruffled pride (a feeling with which Sandy himself could empathise), that the silk in an instant rather regretted his rudeness and made a curt half-bow half-nod by way of amends.

"Forgive me," he said in an airy tone so as to discourage any more intimacy than he intended, "but I don't believe we have been introduced. Cockburn, Alexander Cockburn."

The young man smiled, or rather he pressed his closed lips hard against his teeth. "Warren, Samuel Warren," he said, in an ill-judged attempt to be just as airy, "we met at Frank Woodvine's chambers last November."

"Ah yes, of course. How could I forget!"

Sandy had now a hazy recollection of the fellow in a gloomy attic chambers: a morose face, drinking steadily at the far end of a table lined with some of the biggest bores in London – everyone of any note or interest having long since returned to the shires – and laden with all of the worst food. Fortunately, the table had also been, Sandy recollected, adequately furnished with decanters of '23 claret. It was largely on account of the excellence of the wine, conjoined to his own lack of funds and the paucity of entertainment to be had elsewhere, that Sandy had stayed much longer than was necessary, drinking and talking rather indiscriminately on a range of contentious topics: the extension of the suffrage; the new class of "Unemployed Poor"; the Repeal of the Corn Laws; the summer riots; Feargus O'Connor's pending trial for seditious libel…

It was coming to him that at the time he had entertained a niggling feeling that this fellow Warren did not care for him. But then if he were a friend of their host that was hardly surprising, since their host was a close associate of the husband whom Sandy had spent a good portion of the year in cuckolding.

Sandy mused distractedly, wishing this nobody who had somehow sought him out in the sanctity of the club would take the hint and go and bore someone else.

"Are you a member?" Cockie sniffed. Ordinarily very skilled in summing up a character in a trice (a talent his rivals often attacked him for), Sandy was now rather regretting his ill-judged expression of mild good will towards this parvenu. He squinted at Mr. Warren, deciding that the fellow was likely to be a Methodist. There was a slight conventicle twang to his speech; northern, thought Sandy, or, even worse, Welsh.

"I'm here as a guest," Mr. Warren was saying. Catching at his cuffs defensively, he dropped the name of a prominent member. "Do you know him?"

Cockie swerved from this unexpected reference to a gentleman widely considered to be the most active and experienced advocate of the Lunacy Inquiry.

"He is the gentleman," the Methodist drawled, "who made a very great impression on the House with his descriptions of the state of wretchedness in which the pauper inmates of Warburton's asylum languish at the expense of the St. George's of Hanover-square rate-payers. He was interested to hear my impression of the extraordinary scenes this morning at Bow-street. He has connexions to the Lunacy Inquiry, and shall have a good deal of influence if it is ever agreed to appoint full-time legal commissioners – *salaried* commissioners, that is, if you follow my meaning."

Sandy did not appreciate the familiarity of tone; it irritated him, deflecting his attention from the content of Mr. Warren's little speech. "I can't say that I do, sir," he said. Deuce! He was thinking: the fellow is a "briefless" barrister – one of those who turn up at the courts each day in the vain expectation of attaching themselves to someone more gifted: someone such as himself.

"Lunacy, as you know, can be very lucrative," the fellow was drawling on. "Think of last year's sensational case of the Begum's son whose wife declared him insane in order that she might lay claim to his fortune. It would be marvellous, would it not, Mr. Cockburn, to be engaged on a *really long* Chancery trial, at a *really excellent* daily rate, on a matter of such *intellectual fascination*?"

Sandy knew next to nothing of Lunacy, and nor did he care to know more.

"That blackguard who brought you in was vehemently opposed to the Slavery Abolition Act back in '33, as I recall," he remarked of Mr. Warren's host. He was pleased to see the fellow demur at the riposte; or was he, in fact, suppressing a smirk? "I had heard that he spends all his time demanding compensation for those who lost their sordid business

– which, I have to say, I find nothing short of appalling."

"His family are from Bristol, and I believe has large estates in West India. Do you not believe in protecting family interests, Mr. Cockburn?" parried the Snob, "or is that a privilege reserved for some and not others? How is your uncle, the dean, by the way? Has he quite recovered from his bout with notoriety?"

Sandy was well used to all the insinuating that his recent defence of one of his uncles on a charge of simony was nothing more than a "job," but there was something in Mr. Warren's manner which made him want to punch his well-defined jaw.

"You know," said Mr. Warren in a deft *changement d'engagement*, "I saw you at Bow-street this morning." He laughed; an edgy, tight little laugh. "Taking a view, were you?"

The fellow had assumed a look of blazing defiance; there was something about him, Sandy felt, which bordered on the unhinged. He decided to affect a great and sudden weariness, and yawned in an exaggerated fashion, casting his eye about the room as if looking to see who else was "in"; but the fellow was evidently very thick-skinned.

"Tell me," he insinuated, "and did you come to any conclusion?"

"I should think it a very straightforward matter," Sandy murmured, "scarcely worth all the fuss it seems to be engendering." He had now resorted to the ploy of fixing his gaze beyond Mr. Warren's shoulder, smiling in mock acknowledgement of some invisible intimate who was not, but might well be, standing just a short distance away.

"But it is a dreadful business, surely, a gentleman, a civil servant, shot in the back on a crowded street in the middle of the afternoon?" persisted the fellow, archly.

"Yes, quite, quite dreadful – but hardly complex… Well, well, I'm afraid that I really must be getting along… you know how it is." He gestured at the invisible fellow.

"Indeed," said Mr. Warren, appraising the pantomime with a sceptical eye. He murmured something under his breath, then bowed stiffly.

"I trust we will have the opportunity to meet again, Mr. – ah – Warren."

"I am sure that we shall, sir."

Sandy, with some satisfaction, detected the unmistakable whiff of singed pride; but as he watched Mr. Warren's retreat towards the door he began to feel uneasy. There was something in the way that one or two in the clumps nodded and even smiled at the prig as he passed them – something that prompted the disconcerting thought that perhaps Sandy had been a little *too* dismissive. Men such as he supposed this Warren to be were the kind who sought to catch one out. Men like that, he knew, would make it their business to do irreparable harm to the reputation of one who was admired chiefly because he always seemed to escape scot-free. Sandy considered following Mr. Warren out onto the street and making a great show of friendship, but he could see that in the dining-room the Chief Whipper-in of the Parliamentary Whigs was already on his feet, beckoning him over with a degree of impatience, while Mons. Soyer hovered close by with the menus. He took a deep breath and sauntered towards them, thinking all the while how he could not wait to get away. Arriving at the table, he made a deep bow to his host, who did not return the gesture. "I see you know Samuel Warren," said the Chief Whipper-in, settling into his chair. "My wife is a great admirer of his scribbling. Can't see what all the fuss is about m'self. *Diary of a Late Physician...* madness, body-snatching and the pox..."

"I've never read a word," said Sandy, whose tastes in literature, as in music, did not extend to anything light. He was relieved to discover that Mr. Warren appeared to be nothing more substantial than a writer of sensationalist clap-trap.

"O, come, come," said the Chief Whipper-in, "you must know who he is! He wrote that periodical novel everyone was reading a while ago – the one that makes fun of lawyers."

"That fellow is the author of *Ten Thousand a Year*?" said Sandy. He was surprised to discover that he knew the name of Mr. Warren's literary effort. He had heard it was shamefully ill-written, but succeeded in making for its creator a decent sum of money, nevertheless.

"That's the blackguard," said the Chief Whipper-in.

"Is he being put up for membership?"

"Good heavens, no! He's an Ultra, or whatever the deuce they call themselves these days. He is regularly exercised on the topic of corn in *Blackwood's* – under the pseudonym *FIAT JUSTITIA*."

Sandy felt a presentiment sour in his gut, his heart sink: he knew exactly who this "Warren" was. It seemed he had committed an egregious *faux pas*.

"*FIAT JUSTITIA*?" he repeated. The wretch penned pasquinades for the *Review*: humorous sketches of legal types. Sandy could all-too easily imagine the sketch that Warren was, even now, no doubt, composing on the subject of Alexander Cockburn, Q.C. He pictured Warren in his miserable attic chamber, scratching out the lampoon with a pen dipped in the purest venom, and for a moment the doominess that Sandy always carried in the pit of his stomach threatened to overwhelm him. But the threat posed by the scribbler to his vanity, and quite possibly his reputation, must be cast out for the time being: his host was a very important man, and Mons. Soyer was invoking salmon with shrimp sauce, mutton cutlets Reform, roast quails, *gelée de fruits marbré*, claret and damson cheese, coffee and brandy. "So," he asked, in what was, he trusted, a bright tone, "what does the new session have in store?"

His host mumbled something about the Palace being a damnable site of excavation, with nothing in the right place and a truly dreadful smell of the river, wet sand, wood-smoke and rats' piss hanging over everything. All of which was quite true. Then he declaimed against Peel and the Corn Laws.

"The coming session shall be one of the most decisive in history!" he expounded. "The end of the Corn Laws is in sight, Cockie. The Tories cannot withstand the popular will any longer. In less than two weeks Peel shall have to state his opinion of the sliding scale. I tell you, they are done for! If Peel decides to keep the tariffs as they are, there will be more riots; if he decides to drop 'em altogether, he shall lose the support of more than half of his party. Within a week of the Queen's Speech he shall be dependent upon us for power. If that ain't so, I shall eat my hat."

A steaming slice of rose-pink salmon coated with a glistening buttery sauce, in the pools of which plump shrimps slithered about, was placed in front of the gentlemen. Sandy eyed the dish despondently.

"Do you really suppose that Peel gives a fig for the will of the People?" he said. "After the summary way he dealt with the summer disturbances I should think it quite plain that there is nothing to fear any longer on that front. And you know as well as does any Ultra that the

Corn Laws are a good bit of business – have been for almost thirty years. The Landed Interest will not be induced to give up a quarter of their profit – even if the People were to start building a guillotine in Trafalgar-square…"

The Whipper-in stuck out his bottom lip and harrumphed into his sauce. Sandy chewed on a shrimp and contemplated another wasted evening. He knew as assuredly as the tang of cayenne on his tongue that after listening to all the usual rot, the blusterings of the losing side, he would rise shortly after ten and, home again, feel more than ever that nothing was resolved, that all was stalled: that nobody gave a damn, except for those who do not have any bread to eat.

"So, what did you make of the hearing?" his host asked of him, waving aside the attentions of the chef.

Sandy stifled a yawn. He had been picking at a loose strand of the brocade on his waistcoat front, and was suddenly aware of the hum of the dining-room dropping, eyes turning in his direction.

"That rather depends," he said. "What would you have me make of it?"

"It is being mooted," said his host, "that the fellow is a fanatic for cheap bread, and that he meant to shoot Sir Robert Peel."

"Is it, by Jove?" said Sandy. He speared another of the shrimps on the end of his fork, and idly skated it about the sauce.

His host frowned. "We must not allow Peel to make of this a Corn Law affair," he said. "He could be lashed this session. The Tories will seek to use this unfortunate incident to discredit the Anti-Corn Law League, and by inference, anyone in the country who supports Repeal: a number which includes, I need hardly remind you, Lord John Russell and the majority of the Whig Party. And we simply can't have the Tories turning the public favour against Repeal. Gad, Cockie, are you listening to me? This is important – the misery of a family constrained to live upon eight shillings a week cannot be made light of."

Unmoved by the Chief Whipper-in's sudden conversion to concern for the plight of the poor, Sandy popped the shrimp in his mouth. "Do we know how the prisoner voted in '41?" he asked.

The Chief Whipper-in's eyebrows shot up.

Sandy shrugged. "He appears to be an independent tradesman taken with a deal of money on his person," he said. "I presume, therefore, that he must be a ten-pound householder and a registered voter. And that it is most likely, given his station in life, that he voted Whig."

"Or Radical," exclaimed the Chief Whipper-in. "The Radicals have Glasgow by the throat."

"That may be," said Sandy. He was drawing on his deep knowledge of the late election, gleaned from many tedious hours spent in the committee rooms. "But I think it unlikely that you would be calling upon me to defend a Radical."

His host set his knife and fork at an angle on the plate. "Now look here, Cockie – what the devil does the election have to do with the shooting of Mr. Drummond?" he demanded.

"In his statement this morning McNaughten spoke of having been persecuted by the Glasgow Tories," Sandy continued. "As you well know, Glasgow is notorious for corrupt practices. The Tory agent is a most assiduous challenger of registrants. He has used every trick yet devised to prevent Whig householders from exercising their right to vote."

"And as you well know," said the Chief Whipper-in, *sotto voce*, "the Whig agent is at least as adept as his Tory counterpart in deterring those householders who cannot be depended upon for their support." The gentleman resumed his dinner. "I was hoping that it would be possible to develop an argument that will prove to the detriment of our enemies – without bringing any ill effect upon ourselves," he said. "Prevent Peel making capital out of a possible Anti-Corn Law League connexion – preserve the interests of the Party. You know the sort of thing."

"Have you consulted with Mr. Oswald, the Glasgow Member?" Sandy mooted. "I wonder what he has to say about the prisoner's allegations in respect of the Glasgow Tories?"

His host's furious head dropped like a bull about to charge. "Mr. Oswald quite sensibly in my opinion wants nothing to do with this matter," he whispered ferociously. "And you are to keep him out of it. What would you do? Hand Glasgow to our enemies on a plate? It may be your area of expertise, Cockie, but Lord John Russell is most anxious that you steer away from any scrutiny of sharp practice, poll books and the like."

Sandy was beginning to tire of all this shallow information.

"And the Tories," said the Chief Whipper-in, "have already bought most of the newspapers."

The salmon dishes were whisked away and a plate of lamb cutlets, each bedecked with its own little chef's hat, set in their place.

Sandy eyed them circumspectly. "Do we have any evidence that the fellow is a hired assassin?" he asked.

"He was taken with a large sum of money on his person," said the Whipper-in. "He is ten times more affluent than the vast majority of his class."

"Perhaps he is industrious and frugal."

The Chief Whipper-in's eyes narrowed once more and his bottom lip drooped. "The Permanent Under-Secretary of the Home Ofice has received *certain assurances*."

Sandy laughed. "The testimony of spies and agents provocateurs," he said. "I asked what *evidence* is there?"

"You damned lawyers and your subtleties," said the Chief Whipper-in. "The fellow was taken in the act of firing pistols at a Treasury secretary a few feet from Scotland-yard in broad day. What other evidence do you require?"

"Ah, yes," said Sandy. "The pistols. It might interest you to learn that they were the object of an intriguing discrepancy in the evidences presented to the magistrate this morning. The shot which the surgeon claims to have removed from Mr. Drummond's person yesterday evening does not appear to have been fired from the weapons taken with the accused."

The Whipper-in's thick brows knitted together. "What the devil does that mean?"

"It might mean everything in respect of presumptive proof," said Sandy. "Perhaps someone else fired the shot that wounded Mr. Drummond... Perhap the peelers are bigger fools even than they are customarily taken for... Certainly, as McNaughten's counsel, I would be failing in my duty if I did not do my damnedest to argue the point."

The Whipper-in dabbed angrily at his chin. "And what of your duty to the Party?" he cried. "The Tories shall have a field day with this! There is a League conspiracy to kill Peel! We shall all be murdered in our beds! You know how it will run on as well as do I. What is more, the wretched fellow took his pot-shot outside the Salopian, where many of our country members are wont to resort."

Sandy was unmoved. "Where is the evidence that McNaughten is in the pay of the Anti-Corn Law League?" he asked.

The Whipper-in looked dismayed. "Cockie, old man, what is the matter with you tonight? These are precarious times! What was said at the League's conference last year? 'The contest has begun between the aristocracy and the People'...?"

Sandy contemplated the depths of his glass. "We have a whole arm of the police given over to spying on the populace," he said. "Every word Mr. Cobden of the League writes is read by a half a dozen peelers in Scotland-yard; there are over a thousand men sitting in hulks at this very moment awaiting transportation, and all for the *crime* of asking for the vote and the right to be paid a living wage. We have respectable tradesmen – perhaps, as you appear to have already decided, this fellow McNaughten among them – reduced to making cheapjack threats against government ministers in the cause of nothing more innocuous than cheap bread for the starving masses!"

The Whipper-in laid aside the bone of his final lamb cutlet.

"Lines have been drawn, Cockie," he said. His eyebrows were drawn together in genuine perplexity. "Lines which must not, cannot be crossed. *Ever*."

"So you will have me concoct a defence for the prisoner that does not touch upon politics."

"You are to concoct, as you put it, a defence that will look after the interests of your Party."

"And what of the interests of the client?"

"Damn it, he fired pistols at a Treasury secretary! He's lucky not to have been strung up on the spot!"

"To lay the blame for the consequences of injustice upon the victims of injustice is an old trick, sir, and a low one," said Sandy. He was gratified to hear a few murmurings of approval come from a nearby table of young blades. "Peel understands very well how the present situation arises from the want of adequate sustenance in consequence of the high price of bread and the low price of labour. They ought to do the right thing. Capitulate over Repeal of the Corn Laws and hang the conse-quences to themselves. And Lord John Russell ought to be persuaded to do the same. A coalition on the sliding scale is the only way forward."

"Stop there," commanded the Chief Whipper-in. "Don't run on in that mad way."

"But millions are starving, sir, in the richest nation on the earth, at the mid-point of the nineteenth century." Sandy paused as Mons. Soyer brought forth the fowl. "It is not meet to make political capital out of such misery."

There was a smattering of "hear hears!" which made Sandy smile and put to one side any doubts he might have entertained that he was sounding preachy – as he was so often accused of doing. It was difficult not to resort to proselytising in a society where radicalism had become a term of derision – a thing no gentleman would ever own to – when there was never any proper debate to be had, and when one's perfectly reasonable ideas were routinely dismissed as the ravings of a maniac.

"What is the matter with you tonight?" bellowed the Whipper-in, looking perfectly astonished. Exudations, partly foam, partly lamb cut-let, flecked the corners of his mouth and his eyes were beginning to bulge. And observing all of this, Sandy calculated the likelihood of be-ing the occasion of a second apoplectic fit in the space of a day, before continuing unabated with his argument.

"People are dying on the streets every night, right here in the great-est city of the Empire," he said. "I know it, you know it, Peel knows it. Damn it, Lord John Russell knows it. If this fellow McNaughten has fired a warning shot, then I say give him his day in court and let him say as much. I shall defend him as a matter of principle…"

There was a splatter of applause; an explosion of "disgracefuls!" The Chief Whipper-in brought his fist down upon the table with such force that the claret slopped over the edges of the crystal onto the snow-white linen cloth. Sandy watched the wine stain spread, feeling by turns ap-palled and gratified. The dining-room fell silent as all around men froze in mid-conversation, forkfuls of food poised between plate and mouth, glasses approaching lips, their contents reclining at steep angles.

"We must ensure that the Constitution is not permitted to go down in a sink of degeneration," growled the Chief Whipper-in. "If we do not take care, it will disappear beneath the shoal and quicksand as fast as the foundations of the new St. Stephen's tower did over the summer."

There was a round of applause. Sandy sat quite still and sipped at his claret. The Chief Whipper-in drew in so close that the little silk could smell the piquant sauce on his breath. He fixed Mr. Cockburn with a look as straight as a wavering rheumy eye permits and dropped his voice to a thick catarrhal whisper.

"You sound to me very like a man who thinks he has a choice in the matter," he said. "Might I remind you of how very dismayed the Queen was to learn of your notoriously bad moral character? Lord John Russell had personally to intervene. He was very impressed by your efforts on behalf of the Acts concerning bribery in elections; very grateful for the arguments you have made in support of our challenged Members, and those who lost their seats through Tory sharp practices. He thinks you a very able and principled man, Cockie; but you know in public life, nobody is ever missed. There are a hundred young men who could do just as well as you; better even – and without the threat of scandal perpetually hanging over them: unimpeachable young men; clean, decent young men."

"Then pray make one of them the tool of the Party." The dining-room was already returning to its thrum, rippling with laughter, denials and shared confidences. Cockie could feel the attention leaving him.

The Chief Whipper-in laid hold of his quail in thick hands and smiled slowly to himself. "You know Lord John Russell was most dismayed to learn about the little shop-woman in, where was it, Chesterton? Naturally, he is most anxious to keep it from Her Majesty. He is of the opinion that things have reached a sorry pass if we are all to be held to account for the indiscretions of our undergraduate days." The Chief Whipper-in snapped the fowl in two. "He will do all he can, of course, to prevent a scandal – but you know, my dear fellow, protection, patronage – these things come at a price. Compromises, Cockie," he said. "We must all make compromises. It is the way of the world."

"I see," said Sandy.

"Yes," said the Chief Whipper-in, crunching bone into splinters. "I rather thought that you would."

Sandy took a drink of wine. He had scarcely picked at the salmon or the lamb, but he took a mouthful of the roast quail. It was very good. He was thinking how some way out would present itself: fugue... suicide... a wealthy widow... As the dessert course was delivered to the table, he heard himself agree to consider, with less fatuity than he had hitherto demonstrated, the manner in which the matter of Mr. Drummond's shooting might best be exploited in the Party's interest. Mons. Soyer released slivers of fruit from their gelatine prison just as pervasive influences slipped down corridors crooked with centuries of intrigue. Before the last crumb of cheese had been swallowed along with a mouthful of an excellent port, older than either of the two diners, Sandy's name was being dropped into well-connected ears in the saloon and the library.

"There is, of course, the matter of the fee," he heard himself say in a far-off voice.

"That will all be taken care of," said the Whipper-in. "After all, it is not as though the prisoner is without the means." And he folded his hands upon his paunch and nodded in a thoroughly satisfied manner, as if doubting that there were ever any hungry people anywhere in the whole world.

Afterwards, over coffee and brandy, Good Old Cockie drew on an expensive cigar and puffed perfect rings of smoke at the ceiling. A coterie of his admirers, all of them capital fellows, gathered about, laughing uproariously at his delicious satire on his recent encounter with FIAT JUSTITIA; they nudged and winked, the cards pressed close to their patterned waistcoats, the dice pattering in their white-gloved hands. And as he listened to the odds shouted out above the coloured cravats and gleaming pins, the flattering cajolements that could turn with malignant abruptness at any moment, the Buck of the Bar, Clever Cockie, the coming man, leaned back against the morocco leather and stretched out his legs. He was wearing the expression of a man playing for a large stake with the game in his hand as he tried to picture himself wreathed in glory; but try as he might, he could not dislodge a sobering thought that came to him over and again. He could not dislodge it because in a world of lies and dissembling it was the truth. The thought was: play on, old man, take the chances without flinching; but never, ever forget that the dice is cogged.

In which the Inspector ponders the ramifications of a mistaken identity, prompted by the troublesome visitation of a stunted Scotchman to Whitehall.

Inspector Hughes held a stick of sealing wax in the flame of the candle 'sconced on the ledger desk, and let his mind slip as it bent and twisted. He was thinking about the difference between guilt and blame – which, when it came to marking down a villain, was a most essential distinction. All manner of blame might attach itself to a suspect; but the delineation of guilt – ah, now, then – that was a very different matter. Guilt required proofs.

Proofs.

The sealing wax dripped onto his fingers and splashed onto the pile of evidences teetering at his elbow: all of the day's newspapers; a stack of informations pertaining to villainous Scotchmen pricked out of the *Police Gazette*; a brace of letters from concerned gentlemen ratepayers. Upon the desk-top the plausible and well-founded jostled with the thoroughly specious, yielding not one solitary *proof*: that is to say, nothing that could with any certainty be set before a judge and jury.

The first two days of an investigation were always the most important: after that it was like trying to get smoke back into a bottle. But with rumour and gossip idling about the gleaming strip, filching reason like a pair of sneak thieves, blame was spreading faster than ever. It sprawled across the metropolis in newsprint and club-rooms, in coffee-houses and gin-shops. Everywhere the Inspector came in search of informations, rumour and gossip had already been, leaving behind them suspicious circumstances and alarming intimations.

The so-called *confession* which Inspector Tierney had extracted from the prisoner the night before had sprung from Gardiner's-lane station-house to seize with a perfect convulsion of certitude the minds of the majority. There were no witnesses to whatever it was the scranning cove claimed to have heard the prisoner say; it hadn't been written down anywhere; and the prisoner certainly hadn't set his mark upon it. As it stood, it could never be set before a magistrate as evidence; and yet the notion that the prisoner McNaughten had believed himself to be firing pistols at the Prime Minister, rather than the Prime Minister's Private Secretary, had transfixed everyone from the Commissioners down to the lowliest street-crossing sweeper. The so-called *confession* had become the essential, misty truth at the heart of the whole matter: the thing that everyone knew *for a fact*.

Inspector Hughes had strong opinions on confessions at the best of times. To his mind, they were nearly always to be taken with a grain of salt. A confession, you see, could be drawn out of anyone by any number of means: threat, inducement; even a simple desire to please would do it. And a police inspector should never forget that puzzling class of person who took it upon himself to walk into a station-house and confess to a crime that he could not possibly have committed. That scranning cove, Inspector Tierney, knew all of this as well as anyone: better, in fact – which was why he weren't being explicit. He knew how a miserable thing such as was this "*confession*" needed to be fostered in the drab alleys, kept out of the gas light, and be ready to show a clean pair of heels at the first sign of a scuffle.

It was now generally accepted that the prisoner was a hired assassin who had been paid a small fortune by the Anti-Corn Law League in exchange for shooting the Prime Minister. It had a nice plausible ring to it, and most people would soonest believe a lie that had about it the aura of likelihood, than they would a strange-seeming truth. And so it was unchallenged fact that there was a master plot, a heinous conspiracy behind what the prisoner had done, and the entire focus of the investigations was not simply to determine the extent of that conspiracy, but to turn up anything that could be taken as proof of such a thing. Which was all very well – unless, that is, you happened to be the poor devil to whom the heavy burden of this chimerical task must fall.

Inspector Hughes found himself in charge of an investigation he didn't believe a word of.

The daily report was open on the desk before him, his large clumsy penmanship sloping across the ledger page. He read it through once more before sealing it, to make sure that he really did have nothing else to tell.

1. *A Scotchman has frequently been seen dining in the Elephant and Castle upon a chop and some whisky toddy, but always alone.*

This, Inspector Hughes reasoned, was most likely not the prisoner, who, all other evidence indicated, was a teetotalist.

2. *A Scotchman has been noticed at breakfast every morning – until the last that is – at a coffee-shop in Newington Butts, but always alone.*

He was prepared to accept that this may well be a genuine sighting of the prisoner – indeed, witnesses would be brought forth to identify him; however, the Inspector was aware of no law against a Scotchman eating rolls and drinking a dish of tea.

3. *There is a seedy-looking Scotchman, height about five feet four or five, who frequents the houses of parliament to solicit Conservative members on the topic of cheap bread. He wears a battered slouch hat, very curled up at the sides and a red neckerchief. He sometimes carries a loaf of bread on a pike. He does not resemble the prisoner in anything other than Scotchness. He has never been seen by anyone with the prisoner McNaughten.*

4. *Scotch Societies are regularly held at the British coffee-house on Cockspur-street, along with meetings of the Anti-Corn Law League, but none fitting the description of the prisoner McNaughten has ever been seen there. Spoke to a serving maid who says, and I believe her, that the Scotch meetings are to discuss the situation in Paisley, and to raise funds for the relief of the poor there.*

5. *Mr. Oliver, senior clerk, Drummonds counting-house, says a former cashier had the confidence of his employers withdrawn after it was discovered that he was in the habit of frequenting a whist club held at the Crown Tavern in Old Cavendish-street. The fellow, who is not a Scotchman, has been seen on a number of occasions begging outside of Drummonds, but not for some time past by now. It is widely believed he took his own life, and indeed, may well have been the subject of a FOUND DROWNING bill a year ago. Mr. Oliver*

knows of no other possible grudge-bearer towards the family, or
Mr. Drummond, who is by all accounts a very amiable gentleman.

The Inspector turned down the corners of his mouth. It was without exception the worse daily report he had ever written.

It ain't right, he grumbled softly to himself, making a man doubt his own reason. He wondered what Sir Robert Peel would make of it all. Where in that gentleman's Nine Points of Policing, to which the Inspector adhered as faithfully as he did to his own marriage vows, did it say that it's right to jump to conclusions in respect of a man's guilt? You must have proofs, he told himself, as he had over and over throughout the day: *you must have proofs*. But then what was proof when it came down to it? An arbitrary thing, dependent on the feelings of the judge and jury, the honesty of witnesses; only that which we feel – on account of everything that life has to teach us about ourselves and others from the very moment we are pitched neck and crop into this world and all its troubles – only that which we feel oughter be *right*. Yes, he thought, his well-regulated mind turning over the notion, cautiously – and ever since I first clepped eyes on the fellow, didn't I think to myself there's something not quite right about him? McNaughten – a felon taken in the act – did not look, behave, or speak like any other guilty man the Inspector had come across in thirteen years of policing the metropolis. What sort of man, he wondered, what sort of man fires a pistol at a gentleman on a crowded thoroughfare in broad day, and never betrays the smallest iota of guilt in his countenance?

It was surprising to him that this observation did not make him think ill of the prisoner. He was perplexed by him, but not appalled. He rubbed his chin and gave himself over to remote impressions, which, when they came, had nothing to do with hired assassins, Scotch Chartists, the Anti-Corn Law League, or Glasgow thuggery. His remote impressions were of a famished boy in ragged clothes and busted boots; a respectable person apparently reduced in circumstances with a fortune in his pocket; an ancient Bible open upon an improvised altar in a cold, dark kitchen; a poor mad threadbare little woman; a boat bobbing beneath the crude imprint of a rainbow.

He had gone far beyond what he could possibly hope to comprehend. He was tired, perhaps even on the cusp of cynicism. He had stalked the grimy alleys of the Devil's Acre in search of ken-crackers and magsmen and never felt a quiver; he had fearlessly cast about for villains in the unsavoury hurly-burly of a low tavern; he had stomach enough to lift up a greasy canvas without looking away, no matter what he found there; he had the nerve to stay alert in a smoky gin-shop while others lost theirs; he had the wits to watch his back knowing all too well that the over-familiar coster in his cap and Belcher kerchief could all of a sudden take it into his head to bash you over yours with a pewter pot. He could do all of this – and more – without losing a shred of courage; but he had not the mettle for secret nods and coded handshakes, for informations that sprang up out of nowhere and ran amok all over the place.

A thought came to him. He dipped his pen and carefully nibbed another despatch. It was one more description of the prisoner, together with a request for information about the two Scotchmen wanted in connexion with him: Gordon and Carlo. He had already determined that the former was a known associate of the prisoner; the latter perhaps a fellow lodger – the landlady had made mention of him, yet no further account of him could be fetched up in the vicinity of Poplar-row. He had an inkling that one or other of them might turn out to be the short Scotchman in the battered slouch hat who had so plagued the steps of the government offices in recent weeks.

Any connexion between these men and the prisoner Daniel McNaughten to be investigated by order of Superintendent May. If you are able to assist in the investigations kindly direct your reply to myself c/o the station-house, Gardiners-lane, Whitehall.

Sincerely, Saml. Hughes, Inspector, 'A' Division.

He blotted, folded and sealed the letter-sheet; then he turned it over and wrote upon the front: "*Urgent Attention of Inspector Harvey 'R' Division*". He considered for a moment or two before adding "*CONFIDENTIAL*" in the top left corner. He underscored the word three times.

"Take this to the river patrol quick as you can," he asked of a constable passing the desk. "And make sure they know it's to be handed over to Inspector Harvey at the Greenwich station-house and no-one else."

"Going down to the river, Bob?" said Constable Silver to the message-bearer as he passed him in the doorway. "Oooer! Rather you than me!" He placed a can of hot coffee in front of the Inspector. The icy rain was dragging its fingers through the dust of his oil-skin cape. "It's filthy out there," he said. "Wind, hail – the whole bloody lot!" He took a sip of his coffee. "What's that you're sending to Greenwich, sir?"

Inspector Hughes straightened the edges of a pile of *Police Gazettes*.

"Routine inquiry," he said.

"Had one of your notions, have you, sir?"

The Inspector shifted his weight and lifted the coffee, savouring the warm steam. "'R' Division oversees prisoners sent off the hulks to work in the Royal Arsenal," he said, "a good many of whom happen to be Scotch Chartists awaiting transportation for their part in the summer disturbances. Seems to me there's a chance that one of 'em might know something of the prisoner, or his associates."

"Lor'! That's good detecting, Inspector," said the constable admiringly. "And them poor devils ain't a thing to lose by talking to the police..."

It was quite true that a man sitting out his time on the hulks would happily deal the secrets of his soul for an extra ration of hard-biscuit, or the promise of a morning spent in a nice dry store-room rather than up to his waist in the river repairing chain moorings.

"Keep it to yourself, Constable," said the Inspector. "There's too many round here eager to exchange informations with newspapermen for a ha'pennies."

"O, they pays more than ha'pennies," said Silver. He buried his nose in the coffee can. "Leastways, so I've heard," he said.

"Yes, well. Drink up your coffee, boy; we have work to do."

"Shall we be kept out late again, sir?"

"The way this case is ramifying we oughter be out there every blessed minute o' the day and night." He looked hard at the young constable. "Why, you got something better to do with your time?"

"As a matter of fact, I has."

"Wouldn't have nothing to do with a certain cook up on Spring-gardens, would it?"

"It might do at that," said Silver with a grin.

The Inspector took a draught of the coffee: it was hot and sweet. "I'll tell you what," he said, "you accompany me to the Acre – no grumbling, mind – and I shall let you off the rest of the evening."

"You're a decent cove, Inspector Hughes, and no mistake!"

"I haven't always been married, y'know."

After a few amiable minutes had passed between them, Silver said, "Sir, I heard how the Home Secretary has a pile of informations taller'n a stove-pipe hat. He has a list of all them what signed the Chartist petition, and another on which is writ down every one what's ever given a penny to the Anti-Corn Law League. It seems to me it oughter be a simple enough task to go through 'em in search of the prisoner's name."

"I'm sure they has, Constable."

"Then why ain't they said so?"

Inspector Hughes didn't answer.

Silver frowned at his can. "You don't suppose it's because they never found him there, do you?"

Inspector Hughes ran a hand down his long face. "It's our task to proceed from information to information in accordance with the proper procedures, Constable," he said. "I don't think much of forming opinions before I has seen all the evidences – and neither should you."

"But you must have an inkling, sir; you always has an inkling."

"My inkling is that you can't prove what ain't there, and only a fool or a deep 'un would try and do as much."

"Sometimes," said Silver, "it seems to me it's as if McNaughen wanted to be taken."

Inspector Hughes drank the last of his coffee. It was already turning cold. "Yes, well," he said, "it would've all been a sight easier if you'd had the sense to gather that second bit o' shot from the paving…"

Silver set his empty can down upon the ledger desk, taking care to avoid the Inspector's admonitory eye. "If McNaughten hadn't meant to do for Mr. Drummond, why did he have all that shot and powder in his lodgings, then?" He wiped his mouth with the back of his hand. "Eh? Tell me that."

There was something a sight dismaying in the gesture and the re-mark.

"Better hope, Constable," said the Inspector, reaching for his oil-skin cape, "that the prisoner don't get taken up by a clever barrister."

A few minutes later they were out on the hard, cold gray of Gardiner's-lane heading towards the Devil's Acre. It was snowing rheu-matism. A coster wheeling his empty barrow along the icy cobbles was soon lost in the bleak shadow of the abbey looming up before them: a few more paces and they too felt its chill fall over them.

"Fire up your bull's eye, Constable," charged the Inspector, "and be prepared to spring yer rattle."

Silver unbuckled the lantern from his waist, releasing its angry glare into the dense maze of crooked alleys. Arm in arm the two policemen disappeared into that ill-lit and obscure part of town, past the maggot children of the Acre, the squint-eyed lurkers and the unsteady women, their naked shoulders vulnerable beneath paper-thin shawls; through unventilated narrow passages and cramped quadrangular courts, the crumbling archways from whence came the stench of crime and despair that filled their nostrils, clasped their throats and their thoughts.

They walked on in silence for the most part, through the very worst of the Old Sanctuary, alert to every sight and sound: a sudden shriek opening the sky; the unseen menacing of dogs in the near-distance; glass shattering; a tin rolling across frozen waste ground.

They had walked a good long while and were now picking their way across a frozen patch of broken glass and filth, towards a row of bent hovels from which ragged scraps of smoke rose now and again against the frosty night.

They came to a stop before a pile of old bricks with a few planks of rotten wood slung across the top.

"Mr. Railly," called the Inspector gently. "Are you there?"

Silver held out the lamp as a figure emerged uncertainly.

"Who wants him?"

"It's me, Mr. Railly; Inspector Hughes."

They were looking into a gaunt and faintly whiskered face. "Your honour! Well, well, well!" The old man made a bow, but the Inspector clutched his bony hand and shook it warmly.

"Constable," he said, "this is Mr. Railly – the only honest man in the whole of the Devil's Acre."

Silver moved the lantern beam to reveal a very small, thin man. He looked about sixty, but might have been much younger, so great was the impression of hardship he made.

"Are you come on account of the rising, yer honour?"

"The rising?"

"O, God bless ye, sir, the End is comin'. Naebody hereabouts is in any doubt of it. Second of February. I've a handbill here somewhere if ye'd care to see it. An end to pauperism. Amen!"

"Second of February, eh…? Well, well…"

"O, 'tis the talk of all the street-dwellers, yer honour. I wonder you han't heard about it… O! There's so many looking forward to their deliverance."

The Inspector slipped a couple of browns into the old man's bony hand. "I've come to do a little bit of business with you," he said. "I know you would have been up at Charing-cross yesterday afternoon. I take it you know about the incident – and I know that if anyone can be relied upon to say what went on, it's you. I know you never miss a thing with them keen eyes of yours…"

Mr. Railly glanced about him before raising a palsied finger to his lips and gesturing the two policemen into his home. They stooped in the low doorway, and since neither dared remove his stove-pipe hat in the Acre, set their heads at awkward angles against the precariously sloping sack-cloth ceiling. In one corner a greasy stump of candle was giving off more smoke than light, and in another a coal-dust fire smouldered miserably on the dirt floor.

"I han't always been so low, yer honour," Mr. Railly was saying. "Sure, and at one time wasn't I a provision merchant up in Soho?"

"I ain't forgotten that, Mr. Railly," said the Inspector, "never you fear."

"Only I 'as a liking fer a drap, and sure 'tis been the ruin o' me – that and the slump in trade, or so I should say."

"There's been a good few caught between them two snares."

"I couldn't do a thing about the second misfortune, but sure the drink, that I could have helped. Stay away from strong liquor, young feller. That's my advice to you."

"That's good advice, which you'd do well to heed, Constable Silver."

Silver sighed, an impatient restless sigh that told the Inspector straightway what the young man was thinking: he was thinking – and he was right – that the Superintendent would never permit a derelict 'ibernian to take the stand as a police witness. But the young constable had still a good deal to learn about police work.

"Yesterday afternoon, Mr. Railly," the Inspector gently pressed, "up at Charing-cross between half past three and four o'clock – what did you see?"

Mr. Railly rubbed his chin.

"If you mean that young feller with the pistols, well I seen him alright. Sure and wasn't he waiting outside the counting-house for a good long while round about the time I was gathering me cigar-ends. He followed the large gentleman up the road towards Charing-cross, though after that I couldn't tell you what occurred. I heard all the commotion – o, a terrible deal of fuss. And sure I saw the large gentleman come back and go inside the counting-house."

"How long was the young man waiting there outside the counting-house?"

"O now, to be sure that would be a good half an hour, so I should say, yer honour. See, I generally takes a turn about that end of Charing-cross round about half past three of an afternoon – it's not allowed for the gentleman to takes their smokes inside the bank, and there's always a great flow of 'em in the last business hour. And sure isn't the outside of a counting-house the finest place in the world for long ends? Why, you can fetch in any number in as short a span of time. A feller down by the Tower gives me sixpence a pound fer 'em. 'Tis a living."

"It sounds like a very good trade, Mr. Railly," said the Inspector. "But I'm interested in the young man with the pistols."

"Ah! To be sure, I should never forget him, yer honour. He gave me a shillin'! Though he looked like he han't two ha'pennies to rub together." Mr. Railly chuckled wheezily at the recollection.

"A shilling, eh," said the Inspector. "That was certainly very generous of him."

"That it was, yer honour; that it was."

"And had you ever seen him outside the counting-house before?"

"I've never seen him in me life before, yer honour – sure and I'd remember if he'd ever given me a shillin'!" He chuckled so hard he had to gasp for breath.

"I dare say you would, Mr. Railly. And you'd never seen him any-where else in the vicinity – say hanging about the government offices, for example?"

"Ah, but the plainclothes fellers don't suffer you to hang about the offices, yer honour. They soon see you off if you venture so far down Whitehall. No, I keep to the counting-house. Those fellers has their job to do, but how some of them choose to go about it – well, it isn't right. There's one, a devilish-looking feller he is – a Scotchman – he oughter be reported."

"Is that so..."

"He stands up by the King's statue most days with a great gang of bullies, looking like he owns the street. The way he talks to people, well, to be sure, you wouldn't talk to a dog like that. See, I'm used to a better class of person, yer honour. O, I'm brought very low just now, but, to be sure, I haven't always been like this. I know how to present meself. But that feller has no respect."

"Tell me, Mr. Railly, what does the plainclothesman look like?"

Mr. Railly scratched his chin. "He's not a big feller – about my height, I should say, but wiry."

"How old would you say?"

"Sure and that's awful hard to tell, yer honour. Maybe thirty… He's awful dark of complexion, grimy like. And he wears a sort of slouch hat that he likes to keep pulled down over his face."

"A slouch hat, you say?"

"Well now, it's a rum concern, I should say – sort o' like a preacher might wear – with the sides all curlin' up and very shabby, so you might say, yer honour, sir. And he wears his hair long, lying all about his shoulders there, and he ties a red kerchief about his neck."

"A red kerchief, eh," said the Inspector.

A short while later they were making their way out of the Acre in silence, the Inspector ruminating upon plainclothesmen in slouch hats and red neckerchiefs. They walked on, turning into a filthy courtyard – the bull's eye glancing off half a dozen brute faces huddled in a dark corner. In the distance someone was crying. A dog barked. There was the unmistakable scrape of a window being prised open.

"Queer-seeming slouch hat, short, Scotch," mused Silver. "It sounds to me as if the peery cove your whiddler Mr. Railly saw is the same one the gentleman office-keeper told us he saw on the steps of the Board of Trade. Which means that, most likely, that fellow really *was* a plain-clothesman after all! Busted Active Duty – there's always some jig with them chizzlers, ain't there?"

In the hard and icy brilliance of Parliament-street they bid one another a good night. Inspector Hughes watched his constable disappear into the blur of the street in the direction of Spring-gardens, standing alone on the corner. A smart carriage dashed by, sending up a shower of dirty water against his oil-skin. Across the busy street someone was singing "O! Don't I Love the Bobbies", the melody soon lost in a chorus of bad laughter.

No. 19, Lower Grosvenor-street, Mayfair,
Later that evening

In which a great fire is set and the **haut ton** *come to pay their respects, and show their gratitude for services rendered.*

The portmanteau that Miss Drummond had been expecting to come to the house on Friday afternoon had finally appeared that morning. She left it to her brother Georgie to dispose of its contents. She had other, more important matters to which to attend than the destruction of some parchment scrolls of the King's Remembrancer; and Georgie's Very Large Self-Esteem – the principal attribute of which is overweening conceitedness – best suited him to any task requiring unbearably smug extenuations of self-satisfaction. It galled her to hear him go about the house crowing that he and he alone ever did a thing to preserve the interests of the family; but being unwilling to share with him the shot and the vexatious volume, Miss Drummond had no choice but to content herself with a little face-pulling whenever his back was turned.

As soon as the surgeons had departed for the morning to make their rounds of their other patients, Georgie enlisted Parrott to help him set the fire in the drawing-room grate. Within minutes clouds of choking black smoke were filling the downstairs drawing-room and the hallway, and Mrs. Gaff and Lizzie, the girl, had had to run around the house throwing open doors and windows, all of which prompted a great agitation in Miss Drummond's already overtaxed disposition. She was greatly relieved when it came to Parrott that the application of a double sheet of that morning's *Times* across the open fireplace would do much to divert the smoke out of the house and up the chimney. He succeeded, too, in coaxing a little lick of flame that grew and grew until there was a great blaze roaring in the hearth, giving off an intense heat which lasted the better part of the day.

"Such a splendid fire," observed the Austrian ambassador, as he drank the last of Papa's Chateau Margaux, "so cheering on a cold day." Indeed, the blaze was met with equal cordiality by several persons of *ton* who called that afternoon with kind considerations. Miss Drummond was moved to consider that the burning of the parchment scrolls, necessitous of itself, had evidently turned out well enough in this respect, too – even if she had on several occasions to go into her boudoir and hang her head out of the window, seeking the comfort of cool air for her flushed cheeks.

People of Quality came and went for most of the hours between two and six; but although she eagerly anticipated the arrival of the Duke of Wellington each time she heard yet another carriage rattling to a halt outside the house, unfortunately – or perhaps advisedly, given the circumstances – he did not come, even though she knew him to be in town. Indeed, she had no idea so many of the Carriage Class *were* in town. Lord and Lady Lyndhurst, the Earl of Beverley, the Countess of Falmouth… As she remarked to Lord Kilmarnock, the season seemed to her to come by so much sooner these days than ever it did in her youth.

Lord Kilmarnock was, as ever, quite charming, but in most other respects Miss Drummond found the afternoon to be a great trial. Expectation of the Duke of Wellington's imminent arrival proved immensely wearing, and Cousin Henry's lengthy disquisition upon the Conversion of the Jews quite upturned all of her efforts to create a delightful occasion of engaging insouciance. Much to her discomfiture, Henry failed to notice when the Countess of Falmouth hid a gracious yawn behind her fan and attempted to win him to conversation by resorting to the weather.

However, she had been far more agitated to hear Lady Lyndhurst – upon being offered one of Mrs. Gaff's anchovy sandwiches – remark to the Countess of Beverley *"How very quaint!"*, prompting a smile of unmistakable *slyness* from dear Lady Beverley. Miss Drummond was quite prepared to accept that the impromptu gathering had not been of the order of one of Lady Blessington's *salons*, but the anchovies came from Fortnum and Mason. It was indeed unfortunate that the ensuing conversation afforded no suitable opening within which she could insert this reassurance.

What a relief it was, she was thinking now, that such people were not in the habit of staying too long. The ladies perched on the edges of their chairs, faintly nodding over their teacups; the men discussing bullion, rates of exchange and depreciation of currency in muted tones, without ever once looking at one another; Cousin Henry in the midst of it all, boring everyone to tears with his gloomy prophecies; and poor, dear Neddie, propped up on the bed, looked like his own wax effigy as he tried, with an immense effort, to receive politely all the kind considerations.

Doubtless, if Miss Drummond had been gifted with reliable servants, the afternoon might have passed a sight less wearisomely; but it was her great misfortune to keep the worst household in London. The wretched Parrott, having earned to himself a measure of approval by saving the drawing-room wall-dressings from the ravages of the parchment bonfire, quitted it all at once by making a great deal of having to don the livery suit. O, she saw him frown! Her sharp little eyes did not miss a thing, especially where her aberrant footman was concerned! It was true that the livery suit did not fit him as well as it might, for Parrott was both shorter and fuller of figure than any of his predecessors in the post, but a servant ought not to quibble with his mistress. And needless to say, Georgie had not helped matters by laughing so uproariously at the spectacle the footman presented. What, she inquired of him, somewhat peevishly, did he suggest they do else? Surely there was a certain expectation that her footman be appropriately attired when accepting the gracious inquiries of Their Royal Highnesses the Dukes of Cambridge and Sussex, Prince George of Cambridge, the Dukes of Buckingham and Dorset, the Duchesses of Somerset and Norfolk, the Earl of Aberdeen, and the Earl and Countess of Errol, &c., &c. Perhaps, she suggested tartly, Georgie might care to increase the allowance paid for her household expenses in order that a new livery suit be procured. That soon put a stop to his laughter, as she had known it would.

She was watching Parrott keenly as she recollected all of this. He was dabbing at Neddie's feverish brow with a cool flannel, and something in the gesture made her resolve once more to dismiss the footman just as soon as the wretched business was over and done with.

"It shall be revealed by the flames," said her brother the Reverend Arthur in his church voice. He was on the landing outside about to enter the bedchamber.

"Good heavens! I sincerely hope not," said Georgie in his customary tone of mild irritation. "You are forgetting the first rule of the counting-house, dear boy: the welfare of the customers is the first object. We have taken measures this day that will ensure that their interests have been represented to the utmost of our ability."

How very pompous he was!

"He who hath given forth upon usury, and hath taken increase," intoned the Reverend Arthur piously, "he shall not live; he hath done all these abominations; he shall surely die; his blood shall be upon him. Ezekiel chapter eighteen verse thirteen."

Georgie was laughing as the pair of them entered at the door. Her older brother crossed to the foot of the bed, where he stood in a perfect gloat.

"Doubtless you'll be pleased to learn that we need concern ourselves no longer with the inquisitorial imposition," he declared to Neddie. "I have burned the scrolls of the King's Remembrancer –every one! – and now not one record remains of our liability with respect to that wretched tax. Sir Robert Peel shall have to come and inspect our ledgers himself if he wants to purloin a penny. We must preserve the Landed Interest – more than ever in these troublesome times! "

Neddie made a queer choking noise.

Georgie could be so unkind, and poor dear Neddie – in whom loyalty was such a powerful attribute – had always been so adoring of him: except, that is, in the irksome matter of the income-tax and the wretched parchment scrolls of the King's Remembrancer.

Georgie had received the news that, after a forty year respite, Sir Robert Peel was to re-inflict the lancinations of Income Tax at seven-pence in the pound in a very ill frame of mind; and when it was brought to his attention that the King's Remembrancer had kept a record of all the taxes paid back in '16 – the last time Income Tax had been owed – he had made Neddie the object of his fury.

What was the point of having a brother in the Treasury, he had de-claimed, if such an outrage was permitted to occur in the life of a Tory parliament? Over the past few months it had become a sort of mania with Georgie, which Neddie's stubborn persistence in defending the policy had greatly exacerbated. Indeed, she had often thought it very fortunate that Neddie was both too old and too large any longer to be roasted in front of the nursery fire until he recanted his avowed belief that the Income Tax was the only sure means of assuaging the present State of Danger.

"These delatorian scrolls constitute a dangerous record of liability," Georgie had declared. "They will be used against us. Many of our cli-ents are alert to the threat. You will have to do something about it – that is, if you care a damn for the continued survival of the counting-house and this family – not to say the status quo."

Neddie had made his little half-smile. "The scrolls of the King's Remembrancer! Well, well!" he had said. "Are you quite sure they are still in existence?"

But Georgie would not allow the matter to end there. He had bul-lied, threatened and preached; he had invoked the ghosts of their Papa and Grandpapa.

"I would remind you, George, that the deficit inherited from the Whigs stands presently at eight hundred millions, three hundred and thirty-four pounds," Neddie had argued, all in vain. "This is the principal cause of the deplorable circumstances in which many of our fellow Englishmen now find themselves. And it is the opinion of Sir Robert Peel that those who have lived so well off the funds loaned to the government during the Wars ought to give back but a little in the interest of their suffering compatriots…"

"Damn it, Ned; you sound like a confounded Jacobin!" expostulated Georgie. "I do not expect that meddlesome *parvenu* Peel to appreciate how the interests of the aristocracy are the same as those of the entire nation – he is the son of a northern mill-owner, after all – but I would have expected more of you."

Miss Drummond would never admit to it, but she was in agreement with Georgie on this matter. If Papa and the bank had been good enough to loan to the government the money it had required in order to defeat Napoleon and the Jacobins, then why ever should their descendants not reap the benefit? After all, as Georgie put it, if the government had gone to the Jews at the time of Trafalgar, you may be sure that they would have had to repay the full amount *and* a pound of flesh for every guinea loaned by now!

"It may have escaped your attention, George," snapped Neddie, "but the People are starving."

Georgie had laughed his horrid, sneering laugh. "Why, I dare say you shall be 'turning out' in support of the Anti-Corn Law League next!" he said.

The argument had raged for several months, but in the end Georgie had had his way. Against his better judgement, Neddie had collected the parchment scrolls yesterday afternoon and delivered them to the counting-house. He had been making his way back to his office at Downing-street, when calamity had overtaken him in the guise of a pistol-wielding Scotch maniac. Well, it was done with now, she thought, frowning at her brother's pallid features. The idea of divine retribution crossed her mind as she pictured the dense pall of smuts and ash that had hung over the house all afternoon.

She shuddered. Surely God shared her own immense anxiety on the question of the savage poor and its predilection for envy and violence. Goodness, she thought, pulling her spencer about her shoulders, it is not even as if we live all that well…

When Mr. Guthrie senior arrived for the night-time attendance, he observed a change of a most unfavourable character in Neddie's demeanour, which he attributed at once to inflammation. Miss Drummond kept private her concerns that it might have something to do with the aggravating business of the parchment scrolls – all that awful smoke, not to say Georgie's bullying – and watched in prudent silence as Neddie's right arm was bound tight to the elbow with a broad tape. Mr. Guthrie senior selected a thumb lancet from his case, and grasping the blade, steadied his hand by placing three fingers on Neddie's forearm, applying the sharp edge to the vein in a swift downward stroke. The blood which came seeping to the surface was not as copious as on previous occasions and so the front edge of the lancet was pulled in a straight line across Neddie's left breast. The flesh dropped open and a dark red trickle appeared. Mr. Guthrie senior murmured querulously, laying the thumb of his left hand firmly upon the vein in Neddie's left leg and once more drawing down the blade. It was all very skilfully executed, but still the blood did not come gushing forth.

Neddie groaned and tried to lift his arm, as though to signal to her; but it proved too heavy for him.

"Hush, dear," she whispered, "you must preserve your strength." Soon, soon, she thought, you shall be in that vague, distant place, utterly forsaken and hearing nothing save the thud and gush of your life-blood quitting. He fell quiet once again and she settled back in her chair, picked up her sewing and wondered whence goeth the life-force...

She must have dozed off. When she came to it was shortly after midnight and Mr. Guthrie senior was making an incision just above the left ear, plying the blade close by Neddie's Secretiveness. He was, he said, about to pierce the *temporal artery*. She watched from the corner of one eye as blood spurted forth into the pewter basin which Parrott, weeping piteously all the while, was holding up at the surgeon's commands. She congratulated herself on having thought to protect the shredded livery with the leather apron, and calmly worked a single stitch in the crewel work resting upon her lap; the first of the day: a tiny cross of purple in the charcoal outline of a sprig of heathers tied about with a riband of Clan Drummond of Perth tartan.

"It would seem that the inflammation is lowering somewhat," observed Mr. Guthrie senior with evident satisfaction, "I should say that the symptoms of immediate danger are averted, for the time being."

But Miss Drummond knew that it was all – as is everything in this life – only a matter of time. She had seen Neddie's secrets gush forth from the unwise opening. It was over with: the secret part of his life was flowing in an arc, rising and falling there against the soft white clouds of the bed-linen; and without the secret part, she thought, unpicking the stitch with a sigh, there is nothing, nothing to bind us to the earth.

GARDINER'S-LANE STATION-HOUSE,
A SHORT WHILE LATER

In which Inspector Hughes pursues the understanding that the revelation of the true identity of the stunted Scotchman in the queer hat will prove the sturdiest axe in laying unto the root of all the trouble.

Back in the station-house Inspector Hughes had devoted his attention to the writing of a route-paper – one of those comforting aspects of the proper procedure. Writing a route-paper was something he knew that he could do, and do very well. He nibbed it quick – while the image of the subject was still powerful before him – and read it through with measured satisfaction.

"Somewhere about 30 years of age, 5/4 or 5/5. Scotch. Dark countenance, dark complexion. Hair dark brown and worn loose. Wearing a red kerchief. Good quality boots, either Blüchers or Wellingtons. A singular-shaped hat, like a shovel hat with curled-up sides and very battered. A man matching this description has been reported frequenting the Houses of Parliament haranguing Conservative Members. An office-keeper of the Board of Trade spoke to a man 2 hours before the occurrence on Friday who had a hat on which answers the description."

He set it down on the desk before him and considered. It was a perfectly good route-paper: perhaps not the best he had ever composed, but certainly there was nothing wrong with it in that regard; and yet looking at it, he could feel such boldness as he had hitherto entertained flow and ebb. Putting down in pen and ink the details of a known plain-clothesman was a bold strategy: he knew that, and he weren't at all certain that he was clever enough to follow such a bent, or to suffer the consequences. But he was acting in the best interests of the prisoner, and justice; and, he reassured himself, that of the Force. Perhaps this little act of defiance, coaxing into the open the dark practices to which the Active Duty habitually resorted, would go some small way towards making things fairer.

He wiped the extraneous ink from the nib of his pen, and told himself that in the absence of any further proofs – proofs that might well cause the investigation to take off in a different direction entirely – he could do a deal worse than to stick as fast as he could to his poor ink-lings, wherever they might take him. He could only do what he held to be right; he couldn't do no more; and did not care to do any less, neither.

"This to be read to every man in the Division," he wrote. "It must be ascertained whether a man matching this description was seen near the public offices in Whitehall or Downing-street over the past week or two, and whether or not the above is a Scotch wood-turner answering to the name of Gordon, or another Scotchman known to be in the metropolis who goes under the name of Carlo, or some other person altogether."

This done, he leaned against the ledger desk, settled his chin upon his fist, and gave himself over once more to remote impressions.

The station-house fire was no more than a pile of gray dust with a couple of embers glowing weakly in its midst, and the candle on the ledger desk had declined into thick folds of yellowish fat, slumped at the foot of the candlestick. The clock ticked and tocked another hour into the past and the latest succession of night charges came and went in a thin straggle of misery and wickedness.

"Take him down to the cells and make sure you take his boots off him," pronounced the Inspector against the last of them. Then he tipped himself forward onto the hard unyielding toes of his regulation-issue

Wellington boots, threw on his great-coat and started for home.

In which Mr. Cockburn settles upon a plausible Argument.

On his way home from the Club, Sandy looked in at Evans's supper rooms in Covent-garden. The place was packed to suffocation, but nobody of any real interest was "in", apart, that is, from the "Lord Chief Baron" himself – the soubriquet by which all oflegal London knew that scurvily entertaining rogue, *alias* Renton Nicholson, Old Peeping Tom of London Town &c., &c. Sandy was in need of diversion, and so he settled himself on a bench alongside the Baron and inquired whether the Judge & Jury Society was to be convened on Wednesday next at the Garrick's Head on Bow-street.

"O, bless you, yes, sir," said Mr. Nicholson. "To be sure, the finest wits of a legal bent that the metropolis has to offer shall duly assemble – in whatever masks they please – for an evening of perukes and potations. They shall submit to unscrupulous scrutiny the more piquant crim. con. occasions of recent times. And yes, sir, before you ask, ballet-girls *shall* disport 'emselves in gauze petticoats and pink tights!"

Sandy gave his assurances that in that case he would be in attendance, which response the Lord Chief Baron declared himself delighted to hear; for the immaculate little silk was a prime cove, and no gathering of the Judge & Jury Society would be worth the twig without him.

The pair of them sat in perfect amiability, listened to the Boys' Choir sing a couple of glees, downed a glass or two of punch, and then Cockie leaned across to tap the Lord Chief Baron on the knee.

"What d'ye make of it all, M'lud?" he asked, coming straight to the point.

The Lord Chief Baron shifted his judge's jacey, sinking it low upon one half of his brow as if to save himself the trouble of winking.

"'Tis a tangled web, Mr. Cockburn, sir. A tangled web."

"Intrigue?"

"Indubitably."

"Mistaken indentity?"

"Assuredly."

"Then, perforce, who and why?"

The knave looked down at his very battered boots with a great comical sigh that always put everyone who heard it in mind of Joey Grimaldi, giving rise on this occasion to a great uproar of laughter.

"These crab-shells have seen better days," he said mournfully. "That's for sure."

"What?" cried Cockie. "Would you have me buy you a pair of boots in exchange for information? Is that your rascally game? Why, then I shall wait for Wednesday and the new edition of *Peeping Tom*, where I may have the same for fourpence!"

The pair of them was engulfed in another blast of hilarity, under cover of which Sandy learned in a quiet corner – and all for the promise of an old pair of elastic-sided boots, of such quality that a man on good terms with his pawn-broker might happily live off 'em for a month – the substance of the pure sensation that had all of London in its grip. How the assailant was doubtless a follower of the Chartist rogue, Feargus O'Connor, despatched to sow discord and strife in advance of the Great Trial; a hapless lackey of the Anti-Corn Law League despatched to sow discord and strife in advance of the Prime Minister's statement on the Sliding Scale; an assassin hired by a secret society dedicated to overthrowing the state; or a supporter of the distressed Paisley weavers protesting against Indian silk imports.

"Have you anything," Cockie said when he had heard all of that, "that points away from *politics*?"

The Lord Chief Baron scratched his chin and considered.

"I had heard," he said, "that the fellow was the experimental victim of showground mesmerists."

"*Indeed*." Sandy hardly considered the likelihood.

"How about a dismissed footman extorting the Secretary over some *confidences trop intimes*?"

"That's *better*..."

"An assassin hired by a secret society dedicated to the cause of the

King of Hanover and his claim to the throne?"

"Hum. Not quite right, I think."

"A novitiate of Henry Drummond's secret priesthood, who had gone clean mad due to the exigencies of Apocalyptic contemplations, &c., &c."

"Is that *really* a possibility?"

Mr. Nicholson assumed a perfectly grave expression. "Were you aware," he said, "that the banker Mr. Henry Drummond – *cousin to the unfortunate victim* – is a shameless vaticinator who believes that the world shall end, and end soon? Have you read his *Dialogues on Prophecy*? You ain't? Well, I recommend 'em to you, Mr. Cockburn, sir. They sheds interesting light upon the present crisis. And did you know, sir, that it was a fatiloquent *Scotch* woman who first convinced Henry Drummond back in '30 that the world is almost at an end…?"

"Enormous wealth is no safeguard against perfect lunacy," said the silk. "And I have heard that Henry Drummond's son is dying. Grief does upturn the mind."

The Lord Chief Baron laid a great thick finger alongside his large red nose and glimpsed about him craftily, before withdrawing from his pocket a small scrap of creased and very dirty paper which he smoothed out as best he could upon the table. Then he reached into another pocket and retrieved a handbill which he palmed off on a bemused Mr. Cockburn.

Sandy glimpsed at the handbill. It was one of those crooked efforts that street ranters wave in your face when you are trying to cross a busy carriage-way: the gloomy content – Democratic Chapel – Newington Butts – Thursday 2nd February – Utter Ruin – Writing on the Wall – Judgement Visited Upon the Citadel – People Freed From Bondage – set beneath a primitive representation of Noah's Ark.

"See here," said Mr. Nicholson. "Mark the *D* and the word *Judgement* and here a 2nd." He indicated one or two similarities between the dirty scrap and the handbill.

The oily fragment was barely legible, but it did indeed appear to have been torn from another issue of the handbill.

"I found *that*," said the Lord Chief Baron, indicating the torn section, "on the pavement where the prisoner was taken – at the very spot where the peeler claimed to have caused the second pistol to be discharged."

"Really," said Sandy airily. "It is a most curious thing, to be sure, this business with the barkers." He made the observation because it was a matter of fact, though following his meeting with the Chief Whipper-in, it was the case that Sandy no longer felt inclined to set at much store the evidence of the pistols.

"And did you mark the address on the handbill, sir?" asked the Lord Chief Baron winking heavily. Sandy had not, though he nodded as if he had all the same. "Rum, ain't it?"

Sandy agreed that it was, although he had already discounted the relevance of the handbill to his argument in the prisoner's defence.

"Of course," said the Lord Chief Baron, "a good deal of *Scotch* are mad when it comes to religion. Perhaps you will recall that, before he had his own church, Henry Drummond worshipped at the old *Scotch Church*, along with Spencer Perceval, the son of the assassinated Prime Minister? The two families are very close, sir, as I am sure you are aware. A remarkable set of contiguent circumstances, is it not?"

Sandy smiled. Mention of the Scotch Church had restored to him an amusing memory.

"You know," he said, "I went to the Scotch Church in Regent-square a few times at the height of the – ah – controversy. It was the fashion to go there on a Sunday morning, still sucked from the night before… I have fond recollections of those bedevilled women speaking in tongues and writhing on the altar steps. One or two of them were rather good-looking, I seem to recall…"

"I was there the morning the peelers were sent to keep the peace," said the Lord Chief Baron, falling into a fond reverie of his own.

"Henry Drummond's church at Albury is a far less spectacular occasion," said Sandy. "Pity! Were it other it might awaken in one a long-neglected propensity for observance."

"O, I am sure it holds other fascinations, sir. Did you know that Henry Drummond and his eleven apostles have divided the Christian nations between them? It is their intention to be received among the Elect after the Second Coming."

"Good heavens…"

"The banker has taken *Scotland* for himself." He made the observation in tones of the utmost circumspection.

"What the devil would he want with Scotland?" said Sandy. "He won't find anything worth saving there..." But beyond this, he chose to demur – at least for the time being. He had known the Lord Chief Baron a long time, and understood all too well the rogue's proclivities to mischief-make.

The Lord Chief Baron's attention being momentarily occupied with indulging the supper-room's prevailing taste for small ribaldries, Sandy took the opportunity to consider the various theories that had been set before him, rapidly springing from interest to astonishment before finally lighting upon, so it seemed to him, a very proper scepticism.

"Y'know, M'lud," he said at length, lounging against the bench with his legs stretched out before him, and with one arm folded behind his head, "the propensity of the groping crowd to settle upon the most arrant nonsense never fails to amaze one..."

"Yes indeed, sir," said the Lord Chief Baron, looking suitably judicial. "There is an abiding mystery in the way one mind'll work upon another. D'you recall how, not long ago, a tulip bulb named for Miss Fanny Kemble went for £75 at a public auction?"

Sandy made a pyramid of his delicate primrose-gloved hands, bringing the points of his index fingers together at the tip of his nose. "Tell me, M'lud," he said. He was recollecting something that that impossible swank, Warren, had said to him earlier that evening at the club. "Do you believe the prisoner to be a lunatic?"

Mr. Nicholson pursed his lips and gazed into the bottom of his empty punch cup. "Well now," he said, "I believe that's what they call a leading question, ain't it?"

And Sandy had to agree with him that it was.

After paying some attention to a very pretty boy singing first tenor in a well-executed rendition of "Hail Smiling Morn", and abjuring several requests that he take the platform himself, Sandy left the supper club and returned home, alone, in the cabriolet.

That night, a terrible storm; the room in which he slept rocking like a vessel on a troubled sea. Awakening yet again at a certain hour, he found himself in very low spirits, and guided by them was unable to prevent himself removing darling, darling Polly's letter from the pages of his bedside *Leviathan* wherein he had secreted it.

He held the paper in his hand for a while, without reading. Then he pressed it to his heart, his lips and, with a sob, crumpled it in his fist and crossed to the fire. He waited as the amber-edged specks of paper floated up the flue and out across the London sky. Then he returned to bed, to lie there helpless as his loquacious conscience taunted him with a heated disquisition of scoffs, and jaunts, and jibes.

It was, he told himself, no more than a kind of hypochondria, a violent depression of the spirits brought on by some inner imbalance: perhaps the shrimp sauce, or else the Stilton. Shortly before four he rose again, took five tinctures of laudanum in some water, and finally lost himself in sleep.

But when it came he did not dream of love. For in those days, you see, he never dreamed of love.

The Third Meeting

McNaughten was already waiting for me in the room when I entered. He welcomed me with an outstretched hand, a gesture which put me in mind of a prosperous tradesman greeting a favoured customer. The faint smile flickered yet upon his lips, lending to him that somewhat feeble-minded impression I had observed before.

Indeed, the strange smile was, it seemed to me, often the only manifestation of the alleged diseased condition of his mind (I have seen it present even whilst he was giving consideration to the gravest of subjects); an observation which of itself might appear sufficient to lend credence to the somewhat fashionable and *French* diagnosis frequently (and, dare I say, carelessly) made at the time of the shooting of Mr. Drummond – namely, that of Monomania. My faithful readers will know that I have remained all this while utterly unconvinced by the defence of "partial insanity", and have challenged its application in respect of McNaughten and every other case where it has been used in mitigation against the strictest penalty allowed under the law. For it has always seemed to me to be a great weakness to exempt the insane from punishment on the basis of an *intellectual* test. The question ought always to be asked if mental unsoundness was the cause of the act, or not. It is a simple enough point. If we begin to admit the possibility that one might be insane yet "still take a hand at whist", then the Law shall never be able to ensure the safety of society at large – not so long as it is the case that any common criminal may study sufficient to persuade a host of mad doctors that he is a frenzied lunatic but on one point only, and in all others is capable of all the operations of the human mind, undisturbed by evil or excessive passions.

For if one may smile, and smile, as it were, and yet be found to be insane by the leading authorities of his age, then how are we ever to determine the precise line of demarcation between the extremes of bad temper, fanaticism, or moral depravity, and the point at which the individual mind embarks upon a voyage towards its utter destruction? That smile of McNaughten's, or so it seemed to me, might well be the most villainous ploy yet devised since King David first simulated insanity to avoid King Achish, or Ulysses essayed the same means in order to escape the Trojan Wars. It might evince a mastery of the fictitious "signs of insanity" as depicted (with wanton recklessness, and so little heed to the inherent dangers and likely consequences) by Mr. Charles Dickens in his *Barnaby Rudge* – viz. a vacant stare, skulking in a corner, &c., &c.: a good assortment of which follies McNaughten had certainly exhibited on numerous occasions.

"And how are you today, McNaughten?" I asked him.

"I am very uncomfortable," he began.

"Yes, yes – so you have said before."

"I should like –"

"– you should like to return to your native Glasgow."

"That is all I ask. Do you think it will be possible? Have you seen what may be done?"

I nodded, in a vague, indeterminate way, and selected a nib for sharpening.

"That might depend," I said, "upon the consideration you have given to the conditions that brought you here."

This time his reply was immediate.

"Fate," he said.

I confess to being taken aback, somewhat, by the earnest and very directness of his manner.

"And what is fate?"

"The will of God," he said, "or perhaps of the devil – or it may be of both?"

"Not of man?"

He glanced rather quickly at me. "Ah," he said, "it is quite useless to talk to me on *that* subject: you know quite well I have long and long ago made up my mind never to say one word about it. I never have, and I never will; and so it would be quite childish to ask any questions."

"That is a great pity," I exclaimed, "for a good many people are interested in that very subject, and it would be counted a great shame if, after all our endeavours, these memoirs we are constructing were, for want of a little elucidation, to end up as pipe-lighters!"

He fixed me with a look, so level and unwavering that I felt myself retreating from its scrutiny.

"Have you decided yet?" he asked.

"Decided what?"

"Do you believe that I am mad?"

"Do you believe yourself to be mad?" I responded.

"Others more qualified than I am suppose me to be."

He lowered his head, gazing at the floor.

"And what do you understand by their diagnosis?"

"It is a disease," he said, "unlike any other – a fitful and dismal dream from which the sufferer ma never awake. But you already know that much."

"Know...? What do I know?"

"I believe," he said, "that were you to look into the hindermost portion of your own heart and thoughts, you would discover that you have already understood everything – all this time – and have no need to ask of me any more questions."

He was smiling at some indeterminate thing or point in space.

"I can see it," he said. "I have seen it in your eyes."

He would, he said, *have been about nineteen, twenty, one-and-twenty.*

The incident he was about to recount was one in which there was a confluence of occurrences, such as appear in retrospect to be endowed with a momentum, a significance that cannot be denied. To begin with, there was his decision to tramp to Paisley to hear his father's journeyman Abram Duncan address a chapel meeting. He had gone on the spur, after having swithered above an hour at the Broomielaw in the pouring rain. It was the second biggest journey he had ever made, and the first time since being brought there as a child that he had ever left Glasgow. Each step along the road had filled him with equal measures of trepidation and arousal; and at every mile he had considered turning back. But, as he entered Paisley, he had felt such elation as he had never before experienced. What, he wondered, what inhibition of the mind was it that had prevented him from going away before?

The sense of vigour and purpose remained with him throughout the entire course of Mr. Duncan's address, which was before a large and enthusiastic assembly that hung on his every softly enunciated word. By this time, Duncan had acquired to himself no small measure of popular appeal in Glasgow and the towns and villages beyond. He was regarded as a stirring orator and visionary, but gentle and distinguished, and quite unsullied with any of the rabble-rousing tendencies of many of his cohorts. He was not yet associated with the notoriety which was to accrue to him at the height of the Chartist disturbances: he was still held by one and all to be a good man, serious and religious and learned, all of which, in truth, he was.

The lecture was taken from one of the Psalms, and had something to do with responsibility to one's fellow men; but Dan paid little heed to it. His adventure had filled him with a new sense of assuredness. He spent the hour mulling upon the possibility of how he might finally leave his father's shop and set up on his own account, such as he had often thought of doing. The scope of his ambition, however, always defeated him. It ought to have been a simple enough matter to board a barque headed for Canada or the Indies, but for some reason he could not determine, it was not. Now, though, as he stood in the crowd, letting the murmurings of assent sweep over him, it came to him that he need not go so far afield. His father had recently come by the leasehold on a pair of workshops, which he had been minded to let to men willing to register in the Conservative interest. Trade being so poor, there were few who could afford the ten-pound rent; but Dan wondered if his father might be persuaded to let one of them out to him. He would not be in competition to McNaughten & Son, since it was his plan to leave off turning spindles and spurtles, invest in a rose-engine lathe, and take to turning decorative embellishments – a line that did not appeal to his father. Mr. McNaughten senior did not care to see the way the turning trade was going and had a distrust of the machine lathes, whereas Dan saw in them a dazzling future filled with all the patterns with which his head was stuffed.

His thoughts were running on in this way, when he became aware of a growing restlessness in the crowd. He had already decided soon after his arrival there that the meeting was not meant for a man such as himself – one with a store of money put by and a good coat upon his back. And he had felt uncomfortable at the manner in which some of the working men there had lifted their hats to him as he passed among them, although he was but a boy. It was, he knew, chiefly on account of the good coat, which marked him out as a shopkeeper, an employer, not any longer a *journeyman*. Embarrasment grew into the first stirrings of concern at finding himself among so many who were beginning to bristle with the injustice of their circumstances.

On the platform Abram Duncan was speaking in his compelling, yet mild tones of the wicked, the tyrants who thought nothing of keeping a poor man in his place. A great roar went up, almost drowning out the rest of the invocation.

"– but we must no' attack them wi' weapons!" cried Duncan above the hullabaloo. He raised his hand and the tumult was immediately quelled. "We maun attack them in their conscience. God in His judgement will look upon each o' us according to what we have done. He will shake from their fine houses all those who do not perform their duty to their brethren. I tell you, they shall be shaken out and emptied."

There was a great stirring, a mighty heaving in the room. Dan felt himself lifted onto the swell. When he was set down again he found that he was wondering who it was that Abram had meant by the wicked. He looked about him at the care-mapped faces and found in not one of them a sense of his own belonging. He felt pity, he felt shame, he felt alarm; but he did not feel himself to be a part of their understanding.

He confided none of these thoughts to Abram Duncan as they walked back to Glasgow in the early hours of the morning. Instead, he discussed with him the plans he had laid. He was seeking the older man's counsel, as he always did, and was overjoyed when Duncan turned his gray eyes upon him, filled with understanding, and declared it an excellent scheme.

"Mind, dinna be led intae the slough o' carnal reason and profligacy," he warned. "Keep away frae strong drink an' meat an' other temptations o' the flesh; read guid books and think much on their content; discuss them wi' men o' tempered thinkin'. Follow a' these precepts, son, an' ye'll no' go wrang."

It was just before first light when the pair of them reached Stockwell-street – and, o, what a dismal spectacle was waiting for them there! A desultory crowd was gathered about and Mr. McNaughten senior and young Neil were poking about in the charred and smoking remains of the shop. The watch had fetched them over from Gorbals village as soon as the blaze was reported; several folk had turned out to help stave off the flames, but the fire had caught too quickly, as a fire in a wood-shop will do.

"Just think, Dan," said his half-brother, "if ye hadnae gone tae Paisley ye'd huv been burned tae a crisp."

Their father was raking through a tally of the damage, muttering dark threats. "There was nigh on two hundred pounds in here," he said. Dan knew this to be quite untrue, as his father had a week before deposited the quarter's takings at the bank.

Abram was sweeping the piles of ashes, his good coat hanging in a filthy corner. "I'll no' be able to pay ye, Mr. Duncan," his father was saying. "We maun wait fer the insurer to pay oot, an' ah dare say that'll tak' a guid few weeks."

Abram responded with nought but a soft smile, and carried on sweeping.

His money was safe enough, but the fire had destroyed a good portion of Dan's possessions, including his books. He found what remained of his cherished copy of Playfair's Euclid beneath a heap of cold ashes, the pages whereon he had drawn his patterns were curling, useless, half of them gone for ever. The only thing of his that had escaped immolation was an ancient Bible. Abram bent his head over the book and declared it was a miracle, but Dan was thinking how he would far rather the Euclid had survived. The Bible belonged to the life before, and mathematics to the life that was still to come: it was dispiriting to think that only the past should emerge from the ashes.

The City Marshall quickly identified the cause of the blaze. A canister stuffed full of combustibles and ignited had been thrown through the bars of the wee window above the lathe. The charred remains of just such a canister were discovered lying in the centre of the room.

"Whit did ah tell youse?" said Mr. McNaughten senior. "It's the Rads that're behind this! They idle slaipers dinnae care for my Toryism. Ah've bin the subject o' their spluterin' fer years by noo."

Abram leaned on his broom, mutely exuding disapproval.

The Marshall agreed with Mr. McNaughten senior.

"Those bastards have thrown fireballs into workshops and private dwellings in every street of the city," he said. "And thrown vitriol in the face of many a good man who took work for less than the going rate. Some masters have even taken to wearing masks as a precaution. I wonder you've not thought to do the same, Mr. McNaughten."

"Hech! Nay kirnie lad wi' his heid stuffed fu' o' claivers an' havers picked up at some meetin' hall is puttin' the jinx on me."

The Marshall shook his head. "Times are hard, Mr. McNaughten," he said, "these turned-out hands have nought else to do save make trouble – and they have precious little to lose by it. They care not a tinker's cuss for being imprisoned, or even transported. Why, you'll see any number of them at the Debt Court any day of the week, bold as brass. They know any attempt to poind 'em is quite futile when half the time they've nothing in their rooms worth the candle."

Mr. McNaughten senior waved him aside. "An' whit's ony o' this tae dae wi' me?" he said.

Abram lifted his head. "Remember," he said, "that thou in thy lifetime receivedst good things, and the beggar at yon gate evil things;

[199]

but there will come a time when he is to be comforted, and thou tormented."

"Barmpot," said Mr. McNaughten senior.

It was a few days later that Dan came by Carlo quite by accident. That was how it always went with him: you'd go a good while with no sign, then he'd suddenly turn up when you least expected him, carrying on as if he'd only seen you the day before and nothing much had happened in the whiles. He would sidle up to you, catching you unawares, and then he'd follow you about for the rest of the day, begging pies and drams off you, asking for a few bawbies, or a pair o' boots, or a place to sleep. The feeling he imparted, that you were the best of pals and had everything in common, tantalised and made you feel as though you were alright: a lad daein' lad's things; a man o' the world, swaggerin', wi' opinions and a place in the world. The feeling lasted for just as long as you needed it to. And when it left there was always that threat in Carlo's black eyes that made you glad he had decided to be on your side rather than against you.

This time the encounter was at the quayside where Dan was waiting to take possession of a delivery of wood. They went together to a howff up in Rottenrow. For once Carlo was fouthie wi' silver and standing rounds like it was Ne'er's Day.

He smirked when Dan told him about the fire.

"Aye," he said, "ah had heard that ol' man McNaughten set it himself fer th'insurance."

Dan was shocked to discover that his family's misfortune was become a matter of gossip and speculation. "An' who told you that clishmaclaver?" he demanded.

Carlo was bung-fu' by the look and the smell of him; he most likely hadnae an idea what he was saying. He yawned. "Ach, youse gets to hear things," he said. "An' whit youse dinna hear youse can aye find out – if youse know who tae ask."

"The polis think it's the work o' some secret combination."

Carlo spat a plug of brown tobacco on th`e floor. "Ach, they cunts set everythin' at the door o' the poor. Whit's the fash? Your pa'll no suffer. He can save on wages an' bide his time wi' his other propositions while he waits fer the compensation." He retreated beneath the shade of his hat-brim, keeping his blaeberry eyes down. "I told youse," he said, "old man McNaughten's time would come."

There was a knot of confusion in Dan's breast, and he could sense the beginning of a headache. He didn't want to leave until he was able to determine what it was that Carlo meant by this; but nor did he wish to stay. They sat drinking in silence for a while, then Carlo glanced him a darting look. He was unsure whether it was a conciliatory look or a scornful one: he fancied that he might have glimpsed something in it that spoke of attachment.

"If youse like," Carlo was saying, "ah can find oot wha fired yer paw's shop and mak 'em rue the day." He was smiling. "Mind, I'll need tae charge somethin' fer ma expenses, and fer the risk." Dan felt a quiver of anxiety. "Ah had heard there's a reward..."

Carlo's teeth looked almost savage.

Sunday 22nd January, 1843

The third Sunday after Epiphany
No.19, Lower Grosvenor-street, Mayfair,
early morning

In which much blood is split, a family scandal is raked over, and a very important visitor loses his hat.

"The poor," observed Mr. Guthrie senior, as he scarified the flesh on Mr. Drummond's back, prior to applying the cups, "do not like the skin to be broken. It is a most curious thing with them."

Neddie groaned softly.

They had laid him out once again upon his front, the better to attend to the vicious cleave of blood and fester above his hip on the left side. It was more difficult for him to signal his distress from that position. His eyes now resembled those of a baked trout, and his forehead glistened like the glaze on a ham. Since the blood-letting, administered shortly after midnight, he had scarce stirred at all, apart from the occasional manifestations of pain and dread: the babblement of the dying.

Miss Drummond was all too familiar with death, and so she directed her attention away from her brother, and kept a beady eye trained all the while upon Parrott. The footman had assumed the guise of a devoted lover sitting at the side of his dear beloved's death bed, and would not leave Neddie, no matter how many of his general household duties he neglected. It had become a point of abrasion between her and him. She watched him dip a scrap of muslin in a cup of Madeira, marking the sickening *tendresse* with which he applied it to his master's lips. Her mob-capped head bowed all the while, as if intent upon the sewing that was spread out upon her lap, she slantingly observed how each raking of her brother's flesh prompted the footman to flinch as if it was he who was suffering; how the anxious cares of the past day or so had degraded his smoothly handsome features, almost beyond recognition.

She observed all of this, but not with any sense of pity.

"Indeed, the lower orders," Mr. Guthrie senior continued, heedless of Neddie's pillow-stifled moans, "much prefer to be *dry-cupped*."

Mr. Guthrie senior's observations were perfectly fascinating. She would miss them very much.

"Indeed," ventured Mr. Bransby Cooper, "I myself have observed that the lower orders respond most favourably to the leeches."

At the mention of the leeches, a great number of which had been applied to him in the night just past, poor dear Neddie emitted another weak groan into his pillow.

"O, you have observed, have you?" said Mr. Guthrie senior in the cutting tone he had taken to whenever addressing Mr. Bransby Cooper. The object of the sarcasm responded with a wan attempt at a concilia-tory smile.

Mr. Bransby Cooper was a buffoon: of that there could be little doubt. Indeed, she had overheard Mr. Guthrie senior remark to Mr. Guthrie junior that Mr. Bransby Cooper was entirely responsible for the marked deterioration in Neddie's condition. The knowledge did not pain or alarm her: it was one more secret to be preserved, that was all: a surety to be deployed should any of the doctors ever reveal – unwittingly or otherwise – the truth of the piece of shot that they had removed from Neddie.

She felt for it in her little pocket, rolling it between the layers of soft lawn cotton. It is essential, she thought, that we all stick together; we must stand firm against the snarling Terror that is coming. Her valiant efforts with regard to the bullet, not to mention Neddie's horrid volume, were a shot across the bow: a warning signal to all of their enemies.

"The lower orders are differently constituted."

She was not sure if she had said it out loud or not; certainly, nobody marked her. If they had, she might have gone on to observe how God had endowed such a vast number of people with Small Wonder and Full Cautiousness for a purpose. It perplexed her to consider *why* He had seen fit to create so many starving villains who would fly in the face of their Maker, but she had not the strength to pursue the discussion with herself. It was not possible to question God in his divine wisdom, she decided, even if one could so easily direct Him to do better.

"They that trust in their wealth and boast themselves in the multitude of their riches, none of them can by any means redeem his brother." On the far side of the room her brother, the Reverend Arthur, had arrived at Psalm 49. He was intoning in his church voice.

Georgie shook his *Observer* at him in an admonitory fashion.

Her brothers had been obtruding upon her consciousness all morning: their batings and irrelevancies disturbing the confluence of her thinking. And the youngest of them, Colonel Berkeley, had irritated her beyond endurance with his wretched blubbing. He had been blubbing since his arrival, late last night and still in his fusilier's uniform, straight from the Queen's side at Windsor. And he was blubbing now. Miss Drummond, who considered all despair to be very weak and very foolish, wondered for how much longer he intended to keep it up. She grimaced at the fusilier uniform, fighting a strong compulsion to stick out her tongue. Heavens! Such a display! Don't you know, all flesh is grass? she thought. All flesh is grass.

When, she wondered, would they all return to their tolerable worlds of ledgers and sermons and courtiers, and leave her and poor dear Neddie to the dismal business of dying? Would they care for her turning up at the bank, or at St. Luke's Church, Charlton, or the guard-room at Windsor? No, they would not! And no more would she care so to do. *This* was her domain: *hers*. She did not care to forsake it for the dubious rewards of the world outside.

It occurred to her how it was never more apparent than when at the side of a death-bed – this riving of the world into two distinct halves: the one knowable, warm and, in general, quite pleasant; the other full of darkness and unwelcome surprises. Over the years her encounters with that other world – for instance, the time a soldier stood very close to her in the picture gallery of the Soho Bazaar – had coalesced into a morbid apprehension of ever again leaving the confines of 19, Lower Grosvenor-street: not even to attend church. It never occurred to her that God would fail to appreciate her desire to remain indoors.

And so, as her parents used up first her twenties and then her thirties in the prolonged business of dying, Miss Drummond had remained, for the most part, within the walls of this house where every horror lay within the scope of her expectation. She was fifty, her life behind her. And, as befitted one who had sat patiently hour upon hour, witnessing his progress steal across the forms of loved ones, Miss Drummond did not count Death among her foes. Why, she thought, death is nothing more than sadness, loneliness, and regret, which are altogether familiar sensations. And the *familiar* did not make her want to blub – even if she had ever been given to blubbing.

"Be not afraid," the Reverend Drummond intoned, "when one is made rich, for when he dieth he shall carry nothing away."

"For heaven's sake, Arthur," barked their eldest brother. He shook his newspaper and the Reverend shut up at once.

"Cousin Henry recommended the reading of the *whole* of Psalms," said Arthur, waspishly.

"Cousin Henry is a perfect lunatic," said Georgie.

"He believes most earnestly that Neddie's catastrophe is a sign that Christianity is soon to be challenged!" said the Reverend Arthur.

"Cousin Henry has been saying that the world is about to end since the '32 Reform Bill," said Georgie, "and yet here we are."

"He did not say that the world was to end," said Arthur. "What he said was that Church and State are to be destroyed – just as the Jews were."

Georgie harrumphed. "If you spent any time in the City," he said, "you would know that the Jews have not been destroyed. Why, Cousin Henry himself dines weekly with a de Rothschild who always seems to me to be in a very solid sort of way."

"Why must you be so facetious?" said Arthur. "Can you deny that Christianity is in spiritual distress? Apostasy is rampant; revolution and godlessness supreme among the masses. I tell you, George, after what has happened to poor Neddie – when Henry says that a judgement of God is imminent, I, for one, am prepared to give him the benefit of the doubt. Our Blessed Lord will return soon. He will come to silence the raging of the sea and the roaring of the People. Amen."

Georgie snorted and returned to his newspaper.

"Well, certainly Her Majesty is a little hipped," piped up stout little Berkeley. "The Palace Guard has been in a constant state of prepared-ness since before Christmas. And everyone is in a frightful funk over the opening of Parliament. There is sure to be a great outcry over the Corn Laws – worse even than that over the Charter. The Office of Home Affairs has informed Her Majesty that the peace cannot be guaranteed another four-and-twenty hours!"

"O, have a little sense, do!" cried Georgie. "You're worse than a pair of old women gossiping at a gate! It is small wonder that so much nonsense about Neddie's accident is being buzzed in the clubs when members of his own family are prey to such idle speculation."

Arthur looked aghast.

"What is being buzzed in the clubs?" demanded Berkeley.

Georgie sighed. "That Neddie's accident might be accounted to Cousin Henry and that dreadful business with the Scotch Church."

Berkeley and Arthur gasped.

"O, they treat everything as sport in Pall Mall," said Georgie. "It doesn't mean a thing."

"Only think of it, Arthur," said Berkeley, his voice wavering on the cusp of another sob, "the fellow who shot Neddie was a *Scotchman*, was he not...?"

Miss Drummond made a little cough, and nodded tellingly in the direction of the surgeons; but nobody paid her any heed.

"Yes," said Arthur, "and it cannot be denied that Cousin Henry did immense harm in encouraging Dr. Irving and his congregants at the Scotch Church! It was quite misguided of him to give such credence to the fellow's deluded notion that he could predict with accuracy the precise day on which the world was to end. A great number of very impressionable people were led into spiritual jeopardy."

"Those dreadful displays at the Scotch Church!" said Berkeley.

"Shameful!" concurred the Reverend.

"All those women jumping up and down and babbling in tongues!"

"A *ludicrous* spectacle... It was a great relief to many of us when Dr. Irving was finally declared unfit to remain a minister, and Cousin Henry had no choice but to drop him." Arthur's eyes were half-closed in that pontificatory way of his. "But I must confess to feeling a measure of pity for Dr. Irving: imagine how it must be to hear oneself denounced as a heretic, turned away from the door of your own church..."

Mr. Bransby Cooper's features had elongated into a mask of sympathy.

"They say he died of a broken heart, you know," he said.

"No such thing," snapped Mr. Guthrie senior. His eyebrows clashed together furiously at the foolish suggestion.

"Quite so," averred Miss Drummond, with the merest inflection, such as to imply that the conversation ought to move on.

"And let us not forget," said Mr. Bransby Cooper mournfully, "how dreadful it must have been for those of the Scotch congregation put out with Dr. Irving. The Celtic peoples, especially those of the lower orders, are very easily led. They are child-like and simple; and take matters very much to heart..."

"That is very true," concurred Arthur.

"What if this Scotchman – this McNaughten –" said Berkeley, growing a little flushed, "what if he should turn out to be one of those so disappointed in religion...? What if it were to be shewn that he had assumed unto himself the role of *avatar*?"

"O, for Heaven's sake," groaned Georgie.

"But it was Henry, not Neddie, who gave encouragement to poor Dr. Irving, and hastened the church's destruction!" objected Arthur.

"O, but Neddie attended there more than once – I recall that he went often in the company of Sir Robert Peel," said Berkeley, who had grown quite agitated.

"It was the fashion so to do!" said Mr. Bransby Cooper. "Why, which of us here cannot say the same thing?"

"I was never once there," said Mr. Guthrie senior.

"Nor me," said Arthur.

"Do not forget that we are talking here of a shootist with a fevered brain," counselled Mr. Bransby Cooper. "Who knows what such a poor unfortunate might make of the sight of his social betters deriving sport from his earnest and most sincere beliefs?" There was a moment or two of blessed silence.

"O, just imagine!" exclaimed Berkeley. "Why, it might have been any one of us!"

"I have never heard such utter nincompooperie!" said Georgie from the shelter of his newspaper.

"O, but it is too horrible to contemplate!" cried Berkeley. "Poor, poor, dear Neddie! What harm has he done? None! None whatever! He has given the prime of life to the service of his country, and this – this is how he is repaid!"

"Desist! Desist at once!" barked Mr. Guthrie senior. "The patient is becoming quite agitated!"

Miss Drummond was experiencing a marked depression of spirits. She poured herself a cup of hot water and Rowland's Aqua d'Oro, turning away from the moue of anxiety flickering across the waxy face that was half-turned towards her. Neddie had been trying to attract her attention all the while, his lips moving incoherently. Perhaps, she thought, he wants to box Berkeley's silly ears, or to bang his and Arthur's heads together.

"Was there anything of interest in the newspaper, Georgie dear?" she asked, seeking to put the recent disturbance behind them. "Surely," she continued, "there is some matter concerning the calamity that has befallen Ned."

Georgie frowned at the newspaper. "*Mr. Drummond, who is a bachelor,*" he read, "*bears his suffering with great fortitude...*"

"Did you hear that, dear?" said Miss Drummond, inclining towards Neddie, "it says in the *Observer* that you are a bachelor and that you show great fortitude. Is that not well put?" She leaned in a little closer, close enough to catch his hot frantic whisperings: relieved to ascertain that they were merely the product of febrility.

She sipped her tincture, glaring at the three of them: sanctimonious Arthur, stout, snuffling little Berkeley, horrid Georgie. All those times they had never let her join in as they had torn lines of regiments from *The Times* before the nursery fire! All those games of Highland Battles, when they had chased her through the house shouting, "*A Redcoat! A Redcoat!*"! All those times they had tied her pinafore strings to the door-knob so that she could not race them to clamber onto Papa's knees when he came home from the bank... She had not forgotten a single slight. How they had snickered whenever Mama bent over her at night to whisper, "Sleep well, my ugly little dumpling!" And where had they been all those years later when the ugly little dumpling had been left alone to whisper, "Sleep well, dear Mama" into those poor age-dinned ears night after night – with never a word of praise or thanks slipping from those thin, receding lips?

Only dear Papa had ever shown her the slightest gratitude.

"Ye're a guid wee lassie," he used to say, as she soothed his fevered old brow and lifted cup after cup of barley water to his parched and maundering lips. O! She had waited so long to have him to herself!

Miss Drummond was surprised by a tiny tear that sat precarious in the corner of one eye. It splashed onto her sewing. "It is done with," she whispered, "over, over."

"*He is surrounded by members of his family*," read Georgie, "*who are plunged into the deepest distress by the melancholy incident.*"

Miss Drummond smiled kindly at Neddie. He was hers, now – just as Mama and Papa and Charlotte Matilda had eventually been. Perhaps, she thought, with a conciliatory sigh, they shall all be mine in the end. She was the baby, after all.

"O, good God!" Georgie's expletive rallied her. "It's Harvey," he cried.

"Harvey?" Miss Drummond had very little time for her nephew. He was too cheerful to be tolerated.

Writ plain upon Georgie's face was the horror of seeing his son and heir mentioned in the newspapers. "The damn fool is quoted here!" he said. "It's claimed that he told the police that he had sight of Neddie's injury at the bank on Friday and thought it nothing more than a burn – *which he did not think had been made by a ball!*"

She glanced at the surgeons. They had both grown rather pale.

"What the deuce does *that* mean?" said Berkeley. "Do I not see my poor brother here before me, breathing his last all as the result of some madman's bloodlust?"

"How dare the damned newspapers misrepresent us!" said Georgie. "The editor ought to be horse-whipped!"

Arthur put on his placatory mien. "Harvey must have been mistaken," he said. "The light in the bank is rather weak at this time of the year. I trust you will caution him on the dangers of speaking to the newspapers."

"Harvey did not speak to the newspapers," said Georgie in defence of his first-born. "He would never do that. It must have been the wretched police constable who took down his account!"

"Why, then you ought to complain to Scotland-yard," said Arthur, quite unnecessarily. "They may attempt to call him as a police witness."

A collective gasp went up. Miss Drummond met the furious glare of Mr. Guthrie senior.

"Mr. Drummond has been shot," the surgeon said. "To imply anything else is to contradict the evidence of science – and, what is more, risk mollification of the charges laid against his assailant."

"Quite so!" said Georgie. "The villain who fired at Ned must face the strictest penalties. We cannot allow these murderous devils to get away with it a moment longer!"

"Indeed," said Arthur, "there is far too much of that sort of thing at present."

"Her Majesty and Prince Albert are quite determined," squeaked Berkeley; his colour was almost as up as his regimental scarlet. "If that rascal Oxford who fired at the Queen a year ago had been hanged, instead of being set down in Bethlem to idle away his days, there would have been no Francis, no Bean – and no *McNaughten*. On that you may depend!"

Poor, dear Neddie had grown increasingly agitated. He was gesturing blindly with his hand, as if urging one of them to come closer to him. None of them did.

"What of the cupping?" asked Miss Drummond of the surgeons. She was anxious to move the conversation along, and this was the only remedy that sprang to mind.

The stratagem succeeded admirably. Mr. Guthrie senior peered at Neddie's behind. "I have seen other cases before now," he said, deftly concealing any anxiety he may have experienced with a tone of infallible authority, "of cupping with the application of the scarificator where the blood does not flow very readily – but those were all cases where the patient was quite depleted."

"Yes, yes," conjoined Mr. Bransby Cooper, who was altogether more flustered, "we should not have had that problem here. Mr. Drummond is a man of very full habit."

"What an absolutely *first-rate* observation." Mr. Guthrie senior clicked open his lancet case and selected an instrument. He pricked the thick white flesh at the point of the rakings, nodding with satisfaction as scarlet came bubbling to the surface. "There we have it. Mark the colour, Cooper. Mark the coppery tinge."

"Just fancy," remarked Miss Drummond. She was feeling calmer. Her brother had turned his head towards her, his mouth a perfect 'O' of anguish. He has breathed in the black vapours, she thought. She kept her head bowed over her sewing all the while, watching askance through lowered lashes as Parrott applied the Madeira-soaked muslin to Neddie's lips.

Neither of them heard, at first, the loud peremptory knock at the front door. The spectacle of Neddie trying to smile at the footman, his eyes so full of gratitude, subsumed her senses. A pain was spreading across her chest, hatred seeping across the void that lay between her and the footman, across her dying brother's bed. And then there came another knock at the door, undeniable, snapping her back to the love-less, loveless space.

She was dimly aware of Colonel Berkeley leaving the room to attend to the visitor, but she was too transfixed by the action of the surgeon to pay much attention. Mr. Guthrie senior placed a piece of paper inside one of the cups, applied a few drops of pyroxilic spirit, set a burning taper to it. A sudden burst of flame made her gasp. Mr. Guthrie senior held up the glass to inspect it, the brilliant flare momentarily illuminating the grave lines of his face.

Parrott winced as the first of the cups, with the smouldering paper adhering to the bottom, was suckered to Neddie's back, the smell of cauterised flesh filling up the room; then the second cup, the third, and so on, until port-wine-red protuberances were all over the thick, white succulence, and an image of bloody stump-prints in the snow from some ghastly, long-suppressed nursery tale came to her.

"Fascinating," she murmured.

Neddie moaned softly; quivering like aspen in the forest.

"Is there pain?" said Parrott, his large dark eyes glistening. "Can Mr. Drummond feel it, at all?"

The blood was flowing now, in thick rivulets, filling up the rakings of the scarificator.

"He will feel a little bruised," said Mr. Guthrie senior, "as if he has had a beating."

"Live and declare the works of the Lord," intoned the Reverend Arthur, who had come to stand at the head of the bed. "The Lord hath chastened me sore, but he hath not given me over unto death. Open to me the gates of righteousness: I will go unto them and I will praise the Lord."

"Amen," said Parrott.

"O – o-o-o-o!" cried Neddie, piteously, and she and Parrott caught one another's eyes, the concern, the regret, mirrored there; a pang of doubt, suppressed, vanquished.

And then all of a sudden Berkeley was at the door, flushed and beaming, and in another minute they were all shuffling to their feet, lopsided grins upon their faces, as someone unmistakable entered the room behind the stout little chap.

He had come: he had come at last, clutching a bottle of spirit and rattling a box of fusees. He had come, chortling uneasily, wearing a smile as though he were breaking it in. She strained to hear the grating voice, found herself crossing to the door to greet him. The Queen is quite right was all she could think; he is exactly like a dancing master: why cannot he keep his wretched legs still!

"Now then, Ned! And what a pretty mess is this? You see, I told you what would coom of all that gadding about, did I not? Now, now, old friend, you moost let us know plain and full, what mischief is this? Eh? You may not leave us until we have winkled it out of you! No, no, not at all. I forbid it!"

The Prime Minister crossed the room to Neddie's bedside at once, handing her his hat and gloves without so much as a word or glance. And she, in a blur of surprise, meekly accepted them.

"Coom, coom," Sir Robert Peel was saying to Neddie, "we've been through too mooch together – have we not? – t'have it all end like this. Coom, coom, now, my good fellow, you moost not think that you can leave me now, so easily!" And when he looked up and about the room at them all, she could see that he was crying; that tears were running freely down both cheeks.

It was much cooler on the landing. Her face was scalding with indignation, her nerves, despite the Aqua d'Oro, in a great fluttering of agitation. Fanning herself with the Prime Minister's hat, which she was still clutching, she went downstairs to the basement and alerted Mrs. Gaff. There was not a drop of the Chateau Margaux to be had, but there was a decanter of a rather decent sherry and a plate of anchovy sandwiches left over from the previous day.

The kitchen attended to, Miss Drummond went to hang Sir Robert Peel's silk hat in the vestibule. She was not at all surprised to discover that it was one of those dreadful modern ones the gentlemen called a "crush". Only a very vulgar sort of person would wear a *chapeau claque* – a hat meant for the opera! – whilst making a private visit, and on a Sunday at that!

Miss Drummond examined the mechanism, several times pressing the hat against her cushiony bosom until it folded; then beating the brim against her doughy hip so that the top popped out with a dramatical flourish. She had it in mind that she would continue in like manner until irreparable harm had been done to the spring, but another idea came to her, and she set the crush in its collapsed state upon the floor and carefully stepped upon it. Then she lifted her skirts a little and turned a series of dainty pirouettes – first one way and then the other – over and over, until she was quite giddy with exhilaration and the Prime Minister's silk hat utterly despoiled.

EN ROUTE TO THE SCOTCH CHURCH, REGENT-SQUARE,
AT ABOUT THE SAME TIME

In which Inspector Hughes considers the folly of prophecy and the madness of conviction, and encounters a footman with a conscience and a black-hearted villain with none.

It was a morning designated for church-going. Inspector Hughes had small hopes that his visit to the Scotch Church would yield anything conclusive, but he made his way there, nevertheless, along the bell-heavy, snow-dimmed Sunday streets. A lesser man might have felt thwarted, but Inspector Hughes let his impressions sift and settle like pebbles in the tide, content in the knowledge that something would occur to him in time. A church, he thought, has *plausibility* set in its very stones, and a visit to one could settle even the most disquieting doubts of the most practised doubter. Not that he hadn't plenty of other things to do with his Sunday morning. He was considering, with a little despondency, how he could have been, at that very moment, at home eating a bit o' bacon and some toast and marmalade; or lending his assistance to the mangling.

"Lor', Sam," Mrs. Hughes had begun, the moment he had attempted to slip unobtrusively from beneath the counterpane and retrieve his boots from the window ledge. "I've been lying awake for hours."

"Well, you always find it hard to sleep when you're near your time," he said.

"O no, it ain't that. I can't stop thinking about wash-day. I'm worrying myself half to death with the thought of it. With all this weather I can't get it dry – not without a good deal of mangling. And I can't abide the mangle just now. My arms and back are still aching from grinding them great piles of linens last wash-day…"

Her words found out the Inspector's conscience and pricked it. "What do we pay the girl half a crown a week for?" he had asked.

"That skinny little thing! Lor', it's a wonder she don't run herself through the mangle along with the bedsheets!"

"All that crankin' of the 'andle'd be good for her," he said. "Build her up."

He wasn't proud of himself: he was tired and altogether lapidated, and for some reason had been obliged to dig himself in deeper and deeper – declaring with wanton casuistry how he should like nothing more than to stay at home and help with the mangling if he didn't have a living to make. He had added a conciliatory "my dear" for good measure. He was genuinely surprised to hear how acuminated and barbed it came out.

Mrs. Hughes had folded her neat little hands over her swollen belly and lain there in aggrieved silence, watching his shadow move across the ceiling as he dressed. It was a calculatedly aggravating display of patient forbearance, of which Mrs. Hughes was a master.

"There's a poor woman up on Queen's-street," she said, "who'll do the whole lot for two bob. I reckons we can manage it – at least until the baby's born – if we all just stint ourselves a little. No unnecessary outgoings. For instance, instead of me giving you half a crown for yourself, you can make do with one and six."

It never occurred to him to raise an objection. The Inspector, unlike his good lady wife, had no idea of the price of things; and, even if he had, he knew that it weren't right that a woman in her condition should wear herself out grinding mangles and lifting coppers full of boiling linens, just so's he could enjoy the odd glass o' grog, or a nice meat-pie. And unless the boy could be persuaded to stop growing out of britches and boots for a few months – in which case they might all catch up on themselves – he could see no way around his inevitable sacrifice.

He was stifling a yawn. The morning had been a long one. He had been outside the station-house by half-past five o'clock, in the pitch dark and biting cold, pinning one of those mournful *BODY FOUND* notices to the front door, along with the bill he had prepared the night before carrying the description of the peery cove in the queer slouch hat and the red neckerchief. He revived himself with a can of hot coffee, as he raked together all of the newspapers that had carried accounts of the investigations. He knew that the Commissioners would ask for them – just as soon as it came to them how many privileged informations had been written up by grubby hacks. Not all of it in the least part complimentary to the Metropolitan Police Force. When he had done clipping the newspapers, he wrote up a minute of all the communications received overnight, checked the cells, received the informations of the men coming off duty, and detailed the men coming on duty. It was past seven when he finally set out for the Scotch Church.

Inspector Hughes could never claim to be an especially observant man. He'd been sent to Sunday school, whenever his pa had the browns to spare, where he had learned his letters by spelling out the Gospels; but he had long since fallen out of the habit of attending church as regular as some would say he ought. He would have counted himself lucky to have had off the one Sunday in three, and whenever a day of rest did chance along, there was always plenty for him to attend to at home.

He had reached Charing-cross, and the niggling doubts were beginning to assail him. He could not shake off that sinking sensation: the same gloomy prescience that had come to him as he lay in bed the night before. On the far side of the carriage-way he could hear a sad whistling. The melody hung in the air; something familiar.

The Ranter must have been standing there all the while, on the corner where the Strand met Charing-cross, outside of Coles's Truss and Rheumatic Belt Depot. He could not account it to anything tangible, but it seemed to the Inspector that the Ranter had been waiting for him to come: as if there were some unspoken pact between them. He was beckoning now to Inspector Hughes to cross over: a man with an unclean spirit; ancient and decrepit, standing stock-still; the bitter wind whipping up his filthy rags, his gaze fixed upon the heavens.

"You can't stay there – you shall have to move on," called the Inspector as he crossed the carriage-way. The fellow was all skin and bones, his long gray hair sticking up like the leaves on a pineapple. A filthy bit of cloth that might once have been a cockade drooped on his left breast; and in his right hand he carried a small tattered flag of blue silk, with the crudely drawn image of a boat upon it, floating upon a zig-zag of waves and set beneath a monochromatic rainbow.

The Inspector watched the flag fluttering in the desolate wind.

"Behold! The Lord cams wi' fire," said the Ranter, in a thick Scotch brogue.

"Well, and let's hope He won't be required to present himself before the magistrate at Bow-street."

The Ranter frowned at him. "The Second Comin' o' the Shiloh is imminent," he said. "Ah've bin sent to mak' the proclamation – three times in the midst o' the city – by the soundin' o' a trumpet."

"A trumpet, eh?" said the Inspector. "Not on Whitehall, I'm afraid. Not at the present time."

The Ranter clutched his arm with claw-like hands.

"He'll gather wheat into the garner," he said, his eyes glittering alarmingly in the gas-light. "He'll burn up the chaff wi' unquenchable fire!"

The Inspector turned down the corners of his mouth. "I'm afraid we can have no talk of wheat," he said, "nor corn neither, come to that." He fixed the Ranter with his steady gaze. "Come along with me," he said. "You mustn't stand so close to Whitehall." He took the fellow by the arm and led him across the Strand towards St. Martins-lane.

A few pigeons before them on the unpeopled street rose up, startled. "But the End is not yet!" cried the Ranter. He was searching the Inspector's face with his madly gleaming eyes.

"No, so I gather," said the Inspector, "Thursday second of February."

"Repent! O repent!" cried the Ranter. "Fire an' smoke an' brimstone! Then by these three will the third part of man be killed! By the fire, an' by the smoke!"

"Tell me," said the Inspector, "that symbol on your flag there – the little boat, and the rainbow – does that have anything to do with Genesis nine thirteen?"

A smile came to the Ranter's etiolated lips, and for an instant all the crazedness went from his eyes. "Neither shall there any more be a flood to destroy the earth," he said with perfect simplicity. "It is for a token of the covenant between God and the earth."

On the other side of the carriage-way, the Ranter gathered his rags about him and headed west, away from the gleaming strip and towards the ravages of High-street. The Inspector watched him disappear, and then he turned and traced his own solitary route, towards Regent-square and the Scotch Church, wondering, vaguely, if the Ranter had been working the old Tom o' Bedlam mooch. He had had occasion to see a good many raving lunatics in the course of his duties, a number of which proved to be as sane as you or I.

He sighed.

It was impossible to tell for sure whether what you saw in a man's eye was real and true.

He arrived at the imposing porch door of the Scotch Church, just as the snow began again to descend in thin, wheedling drifts against the dismal excrescence of daylight that was spreading across the sky from the far side of Gray's Inn.

Inspector Hughes stepped into the vast cheerlessness of the Scotch Church, shaking the snow from his overcoat and frowning at the gleaming regulation-issue Wellingtons planted in a puddle of their own making upon the sanctified flagstones. He looked up and discovered a straight-backed, stiff-necked gentleman standing before him, and displaying a remarkable absence of surprise at finding a policeman in his church. The minister bore an expression of such long-practised funebriality that at first glance he might have been taken to be far in advance of the five-and-forty years that the Inspector reckoned him to be. His lips were set in such rigid seriousness that it was hard to imagine them ever parting in a smile, and his two dark eyes of such unsullied graveness, as though they had only ever looked upon the weightiest and most serious parts of life.

After exchanging a few words of greeting and explanation, Inspector Hughes brought out his notebook and opened it on the page that bore the rubbing of the queer token found on the prisoner. "Aye, it certainly looks verra like a communion token," the minister conceded in sombre tones, "but it is verra rare to see one wi'out the name of the issuing church upon it. I should say it most likely comes from one of the wee kirks."

"Such as a Democratic Chapel, for instance?" ventured the Inspector. "The sort of thing Chartists like to establish?"

At this the minister frowned, and his thin lips drew together tighter than the opening of an offertory.

"A good many Chartists wanted in connection with the summer disturbances are still at liberty," said the Inspector. He was trying, without much success, to read the dark occlusions of the minister's features. "One or two of them are Scotchmen..."

He looked about the cavernous interior while he waited for a response.

"I have let it be known," said the minister, "that that sinful crew need not come here seeking absolution!"

"Do you know anything about a Democratic Chapel in Newington Butts – run by a Widow Dutton and a Reverend Duncan?" Inspector Hughes settled his knowing eye upon the stern features of the minister.

"These are dark times for the Church," said the minister. "Anyone can style himself minister, and set up a noisy and irreverent prayer-meeting in his shop or front parlour. And you may be sure, Inspector, that they do not keep their thoughts upon the spiritual domain." The minister's eyes were blacker than a Bible. "There are many blasphemers among that rising crew. They dress up their faithlessness in false oaths, in the cant espousals o' beliefs and testimony; they cite scripture to suit their godless ends – but in truth they have nae a drap o' religion in them."

"So," ventured the Inspector, "there are unlikely to be any Scotch Chartists among your congregation here?"

"This building," said the minister, "was consecrated for the ministry of over eighteen hundred souls, but now there are not enough faithful to fill it. A decade ago it was an entirely different matter..."

"Ho! And don't I know it, sir," said the Inspector. In the gloom he could pick out no more than five-and-forty people, mostly of the shabby-genteel sort, sitting in the pews with their heads bowed and disconsolation settled all about them. It was difficult now to imagine that anyone had ever babbled in tongues there, or writhed in an unseemly ecstasy. "I was part of the police guard here many a time when all them poor ranters was attracting so much undue attention to 'emselves," he said.

"It was a shameful episode."

"All them crowds," said the Inspector, shaking his head, "mostly quality at that – all come to laugh and to jeer. It weren't right, to my mind. A church, after all, ought to be a place of sanctuary."

The minister was looking very grave, giving the impression that he did not agree entirely with that understanding of the matter.

Inspector Hughes slowly turned the brim of his stove pipe hat in his hands. "What's an Episcopalian?" he asked.

The minister gave him a very queer look. "*Episcopalian*?" he repeated. "A trumpery bit o' a half-Papist sect!" He spat the words out. The Inspector hadn't taken the prisoner for a Papist; his mind was running on, as that of an "A" Division man's was wont to do, to thoughts of Guy Faux and gunpowder plots. "Episcopalianism has become a fashion wi' the sort o' hot-headed young gentleman who thinks it a splendid thing to ape the long-haired, wild-eyed Jacobins of old, going about the place decked out in plaid, bewailing Culloden field in maudlin tunes, drinking toasts tae the bonnie Prince Charlie!"

"Jacobins, eh? Well, well, that is certainly most interesting," said the Inspector, trying to make sense of the minister's revelation.

"This *shamelessness*," the minister reiterated, "this utter *shameless-*

ness has been encouraged – I'm sorry tae say – by the Queen's visit tae Scotland last Autumn. The wearin' o' tartan trews by the Prince Consort in particular has promoted an *unnatural excitement…*"

"And might such a young gentleman be interested in a shameful book that accuses the Bible of absurdity, inconsistency and immorality?"

The minister was appalled. "Such a volume ought to be condemned tae the fiery pits o' hell," he said.

"I couldn't agree more, sir," said the Inspector. "One more thing, if I might prevail – " he showed the Minister the rubbing of the token once again. "Genesis nine thirteen – what's the significance of that?"

The minister softened a little. "The rainbow," he said, "appears at those times when we have most tae fear frae the skies. It marks the covenant between God and the faithful – that is to say, the promise o' his love for us."

"So," he said, "a person who was found to be in possession of that particular token – might it be assumed that they was *good*?"

"We are all sinners, Inspector," said the minister. "You, for instance, are a Sabbath-breaker; perhaps, too, a profaner and blasphemer, a frequenter of taverns, a fornicator…" The Inspector was moved to voice a slight objection. "We all must acknowledge our guilt," continued the minister, raising his hand. "Seek admonishment. Find absolution. Know that the Spirit may quicken a dead soul."

"Yes, thank you," said the Inspector.

"And above all, beware of false prophets!" The minister turned away from him, and began to climb the steps leading up to his great pulpit. His words rebounded from the sounding-board above his head and rang around the walls of the church, lodging themselves in the brick and in the bones of every soul that heard them. "They shall deceive the very elect!"

The Inspector sighed. He took a final look about him, and concluded that even though the Scotch Church was conveniently situated for the Birmingham railroad, it was as unlikely a gathering place for a dangerous conventicle of Scotch Chartists and Anti-Corn Law Leaguers as he had ever stumbled across. The Minister had seen to that.

He made his way down the aisle to a dismal "Hallelujah!", and on that found himself cast out of the temple.

He had accomplished no more than a few yards in the direction of Westminster, when it came to him that perhaps he ought to walk over to Mr. Drummond's home on Lower Grosvenor-street and inquire as to the piece of shot. There was a very smart carriage waiting outside No. 19: the horses, stamping and snorting in protest against the cold air, were the very best-bred; and the coat of arms upon the carriage door instantly recognisable to an Inspector of the "A" Division. He took a step backwards into the carriage-way and looked up the whole length of the house. When he was satisfied that none of the curtains were drawn and that there was no cloth muffler tied around the knocker, he proceeded to rap upon the basement door. He was still waiting for a response when a curious metallic scraping coming from the front of the house took his attention.

Looking up and in the shiny door of Sir Robert Peel's carriage, he caught the reflection of a pair of maroon velveret britches drawing back sharply behind the railings in what seemed to him to be an altogether *furtive* manner.

"Hullo there," he called, drawing level with the front step.

A liveried footman of the negro persuasion, five foot six in height, not more than two-and-twenty, with a handsome brow and large almond-shaped dark eyes, was polishing an old brass link-light extinguisher that was hanging on the railings there. The Inspector noticed at once that the fellow did not have a chamois, and appeared to be using one of his sleeve-covers for the task. What was more curious still, the leather apron he had on over his livery suit was smeared with blood.

He tipped the footman a salute.

"Bitter morning, ain't it?" he said.

The fellow looked down at once in that particular manner of people who have something that they oughter say, but have since thought better of it; or who have been caught in the commission of some act which they feel requires an explanation, if it is not to be taken in the wrong way. The Inspector followed the look down to the ground, where he lighted upon an ash-pan lying at the fellow's feet, as if it had been hastily dropped there. Some of its contents had spilled onto the path and were scattered about the dinted snow.

"Dropped something, have you," he said. He could make out some pieces, old burnt parchment and a few scorched scraps of red ribbon – the sort that legal briefs are tied about with. He stooped and picked up a few pieces, brushing the snow from them. They were all burnt beyond recognition.

The footman shuffled awkwardly. "It's just the ashes from the fire," he said. "Master George was anxious that the grates be cleaned, on account of the Prime Minister's visit to see poor Mr. Drummond."

"Parchment, eh?" said the Inspector. "Must have blown up quite a cloud..."

"O, that it did, officer. Miss Drummond was most annoyed by the smoke, but her brother was insistent it be done."

"I see," said the Inspector, frowning at the blood smears on the footman's apron. "And how is your master?"

"He – he – he has suffered very much, so much, the poor gentleman."

Inspector Hughes's gaze softened as it made contact with the footman's own.

"I had heard that the surgeons removed a piece of shot," he said.

"Yes, sir, on Friday night."

"The policeman part of me is very pleased to hear it – though I can't help feel it might've been better by far for Mr. Drummond if they'd let it be. After all, it weren't as if it were that large, was it – the ball, I mean..." He made a sphere with his thumb and forefinger the size of the shot discovered in the prisoner's lodgings.

"O, it was bigger than that, sir."

"Was it now...? And how much bigger would you say?"

The footman indicated a sphere of his own; one about twice as large as the Inspector's.

"As big as that, eh? Well, well... And what did you say your name was?"

The footman blinked a few times.

"Parrott, sir," he said.

"Yes, well, as I was saying, Parrott, to my mind surgeons has a way of making things a good deal worse, don't they? I mean to say, a bit of shot in the rump, never did no-one much harm, did it now?"

A look of great anguish fell across the footman's face. "They took the shot from Mr. Drummond's front."

"So I gathered from the surgeon's testimony."

"They turned him on his back, and now the burn on his hip has festered, poor gentleman... He is very close – " the footman faltered, suddenly overcome.

"You know," said the Inspector, "it might be an idea for me to have sight of that bit o' shot. Perhaps Mr. Drummond'll permit you to bring it by the station-house next time you're passing."

"I – I'll put it to Miss Drummond. She has it now."

"Yes, please do that."

The Inspector tipped another salute at the footman, and then another at Sir Robert Peel's driver, who had been dozing on his perch all the while, well wrapped up against the cold. He stood for a while making a few harmless observations pertaining to how very fine was the pair of horses, looking towards the house from time to time. A little round lady was standing at one of the upstairs windows. After a few moments had passed in this way, the Inspector started down the road, and then suddenly halted and turned back. The footman was picking up the ash-can and its contents and the little round lady was still watching.

"Please be so good as to convey to your master the very best wishes of Inspector Hughes of the 'A' Division," the Inspector cried.

"I will, yes, of course," said Parrott.

"He knows me – we often pass one another on Whitehall. Inspector Hughes, 'A' Division. Gardiner's-lane station-house."

"I'll let him know, sir. Thank you, Constable."

"Good day to you, Mr. Parrott."

"Good day to you, sir."

The Inspector tipped his hat for the final time and continued on his way. He was halfway around the Trafalgar-square, heading in the direction of Whitehall's gleaming strip, when his eye was taken by a line of bills posted all over the palings surrounding the half-constructed statue of Nelson. The paste on the bills was still wet, and the image upon them was of an ill-judged depiction of a sail-boat set pitched precariously between a triad of zig-zag lines below and three thick black arches above.

TIME IS RUNNING OUT! declared the legend boldly.

Is it, by thunder? thought the Inspector, who was beginning to tire of these crooked invocations announcing the End of the World.

Current events clearly indicate that it is God's purpose to overthrow
the present order.
PUBLIC MEETING Wednesday 1st February
Commencing at 8 o'clock
ATTEND IF DESIROUS OF A FULLER LIFE IN THE GREAT
HEREAFTER!
Democratic Chapel, Poplar-row, Newington

He noted the address frowningly, and then some instinct urged him to sweep his gaze towards the Queen's Palace. A few yards on the other side of the square – and as bold as a hussy on fleet pay-day – a short swarthy fellow was engaged in the activity of pasting the bills onto the palings. He was dressed in a buttoned coat, very seedy, drab trowsers, with a red neckerchief tied in a careless, unstudied way around his neck, and – which was pulled down very low over his face – a slouch hat, very greasy and battered.

Inspector Hughes stroked his chin, keeping a steady eye on the fellow. He watched as the rogue, having reached the end of the palings, calmly put away his pot of glue in the satchel of bills he had slung over his shoulder and sauntered across the road to King Charles's statue.

"Y'know, bill-posting is an offence," said Inspector Hughes when he had joined him there.

The rogue grinned at him and then, with a most insolent expression, looked down at the ground – his black, black eyes settling upon a pair of regulation-issue Wellington boots that were every bit as hard – though not quite so gleaming – as the Inspector's own.

"I've been looking for you," said the Inspector, mild as he might. The short, swarthy fellow shrugged. "There's a young fellow who's looking at a mighty long stay at Her Majesty's Pleasure – at the very least – and I have reason to believe you might have something to say about that."

"Are youse gonna nab me fer bill-stickin' or no'?" said the villain.

He was grinning at the Inspector, his teeth sharp and savage.

"I wonder that you ain't the common decency to come forward and say how it weren't Daniel McNaughten what's been seen loitering about the offices on Whitehall, looking shady and suspicious, over the past week or two." The Inspector gestured towards the palings. "And what's the game here? What's a member of the Active Duty doing posting bills on behalf of a Democratic Chapel which happens to reside at the prisoner's lodgings in Poplar-row?"

"Youse mak' it worth ma while," said the bill-sticker, "an' ah might be persuaded tae blab. Though it'll cost a wee bit more than the boabies youse throw tae yon cigar-finder."

The inspector felt his gorge rising as high as his leather neckerchief. "Lor'! Ain't you got no conscience? Don't it trouble you one jot what's bein' made out of all o' this? You need a damn good hiding, you do."

The stunted plainclothesman made a devilish laugh. "An' are youse gonna gi'e it tae me?" he said. He made an unpleasant gesture towards the Inspector and, still laughing, strolled in to the carriage-way.

Inspector Hughes watched the progress of them Wellington boots all the way down the Strand towards Waterloo-bridge. He watched them until they were a speck in the frozen distance. The End of the World. Queen's Speech Day. Poplar-row. Adumbrations of something fearsome sprang up before the Inspector, as he crossed towards Whitehall and made his heavy, plodding way towards the station-house, leaving Trafalgar-square behind him, as quiet and resigned as the last sigh of the dying.

On the Surrey-side,
EARLIER THAT DAY

In which Mr. Warren ponders the intricacies of the case in hand, considers how they might best be exploited in his own interest, discovers that landladies are the surest indicators of a man's true nature, and learns how all the secrets of their hearts may be bought for little more than the price of a week's lodgings and laundry.

After a restless night, Mr. Warren had set out once more in the unstinting pursuit of the truth, his destination that dreary region where the prisoner kept rooms: the unsavoury locality that lies in the shadow of Bethlem Hospital. He was not aware of the puddle until he felt the ice seep over his elastic sides; confirmation, as if any further proof was required, of how much he hated to cross the river. Cabs, along with all of the other trappings of civilised life, appeared to stop at the Embankment, and Mr. Warren was not yet well enough off to keep his own carriage – and still at that delicate level in society where it would not be appropriate to be seen riding in one of the new omnibuses. And so, he had little alternative but to traverse the water on foot: an activity forever associated in his mind with the darkest forebodings. To take one's chances with the man-sized rats that lurked in the bridge's black, black shadows; the river, murky as death itself, swelling but a few feet below; those unnerving plashes, so like the sounds of drowning, summoning the image of *suicide* (Mr. Warren could never approach the middle point of Waterloo Bridge without thinking of suicide) – all of this the legacy of a dismal encounter a few years previously with a deranged water-man. It had been a late hour at a Deptford tavern, and a thick river mist had rolled in, rendering it a folly to venture abroad, even if sober, for fear of falling foul of the ack-ruffians who loitered on the incoming tides. And as Mr. Warren had sat waiting for the first ray of daylight to penetrate the gloom, the water-man had regaled him with awful tales of the Thames, imparting in the course of which the sobering intelligence that a good many people made the error of jumping from the middle part of the bridge.

"They are as a rule dashed to bits agin the buttresses long afore they 'its the water," he had confided. "So my advice is it be better by far to jump orf the sides, should you ever have cause. That way you shall be sure to be dredged up *in one piece*…"

It will be recollected that the previous morning when Mr. Warren had stalked from the courts in a huff, he had intended to head across the river and go straightway to the prisoner's lodgings. However, no sooner had he reached the south end of Bow-street than he had become aware of a general hubbub on the pavement behind him, which commotion he had been turning to take stock of when the boy who took down copy for the *Gazette* had knocked him sideways.

"Now look here, what the deuce is going on?" Mr. Warren had been quite winded, but he had cried out as best he could in the direction of his young assailant, who had called back over his shoulder.

"Can't stop, guv'nor! Lunatic's just said Tories are persecutin' 'im!"

The astonishing revelation had understandably caused Mr. Warren to abandon his original plan to journey to Newington Butts and return at once to the police courts, where he had been disappointed to learn nothing more of any consequence. He had then repaired to Charing-cross, whiling away an hour or two at the Ship Hotel where interest in Mr. Drummond's catastrophe was still bubbling like a hookah, and where he had fallen into conversation with a pharmacist who had been summoned to the counting-house within minutes of the incident, and of whom he had the information that the victim had been *perfectly sensible at the time* and, though a little taken aback, in the same *robust health* in which Mr. Warren had left him scarce an hour before. What was more, it appeared that there had been *very little to show* on Mr. Drummond's person that he had been shot at – save for a burn situated above the hip on the left side, where the flaming missile had caught his clothes.

Feeling the need to distance himself from this line of speculating, Mr. Warren had retired to a quiet corner with a bottle of port wine, there to ponder the substance of these curious intelligences. He decided that it did not suit his argument to consider that the prisoner may not, after all, have fired a bullet at Mr. Drummond. He was concerned that less perspicacious minds than his own might discern a similarity with the *modus operandi* of the would-be regicides, Oxford, Francis and Bean (of whom it was frequently claimed that they had fired at the Queen with unloaded pistols), and concluding that this would not be helpful to his own design, he decided not to write about it in the newspapers.

After spending most of the afternoon at the Ship, Mr. Warren had gone on to the Reform Club, where he had been invited to dine by a prominent Whig Member who held a good deal of sway in the Lunacy Commission, a salaried position which Mr. Warren had long canvassed for. The conversation had soon got on to the shooting of Mr. Drummond, and the gentleman's own belief that the shootist was "clearly a lunatic" (a position that Mr. Warren had no choice but to pooh-pooh mentally, not wishing to turn the well-connected fellow against him).

"I cannot help but think," said the prominent Whig Member, "that if one positive were to be derived from this *unfortunate* matter concerning Mr. Drummond, it would be the opportunity to set out a table of measures by which *greater precaution* might be *universally applied* to the treatment of the *criminal lunatic* – a means by which such unfortunates might be safely removed from society at large."

Mr. Warren (who, on recollection, had perhaps committed the error of drinking rather too much claret) could not conceal his dispproval. "I should say," he had said, attempting to choose his words carefully, "that what is required is a proper deterrent rather than a *table of measures*."

The prominent Whig Member had grimaced – and anxious for his chance of attaining any sort of guerdon that lay within the fellow's gift, Mr. Warren had thought it best to make his excuses and leave before he jeopardised his future any more. It was as he was leaving that he had encountered that dandiacal nuisance, Sandy Cockburn, in the lobby.

It had occurred to him at once that Cockburn would almost certainly be pushed towards the insanity defence, were he to take on the case. It was plain from the conversation he had just quitted, that the Whig sentiment inevitably tended towards the perpetrator, rather than the victim; and there was so little inclination on the part of a Lunacy Commissioner to consider for even a moment that what they had before them was undoubtedly a case of "pretended insanity" on the part of the prisoner McNaughten – the sort of soupy thinking that Cockie was constitutionally inclined to fall in line with. Moreover, as his meeting with the prominent Whig Member had just demonstrated, there was a section of the Party given over to meddling with the Penal Code, and the prospect of picking apart the law in respect of Lunacy would undoubtedly appeal to an *enlightened* Whig of Mr. Cockburn's stamp. Mr. Warren had shuddered at the thought, inducing a bout of dyspepsia that only imaginings of the *petit* barrister's downfall were able to soothe – proving more efficacious by far than the teaspoon of bicarbonate of soda and slice of ginger in hot water prescribed by Mrs. Warren that morning.

Mr. Warren was still ruminating upon what Cockie might make of

Mr. Drummond's shooting as he foraged for a ha'penny, passed through the turnstile and sallied towards the Surrey-side. The very bad air assailed him at once, almost setting him back on his heels. Up until that moment, the morning had passed in a most satisfactory fashion. He had visited the chapel of the New Bridewell at Tothill Fields – obtaining, in exchange for a shilling, a seat close by the rail that afforded him an excellent view of Mr. Drummond's would-be assassin at his prayers. And he had filled up several pages of his notebook with lucrative observations: the prisoners filing in, according to their rank; the many ways, in defiance of the Silent System, in which they sought to communicate with one another; the appalling realisation that so many of the drab-suited caitiffs were little more than boys. He had witnessed a guard berating one, a small, blue-nosed, white-cheeked child, perhaps no more than seven or eight years old, who had come to church without the kerchief the boy prisoners wore threaded through their buttonholes. As the forlorn scene played out, Mr. Warren had watched the prisoner McNaughten, motionless upon the bench, an expression of the utmost pity upon his face. As the terrified child was hauled off to receive his punishment, the prisoner had bowed his head and covered his eyes with his hand.

Such an unguarded display of refined sensibility – in such a place – had impressed itself upon Mr. Warren, and he had congratulated himself on making such a striking observation. It was, he believed, worthy of a Continental *roman-feuilleton*, and unfortunate that the newspapers for which he was fashioning his description had no use for such a morally ambivalent *aperçu* – FIAT JUSTITIA's loyal readership being not at all disposed to subtlety.

Putting aside his artistic scruples, Mr. Warren had applied his skills instead to shaping the information – supplied by the gatehouse-keeper in exchange for another shilling – that the prisoner was occupying the very cell in which the Swiss valet Courvoisier had been remanded three years before upon the murder of his master, Sir William Russell. He had no doubt, as he walked along, that *that* ought to whip up into something suitably ominous. Until the shooting of Mr. Drummond on Friday afternoon, there had been few other instances where so much alarm had been occasioned than the news that Sir William Russell, an elderly

[229]

gentleman, had had his throat slashed as he lay asleep in his Park-lane residence. And Mr. Warren had had the opportunity of witnessing Courvoisier in the observance of his last Sabbath in the Newgate Chapel the day before his neck was wrung. He recollected now how every prisoner brought into that dismal place had looked with terror upon the black bench reserved for the condemned man, and the ominous silence that descended upon one and all as the chaplain entered; a silence broken only by the sound of heavy bolts drawn against the door. The turnkey had led the Swiss man to the seat, and placed a glass of water near him in case of faintness. The murderer had knelt, taking the prayer book offered to him with a firm hand, and then – if Mr. Warren's recollection was correct, and he had no reason to suppose otherwise – Courvoisier had covered his eyes for a moment or two – just as he had seen Mc-Naughten do that very morning.

What was one to make of such self-possession! The motions so controlled, deliberate and utterly devoid of passion; the features bearing nothing but an expression of pensive good nature! The uncanny similarity between Courvoisier and McNaughten was not lost on Mr. Warren. He seized upon it in an instant – certain that only assured guilt could provoke such impassiveness.

It was not a great deal, but it would have to do; for the truth was Mr. Warren had nothing more lurid to report. Setting to one side his outburst in the magistrate's court, McNaughten had proved nowhere near as obliging as Courvoisier – or that vile wretch Oxford, come to that. When Mr. Warren had had occasion to observe him in the chapel at Newgate back in '40, he had been horror-struck by the way the impudent puppy – fresh from having fired at the Queen! – had stretched out upon the steps beside the pulpit with all the insouciance of a baron's eldest son settling beside the woolsack! He had appeared to admire his legs, Mr. Warren recollected now… But let us not forget that Oxford had been *playing* at being mad! It was evidently a role he performed to perfection – for he languished yet in Bethlem at the public expense when the whole world knew he deserved to be hanged or, at the very least, flogged for what he had done. Such wickedness!

The oppressiveness of the Surrey-side was pulling him down, urging the darkest thoughts, the dullest presentiments to scud across one's conscience. As he made his squelching progress towards the Cut, it was a retreatist consideration of his accomplishments that occupied the greater part of Mr. Warren's cogitations. Even his enemies would not have denied that he was a fount of *pensées* upon the numerous infatuations of the time, but the disparaging voices in his mind were stubborn in their refusal to be quelled. The *unprecedented augmentation* of England's taxes since Sir Robert Peel acceded to the premiership; the *true nature* of men who applied Kalydor's preparation after shaving; the needless rapidity of the locomotive: these were all, undoubtedly, subjects worthy of the utmost consideration, but Mr. Warren had his eye on posterity and he yearned for a more lasting legacy.

It was true that his novel *Ten Thousand a Year* had been an undeniably popular success; yet Mr. Warren found himself in that class of authors who, although beloved of the general readership, were the object of the inexplicable derision of their peers. Indeed, he had felt broken by the reviews. "Shamelessly ill-written"; "excessively banal"; "heavy-handed"; "simplistic and simple-minded"; "farcical"; "almost completely lacking in the higher qualities of imagination and passion". He had memorised them all, every word. Bah! Did these so-called *critical reviewers* never imagine that he had not inflicted upon himself the very worst and most shaming admonition, far beyond anything that they could ever describe?

He frowned at his sodden boots, his thinking lapsing into a perfectly morbid dwelling upon these unkind remarks. It mattered not to him at that moment that others had said in his hearing that he had provided the public with "a capital read", "entertaining and true to human nature"; how his green-grocer's wife had declared that he had "beat Boz hollow". It mattered not a jot to a man who wished so intensely as did Mr. Warren for a *succès d'estime*.

He was now descending into that nest of degeneracy that constitutes the six streets of steaming and vice radiating in every direction from the obelisk of St. George's Fields. There was to be no turning back. Torn and tattered fly-posts jaggedly proclaimed THE END; goggle-eyed women gawped out of their tenement windows; and everywhere untidy groups of wastrels lolled on corners in their dusty corduroy, their skulls close-cropped in the convict fashion.

Philanthropic Society, indeed, he scorned, as he passed the gateway of that well-meaning institution. And what, pray, might Philanthropy hope to achieve here, amongst these wretches for whom life was a sordid procession from gin-palace to prison to workhouse to pauper's grave. These *mauvais sujets* would take Philanthropy by the ankles, turn him upside down, and shake that misguided fellow until the entire contents of his pockets spilled out upon the pavement!

Mr. Warren came upon Poplar-row quite by chance. It was not, by a long chalk, the very worst place running off the north end of Greenwich-street (that is to say, the New Kent-road, as he supposed we must all accustom ourselves to calling it). It was ancient, collapsed; as if it had been overlooked in all of the hurry and haste to throw up buildings in the chaos surrounding the Elephant and Castle.

When she opened the door to him, he quickly surmised that the landlady was one of those who strove, without much success, to occupy the solid middle part of the spectrum of respectability. She put him in mind of one of those little illustrations in the pamphlets of the Total Temperance Association, and he would not have been surprised to have seen a scroll materialise beneath her, bearing the words "the innocent victim of inebriety".

"I am *FIAT JUSTITIA*," he announced.

The little lady lay her head to one side and searched his face earnestly, her bright eyes darting about like fireflies. "D'ye seek the New Moral World?" she inquired in broad Scotch.

She seemed not the least part perturbed as he swept past her and up the stairs. He had gathered that McNaughten lodged in the garret and he made his way there without hesitation. He was extremely put out of countenance to discover the beefy fellow from the police courts standing in the middle of the room, sniffing the musty air.

"Indian hemp," said Mr. Nicholson authoratively. "Cannabis indica." He gestured towards the mantel-shelf where a long clay-pipe was settled upon two tins. "It would seem that the fellow was in the habit of smoking it." Mr. Warren raised his eyebrows. "Hashish," said the Legal Correspondent of *Peeping Tom of London Town*, "relieves oppressiveness."

"Does it indeed…"

"The Persian Sultan al-Hassan ibn-al-Sabbah fed it to his assassins – to keep them in thrall to him."

"Really, you don't say…" Mr. Warren raised one corner of his mouth very slightly. "And have you discovered anything else of interest?" he asked.

The square-rigged fellow scratched his whiskers. He was wearing an extraordinary muffler, the exact colour of mustard, which, though it was wrapped around his thick neck a good many times, reached almost to the floor fore and aft.

"Apparently he was in the habit of cleaning his boots every morning in the kitchen," he said. "He had only the one pair – Blüchers – and very shabby they were too. But then, I ask you, when are Blüchers anything else? Eight and sixpenn'orth of podiatrial discomfort, to my mind. O, and he always paid his rent on time: half a crown, every Friday without fail."

Mr. Warren was casting his novelist's eye about the room, looking for suggestions by which to unlock the inner, hidden portion of McNaughten's character. There was not a great deal on which to go: the wall above the bedstead worn shiny by the shoulders of previous occupants; the ceiling brown with the effusions of fire, candle and pipe.

"Nothing very remarkable in any of this," he observed.

"O, I don't know," said Peeping Tom, "it is part of a novelist's stock-in-trade to find something telling in even the most mundane details."

"You're a novelist?" started Mr. Warren. Peeping Tom half closed his eyes by way of assent and folded his hands over his girth. "I thought you were a legal correspondent."

"A man might have more than one string to his bow, mayn't he?"

"Well, yes, I suppose…."

"I wonder, have you read *Ten Thousand a Year,* by chance?"

Mr. Warren smiled. "As a matter of fact," he said, "I have. Tell me, what was your opinion of it – as a novelist?" If was his habit to solicit critiques of his popular periodical novel whenever the occasion arose.

"O, hardly fair to ask me that," said the fellow without a flicker.

"Why so?"

"Well now, I'm the author, ain't I?"

Mr. Warren was quite astounded, and might have challenged the rascal there and then had his attention not been taken by the landlady. She had positioned herself just inside the door, and was smiling benignly, but at whom, or what it was impossible to determine.

"She knows more than she'll let on," said the beefy fellow with a heavy wink, and he drew a circle in the air close by his temple.

"They own half the world, an' noo they seek tae own heaven an' a'," said the little lady.

Mr. Nicholson laughed. "Ha ha ha! O, they'll get theirs, missus," he said, "I shouldn't worry."

"Ye fouter!" hissed the landlady with such force that it caused Mr. Warren to jump. "You can keep *your* gob tight shut an' a'." Mr. Nicholson took out a large handkerchief and ran it over his astonished features, but the landlady appeared to be addressing not him but someone or something that was occupying the gable over the prisoner's bed. "Ah'll say whit ah like – it's ma hoose! By the way," she said, turning back to the pair of them, "it's half a crown fer informations." She was holding out her hand. Her eyes were grown quite wild.

"Half a crown," reiterated Mr. Nicholson, "and cheap at twice the price – if only one could get at what she really knows and ain't telling." And then he mouthed the word "mad" at Mr. Warren, rolling his eyes in an exaggerated fashion for good measure.

"They stole ma prophecies! They told the Presbytery ah was a liar! Aye, they turned me frae the Lord's Table!" There was an unnerving gleam in her eyes.

"Prophecies, you say," said Mr. Warren. "Prophecies pertaining to *what* – exactly?"

"The End," she said.

Mr. Nicholson made a sardonic croak into the mustard muffler.

"The End," repeated Mr. Warren, slowly.

"Aye," said Mrs. Dutton, smoothing her apron.

Old Peeping Tom nudged Mr. Warren hard in the ribs. "She's an Irvingite," he croaked. "One of those poor unfortunates who lost their reason when Henry Drummond withdrew his support for the ravings down at the old Scotch Church a decade or more ago."

Mr. Warren might have slapped his own forehead in frustration. "Damnable ranters!" he expostulated beneath his breath. He was cursing himself that he had not considered the possibility of religion having a part to play in the affair before now.

"It occurs to me, as I'm sure it does to yourself, Mr. Justitia," Mr. Nicholson was saying, "that it is Secretary Drummond's gravest misfortune to have a religious fanatic for a cousin..."

Mr. Warren was forced to agree. He knew all about the goings-on at the old Scotch Church, though he had never witnessed them with his own eyes: due to certain experiences in his boyhood, he had an ingrained horror of religious revivalism.

"My father was a Methodist preacher," he said to Mr. Nicholson, by way of explanation.

"Was he, by Jove," said Mr. Nicholson, sympathetically.

"Yes, and I passed some of my boyhood years in Wales..."

"O dear, I am sorry to hear that."

"So, you will appreciate that I am accustomed to *unfortunate*, credulous women of a certain age, who seek approbation in religion because none is available to them in any other quarter." Indeed, Mr. Warren had stepped over scores of Mrs. Duttons as they lay prostrate upon the floors of the numerous chapels and countless meeting-houses of his youth. He had beheld them quivering, whimpering; their wild eyes; their hair strewn about tear-streaked faces. He had beheld mouths gaping in ecstasy, loosened stays revealing palpitating bosoms.

"I dare say that must have had quite an effect upon an impressionable boy," observed Mr. Nicholson shrewdly.

Mr. Warren stroked his brow as if to expunge the impressions that yet remained. "O! I have seen some terrible things," he murmured.

"I'll no' share the prophecies for less than half a guinea," said the landlady.

"Half a guinea, eh?" said Mr. Nicholson. "I rather think not. Ninepence ha'penny each – take it or leave it – and we want time and date for that an' all."

"Half a crown."

Mr. Nicholson made a show of grabbing Mr. Warren by the arm and propelling him towards the door.

"Och, bide, bide!" said the landlady. "Jings! A shilling it is, then." She spat on her palm and held it out towards them.

"Time and date," said Mr. Nicholson, "and spare us the puffery."

Her small face twisted into a grimace of pure contempt. "Thursday second a Feb'ry," she said. "Mind youse write that in your newspaper!"

"And make a laughing stock of myself," said Mr. Warren, who had been watching the foregoing with a mixture of bewilderment and curiosity. "I think not!"

"That's three bob youse owe me," she said with a careless shrug.

"Why you raddled old bawd!" exclaimed Mr. Nicholson. "Try and bilk us, would you!"

"O! O! O!" cried Mrs. Dutton. "D'ye hear that! These fine gen'l'men is tryina jip a puir widder woman an' her faitherless wean oot a few bawbies!"

"Your bully ain't here," snarled Mr. Nicholson.

The landlady pulled her threadbare shawl about her tiny shoulders. "I dinnae need nae bully," she said in a low resonant voice. "Youse'll no' be spared. Ah've seen tae that."

There was such a conviction in her mad, gleaming eyes, that for a moment Mr. Warren experienced a quiver of fear. He glanced nervously at Mr. Nicholson, and his own fear was redoubled when he saw that he wore only the merest of smiles, sufficient to conceal an undeniable gravity of demeanour.

Without any more to do, Mr. Warren reached into his waistcoat pocket and retrieved a shilling, which he placed with a deploring emphasis in the landlady's bony grasp. It was only when he stepped back that he saw a short fellow of very rough, menacing appearance standing in the gloom of the landing. He had a slouch hat of thoroughly disreputable appearance pulled down over half of his features, a filthy kerchief about his neck and a satchel slung across one of his shoulders. Something about him gave the strongest impression of hunger – not the everyday hunger of the streets, but a vulpine, dangerous hunger, that was entirely at odds with the stiff round toe-caps of the stout Wellington boots that protruded from beneath the ragged bottoms of his trowsers.

"Well, I'll be jiggered," whispered Mr. Nicholson, ably obscuring a fleeting expression of alarm with his mustard muffler.

"This is Carlo," said Mrs. Dutton with an ill-disguised glee. She pushed her open palm towards the two gentlemen, and Mr. Nicholson, with a nod towards the figure in the shadows, tossed a coin into it.

Carlo grinned, a devilish, savage grin. "Why all the questions?" he asked, in broad Scotch.

"We are interested in arriving at the truth," replied Mr. Warren, "in the matter of the shooting of Mr. Drummond. I take it you know Mc-Naughten? You lodge here together, yes?"

"The truth, is it?" The stunted devil laughed, a hard-edged humourless little laugh. "An' tell me, what might that be?"

"Perhaps you can tell me…"

It was very apparent to Mr. Warren that the Legal Correspondent, having coined the landlady's insistent palm, had abandoned his characteristic loquacity and tucked the beefy jaw safely out of sight beneath the mustard muffler. He came to stand very close by Mr. Warren and, much to that gentleman's irritation, began to hiss in his ear.

"Leave it," he said in a hoarse whisper. "Let it go, do."

But Mr. Warren was not at all put out. "I asked you for the truth just now," he said, addressing Carlo. "If you know it, I pray you speak it."

Carlo considered the hard toes of his Wellington boots. "I should say that it's the system," he said, "that's tae blame fer everything."

"The *system*," said Mr. Warren, "and pray, what *system* might that be?"

A malign glint came into the fellow's jet-black eye. "Aye, 'tis a rotten system, is it no', where a man maun sell his birthright fer a mess o' pottage, an' his soul fer thirty pieces o' siller…"

"I know there are evil, creeping, lying thieves who would rob us all of our liberty and justice if they had the chance."

"Well then," said Carlo, "you and I stand shoulder to shoulder in this battle."

"We do nothing of the sort," said Mr. Warren. "Unless you share my abject horror in learning that a man might feel at liberty to shoot another in the back as he goes about his lawful business."

"O, let it go," said Mr. Nicholson. "I beg you, drop the matter."

"Tell me," said Mr. Warren, superciliously regarding the object before him. "Do you work for a living? Or are you – as you appear to be

– one of the great army of Strong Poor? I wonder, have you ever been a member of a Secret Combination? Tell me, what are your views on the Great Charter?"

"For pity's sake, look at his busted boots," came the urgent whisper from Mr. Nicholson. His mustard muffler was creeping higher and higher up his face all the while.

Mr. Warren frowned. "Indeed, I see you've a good pair of boots on your feet," he said.

In the room behind him Mr. Nicholson groaned.

"Aye," replied the wretch with a very insolent shrug of his shoulder. "Seems we've both named oor price."

"I'll thank you not to presume to know a thing about me... Tell me, is the prisoner a Chartist too?"

Carlo ran a finger around the inside of the red kerchief he had tied about his neck.

"Chartist, eh?" he said. "Is *that* what youse've made o' this? Well noo, whit if ah was tae let youse intae a wee secret? Whit if ah wus tae tell ye that it's no' the Chartists you should be mindin'!"

"Aha! Then it is the Anti-Corn Law League!" exclaimed Mr. Warren. "I knew it – I knew it all along!"

"Cheap Bread! Suffrage!" said Carlo. "That clishmaclaver is a' done with. This land is bought and sold, pal, and we maun all grab whit we can, whiles we can."

"Despicable!" gasped Mr. Warren. He was genuinely shocked to hear such fatalism bandied about outside of a French novel.

"Hallelujah!" interjected the landlady.

"How queer!" interposed Mr. Nicholson. He had been poking about in the prisoner's lodging. "It's occurring to me that there's no books. If the prisoner is such a scholar as you was telling me, missus, then I'd have expected books..."

Mrs. Dutton's large eyes were glittering. "The peelers took 'em away," she said in a low, low voice. "They was *Infidel* books."

"Really?" said Mr. Warren, his attention seized by the revelation.

"Ach, Dan reads all sorts," growled Carlo. He had stepped out of the gloom of the landing and come to stand very close beside the landlady. "Why – it's no' agin the law fer a workin' man tae read, is it?"

"But she said they were Infidel books...."

"Can you no' see?" said Carlo. "She's no' all there." He grabbed the landlady by the throat with such savagery that the satchel on his back flew up and a few of its contents – handbills – fluttered to the floor around them.

"Mathematics," said Mrs. Dutton, quickly. "He was aye fer readin' mathematics. An' *Oliver Twist*." Carlo released his grip.

"Aha!" said Mr. Warren, "I've always suspected that Boz appealed in the main to very low types."

"Second of February," said Mr. Nicholson, who had picked up one of the handbills. There was a grim understanding in his eyes, which were all that could be seen above the muffler. "Queen's Speech Day..."

Horror-struck, Mr. Warren turned his attention at once to the landlady. "Has the prisoner ever spoken disparagingly of Her Majesty?" he demanded of her.

"She cannae tell youse a thing," said Carlo. He had retreated once more to the shadows of the landing and was calmly taking a clay-pipe from his pocket. He struck a Lucifer on the wall, his pock-marked face illuminated for but a moment in the flare.

"The Queen wouldnae let the righteous suffer," said Mrs. Dutton."She's *anointed*. But *they* keep her away frae the People – poor lady. When she went tae Edinburgh they raced her carriage past wi' three dragoons thick on each side..."

"That's enough, ye mad auld witch," said Carlo, drawing on his pipe all the while.

"...Dan saw it wi' his ain eyes..."

Mr. Warren was experiencing a curious mingling of dread and anticipation. "Dan? You mean the prisoner?" he spluttered.

Carlo had emerged from the shadows and was standing in the doorway, his fists clenched into two sinewy rocks.

"He said he hoped Her Majesty's visit would dae a wee bit o' guid fer business in Scotland," said Mrs. Dutton, "Ach, it's verra bad there just noo..."

"I warned ye, ye withered auld hag." Carlo's tightly knotted fist was raised against the landlady. He brought it down upon her two or three times, and she crumpled like a bundle of old rags.

"Leave her be, you black-hearted bully!" cried Mr. Nicholson. "The poor mad thing told us nothing we didn't know already. You damnable spy!"

Carlo laughed. Mrs. Dutton was on the floor, crying piteously. One side of her face looked like a piece of liver had been dropped on it, and the spotless white of her pinafore was dottled with blood.

Mr. Warren had seen and heard enough. He put away his notebook, placed his hat upon his head and tossed another shilling at the landlady. Then he let himself out by the front door.

We need not pursue the thread of his meditations as he retraced his steps along the scarred and bullying streets that led from the awful lodgings back to the death throes of the river. Suffice to say, Mr. Warren found himself utterly oppressed by an unintelligible chain of thoughts of which he had to, nevertheless, make some sense.

Think, think, damn you, he commanded himself. It was becoming apparent to him that Carlo was a police agent. In truth, Mr. Warren owed the insight to the beefy Legal Correspondent of *Peeping Tom*, but it was certain that he would have hit on it himself in due course. The Wellington boots alone spoke volumes – never mind the brutal treatment meted to the landlady. Still, it was a very good thing, he thought, that the Office of Home Affairs appeared to be on the trail of Mr. Drummond's would-be assassin. He wondered how long the plainclothesmen had been planted in the lodgings.

And as for the terrible significance of the date – Thursday the second of February – well, once again Mr.Nicholson had hit upon it all too quickly. Queen's Speech Day! Egad! Mr. Warren felt his throat close. He stood for a moment or two, with the noisome fumes of the brewery and the white lead manufactory freezing in the air around him into sharp shards of bitter stink.

The dismal prospect of Waterloo-bridge was looming up before him. He wanted so badly to leave the stark staring madness of the Surrey-side far behind, and to return as soon as possible to the more tolerable derangements of the West End, but he was feeling clammy, queasy, and altogether unsteady as he urged himself on towards the parapet. He fished in his pocket for a coin with which to pay the toll.

A good many *soi-disant* "serving" girls, scraps of scarlet shoddy thrown about mottled shoulders, were crowding the entrance to the bridge – and this on a Sunday at scarce six o'clock of the afternoon! They dangled candles and keys from their skinny fingers and to his horror, as he approached the turnstile, they began to beseech Mr. Warren with their wheedling insinuations, attempting to latch their gin-and-peppermint eyes on his.

"Hallo, my dear," said a rouge-bleared vision in broken feathers, "are you good-natured?"

Mr. Warren buried his chin in his muffler and quickened his pace.

"Lend us a ha'penny to cross the bridge," the harpy of the streets persisted, trying to slip her arm through his, "there's a good sir."

He fumblingly paid his toll and all but ran onto the bridge, the trollop condemning his sober-suited back to an eternal slow-roasting all the while. Within a few minutes more of brisk walking he was approaching the halfway point of the bridge.

Think. Think, damn you! he willed himself.

It came to him just as the Embankment hoved in to view: 39 and 40 George 3, c.94 1800 – *An Act for the Safe Custody of Insane Persons Charged with Offenses*. The Act had been mooted in several places during the trials of Francis and Bean: a wretched piece of law that required of anyone who had assailed a notable person to show but the slightest symptoms of *derangement* if they wished to be spared the gallows. It was the self-same bit of nonsense that had worked so well for that vile wretch Oxford, who had languished in Bethlem at the public expense for the past two years, despite having raised a pistol against Her Majesty the Queen.

Of course! It was quite obvious to him now... The little pantomime he had just witnessed at Poplar-row had a method to it: the carefully laid evidence of a religious delusion – sufficient to make of McNaughten a martyr in the eyes of the deluded masses – the Scotch, the Welsh, the Irish, and any others susceptible to religious primitivism (as a good many of the lower orders were found to be, especially in the present difficulties)!

Unsettling gurglings emanated from the black deeps a few feet beneath him; a desperate floundering, a struggling to shore. And hearing it, Mr. Warren walked even faster, scurrying towards the Strand. As he prepared to set foot upon the north bank, he could sense the slow return of his reason. He would need to proceed cautiously in the assiduous steps of the Home Office and their agents – for there were doubtless many twists in the plot that were not apparent to him, and he did not wish to hand useful arguments to Cockie and the Whigs on a plate. But he was far more concerned that an acquittal for McNaughten – on the grounds which he had just outlined to himself – would throw open the doors of Bethlem to every criminal in the land.

And who, he thought, would pay for their upkeep?

He may not have hit upon the real, the true *political* motive, he had not uncovered any evidences impugning the Anti-Corn Law League, or indeed anything whatever that might best serve his Party's interests in the way that Mr. Drummond had suggested to him; but perhaps he could still make of this a great cause. As he turned the corner on to Exeter-street, he resolved to do his damnedest to prevent the public from being duped into believing that the prisoner was a so-called "innocent maniac". Deep in thought, he sidled past the knots of rough types on the pavement edge and slipped into the warm smoke-haze of the chophouse. He took a good lungful of the comforting steam of fried liver and bacon and ordered a glass of piping hot punch. Then he found a quiet corner and began without hesitation to compose.

"The prisoner," he began, in a phrase which he would be gratified to see repeated precisely word for word in the next morning's *Times*, "may well be practising a great deception on the public in assuming the mannerisms, speech and delusions of a madman..."

A SPORTING CLUB, PICCADILLY,
LATER THAT EVENING

In which Mr. Cockburn learns a great deal about the game of billiards.

The Chief Whipper-in had been most specific in directing Mr. Cockburn *against* making contact with Mr. James Oswald, the Liberal Member for Glasgow, in respect of the matter of Mr. Drummond's shooting; but he had applied no such proscription to that gentleman's near-neighbour, Alexander Johnston, the Liberal Member for Kilmarnock, Dumbarton, Renfrew, Rutherglen, Port Glasgow, &c., District of Burghs. Cockie, therefore, finding himself awake at four, five and six of the morning, spent but a little of one of those fitful hours in composing a letter inviting the gentleman – whom he knew to be in town – to a game of billiards at one of those obscure clubs at the back of Pall Mall, and instructed his valet to deliver it at once.

He was immensely gratified to discover an acceptance by return of post, sitting upon his breakfast tray, when Hatchett brought it to him some hours later.

Sandy had been labouring under a dejection of spirit, far more oppressive than the comparatively insipid bouts of *ennui* that those of a Romantic disposition must periodically endure. Having slept badly (at one stage awaking with the image of himself hanged before a great crowd that bayed *shame* and disgrace and pelted him with filth and pebbles), he had lain in bed until a quite late hour, pulling the distempered bed-sheets about him as the relentless church bells tolled beyond his bedroom window. The destruction of Polly's letter had failed to exorcise the old ghosts; indeed, the action had only succeeded in making him more regretful than ever that the past could not be revisited and undone. He was unable to disabuse himself of the understanding that this would be another day upon which he would achieve nothing and nothing would be changed – save that he would grow older, sadder, more disgusted with himself, &c., &c., – and he succeeded in that state until shortly before mid-day, when his man Hatchett finally opened the curtains on one of those gray, bleak London Sundays that seemed never to end, and set down the newspapers together with the tray bearing some coffee, two lightly boiled eggs, and the note from Mr. Johnston.

"There's a great deal in the *Observer* about Mr. Drummond's shooting," Hatchett informed him. "Apparently a Recruiting Sergeant had spied McNaughten hanging about outside the Treasury a short while before, and informed a police officer of the same."

"Really?"

[243]

"And a nephew of Mr. Drummond's had sight of his uncle's wound at the counting-house moments after the incident and took it to be a burn. Apparently the gent's coat-tails caught fire. Curious affair, ain't it, sir?"

"*Most* curious."

Sandy, whose mind naturally inclined towards conspiracy, could salvage nothing of any great surprise, merit or interest from the newspapers. He tossed the *Observer* aside and let his eyes pass over the handwritten cover of the note from Mr. Johnston.

"Will you be taking your constitutional today?" inquired Hatchett, returning for the tray a short while after. "I've cleaned your top-boots."

"I can't face the park, Hatchett."

"As you wish, sir. It's certainly very dreary. Will you be dining here or at your club, sir? I have a little chicken which I could fricassee…"

"It appears that I will be out this evening," said Mr. Cockburn, indicating the tidings of the Liberal Member for Kilmarnock, Dumbarton, Renfrew, Rutherglen, Port Glasgow, &c., District of Burghs.

Within another hour he had left the shelter of his bed. By three o' clock he was bathed, though not shaved and still in his dressing gown, and sitting at the pianoforte. He had decided to postpone mastery of Herr Mendelssohn's *Variations sérieuses* for the time being; but, still inclining towards the lacrimoso, was attempting something suitably plaintive.

Sandy's entire future now depended upon the outcome of the miserable business of Mr. Drummond's shooting, and yet he had not one iota of faith in his own ability to succeed, and no idea where to commence. What was more, it was looking very doubtful whether he would secure release from the onerous burden in time to retreat to High Beech to join the Easter Monday Cockney Hunt in Epping Forest – even supposing that his uncle the Rear-Admiral had made a full recovery by then (there was nothing to suppose he would have done).

Over and above all of these dispiriting influences, the discordant strummings of his unstrung heart resounded loud and clear. Cockie shut the lid of the pianoforte and sighed.

"Will you take a little soup, sir?" asked Hatchett. The dear fellow placed a consoling hand upon his master's shoulder. And so the afternoon passed.

"I've laid out the tail-coat with the dark blue lapels," said Hatchett, when the time came for him to dress.

"And the peacock-blue waistcoat and stock," murmured Sandy, rousing himself for the city.

He found Mr. Johnston in the Billiards Room, a limber, ruddy fellow – somehow not quite right for the game, though it was soon plain enough that he knew how to place a ball into a pocket, which in essence was all that was required. Indeed, the Liberal Member for Kilmarnock &c., successfully strung for the lead, and he made a good break too. Cockie always liked to suppose that he could tell the strength of a man's game and, up to a certain point, his character as soon as play commenced. Mr. Johnston wasted no time in considering the geometrics of the table, as Sandy liked to do, in walking around it contemplatively as if musing upon the eternal problems of mankind. His was a more robust, practical application of skill and sense. It was a game that to Sandy's mind was somewhat monotonous, being far too reliant upon mastery of the spot-stroke in producing a predictable series of winning hazards; with nothing of the delicacy to which he aspired in his own game; nothing of *panache* or verve. Indeed, there was something perfunctory about the Member altogether; something of the type that Sandy did not in general care for.

"Peel will be in a awfu' *funk*," he informed Sandy, the aromatic zephyr of his Havana curling protectively about his head as he winked at the object ball. "As it was the damned fool spent most o' the last session lookin' up to the gallery to see if he were about to be shot. Ha!" The white clicked efficiently against Sandy's cue ball and then red, which screwed obligingly into one of the corner pockets. Mr. Johnston proceeded to make a series of similar, mild, uncontroversial disparagements of the Prime Minister – without ever once giving the impression that he either liked or disliked the fellow – whilst playing off half a dozen shots with the same air of artless, if assured indifference.

On his final play he ran his ball off the table into one of the side pockets, making a little play of frustration, before yielding.

"So be it," he said philosophically.

Cockie knew full well, and divined that the Member doubtless knew that he knew, that the fellow had deliberately forfeited. Perhaps he was bored, Cockie mused, as he considered his shot, eyeing the cushions.

"Och, ye'll get no play off o' them, Mr. Cockburn," observed Mr. Johnston with a wry puff of cigar smoke. "The water in the warming cups hasna been changed all day. The rubber will be frozen solid."

Sandy chalked his cue with visible irritation. "It is not," he said, "in my nature to play a safe game."

Mr. Johnston watched disinterestedly as Sandy's ball bumped into the rubber and rolled dazedly into the opposite hazard without touching anything else on the table. "Och, I say, that's awful bad luck, Mr. Cockburn," he said.

Cockie took a little brandy and watched the Member make his next two shots with guileless precision, one directly after the other. "How are things north of the border?" he asked.

"Very bad," replied the gentleman. "Very bad indeed. A good many are calling for a Nnew Poor Law."

Click. Winning hazard on the white.

"And here a good many are calling for the New Poor Law to be abolished," said Sandy.

Mr. Johnston paused to scrape the chalk across the large leathery tip of his cue. "Well now, a Poor-law is only a temporary measure at best, is it not? But people canna be left to die, Mr. Cockburn, all the same. And until and unless something better comes along, it is my opinion that Scotland must have a Poor Law. There are scenes of such woe and destitution everywhere, sir. Small wonder so many prefer to take their chances in America or Canada – or even here in London."

"Poor devils," said Sandy, "I dare say there must be a good many Scots who would like to see Peel dead."

Mr. Johnston drew shrewdly on his cigar.

"Aye," he said in a low murmur directed at the table.

"And tell me, do the Tories threaten Whig interests much these days in Glasgow?" asked Sandy. "I am familiar with the Tory agent. His name crops up a good deal in the Election Committees. He has made an art of complaining against Whig registrants to the Registration Courts."

Mr. Johnston leaned against the table to make his next shot, his eyes half-closed as if taking aim at something with an invisible gun. "A very clever fellow, Mr. Cockburn; why, if he'd been minded to go to the Metropolitan instead of the Glasgow bar, I dinna doubt he'd be Queen's Counsel too by now. A cleverer man by far, dare I say it, than our agent." He winced against the cigar smoke.

"Yet Glasgow, so it would seem, is naturally inclined to vote Whig rather than Tory..."

Mr. Johnston smiled. "Before '32 five thousand men in the whole of Scotland had the vote – today twice that number vote in Glasgow alone – an' ye'd be hard-pressed to find a Tory amang 'em, right enough: though it is by no means the case that they may all be depended upon to vote Liberal." The Member made his play amidst robust clouds of blue-gray smoke. He missed the red, sending his own ball once again directly into the pocket. "Now, how did I miss that?" he said bemusedly, giving way to his opponent.

Sandy splayed his left hand in a delicate bridge and nuzzled his ball with the point of his cue, coaxing it forward to glide with exquisite grace into the red. Both balls travelled effortlessly across the table before dropping obligingly into their pockets.

"Good shot, Mr. Cockburn," said his opponent with approval, drawing shrewdly on his cigar all the while.

Sandy frowned at the table. "The fellow who, it is alleged, shot Mr. Drummond on Friday – do we know how he voted?" he said.

Mr. Johnston licked cogitatively a shred of dark tobacco that was lying on his bottom lip. "That is a very good question, Mr. Cockburn. And I am sure that such a skilled counsel would not be putting it unless he had already come to some expectation or other."

"It had occurred to me," said Cockie, "that if a spot of over-zealous Tory press-ganging had inclined the prisoner towards the murderous – as he seemed to imply in his statement to the magistrate – then why did he not target the Tory candidate for the Glasgow burghs, or, come to that, the Tory agent? Mr. Drummond, as far as I know, had nothing whatever to do with the Glasgow election – so why shoot him? I tell you, Mr. Johnston, sir, I have puzzled over it. I cannot make a case out of political harassment, but as one who has spent more hours than I care to think steeped in the corruption of the electoral system, I would have *relished* the opportunity to make of it grounds for attempted murder."

The Member was smiling as implacably as a temple Buddha through wispy strands of holy smoke. "I can tell you," he said, "that there is no record of McNaughten registering for the vote."

"I see. You are doubtless aware that a good many *Chartists* chose to boycott the last election..." Sandy led.

"O aye. They had a popular candidate in Glasgow – a man called Abram Duncan," said the Member. "It was a great surprise – nay relief – to Mr. Oswald when the fellow stood down. A career in politics can be an expensive business, as you well know – at least it seems it was beyond the reach of Mr. Duncan. But I can assure you, sir, that none of *that* has a thing to do with the prisoner." The Liberal Member for Kilmarnock, &c., struck a fusee on the slate underside of the table and concentrated all of his efforts upon re-lighting his cigar as if it were the only thing in the world that mattered.

"How can you be so sure?"

"Because McNaughten himself said as much to Mr. Oswald."

"He went to see Oswald?"

"Of course. Mr. Oswald is his Member of Parliament."

"Why did he go to Oswald?"

"I can tell you that he never mentioned Chartism. He complained of persecution by emissaries of the Tories whom he had offended, as he put it, by 'interfering in politics'."

"And what did Mr. Oswald make of these accusations?"

The Member drew on his cigar. "He thought him mad to say such things."

"Do Members generally think it mad when a ten-pound householder complains of being harassed by the agents of a party for which he did not vote?" Sandy's ball gently kissed the red.

"It appears so in this instance."

"In that case, Mr. Oswald must have a good many lunatics numbered in his poll books; and so must you, sir, come to that."

"It appears that the boy is the natural son of a staunch Conservative who is a close associate of the Tory agent and the Lord Provost. Perhaps one or other of them may be prevailed upon to speak to you, in the family's interest. You might want to make contact with the pa."

"Natural sons are not always afforded the same courtesies as legitimate ones," observed Cockie quietly.

"That is very true."

Cockie took his eye off the table and reached for a brandy from a passing tray. "I must say," he said, "I find it nothing short of an outrage that Mr. Oswald discounted the fellow – when in the past few months hundreds of decent working men, just like McNaughten, have been rounded up and presented to the nation as cold-blooded traitors. Peel has urged the Home Secretary time and again to go to the edges of the law in putting down the Radical press; policemen are spending their days in searching book sellers for seditious pamphlets, and raiding the socialist institutions – even those of the most innocuous colour. I put it to you, that in such a climate McNaughten had every reason to be in terror of his own life and liberty, did he not? And I should say that the same thought must have occurred to Mr. Oswald."

The Member emitted a long, steady stream of smoke. "The Lord Provost is Sir James Campbell," he said. "He was the Tory candidate for the Glasgow seat in the last election."

"Thank you. I am well aware who the gentleman is," said Sandy.

"He attends the same lodge as Mr. McNaughten senior."

Sandy swirled the brandy around the bottom of the glass and breathed in the aroma, raising a querulous eyebrow as he did so. "A spy system is nothing new in Glasgow," he said. He turned his cue gently in his fingers, preparing to spot the red. "When McNaughten visited Mr. Oswald, did he appear distracted, deranged – babbling – incoherent?"

"In truth I cannot say that he did."

"Yet he left the impression of madness...?"

"He appeared to believe what he said. It was his firm conviction. Mr. Oswald reasoned with him, of course; told him nobody was interested in persecuting him and that if he received any nuisances he ought to go to the sheriff and make a complaint. I suppose he said it to get rid of him."

Sandy sent the red ball across the table. "You see my problem," he said. "I need Mr. Oswald to come to court and say this on his own account."

"That he will never do."

"I cannot depend upon the Scottish Tories attesting to McNaughten's state of mind. You must see that."

"What if I were to say that the prisoner wrote to *me*, begging me to intervene on his behalf? What if I were to suggest that the letter was very disordered and full of alarming matters?"

"Alarming matters?"

"If they had been true, that is – that the letter left me in no doubt that the laddie was beset by some species of insanity."

The Member inspected the glowing tip of his cigar.

"And what became of the letter?" asked Cockie.

"I'm afraid I destroyed it, thinking it of no consequence."

"But you recollect the contents?"

"It was – no – I cannot say that I do. I only read it through the once and then discarded it, thinking it a curious thing, not worth the reading of again."

Sandy removed the red ball from the pocket, and cupped it gently, passing it from one hand to the other. "Hum..."

"What if I were to supply you with my reply?" The gentleman reached inside his coat and retrieved a piece of paper from his waistcoat pocket. Cockie took it, unfolded it, read it.

REFORM CLUB
May 5th, 1842

SIR,

I RECEIVED your letter of the 3rd of May, and am sorry I can do nothing for you. I fear you are labouring under an aberration of mind, and I think you have no reason to entertain such fears.

I am, &c.,

ALEXANDER JOHNSTON

To: Mr. D. McNaughten,
90 Clyde Street, Anderton's frontland, top flat

"It's a faithful copy from my own files," said the Member. "Fairly conclusive, I should say."

"I see that you have dated it May the fifth last year."

"That is the date Mr. Oswald supplied to me this morning. It is the date on which the prisoner made contact with him."

"It happens also to be the same day upon which the People's Charter was thrown out of Parliament."

"Really?" said the Member. "A curious coincidence…"

Mr. Johnson was standing at the opposite end of the table, a little outside of the shaft from the gas-light chandelier. He was smoking his cigar in his amiable manner and smiling down on Cockie as if he were some kind of protégé who had just learned a hard but essential lesson.

"My reputation," he said, carelessly striking the ash from his cigar with his little finger, "is neither here nor there, Mr. Cockburn. You might say I have come forward because I read the newspapers and canna stand by idly and watch a poor mad boy be trundled through the town, knowing what I know of his disposition. Och, even if he were the most notorious agitator since Arthur Thistlewood, I should say there's little or nothing to be gained from his persecution – save that his importance in certain quarters will swell beyond all proportion – perhaps even to the extent, dare I say, of making a martyr of him. Mr. Cockburn, it is my sincerest belief that this laddie is nought but a feeble-minded boy who ought not to be made a scapegoat just so's Peel can rebound attention from his own misdeeds. That is my belief, sir, and that is why I have come forward."

Sandy deftly placed the red ball on the pyramid and prepared to play on. "You have no objection to the – er – correspondence being produced in court?" he asked, squinting out his shot, "or to being deposed?"

"None whatever."

"And you really do believe that McNaughten's best interests," said Sandy following through, "lie in his being found mad?"

The Liberal Member for Kilmarnock, &c., appeared to wink at his cigar.

Sandy drew back his cue.

"Well played, Mr. Cockburn," said the Member, watching the progress of the balls across the table. "I should say that is the winning shot – at least by my reckoning."

"The winning shot," said Sandy leaning on his cue as he took another brandy, "will be to preserve my client from the hulks. Might we drink on *that*, Mr. Johnston?"

The Member raised a glass of whisky to eye level.

"*Slainte mhath*, Mr. Cockburn," he said, "*slainte mhath*."

TOTHILL-FIELDS HOUSE OF CORRECTION,
AT ABOUT THE SAME TIME

Wherein the prisoner is examined for proofs of a weakened mental state, whether morally or physically derived.

"I am Mr. Lavies," said the taller and sterner of the two gentlemen, "I am the prison doctor. And this is Mr. Amyot. He is the Chairman of the Visiting Magistrates. I am going to examine you and ask of you several questions, which you are to answer as truthfully as you can, the object being to determine the state of your mind. Do you understand?"

The prisoner sitting on the only chair in the cell was a study in nonchalance: his arms folded across his chest; his legs stretched out in front of him, loosely crossed at the ankles. His lids fell over his eyes, slowly, by way of assent; there was a slight smile playing about his thin lips.

"Have you ever suffered from any nervous diseases, cramps, palpitations or palsy?" Mr. Lavies asked, peering hard at the subject.

The prisoner focused his own gaze upon the flagstones. "My hands sometimes shake," he said, "my head often aches, and since the previous evening especially, I've been much troubled by a palpitation of the heart. I've had a consumption upon me for some time, I believe. Perhaps for five years."

The surgeon frowned, and drew out a large pocket watch from his waistcoat. "Give me your hand," he commanded; seizing hold of the wrist offered him, he counted the pulse beats whilst looking at his pocket watch. The prisoner contemplated the coarse, black hairs which extended all the way down the powerful ridges of the surgeon's arm.

"The pulse does seem perhaps a little faster than is normal," Mr. Lavies said.

Mr. Amyot nodded sagely. "That is hardly surprising," he said, "after the exertions of the past few days…"

The surgeon turned away briskly, directing his attentions to the cell door. "Any inflammation of the testicles – *involuntary emissions – erections*?"

The Chairman of the Visiting Magistrates coughed.

"I have nae venereal disease, sir," the prisoner answered. "I have long since abjured the touch of woman – aye, and man too, come tae that – ah never was one to consort wi' whores."

Mr. Lavies kept his back towards the fellow. "And what of that *loathsome habit* – you know of which I speak?"

"I believe so, sir."

"Are you troubled much by those filthy urges that can fill a body with disease, and leave a mind in ruins?"

"No more than is any man," he told the surgeon's back.

"Do you have any ulcerous sores upon your head, your breast, back, thighs; any fistulas, or cancers; any discharges of foetid, loathsome pus?"

"I do not."

"You know of what I am talking?"

"I believe so."

"You understand the question?"

"Yes, sir."

The surgeon spun round of a sudden. "Does the need of which I speak rule over you like a tyrant," he thrust his face in very close to the prisoner's, "or a *demon of darkness*?"

The prisoner slowly raised his eyes to meet the doctor's own. "I dinnae frig myself any more than is normal, if that's what you're askin', sir," he said, quite plain.

The surgeon's eyebrows shot up in astonishment.

"Ahem. I wonder – might we leave it there?" said the Chairman of the Visiting Magistrates, shifting nervously. "That is a private matter, is it not?"

But the prisoner was not in the least discomfited. "My Organ of Amativeness," he said, "is of quite small size and dimension; you may inspect it if you wish."

"O, surely that will not be necessary," implored the Chairman of the Visiting Magistrates, looking away.

The prisoner offered the top of his head to their scrutiny. The surgeon's mouth compressed: a thin, grimly censorious line. "You are aware, are you," he said, "that self-pollution not unfrequently terminates in death?"

"No, I never heard that said before, sir," replied the prisoner. "That is quite a sobering thought. I thank you kindly for the information and shall bear it in mind."

"The young man seems perfectly sensible, Mr. Lavies," beseeched the Chairman of the Visiting Magistrates. "Might we not conclude the physical examination there – I have some questions of my own pertaining to conditions here…"

Mr. Lavies disregarded him. He was winding his pocket watch absently. "Have you ever been afflicted by *melancholy*?" he asked the prisoner. "You understand the question?"

"O aye, I'm often in that condition, sir. Well, in truth, which of us is not? There is cause enough in this world, or so I should say. I do not hold it to be a necessarily bad case."

The doctor edged towards him, dangling the watch between his thumb and forefinger. The prisoner was careful to keep his eyes fixed upon the ceiling all the while.

"How so?" Mr. Lavies asked.

"I consider the condition tae be a function o' the human soul," the prisoner answered. "Does not Agrippa in *De occulta philosophia* teach that the *humour melancholicus*, when it is combined with the heat of Saturn, produces a *furor* which leads tae wisdom? And Socrates wrote that our greatest blessings cam tae us by way of madness – provided that the madness is gi'en to us by the gods."

The surgeon had a look of pure astonishment upon him.

"Indeed, it is commonly observed that many men who have earned distinction in most branches of knowledge have been inclined tae melancholy. And findin' myself in such august company, I dinnae hold it to be too great a trial."

"That is most interesting," said the doctor, twirling the watch in his thick fingers.

The prisoner folded his hands upon his lap and lowered his eyes. "It is my contention that there is a fluid which forms an arc around us," he began, "and that it is capable of bein' directed. I believe it to be similar to the energy rays emanatin' from the sun. The power of the *humour melancholicus* is so great that it may affect this fluid – perhaps even attractin' tae itself other forces, such as the human will. When the soul is especially inflamed, I believe that higher powers may control it, those frae whom we may learn the divine secrets of the universe."

Mr. Lavies was surveying him with a look of pure alarm. "I think we have seen enough," he murmured.

"And, tell me," inquired the Chairman of the Visiting Magistrates, "do you consider yourself to be in receipt of the divine secrets of the universe?"

The prisoner yawned carelessly. "I might be."

"You seem very well informed upon philosophy," the Chairman of the Visiting Magistrates continued. "Might you be, in a similar way, interested in politics, I wonder?"

The prisoner smiled a strange half-smile, but said nothing more on the subject.

The doctor was standing by the door dangling his pocket watch. He seemed quite mesmerised by it.

"Do I take that to mean that you have an interest, or that you have no interest," gently persisted Mr. Amyot.

The prisoner sighed. "So every carpenter that laboureth night and day," he said at last, "the smith too, and the potter sittin' at his wheel, all these trust to their hands, and every one is wise in his work. Wi'out these a city cannot be inhabited: yet they shall not dwell where they will, nor go up and down. They shall not be sought for in public counsel: nor sit high in the congregation: they shall not sit on the judge's seat, nor understand the sentence o' the judgement..." He broke off here, turning to look the Chairman of the Visiting Magistrates very directly in the face. "But they will maintain the state of the world." Then he paused effectively, waiting a few well-timed moments before lowering his eyes once more to contemplate the hands folded neatly in his lap. If he had peeped out from underneath his pale lashes, he would have caught the two gentlemen exchanging meaningful looks.

"What is your diagnosis?" he asked.

"How so?" replied the surgeon.

"Am I right in my senses or no'?"

The surgeon did not give an answer. He shook his head and called for the guard.

The Chairman of the Visiting Magistrates smiled kindly. "That is not for you to know, prisoner," he said.

When he was satisfied that their footsteps and conversation had faded down the passageway – and only then – the prisoner let his head loll back against the wall, and ended the day as he had begun it: in weeping.

Early edition

THE SHOOTING OF MR. DRUMMOND

FURTHER PARTICULARS RELATING TO McNAUGHTEN

The prisoner may well be practising a great deception on the public in assuming the mannerisms, speech and delusions of a madman; for the impression gleaned by this correspondent from McNaughten's landlady, Mrs. Eliza Dutton, a respectable and deeply religious widow lady by all accounts, is of a man whose previous behaviour and conduct, coupled to his general appearance, *entirely negatived such a supposition.*

Despite giving the firmest impression of direst poverty, the prisoner is not at all known as an applicant for relief, or otherwise, in any public department, and when he was arrested was found to be in possession of a large quantity of money.

The landlady further supplied evidences that the prisoner was a man of some erudition, studies pursued in his native city and doubtless at an institution commensurate with his class. It will be recollected that reports of the League Convention held last year shewed that payments were made to those termed "lecturers", sometimes in excess of £250 at a time.

It has been confirmed that Police removed a quantity of shot and gunpowder from the prisoner's room on Friday evening.

There is some indication that he visited his native Scotland at the time of Her Majesty's visit there last year, and was indeed present during the historic tour of the City of Edinburgh. It would appear that his being in Scotland at that time strengthened the possibility of his having transacted business there, for there can be little doubt of the genuineness of the check or receipt of the Glasgow Bank for £750. The visit, the possession of so large a sum, and the singular narration of Mrs. Dutton relative to his mode of life and habits, attach a degree of mystery to the motive which influenced the prisoner to the commission of his deadly crime, to the solution of which, at present, no clew has been obtained.

It ought further to be noted that Mr. Drummond, previously to this murderous attack upon him, reported to a friend having received letters of a threatening nature.

The prisoner is presently awaiting trial at Tothill Fields House of Correction, where he is incarcerated in the very cell occupied by Courvoisier at the time of his apprehension for the murder of his master, Lord William Russell.

DOWN WITH THE RIVER,
EARLY MORNING

In which Inspector Hughes makes a journey by boat, and discovers some more particulars of the prisoner McNaughten and his associates.

The middle part of the morning found the Inspector with his bony knees tucked up somewhere beneath his chin clutching the side of a four-oared Thames Police galley bound for Woolwich, and shrouded in river-gloom. And ah, but it was cold: as bitter a cold as he could ever remember, slashing his face raw, causing his nose and eyes to water. At least in the depth of winter you don't get the awful stink like you do in the heat, he told himself. Just be thankful for that.

Inspector Hughes didn't ever care to find himself in a strange part of the metropolis, so to be pitched and tossed upon this inhuman element, far from the certainties of muck-strewn pavings and dim alleys was a source of the gravest concern to him. He tried not to think of the journey back, not letting his mind go beyond his arrival at the headquarters of "R" Division (Greenwich), where he was to encounter a Scotch Chartist awaiting transportation on the hulks, whom (upon receipt of the Inspector's own route description paper) Inspector Harvey ("R" Division) had immediately identified as one in his charge – a convicted rabble-rouser who was "in possession of certain informations pertaining to Scotch Chartists still at large…" All of which was good; very good.

And, what was better still, the fellow's name was *Gordon*.

O, please let it come to something, the Inspector implored the thick river-mucculence, rheumatism seeping in at his boots. He hoped that he would not have reason to regret his trip. The much-anticipated communications from the Detective Sergeant who had been despatched to Glasgow on Friday night were expected to arrive at Euston railroad at one o'clock that afternoon, and he was keen to have sight of them; but he dared not entrust the task to which he was currently joined to another living soul. He needed to see and hear certain things with his own eyes and ears – only then did he feel he might move forward with any surety. It was unfortunate that that scranning cove, Inspector Tierney, had been so quick to volunteer for the collection from the Birmingham Railway Mail of the Detective Sergeant's despatches. Inspector Hughes feared what fancies would be spun from all of his redoubtable detectivings once the Active Duty got to work on 'em.

Following his encounters with Miss Drummond's footman and the Scotch plainclothesman the previous day, Inspector Hughes had returned to the station-house to discover a slew of communications from gentlemen rate-payers, Select Vestry-men, and all the rest of respectable society, demanding of Scotland-yard what the *deuce* was being done to protect decent citizens against being shot in the back by maniacs as they went about their daily business. And prime amongst 'em was a complaint from Mr. George Drummond, partner in the counting-house and elder brother to the victim, concerning reports in the newspapers that his son, Mr. Harvey Drummond, having seen the wound on his uncle's rump, had declared that to his mind it weren't caused by no gunshot. Now, assuredly, the only way the newspapers could have known that was either because Mr. Harvey Drummond had told them himself – which did not on the face of it seem at all likely – or because the constable charged with taking down the nephew's deposition had, in exchange for a half a crown, divulged all to an inky inquisitor. The constable in question had been sought out; accused; denied all; had a week's pay stopped.

The Drummond complaint was most vexatious, but it was nothing compared to the number of complaints received pertaining to an account given in the *Observer* of the testimony of a certain Recruiting Sergeant of the 10th Huzzars. Inspector Hughes hadn't been in the least bit entertained to discover that the idle boaster was now claiming to have spied McNaughten not at Charing-cross, as he had told the Inspector, but on the steps that lead to the Privy Council. But what had attracted the hue and cry was the suggestion that the Recruiting Sergeant had alerted a police constable to his concerns only a few hours before Mr. Drummond had been shot at. The respectable parts of society were demanding an explanation as to why these concerns had not been acted upon immediately in the public interest, and so the Superintendent had sent the Inspector straightway from the station-house to the Dove and Mitre public house to confront the braided and epauletted braggart.

The indefinite postponement of the mending of the banisters was a small charge in the face of such an extravagant hobbling of the truth and impugning of the reputation of the Metropolitan Police Force.

"None of my affair," the Recruiting Sergeant had said with a careless wave of his hand. "I told the policeman to keep a close eye on him, didn't I? It's none of my affair if a constable says it's nothing to do with him. You want to go and ask *him* about that."

Inspector Hughes intimated how he should very much like to. "Suppose," he said, "you tell me his name."

The Recruiting Sergeant lolled against the bar, latching his bootheel onto the brass floor rail. "How much is the information worth," he said, cool as you like, blowing the steam off his grog.

Inspector Hughes licked the end of his stub of pencil. "How about a night in the cells for hindering police investigations," he said.

"Smith," the Recruiting Sergeant said.

"Smith?"

"That's it."

"There ain't no Police Constable Smith in 'A' Division." The Recruiting Sergeant shrugged dismissively, giving all of his attention to the grog. "Did you have sight of his badge number?"

"Badge number? Well, now, bless you, he didn't have one, did he?"

"Didn't have one?"

"No. He was in plainclothes see."

"Plainclothes, was he…"

"That's right."

Inspector Hughes felt a distinct prickling. "I see," he said, "so what's he look like, then, this *plainclothesman*?"

"Short, dark. He wears a red neckerchief and a very dirty old slouch hat. It's a good disguise, I'll give him that. Though mind you, their Wellington boots always give those fellows away. You shall find him hanging about the King Charles statue most days…"

"I see. Know him well, do you?"

"O, bless you! I won't have a thing to do with him in the ordinary run of things. He drives a hard bargain, see."

"Does he now…"

"Now, look you, I know better than any man alive how it can take a good few Old Toms to bring a fellow to his senses and make him see how badly he wants to go a-sojering – but ten bob is a deal of rag, see, and I be the one carrying all the risk in that bargain."

"Old Toms? Ten bob?"

"O, bless you, he's a bringer, isn't he?"

"Is he…?"

"Yes, yes – and he's a good eye on him an' all. Why, I should say that he can spot a likely recruit almost as well as I can meself." The Recruiting Sergeant nodded in the general direction of the bar, where a good many of his brethren were to be found revivifying 'emselves. "See, too many hereabouts are content to let such as him do all their work for 'em, and never mind sharing the profits; but not me. I haven't a lazy bone in my body, and I don't care to share my earnings with no-one." He threw his gin down the back of his neck.

"Hold on tight," the boatman nearest to the Inspector was crying. "The current runs very strong just here, and 'tis time to bring us in closer to the shore."

A dismal clunking and grinding was emanating from the very depths of the chopping waters, as the Inspector gazed into the inexorable gray. It was all just water to him. He eyed with a desolating envy the boatman's thick whiskers curled so luxuriously about his chin and ears. So

[261]

comfortable-seeming! But the Commissioners would never suffer 'em – not for a moment. A bitter wind was whipping raw his own close-shaven face. He sunk into the upturned collar of his great-coat and then, not a minute too soon, the gray began slowly to dissipate, and indistinct shapes to take form: buildings, cranes, ships, and soon he could make out the Arsenal pier just a little way ahead of them, pricked out of the gloom by little red lamps strung in a row all along it, and beyond, scattered all about the water's edge, great teetering piles of rotten timber, rusting cartwheels, and pyramids of cannon. They sent into the air a bitter ferrousness, forbidding, forlorn. In another moment the vessel was bobbing precariously at the foot of a set of steps, and he was being helped to shore, clambering up into the murkiness, into a smarting vapour of turpentine and burning.

Inspector Harvey was waiting for him, grim-lipped, his stern composure softened but a little in the steam of his own breath, and together they walked the short distance from the pier to the gatehouse, passing a line of women selling radishes from huge baskets. At the gatehouse Inspector Hughes gave his name and rank to a police guard, and then they returned to the pier and stood watching the progress of a gig pulled through the thick fog by four convicts under the direction of an officer who stood proud at the stern.

On the waters behind them he could just make out the sombre forms of the hulks themselves, jagged lines of washing hanging from the broken masts, giving to them gallant old warships a familiarly human, careworn appearance.

"Are conditions on board as bad as they say?" he asked Inspector Harvey as they stood side by side at the water's edge.

"O, 'tis hard, very hard labour these fellows must endure," came the reply, "and they are soon made hard by it, else they do not last long."

"I'd heard more die as a result of them conditions than do at the hands of Jack Ketch."

"I dare say that is so."

Inspector Hughes turned down the corners of his mouth. "It's a great pity that more can't be done to prevent diseases on the hulks," he said, "the more so when you consider how easily a miasma might drift along the river into the metropolis."

Inspector Harvey gravely inclined his head. "More must die in the workhouses," he said. "Felons receive more in the way of medical attention than do the poor. Better diet too, I dare say."

There was a little silence, which the Inspector filled in marking the slow progress of the gig through the gray. "Tell me what you know of this man Gordon," he said at last.

Inspector Harvey tipped himself forward onto the toes of his Wellington boots. "He's to be transported for twenty-one years," he said, "for inciting riot and treason during the summer disturbances. Back in November an anonymous letter was sent to Scotland-yard stating that he could be found in a common lodging-house in Mary-le-bone – but most likely you know all about that, since it was your Inspector Tierney who made the arrest…"

Inspector Hughes sighed. He wasn't at all surprised at the failure of the scranning cove to mention any of this, even given that the details concerning the search for Gordon had been pasted all about the station-house, in plain view of one and all, since Saturday dinner-time.

"The Active Duty is a law unto themselves," he said simply. "But tell me – this Gordon, is he at all *religious*, so far as you know?"

"Well," came the telling reply, "I should say that in truth he's of no religion whatever."

"A freethinker?"

"O, I dare say, Inspector Hughes. His behaviour is in general very good, but he pays the most marked disrespect at the prison chapel. He never rises from his seat, and he keeps his head up, looking all around him in a most bold fashion, when he should be saying his prayers."

They exchanged muted expressions of disapproval.

The gig had reached the pier, and Inspector Hughes found himself looking down upon a row of hard, glazed hats in the tops of which the red lights of the pier were dimly reflected. A collective, weary sigh went up, as a small figure in a brown suit was brought ashore, clambering with difficulty up the pier steps owing to the weighty irons affixed to his legs at the ankles and the knees. Once on solid ground, he snatched off his hat and stood with his close-cropped head bowed. This was done with a grave defiance. The Inspector had to search his memory for a while before he was able to recollect a sorrier sight than the fist-hard features screwed tight against everything that was before him now.

"Prisoner sixty-eight-fourteen," said Inspector Harvey, "proceed."

They all set off towards a set of long, square stone buildings, at last entering at a door over which the blue ensign of the River Police stirred faintly in the dismal wind. Inside a small fire was burning in the grate; in all other respects the room was bare and utterly cheerless. Inspector Hughes moved behind the desk and took out his notebook and pencil; he set them down alongside his stove-pipe hat, then he settled back in the chair and gave himself a moment or two to consider the wretched spectacle before him. Prisoner sixty-eight-fourteen was small and sickly-looking. He kept his head bowed, his eyes blazing intent upon the desk-blotter, and he turned the brim of his glazed hat with the fervid intensity of a Turkish rhubarb-seller telling his prayer-beads.

"Tell me, Mr. Gordon," the Inspector said at length, "how does a decent working man like yourself come to such a sorry pass?"

The convict slowly brought up his flinty-gray eyes until they were level with the Inspector's own steady, brown gaze.

"I was betrayed, sir," he said.

"That must rankle with you, I dare say."

The prisoner shrugged slightly. "If ye're the pipeman," he said simply, "ye maun play."

"Speak plain, prisoner," commanded Inspector Harvey, and the convict turned down his eyes once more towards the desk. When he spoke again it was in an accent that was strong, yet quiet.

"I huv nae shame fer whit ah've done," he said. "Ah've sons, God save 'em, who maun surely starve now; but if they be spared, then all I did was fer them. Every workin' man has the right tae a guid coat tae his back, a hame, a guid dinner upon his table. 'Tis bad government that keeps these things frae the likes o' us, and universal suffrage, sir, is the only remedy fer bad government that I can fix on. 'Tis a great cause – the greatest – an' I was proud tae fight the guid fight. But I tell you this – as God is my witness, I never was fer physical force. What was said of me in court was a' lies, every damnable word o' it."

The Inspectors exchanged a look that told of how many times they had heard the same arguments and protestations before today. "I dare say," said Inspector Hughes mildly when Gordon had done with his rendition of them. "You was betrayed."

"Aye, by bad men."

"And do you know who they are, these bad men?"

The prisoner's face creased as if in pain. "Spies," he said. "They were amang us all the while like shadows. They stood beside us like brothers at arms, they placed their marks alangside ours upon the Charter, they threw up their hats in the name o' justice – and they betrayed us for handfu's o' silver."

"And yet you never saw fit to betray them likewise. I must say, that is very commendable."

"Ach, they were desperate men tryin' tae scratch a livin', sir. It's the system – the system's tae blame." He had become greatly agitated during the foregoing speech, and now heg began to cough in a manner that was painful to behold. He turned away to spit into a filthy kerchief. Inspector Hughes noted with a pang of pity the scarlet bubbling clot. "The divvil tak' 'em," said Gordon when he had wiped his mouth.

"You made a good impression on Mr. Hedges, the turner."

"Mr. Hedges is a guid man. Before I went to him, I hadnae worked in weeks. He put his trust in me and I failed to repay that trust. That is my only regret. My disappointment at the failure o' a' my efforts was sic tha' I had determined to put an end to Radicalism, sir, and endeavoured to live a decent life. But it wasnae tae be."

"Spies," said Inspector Hughes, "put paid to that." The convict smiled slightly, but would not be drawn. "Mr. Hedges tells me he owes you some wages. He'd like to pay them out. I can see to it that they're sent to your family if you wish…"

The convict smiled with a sad resignation. "Tha' all depends on whit youse're seekin' in return," he said. "I told 'em plain before – I'll no' name names nor condemn ane o' my brethren – no matter what youse're offerin' in the way o' inducement."

Inspector Hughes spread his hands flat upon the desk, contemplating them in earnest for a moment or two. "That's very noble of you," he said. "But I'll come direct to business all the same. Tell me, what do you know of a wood-turner – late of Glasgow – who goes by the name of Daniel McNaughten?"

The Inspector glanced up quickly, in time to catch the convict's surprised expression. It seemed to him to be quite genuine.

"Dan?" said Gordon, amazed to hear that name in this place. "An' whit's he tae dae wi' ony of this?"

"I happen to know that you and he associated in London before you was taken."

Gordon swallowed his words down hard, and when they rose again ,they strained against his better judgement. "Aye, I cam' across him by chaunce up on St. Martins-lane in November, I'll no' deny it. But I had-nae seen him fer a year or more before then an' I hadnae the slightest notion he was in London. Last I saw of him he was carrying on a guid trade back in Glesga' – ornamental turning – though there was talk of his gi'en it up to study fer a surgeon…"

"A surgeon?"

"Aye – or mebbe a lawyer… Ach! Dan's always had ideas ayont his standin' – but he's an honest man, and a verra hard worker – an' he never had a thing tae dae wi' politics."

"How did he seem to you when you met with him in St. Martins-lane?"

"He seemed to me to be in a puir way – he said he'd been taken verra bad wi' a fever – he wus dressed very ill. I supposed that his busi-ness must've taken a turn fer the worse, which shocked me, since it was always guid – but he told me he'd gi'en it up of his own accord and was thinkin' o' goin' intae another."

"Medicine… Or the law…"

"He didnae specify."

"Would you say McNaughten was well-to-do?" the Inspector asked after a moment or two spent in mulling all this over.

"Aye, comfortable – an' why no'? He ay worked hard and nivver spent a penny more'n he had tae… Ask about Glesga' fer 'im – any one'll tell youse the same. Havers! His faither's a Tory Nob, and very well connected – pals wi' the Lord Provost – aye, that's the sort o' stock yon Dan's sprang frae… Mind, he's the natural son. He'll no inherit a penny. He's tae work fer all he has."

"Tell me what happened after you met him on St. Martins-lane."

"We went together tae a tavern."

"Do you remember which one?"

"No."

"What did you do there?"

"I'd a toddie an' a hot meal – the first I'd had in some time. Dan paid – said he wasnae short o' money. Then he offered to tak' a wee tour of the turners' yards wi' me. At Mr. Hedges's shop he demonstrated to me the use o' Ibbetson's geometric curve. Wi'out his assistance I should never have cam' by the work, for which I was verra grateful."

"Skilled at the lathe is he?"

"O aye. Folk say Dan's a wee bit daft in the heid, like, but there isnae a lathe in the world that lad cannae work." The convict broke off, turning his flinty eyes upon the Inspector. "Dan's nae a Chartist," he said. "He's no' a smidgen o' interest in ony o' that. But even if he were, youse'll no persuade me to say a word agin him – I'd rather my wife an' weans go wi'out the wages ah'm owed than betray an innocent man who nivver did me a jot o' harm. Hech, I know fer a fact that he nivver even registered fer the vote. He rented a shop frae Smiths the bell-hangers fer a guid while when I was the manager there, and wouldnae pay a penny more than nine pound ten fer it – even though he could well afford it. O aye, it made a few people wild, did that – tae think that we was all efter strugglin' fer the vote and him too pinchit to pay ten guineas fer it. Aye, he was careful to keep well oot o' all the rabblin's and rousin's o' Glesga', was Dan. I'd swear to that on the life of ma weans."

The words of a convicted or condemned prisoner are not ever to be taken lightly, for they are among the only men on earth who, in general, have little to gain by lying. Keeping this in mind, Inspector Hughes considered what he had gleaned thus far. He could see no reason why the convict would endeavour to protest so much the innocence of another man: unless that innocence was nothing more nor less than the truth...

"Tell me, Mr. Gordon," said the Inspector when he was done with considering and writing in his notebook, "did Dan ever express any opinion in your hearing of the Prime Minister, Sir Robert Peel?" He looked up at the convict with a perfect blankness of expression.

"Sir Robert Peel...? Well, now..." He wiped his mouth on the back of his hand. "I believe that he saw him once."

"Did he now? And when was that?"

"Ach, a few years back. There was a banquet held in Peel's honour – sump'n tae do wi' the university – every Tory in Glesga' was there, including Dan's faither – like I told ye, he's one o' the Tory click. They put up a pavilion across the whole width o' Buchanan-street and Dan's faither worked it for him to fetch in some trade on the decorations. He stole in so's he could listen to the speeches."

"Interested in that sort of thing, is he?"

"I've heard him say a guid many times how, having heard 'em both speak, Sir Robert Peel was a better orator by far than Feargus O'Connor. It always caused a wee bit of a stir – there being very few folk in Glesga' who think well on Bobbie Peel…"

"And it appeared to you that Dan was one of those who did."

"I dinna ken who's telt youse a' this aboot Dan, but ask around an' youse'll find there's a guid many more folk in Glesga' who count him a Tory Nob, like his pa, than believe him inclined to radicalism."

"And what do you think, Mr. Gordon?"

"It's like I told youse, Dan nivver bothered wi' ony o' that. I nivver heard him say a thing either for or against the Prime Minister."

"Where did he stand on Free Trade?"

"I huvnae the foggiest…"

"What about the Income Tax? Nobody cares much for that…"

The convict sighed wearily. "I did once hear him mention how he thought it terrible hard to mak' those wi' small salaries – such as the farmers and the clergy – pay so much."

It was a perfectly common-place observation.

"Did you tell any of this to Inspector Tierney? I mean about Dan's opinions of the Prime Minister and the Income Tax?"

The convict's eyes narrowed. "I wouldnae tell that bastard what day o' the week it was!" he cried.

"That's enough!" barked Inspector Harvey.

"He offered me ma freedom if I'd go over tae the other side – name names, turn spy. Freedom! Whit sort o' freedom is that?"

"I said, that's enough!"

The convict spat more blood into his scrap of cloth. The Inspector waited for him to be done, then turned his notebook to the page bearing the rubbing of the queer token. He held it out towards Gordon.

"Have you ever seen this before?"

The convict scratched his head. "It looks like a wee communion token," he said.

"It ain't familiar to you."

"I've seen the like, but nivver that particular ane."

"Well then, have you ever come across a Democratic Chapel that uses that there symbol?"

Gordon indicated that he had not, and Inspector Hughes returned the notebook to his pocket. He glanced across at Inspector Harvey, as if to say he had heard enough.

"Wait now," said the convict. "Democratic Chapel, you say... Mr. Duncan kept one o' those."

"Do you mean the Reverend Duncan?" repeated Inspector Hughes.

The convict had grown very pale indeed, and he started babbling all at once.

"Dan and Abram – ach – now I see whit youse're about! Well, well – they were close right enough, but never in regard tae politics – I'd swear tae it! Youse've got that part o' it wrang! Abram worked for Dan's pa as a journeyman when Dan was a wee lad – he was like a second faither to him. But Dan hasnae a sliver where Abram has va-moosed tae – he told me he hadnae seen hide nor hair o' the gyte carle since he left Glesga' tae press for the Charter, which is more 'n a year since." His voice trailed off. He was biting his bottom lip and twisting the glazed hat in his hands: a perfect study in anxiety.

"Abram Duncan!" exclaimed Inspector Harvey, "why – that's the Gray Goose!"

"O dear, o dear, o dear," said Inspector Hughes. He was thinking how he oughter have put two and two together when the prisoner's landlady made mention of the name – not to mention the minister of the Scotch Church. "I have reason to believe he may be at large in the metropolis," he said, very grim. "That is to say, Newington Butts..."

"But he's wanted for seditious treason!" said Inspector Harvey.

Cursing himself, Inspector Hughes took out his notebook once again.

"No, no," said Gordon, "Mr. Duncan's a pious man – saintly, you might even say. Whit's been said about him is nought but filthy lies put about by confidential agents, the divvil tak' 'em. He only ever tried tae educate his fellow men in sobriety, and how best tae live and take care o' their families. There wasna any physical force tae him."

"That'll do, prisoner," commanded Inspector Harvey, but the convict had declined into a fit of sharp, piercing coughs that shook the whole of his slight frame, and culminated in a great flow of blood which quite soaked the dirty bit of handkerchief he had clamped to his mouth. He was glistening with perspiration and trembling from head to foot, but he held up his hand, signalling that he had more to say.

"There was a degree o' affection between the two that ordinarily exists only between faither and son – an' ah should say that the manner of his appearance when ah saw him last is proof of how bad Dan has suffered the loss o' a dear companion. Broken-hearted, so he was. O aye! Why else would he gie up a guid business for seventeen pounds!"

"McNaughten sold his business for seventeen pounds?" said Inspector Hughes.

"Aye, last New Year. He told me he'd've put it up for public roup if his journeyman hadnae taken it aff his haunds. Journeyman! Pshaw! If ye can call him that! Slinterin' scouf!"

"And I take it that in your opinion the business was worth considerably more than seventeen pounds." Inspector Hughes licked his pencil stub in readiness.

"Aye, a guid deal more!"

"Any idea how much more?"

"He had a guid engine, a fine set o' cutting tools, a pattern book he'd spent years in makin' up. An' a long list o' clients…"

"And who did he sell it to?"

"His journeyman – Carlo."

Inspector Hughes paused, his writing hand held just above his notebook. "*Carlo*?" he repeated.

"Aye," said the convict. "The worthless yammerin' bampot."

In which Mr. Cockburn comes to appreciate the benefits
of keeping to the Law.

Sandy slept much better following the game of billiards with the Member for Kilmarnock, Dumbarton, Renfrew, Rutherglen, Port Glasgow, &c., District of Burghs. A good many things were still weighing upon his conscience, it was true, but he felt altogether lighter upon waking; and as he lay a-bed waiting for Hatchett to draw his bath, permitted seductive thoughts of victory to course through his mind. He was beginning to see that it might actually be possible to win the case, create a sensation, *and* please the Chief Whipper-in to boot. The thought overtook him to such an extent that he was not at all mindful of the risks that inhered in the venture. He felt a *certainty*, which for once had nothing to do with gambling or sex; and now that the crushing weight of despondency had begun to lift, Sandy had been seized by a powerful determination to understand *everything* about the jurisprudence of madness.

O, he had got up his law plenty of times before, and, as he repeatedly told himself, if that three-bottle man, Mr. Samuel Warren, could boast of mastery of the insanity defence, then just how abstruse can it be?

It was good to have a matter of some earnestness with which to occupy his time, one which he could tell himself was of more import than the endless distraction life had become. Once up and bathed, he laid plans to visit the library at the Middle Temple later in the week in order to look up 39 and 40 George 3, c.94 1800 – *An Act for the Safe Custody of Insane Persons Charged with Offenses* – Erskine's celebrated defence of Hadfield, who had fired a horse-pistol at the King forty years ago. He spent the remaining part of the morning engaged upon an abstracted appreciation, fuelled by the contents of the morning papers, of recent developments in respect of the insanity plea. It was close to lunch-time when the dismaying truth dawned on him that Erskine's arguments were no longer as acceptable as they might once have been.

"I had no idea," he complained to Hatchett from behind his copy of the *Morning Post*, "how profoundly those pathetic attempts upon the Queen last summer had afflicted the public conscience. It seems that the insanity defence has had its day."

"Ah, yes! Francis and Bean," said Hatchett knowingly.

"Those ridiculous incidents appear to have primed the entire population to spy out insurrection and plots everywhere and anywhere – not to say urge the application of stringent penalties against any hapless booby who looks as if he might threaten the status quo." Back in the summer when assassination attempts on the Queen had appeared to be a weekly phenomenon, Cockie – who was not at all well disposed to Her Majesty – had dismissed the actions of Masters Francis and Bean as a matter of no interest whatever. It now appeared that in doing so he had proved himself to be dangerously out of step with the prevailing mood. "Just look at the nonsense that is being written in regard to my client: in paragraph after paragraph I have come across the assertion – laid in a couple of instances at the Bethlem cell door of Oxford himself – that hanging the perpetrators is the only method of preventing attacks on the Queen and other prominent people, and that it ill-behoves the Law to use the insanity defence in such cases. Balderdash!" Sandy exclaimed, and he threw the *Morning Post* upon the floor.

"I had heard that Francis was a confidential agent," said Hatchett, stooping to pick up the newspaper. "And, as for Bean, well, I believe it was proved that he never even charged his pistol…"

"Let the laws of your own land," Sandy said, "good or ill, between ye stand; hand to hand, and foot to foot, arbiters of the dispute." Vigorously quoting Shelley always made him feel better.

"Very well put, sir," said the valet, as he served him his coddled eggs, "if I may say so!"

"Damn it all, my dear fellow – justice is burning on a pyre!" said Sandy, tucking in.

"I'm very glad to see your appetite is restored, sir," said Hatchett. He placed a pot of coffee on the table, and wiped a cup and saucer.

"And the most extravagant rumours are in circulation. It would appear that the government is set upon having McNaughten whipped soundly and transported to Van Diemen's Land, whether he loaded his pistol or not," said Sandy. "And it has deliberately fixed the Law so as to ensure that that is the most likely – nay – the only penalty applicable! The Prince Consort's interference in the trial of Master Francis has ensured that all attempts on persons of quality and note shall henceforth be met with a sharp and degrading punishment – no matter what the circumstances."

"I am sure that you are correct in that, sir; but I can't help but make the observation that if the Prince Consort hadn't interfered, then Francis would have been hanged, drawn and quartered…"

"Damn panic legislation!" cried the master. "Laws ought not to be passed in a crisis. The Law is immutable and impassive!" Hatchett poured him a cup of coffee. "The Law is beauty and truth, old man. It is not to be dictated to, or skewed by emergency!"

"No, indeed it is not, sir," said Hatchett, "though upon occasion the Law might be plain *wrong*."

Cockie took a sip of coffee.

"You do see what is going on here, don't you?" he said. "Why, that lickspittle *FIAT JUSTITIA* laid out the ground with admirable clarity in this morning's *Standard*. Where the devil is it?" He set aside his coffee and snatched up another of the morning papers from the untidy pile where he had tossed it aside a short while before. "Ah, here we have it: '*even the insane are not so utterly devoid of moral and reasoning faculties as to be impervious to proper punishment. The lunatic can be deterred – especially if he is only* partially *insane*'." Sandy frowned, mulling over the stark implications. "Pah! One might as well say that there are very few madmen who are so unbalanced in their minds that they do not fear death or a stiff birching or transportation! How so? Are the poor wretches to be doubly tormented?" He took another sip of coffee and mulled judiciously upon the construction of the argument.

"Is the client at *all* raving, sir?"

"No."

"Does he drool, like them poor souls you see slumped on the thoroughfares?"

"No. There's nothing in the least imbecilic about him. Far from it:

[273]

he's rather refined, delicate; gentlemanly, even."

"Might he be an *idiot savant* – like that Mr. Dickens wrote of in *Barnaby Rudge*?"

Sandy, although a friend of Boz's, had not made time to read the work; but he felt a little hopeful at his valet's suggestion. "And what might that entail?" he asked.

"The chief part of it appears to be an amiable, good-natured disposition, alongside something wild and not entirely sensible – and perhaps some queerness or other, such as a raven sitting on one's shoulders."

Sandy applied the description to what he had observed of the prisoner. "Not a bit of it," he said, "regrettably."

"Perhaps it's the pox," said Hatchett after a moment or two of thought.

"He is quite thin," concurred Sandy, who had seen a good many fellows taken that way, and knew the signs by heart; "though I would have to say that there was evidently nothing *unclean* about the fellow."

"Did he have all his own hair?"

"He certainly *had* hair…"

"Well then, did you get a good look at his teeth?" said Hatchett. "In my opinion, the teeth always give it away."

"O, it's no good, old man," said Sandy with a sigh. "The fellow looked as sane as you or I." He looked again at FIAT JUSTITIA's article, still open before him. "*Partial* insanity," he murmured. "How very singular…" It was quite true that the concept had not occurred to him before then.

"Hatchett, old man," he said after a further moment or two's brooding. "I wonder, would you mind? There's a book in the library – Erskine's Speeches in respect of constructive treason. You'll find it on the bottom shelf near the case clock."

When the valet returned with the volume, Sandy leafed through it until he lighted upon the great advocate's own words. "What do you think of this?" he said. Hatchett was immediately attentive. "'*Reason is not driven from her seat, but distraction sits down upon it along with her. Delusion, therefore, where there is no frenzy or raving madness, is the true character of insanity*'."

"Very well expressed, if I may say so, sir," said the manservant.

"You see, times are changing. It's no longer necessary – or acceptable – to think of the mad as ferocious beasts. A man might appear perfectly normal on first encounter – yet be prey to all manner of destructive impulses – *delusional*, as it were. Such a man may be said to be only *partially* insane, no?"

"Indeed, sir. Although I can't help but think that it must have been a sight easier when we kept to the old-fashioned distinctions in the matter. After all, a good many perfectly sane people might be said to suffer from a great variety of *delusions*."

"You are quite right, Hatchett," said Sandy. "After all, what is life but a desperate pursuit of deluded hopes and dreams – a great gamble founded on the utterly irrational belief that it is possible to succeed at something or other without it costing one too much in terms of cold cash or principle..." Sandy sighed despondently. "Perhaps it is all a far more complicated matter than I had imagined." Erskine's words swam on the page before him: *partial* insanity; delusion. "I need you to go straightway to my book-seller on Chancery-lane and have of him any works upon the subject – especially anything with relevance to jurisprudence."

"You may need to settle your account, sir, before Mr. Benson will allow you any more volumes," said Hatchett.

"Ah! Do you really think so? Perhaps he'll take – let me see, what have I here – four guineas, and the rest on account?"

"I'll put it to him, sir."

"Good man!"

With Hatchett departed, Cockie finished his eggs and coffee and sank into a deep reverie.

The Member for Kilmarnock's deposition was rather a good beginning, he told himself; his letter would serve as strong testimony as to the balance of the prisoner's reason. Furthermore, Mr. Johnston had hinted that the Lord Provost of Glasgow – the unsuccessful Tory candidate for the Glasgow seat in the late election, and a friend of the prisoner's father – might well be persuaded to depose in similar vein. And, moreover, Cockie had no doubt that all of this lay in the direction that the Chief Whipper-in most desired for the case.

That there was something altogether queasy in a defence founded upon the assumption that a man would have to be insane in order to accuse the government of persecution at the present time, and even more so, to fire a pistol (loaded or not) at one of its servants, troubled him immensely; but what was he to do?

"*Faute de mieux*, old man," he murmured, with a sigh. He poured himself another cup of coffee and picked up the *Chronicle*.

"*Some evidence or other*," he read, "*gathered by the peelers on Friday evening has led the Superintendent and Commissioners of Police to conclude that the prisoner had long been harbouring murderous designs against Sir Robert Peel, or some Members of the government.*"

Evidences, my eye! He struck the page with the back of his hand. They had presented no such evidences in court on Saturday morning. Pah! If the peelers had a shred of evidence of that sort we'd have heard no more of McNaughten until he'd been slipped onto the hangman's list first thing today! Blasted subterranean journalism! The hacks swallow every shred of prejudicial speculation, every shady hint and insinuation that those pusillanimous, cringing Scotland-yard puppies feed 'em! McNaughten's tried and convicted before he's even set foot before a jury.

And here am I, he thought, more or less thrown into a conspiracy.

He set down the *Chronicle* and picked up the *Standard*, reading through, for the twentieth time that morning, the report of the Magistrate's hearing. He was looking for a short appended paragraph that considered the bank deposit receipt for seven hundred and fifty pounds found on the prisoner's person.

"*It is well known that organisations such as the Suffrage Union, Sturge's National Association for Promoting the Political and Social Improvement of the People, and the Anti-Corn Law League, pay large fees to lecturers and pamphleteers.*"

He tore out the troubling paragraph, tucking it inside the volume of Erskine's speeches; then he closed the book tight shut and laid his hand upon it in the manner of one swearing an oath. This done, he took the book and went into his study, where he snatched up a pen and ink and some paper from the writing desk, and sat down in an armchair before the fire. On the white border running alongside the incriminating passage he set down a figure that he reckoned to be the typical income of a moderately successful tradesman – something in the region of two hundred pounds a year. He next applied all the faculties of his imagination to calculating how much a frugal and sober young man, with no family or ill habits to indulge, might expect to expend over a twelve-month. Rent for lodgings and laundry: three or four shillings a week, that is to say, nine pounds annually; rent for premises, say between ten and twelve pounds a year; allow something for a meagre diet – with no strong drink – and sundries. To look at him, the fellow evidently did not care much for fashion, but Sandy gave him a pair of short boots at twelve shillings, a pair of unmentionables at sixteen and sixpence, a couple of shirts, an Oxonian coat, and three pairs of stockings: why, he could fit the fellow's entire wardrobe for three or four pounds at the most!

He quickly made the sum.

The whole amounted to outgoings of something in the region of fifty pounds, leaving a nett profit of around a hundred and fifty a year. Five or six years of steady business would have been sufficient for McNaughten to save something in the region of seven hundred pounds – even without interest.

Sandy smiled to himself.

He had begun the process of establishing reasonable doubt.

A few hours later found him intent upon Mons. Marc's treatise, which Hatchett had brought back from the book-seller's in a parcel containing three or four other relevant works. Having an exquisite grasp of the French language (in addition to fluent German, excellent Italian and rather good Latin and Greek), the at times recondite language of *De la folie considérée dans ses rapports avec les questions médico-judiciaires* posed no great difficulties for Sandy. In fact, he found the work to be immensely absorbing – so much so that he had not ventured out of doors once; not to his club, not to his chambers, not even to take his constitutional in Green Park. It was perhaps just as well: one never knew when the bailiffs might tap a fellow, and absorption in a case, though bearing its own rewards, did nothing whatever to restore an insufficiency of funds. But there was contentment. When Hatchett brought him a cold roast beef sandwich and a glass of claret, he was pleasantly surprised to discover his master in the same attitude of concentrated repose, in the same walnut wing armchair, and utterly engrossed in the topic of "Homicidal Monomania".

"I had absolutely no idea that there was so much to madness," Cockie averred, without looking up from his book, "and I speak as one who has been 'madly' in love more times than I care to think; and who has seen plenty of other fellows rendered 'insane' by amatory disappointment, and 'maniacal' in the unstinting pursuit of preferment."

"Indeed, sir," said Hatchett. "It all sounds most interesting."

"This French alienist, Monsieur Marc, holds that Monomaniacs are impelled by a strongly-held conviction – skewed by false reasoning – which is all too apparent to them, yet wholly *irrational* when considered by anyone else." Sandy looked up from the volume, stroking his chin with the quill feather. "I say, Hatchett, old man, if that's true, then I ought to be dashed off to the nearest asylum at the earliest convenience, where I dare say I shall find myself in very good company!"

Hatchett laughed. "I'm pleased to see you restored to your customary good humour, sir," he said, topping up Sandy's glass. "I must say it seems a gloomy topic to me; but then you do have quite the knack for putting a clever and amusing twist on most things."

Cockie took a thoughtful sip of the wine. "I wonder," he mused, "how might one tell a monomaniac from a sane fellow? Diogenes held that most men are within a finger's breadth of madness."

Hatchett nursed the claret jug to his chest. "O, I am sure that one's friends and relations would let it out, sir," he said.

"In my experience one's *enemies* are rather more likely to point at such an unpalatable truth. Loved ones are too susceptible to sentimental indulgence, not to say too well mannered to raise objections. No, I'm afraid that a man must be upon his mettle when it comes to the discernment of the state of his own reason. Why, look at me, Hatchett. Other men's wives were one of the great discoveries of my life: appreciative, discreet, gorgeous, fragrant, inexpensive and undemanding – holding out the promise of the most perfectly amicable transaction it is possible to make: desire and the satisfaction of desire; mutually sustaining; *quid pro quo*." He paused, smiling ruefully at the memory of rustling silk, perfumed corsages, tumbling locks and low, gentle moans. "And yet, my dear old bean, I have abjured it all – and for what? In order that I might proceed in a practice that is not at all affected by how I choose to spend my afternoons; parading about in a periwig and a silk gown, working twice as hard for half the cash, at something which bores and disgusts me beyond endurance. Now, in what manner, pray, is any of that *rational* behaviour?"

"I dare say that there are worse occupations, sir," said Hatchett. He set the claret jug and the tray down upon the occasional table with an unnecessary degree of care, and stood regarding them in a most thoughtful attitude. "I called in at the chambers on my way to Chancery-lane," he said.

Cockie swilled a mouthful of claret around his teeth and gums, savouring the bitterness; the redolence of something rotting. "Did Frayling have any business?"

"No, but seeing him restored to his desk after so many weeks away, your neighbour in the attic chambers had been down."

"Pah! What the deuce did that confounded prig want?"

Hatchett smiled vaguely. He was dusting the occasional table in a somewhat detached manner. "It would appear that a young man called twice in the last week, making inquiries after you." He looked up from the dusting in order to gauge the effect of his words. "He must have had your chambers out of the trade directory."

Sandy pinched the corners of his eyes between a thumb and forefinger. "Well, then the entire Temple will know of my *difficulties*."

"O, but he weren't no bum-bailiff out for a tap, sir. He came on a personal matter." There was a silence that Hatchett carefully broke. "Mr. Frayling wants to know what to do should the young man call again."

"You are right to be disappointed in me," said Cockie with a sigh. His head had slumped onto his breast, and he was gazing in a melancholic reverie at the glass of claret.

"It is immaterial what I think, sir," said Hatchett. He returned to the dusting with a careless shrug; but when his master looked over at him, he could see that the confidential valet had set his dark eyes broodingly upon the shining table-top, and that he was running a chamois over it in slow meticulous circles.

Cockie fancied that he could feel his heart grow cold and hard and heavy. There are times, and this was one of them, when he did not like himself very much. He tried to blame it all upon the World; but the World, ah me!, the World would have none of it; she turned away from all of his entreaties, leaving him to face alone the fact that perhaps he was not a good man, after all.

"I never meant to do harm," he said softly.

"Few men do, sir," replied Hatchett.

This was true; and yet, somehow, it could not be denied, he had done harm. He had turned his heart against all appeals to decency; he had lost control over his own actions; he had sacrificed his moral liberty. Why, he concluded, *'tis the very essence of insanity, is it not*! Certainly Monsieur Marc would have it so; for there it was set out quite plain upon the page before him.

Hatchett knelt on the floor, setting in order the papers and books that were scattered at Sandy's feet. "What's done is done, sir," he said. "You've a duty to attend to now: an opportunity to strengthen the operation of justice and truth, which is a matter of no small importance, I should say, and a sight more than most men could lay claim to for themselves! It is what makes me proudest to be your confidential valet. In fact, I should say that on balance, with all things taken together, you have probably done more right than wrong in this life."

Sandy wanted so badly to believe him. "And in your opinion, dear old man," he asked, "is the boy worth saving?"

Hatchett placed his hands upon his hips; he was shaking his head slowly from side to side, thunderstruck. "Why, he's a human being, ain't he, sir? A human being is always worth saving."

"But surely, if it can be shown that the fellow intended to kill then he deserves to die."

Hatchett fixed him with a look of bewilderment, perhaps dismay. "You oughtn't to take the case, sir," he said, once the moment had passed, "not if it goes against your conscience."

Sandy stroked his face with the quill; he was reading back what he had just written. *Cui bono*, it read. *Cui bono*... "They will crucify me," he said simply, and he crumpled the page into a ball and batted it towards the hearth, just missing the fire. Hatchett stooped to pick it up, committed it to the flames, which he stoked gently with the poker.

"Were you considering dealing me a couple of blows over the head just now?" said Cockie, suddenly and with a wild laugh.

"Not on this occasion, sir." Hatchett sat back on his heels, a faint smile on his lips.

"Ah, but I only have your word for that, don't I?" said Sandy.

"I suppose so, sir."

"None of us can ever know for sure – can we? – what thoughts another might be entertaining."

"That is very true, sir."

"Do you suppose, for instance, that Lord John Russell's uncle had any suspicions regarding *his* valet?"

Hatchett laid the poker on the fire-dog and watched the flames lick at the paper. "I read somewhere," he said with an altogether placid countenance, "that Lord William Russell was a *very* testy old gentleman."

"And think you that that is reason enough for a valet to cut his master's throat as he lies asleep in his bed?"

"It might be reasonably considered as such, sir: if the valet had not been long enough in the service of his master to accustom himself to his ways. I believe that Courvoisier had been in Lord Russell's household just a little above a month at the time of the murder. Also, he was a Swiss, wasn't he? Continental servants are not like English ones, sir."

"You mean they do not always purport to know their place?"

"Yes, sir. That is precisely it."

"And if a servant knows his place, think you he is less likely to cut his master's throat?"

"That would appear to be the way of it, sir."

Hatchett replenished Sandy's glass with a little more of the claret.

"So, is all violent disturbance to be seen as an inevitable consequence of the irritation that exists between individuals – in those instances where one does not play his part in accordance with the wishes of the other: the result of frictive pressure?"

"I believe that to be the truth of it, sir, yes."

"If I were testy would you wish to cut my throat?"

"I might wish it, sir."

"Ah, but you would not do so..."

"Not as a matter of course, sir, no."

"Well then, would you do it for ten pounds?"

"Not even for twenty pounds, sir."

"Fifty?" Hatchett was smiling broadly. "A hundred and my gold watch?"

"You would have to be exceedingly testy, sir," he laughed.

"But what if you had an uncontrollable impulse, something indefinable, as it were, that impelled you to kill?"

The valet had crossed to the door and was standing with his back to Sandy.

"It strikes me, sir," he said, "that your murderous impulse might be drawn out of any reasonable man who finds himself *frustrated*, as it were, by his situation."

"Go on..."

"Well, the loss of some part of himself, as it were: all hope, a cherished dream of the future, an idea he carried of who he was or what he might become – that might succeed in driving anyone out of his senses. The more so if he were unable to give vent to his true feeling in some legitimate form. If that were the case, well then, it might go bad with him – like a fellow who takes to drink, or to beating his wife. A man is a man, sir, after all is said and done; and he don't care to be kept down, no more so if he comes to see how it ain't fair or just."

"I dare say a good many working men at the present time feel this frustration of which you so eloquently speak, Hatchett."

"Men of all classes and occupation might feel frustration, sir."

Sandy took up his claret, breathing in the aroma, deeply. "They won't let me make any sort of political case," he said.

Hatchett turned to face him. "Who said a thing about politics, sir?" he said. And then he bowed deeply, and with an ineffable sincerity, and left the room.

Sandy drained his glass of the last bitter dregs; they stuck to his gullet: gritty, indissoluble. After a few moments he realised that Hatchett had been thinking not of McNaughten, but of Polly's boy: his son.

"My son," he said softly to himself. "My son."

And this time, the first occasion in many years, he did not try to suppress the thought.

Glasgow,
January 22nd, 1843

Honoured Sir,

From inquiries I have made respecting Daniel McNaughten it appears that for the last twelve months he has appeared to be in a deranged state of mind.

I have seen Mrs. Patterson with whom he lodged in Clyde-street and she states that she has known him from his infancy and that he is a natural son to Daniel McNaughten, a wood-turner, by a female named Elsie who died when he was very young from which time he lived with his father, who is married, at his premises on Stockwell-street until he went into business for himself about seven years ago, also on Stockwell-street. During the time he was in business he was very saving, seldom taking more than two meals a day and never drinking anything stronger than water. He was averse to all company, and about two years ago he suddenly gave up the business and tools to his journeyman, a man called Carlo, for seventeen pounds, even though he was doing a good trade and the concern might easily have fetched twice that.

Mrs. Patterson had asked him several times what made him give it up and for such a cheap bargain, but the only reason he gave for it was that he did not like it and wanted to better himself and talked of going abroad. He had left her once and been away about twelve months and told her when he came back he had been to France and being asked, said he went there to get a situation and again being asked what situation he wanted, he said he wanted to get on in the Army but did not want to go as a common soldier.

She has seen him at times very dejected, but supposed it to have been occasioned by being unable to get a situation and has frequently said to her neighbours she was afraid he would commit suicide. He had since been to London and France again, which was at the beginning of last summer and then appeared to be much worse, for he had got a notion that he was continuously dogged about both there and at home and would frequently get up in the middle of the night and wander about the house and would say he could not rest for he was sure he was persecuted. At other times he would go out with a fishing rod and line and remain out all night as well as all day and the only refreshment he would get during that time would be a little milk he would beg at some farm house. Sometimes he would be singing and hollering about the house. At other times he was so dejected that they could but with difficulty get him to speak. At last he took to smoking a hemp pipe and this he would keep spitting into polished tins over the fireplace and about the room and if spoken to would say he had nothing to do but to clean it. Sometimes he would appear rational while at others he appeared otherwise.

I after some difficulty succeeded in finding his father and from inquiries learned that he could not account for his son giving up his business and that as it regards politics he never took any part in them. When he did vote he believed it to be for the Whigs. He himself was a Conservative. The first reason he had for thinking him a little deranged was about twelve or fourteen months ago since, when he called upon him and wanted him to get one of the sheriffs to get him a situation in a West India House here. The father told him his education was insufficient for that but since he had thrown off his business, if he wanted a situation of that kind he had better put himself to school after which he did not doubt he could get him one. The father said Dan then broke out and said: Do you know there is such a thing as a spy system going on in the land for there is. I am persecuted by them. Go where I would so will they watch me about and see me home to my lodging and watch out for me again. His father thus reasoned with him, telling him the absurdness of such a thing that they should watch an obscure person like him about.

He had never taken any political part to make them do anything of the kind for he had never even attended the place where the Members was brought forward nor at any other time or place. And after further reasoning with him, he went away very contented, but returned in a few days more excited than before, complaining that he was exceedingly persecuted, for go where he would, there were persons dogging him. It was the Tories that was persecuting him so, and he begged his father to go to the Lord Provost and Captain Miller, the

Supt. of Police, and get a stop put to it, for he could not abide being so tormented. His father again endeavoured to reason him out of it. "I have endeavoured to find out the residence of Carlo, who has taken to McNaughten's business, but cannot, he only working at the shop, his residence being at another place, and it being Sunday he is not at his shop, but I expect to find him there tomorrow.

I also delivered the Commissioners' letter to one of the directors of the bank, but cannot get the particulars required till tomorrow when the clerks will be there, after which I will follow up the inquiries made, and return by tomorrow's mail, which leaves here at eleven at night. I arrived here at two o'clock this morning and have been out making inquiries since about 9a.m. His father appears to be a very respectable man, and is reported to be a man of good property.

> Honoured Sir
> I remain your obedient servant
> Geo. Stephens
> DS A13

P.S. Most of the persons in business here reside in the neighbouring villages, which has been the cause of taking up so much of my time.

GARDINER'S-LANE STATION-HOUSE, SEVEN O'CLOCK P.M.

In which Inspector Hughes permits himself a little congratulation regarding his progress thus far in the investigations, and is straightway rewarded for his folly with an indication of the hazards yet to come.

Inspector Hughes was perched on the high stool at the ledger desk in the little cubby-hole, his feet resting on his topper, a tin of coffee at his elbow, and the station-house fire winking cheerily at him from the grate. He had just finished the last crumbs of a meat-pie bought for his dinner, and it was with a glow of satisfaction – which as a modest man he never could have owned to – that he considered once again how much pain and trouble the timely interventions of the informations from Glasgow had spared him.

It was most fortunate that Inspector Tierney had not, in the end, succeeded in collecting them from off the Birmingham Railway Mail that afternoon, having been called away unexpectedly to the Office of Home Affairs in pursuance of some urgent matter or other. The task of collection had, therefore, fallen to Sergeant Shew. Inspector Hughes did not for a moment doubt that the contents of the despatch were already common knowledge throughout the metropolis, since Sergeant Shew was on terms of the utmost familiarity with most of the denizens of Grub-street, and would sell the secrets of his own soul for a half a crown; but, for once, he weren't bothered by any of that. He had the Detective Sergeant's letter in his own hands and had read through the contents with his own eyes: which was all that mattered. The proofs uncovered in Glasgow pertaining to the prisoner's deranged state of mind removed a great burden of doubt and anxiety, and life, the Inspector reckoned, would be a good deal sweeter now that he had no longer to fret about covenants and Scotch churches and spies and Chartists and spectral young men and humbugging office-keepers and canting recruiting sergeants and dark terrors in respect of Queen's Speech Day. The nightmare of the past three days was receding from him.

"It would seem," he informed Constable Silver, "that McNaughten might be a lunatic after all." He had just finished copying out the Detective Sergeant's letter for the buff boxes, and, though he was careful not to gloat, he could not deny that he felt, in some way, *vindicated*.

"He could still be an agitator," said Silver, who had come up to the desk to sign himself off on the duty ledger. He was wearing a terrible scowl, and was evidently in that grudging frame of mind in which constables often find themselves when they have been walking the frozen and dismaying streets all day in a pair of ill-fitting boots.

"Well, as to what the prisoner might turn out to be," said Inspector Hughes, "as to that, we don't have no evidences – despite having looked mighty hard for 'em. So far, the Detective Sergeant has only turned up evidences that the prisoner had no strong politics – evidences which happily chime in with everything that we have found."

He was well aware that the evidences also pointed to the prisoner having known that notorious mischief-seeker, Abram Duncan, since boyhood; and it also appeared that he had been lodging with him. But the Inspector did not put too much store by that. There was not necessarily any guilt in the case of a boy, coming to London for the first time, taking lodgings with people known to him and his family. And as to the revelation that Duncan (who had delivered inflammatory harangues up and down the country during the recent disturbances) might well be masquerading as the minister of a Democratic Chapel over in Newington Butts: well, Inspector Hughes did not expect to be troubled any further by the ramifications of that dismal matter. He had passed the information over to the Commissioners, who had doubtless passed it over to Inspector Tierney and the Active Duty, within whose demesne such matters fell.

"All I'm saying," Silver was cavilling, "is that a good many of those Radical fellows are raving mad. Why, look at Feargus O'Connor! I've heard he talks to himself all night long in his cell, and believes he is the object of persecution!"

The Inspector turned down the corners of his mouth. "If them poor devils ain't mad to begin with, I dare say they soon become so once the shadow of the gallows falls upon 'em. As for the prisoner McNaughten, I'm almost certain that once the Home Secretary's returned to London, and has had sight of all of the informations, he will see to it that the poor bugger's packed off to an asylum without any more to do – which is what should have been done at the very beginning. Yes," he sighed, "it would appear that order is at long last emerging from the chaos of informations."

He was a sight disappointed to discern not one jot of enthusiasm in P.C. Silver's countenance: after all, the pair of them had experienced a good many sloughs and troughs since Friday afternoon. He had been anticipating the sharing of something a little *celebratory*, but so dispiriting was Silver's humour that, to tell the truth, the Inspector was rather relieved when he saw that the constable was muffling himself against the rheumy streets in preparation for leaving for the night.

His relief was, however, short-lived, for within a few moments Silver's place in the station-house office was taken by Inspector Tierney, stamping off the slush from his top-boots and calling to the duty sergeant to bring him a soft cloth.

"Lor'!" said Inspector Hughes. "This ain't a blooming Pell Mell club-house you know!"

Tierney sneered as he set his foot upon the rail of the little dock and began to attend to his boots. "Might I ask, Sam," he said, "what it was that impelled you to take your meddlesome ways down to Woolwich?"

"I was just attending to my duty."

"You bumbling oaf," said the scranning cove. "It might gratify you to learn that in turning up the convict Gordon, you have supplied a most useful witness in the case against McNaughten."

It curdled the lifeblood of the Inspector to hear it said. "Why, you devilish ill-conditioned cove," he said, "what have you done to him?"

Inspector Tierney snorted and carried on buffing his boots. "Done?" he repeated. "Why, it was not necessary to do anything. It never fails to astonish me what benefits a few weeks on the hulks will bring to a man's memory – never mind his conscience. You have not the slenderest grasp of this case," he said. "We have *evidence* that a blasted Radical intended to shoot the Prime Minister! We have *proof* that London is in the grip of a revolutionary fervour!"

"Proof? What proof? What evidence? I can tell you, I have boxes and boxes of informations right here, and not one proof is to be found among 'em!"

"Are you aware that it has been requested of Her Majesty the Queen that she does not attend the opening of Parliament next week? And that the Lord Great Chamberlain himself is to conduct the customary search of the cellars of the Palace of Westminster the night before? And here are you – with your nose in your damned buff boxes – carrying on as if none of it has a thing to do with you."

Inspector Hughes would have snorted if he could, but it wasn't in his nature to snort. "Just tell me," he said, "what evidence you have that a Radical intended to shoot the Prime Minister?"

"I told you the other night what McNaughten himself told me."

"So you say..."

"Don't take my word for it, not if you don't care to. The prisoner has, by his own volition, stated in open court that his murderous action was entirely motivated by his hatred of the government."

"You know as well as I do that ain't what he said."

"By thunder, Sam, your own rather ham-fisted efforts down in Woolwich have thrown up proof that he is a known associate of Abram Duncan – alias the Gray Goose – a disgusting and violent vagrant who has sown seeds of the most inflammatory and seditious type the length and breadth of the country!"

Inspector Hughes wearily ran his hand over his chin as tiny clusters of pins and needles shot through his feet and up his legs. "Yes, well, anything might be made of anything," he said. "But what about the evidences? I've just finished copying out those sent down from Glasgow by the New Detective, and it might surprise you to learn that there is every indication that the prisoner never had any political proclivities whatever."

"So why did he shoot Mr. Drummond?"

"It seems more than likely that he's just another madman."

"Dr. Lavies examined McNaughten at Tothill yesterday," said Inspector Tierney, "and found him to be of perfectly sound mind. And as for evidences – what about the testimony of the gentleman office-keeper and the brave Hussar – both of whom saw the prisoner skulking on the steps of the Privy Council and elsewhere in the vicinity on several occasions prior to the attempt on Mr. Drummond."

"They saw *someone* skulking – that I don't deny. I have a witness who says it weren't the prisoner but one of your busted plainclothesmen."

"Ah, yes, your informant, the old cigar-finder..." Inspector Tierney smirked. "Is that really the best you can do, Sam?"

"You know as well as I do how you can't prove something never happened."

Inspector Tierney rubbed his boot briskly. "Well, it's certainly very difficult, I'll give you that. However, not even you can deny that the prisoner fired pistols at Mr. Drummond. That is fact. And that he did so as a result of the vile and reprehensible anti-Tory rhetoric that the Radicals, Liberals, Free Traders, Chartists and all the rest of that band of destructivists have been preaching – is also *fact*! Deny it at your peril! Why, even if the wretch were found to be mad, it would be as a result of this poison festering within his mind. It is *that* and nothing else that has led to the shooting of Mr. Drummond! Now, are you with us, Sam? For if you are not, then, by thunder, you must be against us!"

"I ain't for or against nothing or no-one," said Inspector Hughes, "save the proper procedures."

"You lumbering fool!" Tierney spat on the toe-cap of his other boot, vigorously buffing it to a gleam with the cloth. "I don't blame you, Sam," he said. "These agitators can be very convincing. One needs a degree of cunning to meet them head-on. And this matter has dimensions to it that a simple fellow cannot possibly apprehend. Think of it! How else do you imagine the fellow came by such a vast sum as seven hundred and fifty pounds?"

Inspector Hughes sighed. "All the informations indicate that his habits are very frugal. By my reckoning, since October he has subsisted on no more than thirteen and six per week – and that includes the three shillings and tuppence for lodging and washing and the fifteen bob he laid out for the pistols. Prior to the beginning of last year he kept a well-set turning business for some five or six years, which he worked very hard at and, being so frugal, he may well have saved a good portion of his income for all I know."

"Seven hundred and fifty pounds!" exclaimed the scranning cove. "For wood-turning? In the present market?"

"Alright then, how much do you think a concern like that might fetch?"

Inspector Tierney rolled his eyes in an exasperated manner. "With or without tools?" he asked.

"Let us say, for the sake of the argument, *with*."

"I really don't know – and neither do I care..."

"Well, as a matter of fact, it all depends on the quality and condition of the lathe. Some of 'em are very handsome and might fetch a considerable sum – perhaps even as much as several hundred guineas."

"Is that so?" said the Active Duty man.

"Yes, and it's possible that McNaughten may well have had such a lathe – he has certainly demonstrated a good knowledge of 'em."

"And you have *proof* of this sale, do you?"

"Not as yet, no – all I'm saying is that things ain't necessarily how they appear to you. As a matter of fact, there is evidence that the prisoner did sell his business..."

"For seven hundred and fifty pounds?"

"No... he sold it to his journeyman for seventeen pounds."

"Seventeen pounds?" Inspector Tierney laughed. "Even without a mechanical lathe, it should have fetched more than twice that amount!"

"Yes, it should. And if that ain't a sure sign of some brain frenzy or other I'm a Chinaman."

Inspector Tierney appeared to be brooding on the turn of events. "And how do you know that this isn't all some fabrication?" he asked. "You can't go on the word of a convict..."

Inspector Hughes withdrew the informations from Glasgow from the buff box, and pointed out the relevant section to the scranning cove's attention. "See, it says right there that McNaughten sold his business for seventeen pounds to this fellow Carlo."

Inspector Tierney's eyes narrowed dangerously. "Who else knows about this?" he demanded.

"If you or your men ever troubled to read a single route-paper you'd know that I've been looking for that fellow Carlo since Friday night." Inspector Tierney was looking at him with a most peculiar expression on his face: a perfect mixture of astonishment and dismay. "And I have a strong inkling," continued the Inspector, "that whatever else the Detective Sergeant has discovered by now, he will have found that this *Carlo* ain't in Glasgow. As a matter of fact, I believe him to be here in London: the prisoner's landlady mentioned him by name to me. She said he offered to fetch a pair of boots for McNaughten."

The scranning cove pursed his lips in a shrewd manner. "I wish to make a statement," he said. "Write it down and I shall sign it. Don't look at me like that. Just do it. I, John Massey Tierney, Inspector, 'A' Division, recollect seeing a fellow about a year ago, and again in the past month or so, matching McNaughten's description, standing about Whitehall-gardens, Whitehall Chapel, the corner of Downing-street, and on the steps of the Privy Council!"

"Well, I'll be jiggered," said Inspector Hughes, when he had done writing out the statement and passed it to the scranning cove to sign. "That's just moonshine, ain't it? Is this all about your blessed bounties? You oughter be ashamed. You might not be in uniform, but you're still an inspector of the 'A' Division. What swag do you hope to bag out of this, then? Is blowing the gab on a poor mad Scotchman going to help you keep your rate up next time a provincial magistrate calls on your *services* to help him read the Riot Act? What was it you bilked from 'em last time? A hundred and twenty pounds, weren't it? For turning in a handful of poor Welchies on the word of a starving wretch who thinks his only hope lies with you and your free beer. How many of them deserved to be shipped to Botany Bay?"

"It's not as simple a matter as all that," said the plainclothesman. He had gone to stand by the coat rack, where he was giving all of his attention to scrutinising the items that were hanging there. "It's dangerous work, and I have many expenses to cover."

"O, yes, I'm sure you do, you bleeder. Expenses! You take the lion's share and leave the scraps for your informers to fight over!"

Inspector Tierney did not respond. He had picked out a dusty greatcoat which he threw over his arm. Then, looking as black as a preacher's breeches on Good Friday, he stormed out of the station-house.

No.19, Lower Grosvenor-street, Mayfair,
at about the same time

Wherein Mr. Drummond receives a very important visitor, and Miss Drummond plays a vital role in maintaining the safe governance of the realm.

The liveried footman informed Parrott that His Grace the Duke of Wellington had ventured out into the miserable link-lighted streets with the sole purpose of attending Mr. Drummond, who, upon hearing this, let out a low groan not unlike the cry of a wounded beast. Miss Drummond assumed his apparent distress to be an attempt by her brother to impart to her something of the utmost importance. She stroked the troublous volume, which was hidden beneath her sewing.

"Do not fret, dear!" she said, *sotto voce*. "I know just what to do." She noted with gratification the startled fluttering of his eyelids, which was all that he could do by now, apart from moan. "What are you waiting for? Admit His Grace at once!" she commanded Parrott. The words sent a thrill through her entire body.

The doctors abandoned the blood-letting for the time being, and lent their assistance in preparing Mr. Drummond for his distinguished visitor. Parrott departed sulkily to change into the footman's livery, and collected Neddie's whangee from the vestibule. It was essential that His Grace be escorted from his carriage into the house with all appropriate display. With her brother attired in a clean nightgown and cap, Parrott in costume, with the rolled umbrella in hand, and the surgeons suitably impressed, Miss Drummond laid aside her sewing and patted her hair. Then, with her little feet propped upon the footstool, she folded her fat little dimpled hands in her lap and waited, her heart flapping timorously, just like, she fancied, a poor little butterfly caught in a net.

In another moment he was in the room with them.

"This state of things cannot be permitted to continue," he boomed immediately upon entering. His Grace had been hard of hearing for a number of years by now, following the treatment of an ear infection with illiberal quantities of caustic soda; and his voice had correspondingly grown louder and more commanding. "This has gone beyond hayrick-burning and loom-smashing! The lower orders have passed across our bows and are now raking us with a broadside. Pray, forgive the naval metaphor!"

"Your Grace," she said, inclining her head coquettishly. "We are honoured." From Neddie's bed came a mournful sigh.

"I have come directly from a private dinner with Sir Robert Peel," shouted the Duke, – "sends his regards by the way – he shall call upon you tomorrow!"

"That would be *delightful*," said Miss Drummond.

"I found him to be in a fearful funk. It would appear that the Commissioners of Police have shewn him some alarming materials discovered in the assassin's lodgings here in London! He was taken with a large sum of money on him – a reward, no doubt, for bagging the Prime

Minister. Seems he shot you by mistake, old man!"

The surgeons expressed alarm and disapprobation. Neddie groaned softly. Miss Drummond, with her superior knowledge of all things pursuant to the matter, smiled a satisfied smile and patted the *Population* clutched in her ample lap.

"The Anti-Corn Law League is suspected!" bellowed the Duke.

"No!" exclaimed the surgeons.

"You may recall the report of a Reverend Bailey in respect of the League's Convention last summer – he heard one of those rascals declare in a crowded room how he would draw lots with a hundred others to decide which of 'em should murder Peel..."

"Tsk, tsk," said Mr. Guthrie senior.

"Dear, dear," said Mr. Bransby Cooper.

"...and it seems that your assassin had some sort of lot or token on him when he was taken! O yes! It's the talk of the clubs!" The Duke of Wellington was much too hard of hearing to detect the sounds of evident distress emanating from poor dear Neddie. "Aristocratical government is quite impossible in England. I fear that we are as close to Democracy as we have ever been!"

"Surely not!" said Mr. Bransby Cooper.

"What, what?" barked the Duke, sensing at once that he was being challenged.

The surgeon knew as much of politics as the Duke knew of leeches, but was undeterred nevertheless from expressing an opinion. "I meant to say, Your Grace," he replied insipidly, "that surely a well-ordered monarchy is the best course for strong government." He accompanied the observation with a low, cringing bow.

"Pooh pooh!" said the Duke. "Strong government is quite impossible. Reform put paid to that...!" He had lost a great number of teeth, due to the ravages of age and the battlefield, and not all of them had been replaced, yet Miss Drummond thought him every bit as fascinating as she recollected.

"But surely, Sir Robert Peel has a majority of more than ninety in the Commons?" objected Mr. Bransby Cooper.

"What what? Speak up if you will be heard!"

"It is so very *kind* of Your Grace to call," obliged Miss Drummond. She shot a look at the surgeon as she rose from her chair, delicately slipping the volume inside her leg o' mutton sleeve. She was blushing madly as His Grace took her hand and, bowing low, kissed it gallantly.

"Dear Miss Drummond," he said.

Her colour rose yet more steeply. She was thinking how very handsome he was, dressed for the evening. How dearly she would have liked to study his protuberances, if only he might be persuaded to sit down. His hair was thinner and much whiter than she remembered it, and she was certain that she could glimpse his Extra Large Conscientiousness as he slowly came up from the deep reverence.

He patted her soft, fat, little hand. "A most singular incident – four o'clock on Friday," he imparted, "crossing the park on my way home – a stout-made youth runs into me and all but succeeds in knocking me over!"

"Dear, dear, one wonders what the world is coming to!"

"Scoundrel had no idea who I was."

"Whatever did you do, Your Grace?"

"O, I would brook no apology."

"I should think not, sir."

"Young puppy is to be birched! I tell you, the lower orders have such a taste for plunder – it lies behind everything they do – plunder! Like a fleet of Barbary pirates, they think of nothing else!"

Neddie made a queer little noise: something between a groan and a wail.

"Poor dear Neddie," murmured Miss Drummond turning to look at him. "It was his proudest moment when you were so kind as to announce to the entire House of Lords your good fortune, sir, in having secured his services as your Secretary at the time His Majesty asked Your Grace to form a government. It was your proudest moment, was it not, dear? What say you? O, but he has taken such a shock! Poor, poor Neddie. But he is thrilled to have you here, sir. Thrilled!"

"I blame it all upon the loco-motive," bellowed the Duke. "That infernal machine allows the lower orders to traverse the country causing a deal of trouble. No good shall ever come of it, mark me! I have been saying so for a decade or more!"

"And, pray, Your Grace, how is Mr. Hume?" piped up Mr. Guthrie senior.

Mention of the Duke's own physician caused Miss Drummond's heart to skip a beat. She caught the eye of Mr. Bransby Cooper, grinning inanely at the side of his habitual tormentor. "Loco-motives are indeed fearsome things," she said emphatically. But it was no good.

"What what?" barked the Duke, inclining his good ear towards the surgeon. "You shall have to speak up, sir. I am a little hard of hearing, don't you know."

Everyone expressed their surprise.

"I was inquiring after the health of Your Grace's physician – Mr. Hume," said Mr. Guthrie senior, enunciating each word carefully. It was very importunate of him to inquire in so direct a manner after the health of a rival. But Miss Drummond was far more mindful of the grave dangers of straying so close to the matter of the *duel*. Mr. Hume, acting as the Duke's second when he had sought satisfaction of the Earl of Winchilsea, had been so thoroughly ignorant of protocol that he had supplied *rifled* pistols. She tried to catch the eye of Mr. Bransby Cooper, but he was gazing in a perfectly imbecilic manner at the opposite wall. "I had heard that Mr. Hume spends much of his time making the rounds of the asylums," said Mr. Guthrie senior. "He is quite unwell, is he not? Infirm – through age – or so I am given to understand."

The Duke appeared baffled. "Who is this fellow?" he shouted at Miss Drummond.

"Mr. Guthrie senior has been most kind in attending Neddie these past few days, sir."

"O, but you must allow me to send my own doctor," he said. "Hume. Excellent fellow. He saved my life once, don't you know. I took a bullet in the thigh which he removed. The Earl of Winchilsea, damn his eyes, failed to make his *delopement* wide enough and his shot found me out."

Miss Drummond coughed politely. Mr. Bransby Cooper came out of his reverie and raised his eyebrows towards her in an expression of abject hopelessness. Could it be that His Grace had forgotten, after all these years, the circumstances in which Mr. Drummond came to be attended by Mr. Hume once before – along with Mr.

Bransby Cooper's esteemed uncle, now departed?

"I am given to understand, Your Grace, that the decline in parliamentary standards of late is quite shocking to behold." Mr. Bransby Cooper, smiling in that forlorn, drooping way of his, quite surprised them all with his timely intervention.

"It is a perfect disgrace," yelled the Duke. "Such a dreadful din – the place is worse than a barrack-room! But then you see all is now at the mercy of public opinion – no longer the zephyr breath it once was, but a veritable Thracias, threatening all the uncertain violence of hurricanes and great deluges! How is the Queen's government to be continued? What what? Now there's all the matter! Public opinion shall destroy this country!"

Neddie was attempting to wave his arm about – the one with the tourniquet around it. The doctors succeeded in quietening him, but not before Miss Drummond had caught the urgency in the gesture. She patted the volume lying inside her sleeve. "Do not distress yourself, my dear," she crooned. "You have absolutely nothing to worry about." He was telling her what to do. She was certain of it.

A short time later she had her opportunity as the Duke of Wellington stood beside her in the vestibule, while they waited for Parrott to return from the mews with the carriage. She had her arm linked in his, bobbing at his side like a steadfastly squat buoy alongside a great gun-boat; her heart fluttering, her face all a-flush.

"The lower orders would never have dared threaten property as they did last summer if you had been Prime Minister, Your Grace," she said. "You have always understood how they are rotten to the core."

He bent his head towards her, the better to catch her words. "The problem with the lower orders," he said, "is that they are all rotten to the core."

She smiled, and tried to suppress involuntary memories of the horrid hot potato man who had used her so roughly in High Holborn in the course of a childhood visit to Mr. Hamley's Noah's Ark; how he had stood before her on the pavement and addressed her familiarly as his "Black-eyed Susan", tears coursing through the dust that coated his care-mapped face. She shuddered. It was, she thought, as if in some way he had considered her responsible for his misery...

[297]

"I have something for you, Your Grace," she said. "Something of immense importance to the continued safe governance of the realm."

Wordlessly, she slipped her hand inside her leg o' mutton sleeve and withdrew the vexatious volume. She passed it into the Duke's white-gloved hand.

"It is not all it appears, sir," she confided. "You will find within its pages a veritable trove of informations concerning the secret part of government... Dim and dismal matters which I am sure my poor brother would wish to share with you, and you alone."

The Duke patted the volume, and safely installed it in his breast pocket in the vicinity of his brave heart. "I will give it my full attention, madam, you may depend upon it. I thank you for your confidences."

"O Your Grace, I could never conceal a thing from you." She was thinking how this moment was the acme and pitch of her little life. "And you may ever depend upon my discretion in respect of that other matter." Her little eyes sparkled, her tiny mouth set in a line of thick contentment. "We were always of the opinion that Your Grace was quite correct to pursue that course of action – no matter what the King had to say about the folly of his Prime Minister issuing a challenge to one of his noble lords. A duel is the *natural* issue of a slight to a gentleman's honour – no matter what the law has to say upon the matter."

"Eh," bellowed the Duke. "What's that you say?"

"It was most unreasonable of the Earl of Winchilsea to accuse you, of all people, Your Grace, of betraying the Party and of introducing Popery into every department of the state. Such calumny – whatever one might think of the Emancipation of the Catholicks..."

"Winchilsea," snorted His Grace, "perfect ass!"

"And my brother, though doubtless well-intentioned, simply had no business going to Battersea Fields in the hope of preventing you from defending your honour."

"What? What?"

"My brother, Mr. Drummond – "

"Ah yes, Drummond! Best secretary I ever had! Fine fellow. Very fine fellow! A little misguided in the matter of trade and taxes, but a fine fellow, nevertheless. Very fine indeed! Behaved very well over that unfortunate business with the duel. Mark of a true gentleman."

Miss Drummond felt in her pocket for the shot.

"Of course, I aimed wide," the Duke was reminiscing, "unlike that cad Winchilsea. But the *delopement* was evidently wider off the mark than I had intended."

"It is easily done, sir. I gather the shot struck a tree a glancing blow, before finding its way into poor dear Neddie's *omentum*."

"Never accept pistols from a quack, madam! That is the lesson here."

"A surgeon," she said, "does not have the necessary grasp of these things. And Neddie ought not to have been there." Parrott was at the door, the livery soaked through, ruined. He was shaking off Neddie's whangee as though it were a tu'penny cane.

The Duke clicked his heels together and made a bow. "My dear Miss Drummond," he said, and he took her hand, bringing it to his lips. "I know that I can always depend upon you."

Her colour seeped through, long-forgotten stirrings saturating her heart and her head. "We should not have lasted thirty years at the Treasury, Your Grace," she graciously replied, "if our discretion had ever once been called into question."

The toothless and deaf old man they used to call the Beau took his hat from Parrott, but eschewed the offer of the umbrella on the grounds that it was an unmilitary device, and then without another word or gesture, he passed through the door and onto the freezing street, with the secrets of the nation tucked away where they were surely most safe: *that is to say*, next to his heroic bosom.

The Fourth Meeting.

They found McNaughten in the water closet. I was aware that he was in the habit of hiding himself there whenever a stranger entered the gallery, but it had not hitherto been his habit to resort to such tactics of avoidance on those occasions on which I attended him. He was discovered reading Robertson's *Spinal Diseases* – wherein are to be found, it will be recollected, learned descriptions of the manifestations and symptoms of what are commonly called "nervous conditions". The keeper who found him informed me that McNaughten read widely, but was "*especially interested in medical texts*" – a tendency that was readily accounted to his having once studied surgery in his native Glasgow, although it seemed to me to have an altogether more suspicious origination.

When they brought him forth he appeared to lose himself in contemplation of the flagstones for some considerable time. There was a weary look in his eyes.

"Ah me!" he said at last, "It is all such a waste. An' tae think that in all my life I never spoiled so much as an inch o' wood!"

"I do not doubt it," I replied, thinking that his was a perfectly observed rendering of Melancholia. "From everything you have told me of yourself," I said, "it would seem that you are a man of considerable intelligence and great self-reliance. I do not wonder that you lament this – this *waste*, as you put it."

He thought for a moment.

"Well," he said, "that may be, but I suppose that I must have done somethin' very bad or they wouldnae have sent me here."

"And do you recollect what it was – this bad thing?"

"I was acquitted," he said, "on the ground of insanity to be confined at Her Majesty's Pleasure."

It was, or so I was thinking, astonishing, the cool determinedness with which he played his part.

"Perhaps then," I countered, "– given that you did do this very bad thing – that verdict may have rendered you a service. Perhaps it may even be viewed as a shrewd means of preparing a loophole by which to win to yourself charity, and thereby escape punishment."

He appeared to shake himself into some form of composure, but I was unable to detect any sign suggestive of anything like a bestirring of conscience.

"What if," he said, "what if existence was an Archimedean spiral, turning for all eternity into a distant point that is never to be reached?" He was unable to bring himself to a paroxysm, though his eyes had become quite wild with emotion, and he was wringing his hands in an estimation of some sort of profound despair.

"We must all live in expectation of the eternal life that is to come."

"Aye," he cried, his voice thickening with grief, "but all the beauty that we can imagine isnae there. It is here – *here*! It is now!"

It was the beginning of 1837. He was established in the Turner's-yard premises in which his father had an interest. He had acquired a rose engine lathe and set up in the ornamental line. He slept in his shop; he did not employ any others to help him; he did the work of three men, seven days a week – and in this manner succeeded in saving, he reckoned, above four-fifths of every penny earned. In general, he only drew out very small amounts on which to live – although he did buy himself a fine beaver-skin hat, modelled in the D'Orsay style, and a weskit with sleeves and strings behind, and two pairs of smart-cut drab trowsers. It was important to be presentable. He affected gentlemanly airs when showing his pattern book to prospective customers, emerging from behind the lathe as articulate, careful and neat a vision as the precisely-drawn mathematical structures he so proudly displayed.

And for a while he was actually happy. He would retire each night tired but content, the patterns to which he would soon give shape swirling in his mind's eye. Often he would stir from near sleep to snatch up a notebook and work out the geometry before the perfection of an image faded from him for ever. He had such keenness, such urgency to him! The patterns wreathed him to the earth, cradling him in their tanglings; his days passing in a succession of trochoidal curves emanating from the straight lines of the cutter: all, *all* of it, the pure product of his mind.

But a shadow falls over everything upon the earth.

He had been in business on his own account for about six months, when another election was called with all the usual rowdinesses. Gangs roamed the streets beating drums; banners waved from every window; and on each corner broadsheet-sellers brandished smudged ribaldries at the expense of the Tories, or the Liberal click.

The shop that Dan had had of his father had a ten-pound rent owing to it, and it had been the intention of Mr. McNaughten senior to let the premises to a man who was prepared to register in the Conservative interest. Such men, however, being difficult to come by in Glasgow at the time, his father was content to let Dan bide there on the understanding that if he were minded to vote at all, the boy would not turn out for the Liberal candidate. Dan was in agreement with this – not caring for politics of any hue; but he shrewdly struck a bargain with his pa in any case, having reasoned that as he was being asked to forego his vote, it was only right that he pay a rent set a little below the threshold for election rights. Mr. McNaughten senior agreed on a payment of nine pounds eleven shillings.

When he learned what Dan had done, Abram Duncan declared himself disgusted. To think, he decried, that, for the sake of a few shillings, a man could so unthinkingly surrender that prize for which countless others would have willingly given all they had.

Abram was, by that time, a renowned speaker on democratism, and the author of a popular fourpenny pamphlet, and had garnered to himself a great following in Glasgow and beyond. He might even have considered standing as an independent candidate, had he the funds so necessitous to a political career. His following was not all of the raggit and worn variety – there were one or two tradesmen therein above the middling sort, and some of the lecturers from the Mechanics' Institute; but they were not well-to-do men, such as could cover the costs of a hustings without feeling the pinch; and Abram, being noght but a journeyman, had no great store of wealth with which to fund himself – and not being a shopkeeper or property-owner, he had no vote.

He came to the shop again and again, urging Dan to register and turn out for the Radical candidate.

"Och, but it's just business," said Dan. "I'm after makin' somethin' o' myself, that's all."

He had no need of all the rousin' and urgent talk o' clicks and lordling loons. It meant not a jot to him.

Besides, he had struck a bargain with his father, fair and square.

"The powers that be," Abram told him, "stand in the way o' the urgent an' bitter necessities o' the People. A revolution is necessary, if no' inevitable. At present yon middle classes are arrayed on the side o' oor oppressors, but if sic as ye, Dan, were to join us in oor struggle agin the tyrants ye maun gie to this sweepin' change a peaceful character: if no' then vengeance'll o'ertak' ye an' all your class. Yer warehouses, yer homes'll be gi'en to the flames, an' black ruin'll o'ertak' the country."

Dan had heard it all before. And although it was the cause of great pain to him to suffer the wrath of a man for whom he had so long cared, he believed that he had the right to make a life for himself in the only way he could. He liked his shop. He listened to Abram's prophecies, and gave them full consideration, but he had also imbibed the arguments of his father, to whom the remedy for revolution lay, not in extension of the suffrage, but in supporting the army and the polis as they endeavoured to keep the riff-raff at bay.

It seemed to him that there could be no danger to men such as himself, men who kept above the hurly-burly, who worked hard, and were decent and honest, provided that the rule of law was upheld.

One afternoon as he made his way along the high-street to the Mechanics' Institute (where he hoped to consult a work on geometry that he knew to be in the library), a group of factory girls pushed past him. Their feet were very ill-shod, and their heads and shoulders wrapped in rough-edged squares of tartan shawling. He felt instantly a pang of pity for them; but as they passed, one of them looked back over her shoulder, and cast a look of such scorn in his direction as to leave him quite undone. He walked on quickly, though he fancied that he could hear her laughing about him with her companions. Upon reaching the corner, he prepared to cross over. He looked first towards the stump of the Tron steeple, and then to where the yet rising edifice of the new Sheriff Buildings could be glimpsed behind a maze of smoking wynds. When he looked back, a rough crew was standing on the other side of the road and, although he could not offer any explanation for the thought, it came to him that they were waiting for him. Not wishing to draw attention to himself, he put down his head and decided to keep to his side of the high-road, walking on hurriedly until he reached the safe haven of the reading rooms on North Hanover-street.

That night he woke with a start. It was very dark in the shop, but he was aware of someone moving across the floor towards him. He had scarce time to register the fact, however, before he felt a breath, hot and urgent, upon his cheek.

"Hauld your tongue an' youse'll be taken care of," came a harsh whisper. "Resist and it'll be the worse for ye!"

In another instant a hood of coarse sacking was slipped over his head and he was being forced to his feet with considerable violence of oaths. It being so cold, he had gone to bed with his clothes on, which he now had cause to count a stroke of the utmost good fortune, for he was forced onto the freezing street with no opportunity to put on his boots or hat, and in this dismal fashion was goaded along lanes and byways. He was able to keep some of his fear at bay by drawing in his head the bearings of each twist and turn made before being brought to a halt in a close somewhere, he reckoned, in the vicinity of the Glasgow Cross. He was aware of a sudden gust of warmth and noise which he took to be a tavern, and was then bundled down some stairs, coming into a room heavy with tobacco smoke, where other low voices mingled with those of his captors.

The sack hood was exchanged for a bucket, which was hit with a bar several times, until he shook from head to foot like a bell; foul oaths resounding in the metal echo.

"Fuckin' knobstick!"

"Tory spy."

"Tory cunt."

"Blaw his worthless brains oot!"

Rough hands hauled him to another place in the room. His trowser was pulled down amidst uncouth jeers and impredations, and he felt the heat of a candle thrust between his legs. The pain and terror was immense.

He was blubbing now. "Pity's sake! Pity's sake..." His sobs dimmed against the bucket. They hit him again on the head, and he felt his mind shatter into a thousand shards.

"To the poll, to the poll!"

"Ye maun turn oot fer the Liberal!"

"Tory shite!"

"But I'm no' a Tory!" he protested. "I'm no' even registered fer the vote..."

To his amazement the candle was removed, and he found himself pressed down onto the floor.

"Next time ye cowerin' non-elector," came a whisper close by him, "next time..." And then came a volley of hard fists and heavy boots and harsh jeers and filthy insults, causing him to surrender utterly to the fast-descending black.

When he revived, he was aching, wet through, half-frozen, and lying upon the cobbles of a very bad back-close. He was only a little surprised to find Carlo there: it was as though he had been expecting him. Carlo was proferring a blackened short pipe, oft-used, but warm, which Dan accepted gratefully, inhaling long and hard, the smoke heating his lungs. When he coughed, thick plugs of blood splashed upon the cobbles and everything seemed to rock as if he was on the deck of a ship. He'd never been on a ship, of course, but he imagined that that was how it would be.

"The Liberals maun muster a' the votes they can," said Carlo, "to keep the Tories oot a Glesga'."

"Aye, but I'm no' a Tory."

"Aye, but your pa's fer the Tories."

"Havers, mon, they might a killed me!"

Carlo helped him to his feet and walked him back to the shop. He washed his wounds and fetched brandy from a tavern. Dan cupped his hands around the beaker and urged the contents down his throat.

"Ah cannae watch youse a' the time, wee man," Carlo was saying over and over, like a lament, a prayer. "I should say it's best youse dinnae mention this to a'body, else they shall come again. An' next time ah might not be there tae stop 'em."

After a few days it came to Dan that he had no choice but to give up the shop on Turner's-yard. He took on smaller premises on Stockwell-street, just a wee bit along from his pa. His father thought it strange that he should have given up a very good shop for such an inferior one, and would often stop him on the street in order to inquire after the fact. After a while, Dan took to crossing over whenever he chanced to spy Mr. McNaughten senior coming towards him. He could not bring himself to offer any explanation that was a lie, and he was afraid to tell the truth. What was more, he had come to believe that if he never spoke of what had happened, then, in time, he would be able to forget.

The new shop was leased from Smiths the bell-makers. There being a slough in trade, it was not difficult to agree a rent of nine pounds and nine shillings, and in this way he was able to save a deal of money, and at the same time remove any obligation to register for the vote as a ten-guinea householder.

Henceforth, though he maintained an intellectual interest in political economy – for it was important to understand these things if one was to progress through the world – he let it be known about the town how he could not be induced to lend his support to any man, or cause. And thus he endeavoured to set himself apart, the better that he might get on. He returned to his patterns and gave over all of his energies to trying to restore his previous good life. But he ignored the democratic violence of the streets. Every so often he would read in the newspapers of another shooting, or of a jar of vitriol being flung in the face of a tradesman, but he would always strive to put such fearsome notions as these scraps of news gave rise to out of his head. He would tell himself that there was no saying what these men might have done to deserve their fate, and that what had befallen him was of an altogether different order.

He never told a soul what had happened; and yet he was unable to forget the events of that night. Often would he retrace his steps from the old shop in Turner's-yard to the place where Carlo had found him: a vile spot up by the Gallowgate. And once, his heart pounding, he dared to descend the steps into the cellar of the Black Boy Tavern, his senses reviving every moment of that dreadful occasion so closely that he thought he might die of fear.

Still, life went on. He worked hard and spent his nights in the shop, reading and designing patterns. He saw less and less of Abram, but Carlo would come by occasionally, whenever he was in town, looking for money or a place to stay or an old pair of trowsers. Once or twice Dan gave him some work, although he was a poor tradesman. He did so, he supposed, out of a sense of gratitude. He was aware how Carlo would have fared well enough in the turmoil of street politics, without taking any care of him, and yet the scouf continued to seek out his companionship. From time to time it perplexed him as to why this should be, but he could not deny that he was grateful for the measure of protection the association afforded him.

McNaughten's pale eyes had an uncharacteristic gleam to them as he reached the conclusion of this part of his narration.

"Is it a wise man, or a foolish one," he asked, "who fancies that he can read the signs o' his times?"

I laid aside my pen. "Sometimes," I said, "it is as though the world is changing faster than my cumbersome thinking can possibly hope to keep pace with."

The sky was darkening and in the distance a shriek echoed along the chambers of that place: ghastly and terrifying, causing the hairs on the back of my neck to bristle and to stand up on end. The fearsome memory of the shriek hung in the atmosphere for several moments before succumbing to a profound silence. And when it was no more, it came to me that there had been something of jest and, yes, something *vital*, in the horrid noise, and I found myself longing for it to resound once more – to fill up the emptiness, cruel and irrevocable; that chill, still air that contained more of misery than any cry of beast or man could ever muster.

TUESDAY 24TH JANUARY, 1843

The Times
Morning edition

MATTERS OF GREAT IMPORTANCE

Several cabinet meetings have been held at which it is understood matters of the gravest importance have been discussed.
On Monday Her Majesty's Ministers assembled at the Foreign
Office, and sat two hours. The Home Secretary, Sir James Graham, arrived express from Brighton, for the purpose of attending
the meeting.

In the early evening a second Cabinet Council was held at
the private residence of Lord Fitzgerald and Vesci. Sir Robert
Peel, the Duke of Wellington, the Duke of Buccleuch, the Earl
of Aberdeen, Lord Stanley, Sir James Graham, the Chancellor
of the Exchequer, the Earl of Haddington, Lord Fitzgerald and
Sir Henry Hardinge were present. The Ministers met at three
o'clock, and the council broke up at half past five o'clock.

Late edition

STATE OF MR. DRUMMOND'S HEALTH

Following the medical consultation which took place this evening
at ten o'clock, it has been announced to Mr. Drummond's friends
that the gentleman's dissolution is fast approaching – that, in
fact, mortification has taken place, and that all human aid will
consequently be of no avail.

Although the unfortunate sufferer has been gradually sinking
the whole of the day, the great change which indicated his speedy
dissolution occurred about seven o'clock, when the whole of his
family was immediately summoned.

The inquiries after the unfortunate gentleman's health have
throughout the day been exceedingly numerous.

Conclusion of the life of Mr. Drummond – amidst consideration of the follies and indolence of servants, the Hereafter, and other bumps and protuberances.

Poor dear Neddie groaned upon waking for the final time, and his devoted sister put down her sewing to attend to him. She watched closely as Parrott deftly applied a damp muslin to his master's lips, which were very parched, and then to his brow, which was very moist.

"I do believe he's trying to say something, Miss Drummond." The footman placed his ear tantalisingly close to his master's mouth. "Pray, what is it, sir?"

She felt a curious relief when Neddie's papery lids folded once more over his glassy eyes.

"Parrott, you know as well as do I that Mr. Drummond must not speak." She pretended to turn back to her sewing. The ameliorative effects of the tincture she had taken shortly after four had already worn away – this largely due, she must own, to Mrs. Gaff the housekeeper and her tendency to huff, puff and generally throw herself into an agitated state over practically nothing; not to mention the wastefulness, which required Miss Drummond to spend a good part of every Sunday in the scullery while Mrs. Gaff and Lizzie the girl were at church, plumbing the depth of the flour bin and measuring out the contents of the tea caddy. Her brother lying close to death had occasioned no slight degree of vexation to her nerves, but while poor dear Neddie had been lying there with half of London dancing attendance on him, life in the house had been going on all the same. She could not allow her vigilance in respect of flour and tea and other costly items to lapse. Mrs. Gaff's profligacy; the girl's slovenliness; Parrott's contempt – which over the past few days he had done nothing to disguise – taking all of this into consideration it was small wonder that the lassitude that afflicted her each day upon the onset of evening had intensified of late. And inspec-

[309]

tion of the kitchen had revealed the alarming intelligence that the grate had been brightened with emery paper. That wretched girl! Miss Drummond wondered whether she ought to let her go...

As for Mrs. Gaff: she had been quite worn down by the wretched woman's fussing; and driven to inform her earlier that evening, that she would take nothing more than a pot of chocolate and some Welsh Rabbit for her supper; for which, seeing as Parrott was quite capable of preparing such a repast without a modicum of bother, it was not necessary for the housekeeper *to trouble herself any further*. She had been looking forward to a pair of boiled kidneys and some macaroni, but it was imperative that servants be brought, from time to time, to an understanding of how *dispensable* they were. As she informed the housekeeper, five-and-twenty years of service does not preserve one from the giving of notice!

And as the good Lord knows, she thought, I have expended *quite enough* of my dwindling strengths upon the menus for the coming week. Of course, Mrs. Gaff was – as were all servants – in possession of Small Wonder and Large Cautiousness, a combination which made it quite impossible for her to take any decisions of her own accord – and no doubt made it equally difficult for her to resist the wily *tendresses* of Bugbird the butcher...

"One and ninepence ha'penny for a dish of mutton, indeed! Just fancy!" Miss Drummond tut-tutted over her sewing. "Thank goodness for my Scotch blood, Parrott," she said, "or we should all be ruined. When Mr. Drummond is dead there will be no clerk's salary from the Treasury to pay for such luxuries!"

"Dying..." Neddie said in a feeble whisper; and something that sounded like "is this death?"

"Hush, sir," said Parrott.

"Darkness," said Neddie in a dwindling voice.

"I shall not leave your side, sir. I give you my word."

The blisters behind her brother's ears, at the nape of his neck and all along his back were straining to burst; some of them already suppurating. The pain, she thought, must be very great; blinding poor Neddie, no doubt, to everything else, including the footman's pusillanimity.

She had entertained such hopes for Parrott when he had joined the household, it long having been a point of enlightenment with her that the despised race to which he belonged did not deserve the degradation so often inflicted on it by their fair-skinned masters. Negroes, as she had often averred, made very good servants: that is, *in general*.

"You know, there is no will," she murmured. "The house and a small income is all there is. Miss Matilda bequeathed it to us both equally in the will that Master George drew up when *she* was dying. The remainder passes to whichever one of us, Master Edward or myself, is left – and thence to our nieces and nephews. It was a point with dear Papa never to pay to lawyers a penny more than one had to." She looked sharply at the footman. "There will be no gifts."

"Miss Drummond – how – how can you..?" His voice was breaking with emotion. Barely stifling his distress, he returned to the task of soothing her brother. "Hush, sir. We are all praying for you," he said, "praying so hard. You are a good man – the best: you have no need of fear." He wiped the back of his hand across his eyes. "I think it very harsh," he said; "poor gentleman! Ah me, he has been used very ill. If he were my brother, I should not let the doctors near him again to suffer so."

The doctors had deserted them for the time being. They would be back, but now that there was little else to be done for poor dear Neddie, it had been agreed that they should attend to their other business, so long neglected. Over the course of the day just past – the longest yet in this vigil – they had given constant assurances that they had provided all that human aid could avail. They had grazed the skin on his right arm; scraped the flesh from his left leg; drained him of several more cups of blood; emptied him of urine and held up the murky fluid to the light. They had peered and poked at his stool, and at the festering wound in his front. And then they had rolled him over so that they could do the same to the festering wound in his back. He had suckled a dozen leeches at his breast, and a dozen more at his rump: feeling the life seep from his veins, the coldness enter, the warmth leave his body for ever.

She had watched it all from beneath her lashes.

"O pooh-pooh," she scoffed, "poor dear Mr. Drummond shall be immortalised. They shall write him up in their journals and give talks on him at the Chirurgical Society; they shall recompense him a thousand times over in tuppenny endorsements of cure-alls in the newspapers." It occurred to her that she was, by now, past all pretence at caring. "You are a young man," she said; "you are not used to death. But I am, and it always goes like this."

Neddie's face, turned towards the candlestick, was mapped with tears; his eyes flickering between the tinder-box, and the fire leaping in the grate.

He is drawn towards the flames, she thought, because he knows that he is damned. She flashed another look at Parrott. And how can he not be, after all that he has done?

"Hush, sir," said the footman, weeping. "Let me wet your lips. There, that is better, is it not?"

But Neddie was already in the swamp, among the embers of the old Palace, the burnt tinder-sticks of the temple.

This is it, she thought; and she laid her sewing in her lap, closed her eyes and breathed deeply and contentedly. "This is what makes the leaves in the forest quiver so," she said in a sad whisper.

Beyond the heavy drapes the London sky was soft as lead, and Grosvenor-square damp and musty, heavy with the scent of dead vegetation swept in on the wind from the market gardens; bitter and reeking, showing Neddie the key to the universe.

O! Why not me, she thought over another ill-tempered stitch. Why am I always to be left behind? She had to strain her eyes to see because the wick needed trimming and the light kept dipping, plunging them in and out of shadow. She wished that she had been more rapid of thought, that she had been prettier and not so stout. She wished that she had been more *loved*.

So many mysteries that were not hers to divine! Rather Large Wonder. Rather Large Cautiousness. It was her fate to have a Proper Sentiment conjoined with a Common Propensity, in equal measure.

"Soon you will be at peace," she said, smiling weakly. "Soon you will be with Mama and Papa, and dear Matty. Soon you shall look upon the smiling face of God and hear the trumpets of a golden host."

"Hallelujah!" cried Parrott in a wild sob.

She rubbed her eyes with her podgy fists, but they were quite, quite dry.

"Soon," she said, "you will know all the mysteries and secrets of the universe." And I, she thought, shall be left behind. While dear Neddie floats among the stars I shall be peering into the steamy fissure of the waiting basket, with the clamour of the mob in my ears. For the Duke of Wellington is quite right, of course: it is all over with this ill-fated land.

She closed her eyes against the vision of ten thousand tormenting faces in red caps grinning before her, each of them assuming the features and appearance of the wretched hot potato man, with his awful, sad smile: all, all blaming her, her, for their misery.

And suddenly she felt the burden of lost promise. Her prison, this house, a dry husk with an old maid and her bachelor brother left to rattle around inside it... The parlour taunted her; the nursery luring her back to the place it had been in more propitious times: the swoosh of Mama's skirts, the creak of Papa's top-boots; nine, then eight, then seven, and finally six little pairs of eyes shining on Christmas mornings, brighter than the tapers used to light the candelabra – which, Miss Drummond observed as soon as she dared to open her eyes again, was very dusty.

She thought: Yes! I shall have to let Lizzie go as well.

Parrott was wiping poor dear Neddie's forehead for the last time in this life, crying in a voice that was fractured with grief. "We pray for you, sir. We pray for you."

But she was thinking of the fire, the licking flames reflected in the gleaming blade of the guillotine. Wild men will cavort in Parliament, she thought; the lunatics will run amok in Bethlem. It is written in the hills and crevices; in the valleys and the mountains; in the bumps and protuberances. For if the human soul has its own topography, as it were, which may be read upon the skull, then what may be known of the essence and even the destiny of a nation by reading the mountains and the vales; the sloughs, the tracks and drifts; the shore-lines; the rocks and stones and trees? Then, "It is time," she said. "For pity's sake, let him go."

And she reached across to fill her glass with the last of the hot water from the silver coffee-pot that was practically all that remained of Uncle Georgie's portion of the bank money, after he had lost twenty thousand pounds in a game of whist with "Beau" Brummel at Brooks's.

Unleashing the drops of Aqua d'Oro, she settled back into her chair and sipped and waited and sipped and waited.

And with the last strength remaining in his blistered, bloodless body, with the last morsel of strength, Mr. Drummond seized Parrott by the arm and mouthed the words she thought were: "Burn them!"

"Hush, sir, you must not speak. The doctors say you will not mend if you speak."

But Mr. Drummond clutched the fellow's lapels, pulling him close, closer with the last remnant of strength left to him. "*Forgive him!*" he gasped. Then he lifted his head slightly, as much as he could bear, and with his dying breath planted a tender kiss upon the lips of his footman. This done, he fell, exhausted, against the pillow and never said another word.

The grave was already covering him, the soft earth like liquid, the ooze of the river filling up his nostrils and his eyes and his mouth; but it did not choke him: it glided into his body filling up his veins like mother's milk. And when she looked at him she saw at once that he was smiling: the mild, sad smile of the dead.

WEDNESDAY 25TH JANUARY, 1843

TEMPLE BAR,
SEVEN O'CLOCK A.M.

Wherein Mr. Nicholson arrives at the understanding that strong delusion may be sent as punishment for believing a lie.

And here he was, Old Peeping Tom, the Lord Chief Baron himself, Renton Nicholson, publisher and book-seller, the flashest of flash habitués of gambling dens and boozing kens; the arbiter elegantiarum of fashion and folly; blabber, screever, moocher, scrivener, &c., &c., &c. Burly, square-built, whiskery and dusty in the still half-light of the chilly sunless morn. And there he went, loosely dressed, ill-shod – ambling along those slabs of cold-as-the-grave stone, those thick dead groutings. This morning, not-quite-sober, never-quite-sober, he was on his way to assume the role of proprietor of a shabby bookshop on Holywell-street (quite the shabbiest in that shabby, shabby trade upon that shabby, shabby row); where, under the cunning guise of his own name, an improbably ginger wig, and full complement of mutton-chop whiskers, he would be selling a spicy mixture of pornography and sedition to any who cared to drop by with the wherewithal.

He would clandestinely relish all the frenzy, all the fury, all the bluster, bustle and commotion that ensued once the metropolis had had a chance to smell the rank slops and spills of life in this town as she was lived by those who knew her best. For today was Wednesday and the first day upon which it was possible to "Catch the Living Manners as they Rise" by purchasing the latest edition of that "scurrilous", that "tawdry" popular rag, that journal of cacophemy: *Peeping Tom of London Town* – the only true success of a long career which had all too often been at variance with fortune.

And let his false moustachios fall into a dish of eggs and his ill-gotten set of Waterloo teeth choke him if he wasn't proved justified in his revelations of the humbuggery that had been applied to the shooting of Mr. Drummond in depredation of the truth. Tricky blighter, truth: a

[315]

dodger, a phantom; glimpsed but rarely, in the adumbrations edging the domain of *suggestio falsi*. Ask any peeler worth his salt and you would learn the same. Mr. Nicholson never wasted time on getting at the *truth*. O, dear me no! His only interest was in how it all hung together, and in what kept it turning. For the world will go on turning, be assured of that, my pippins: kept going by all of us desperate souls a-stepping on the old cock-chafer; with them close to the top clinging on lest they be flung off altogether, and a great thrumming mass at the bottom, waiting to be crushed like so many beetles.

In the course of his own frantic bit o' steppin' Mr. Nicholson had already discovered a great deal, though he wavered between believing that *the Irvingites were behind it all*, and the notion that the matter had something to do with getting *our daily bread*. Amen. He always crossed himself whenever the Anti-Corn Law League presented itself in his swirling thoughts.

Mr. Nicholson had instantly recognised the prisoner's Scotch landlady from her glory days when she had tantalised dandies at the old Scotch Church under the aegis of Doctor Irving. She still had a pretty little figure, set off by the neat order of her shining black hair, but the misery of her life since then could not have been read more plain upon her face than if it had been writ in a book. Before Mr. Warren had arrived at the lodgings on Sunday afternoon, he had been ingratiating himself with Mrs. Dutton, sharing reminiscences of the grand old days at the Scotch Church in Regent-square, and that great incarnate, Dr. Irving. But this was as far as Mr. Nicholson had come with the religious connexion. In truth, he had grown a little bored with the story, other matters having taken his attention. The presence of the Active Duty in the lodgings had made him a little wary of maintaining too high a profile. He did not wish to find himself collared at this late stage in the proceedings, and so he had spent the past two nights in a boozing ken on the Ratcliffe Highway, rather losing track of the plot.

His beery breath rose into the hard air of this cold, bright London morning as he prepared to step across the Temple Bar. He had, of course, no idea that Mr. Drummond had expired; no idea that everything was about to take an entirely different course. No idea at all.

He was suddenly reproved into pinching the ragged brim of his hat as a chap-handed, butter-lipped Welsh milk-maid passed him in the op-posite direction, dreaming of home. O! he silently implored her; pause but a moment to wonder who is he who brushes my pail as he shifts by, and sets it swinging sadly in the crisp, frost-sparkled air of the slowly waking city!

"I could love thee till I die," he sung at her in a surprisingly light tenor, "wouldst thou love me modestly." But the milk-maid passed on, seemingly oblivious to his attentions and leaving him to gaze with sin-cere envy upon the empty pails, hanging limply from her yoke either side of her pretty waist. He watched her go sighing down those hard streets, past buildings the colour of smoke; her long, soft plaid shawl and shiny beaver-hat betokening another world altogether. And when she was gone from him, the low mournful wail of a river barge break-ing across the sleeping streets scored his time-worn heart. As the sound faded into the merciless sky, he was a little surprised to find that he was weeping.

Mr. Nicholson travelled on a little further until it was time to make his turning away from the clean, fine double-fronts of Strand, and to duck down the running ulcer that was Holywell-street. The sour decay filled his nostrils at once; at every dull tread he sensed beneath his feet the grass and the rivers, the fish heads and the belt buckles, the dung mounds and the amulets, the rotten and burnt timbers, the spent coals, the tinder-sticks, the piss and shit, the dead babies, the glittering mo-saics, the dinosauruses. Ah! This city, which he loved and loathed in equal measure, laid out neatly upon the mud and oozings of its own making in the brick fields of Highbury and Spitalfields: bricked up; entombed with all those countless others brought here to this great, stinking plague pit.

He crossed the road by the portico of St. Clement Danes, where a notice nailed to the parish board proclaimed: *THE HUMBLE SHALL BE EXALTED, Luke, chapter 8 verse 14*. But when, he thought, reading it. *When*? And there already out upon the pavement, the Jew old-clothes-seller from the premises next to his own was looking up at the sky, across which daylight was spreading in slow, even layers of shimmer-ing glaucescence, as surprising as a pigeon's breast.

"Shamoir yesroile!"

"Good morning, brother," responded Mr. Nicholson, drawing a large rusty key from his knapsack.

There was a crude drawing chalked upon the shop wall: a badly drawn erect penis with comically bulbous testicles armed with three sprouting hairs apiece, and above it a stick-man in a huge slouch hat, hanging from a gallows, a pipe dangling insouciantly from where his mouth would be had the artist troubled to give him one. Mr. Nicholson frowned at the image for a moment or two, then, pulling a frayed cuff down over his hand, scrubbed it out. Turning the key in the padlock he took a deep breath. The sweet biscuit smell of mouse droppings mingled with the dust from the rolls of parchment rose to greet him, as he stepped into the piles of obscene song-sheets, the blasphemous pamphlets, the vile lithographs and woodblock prints pegged out in jagged lines across the interior; the rows and rows of special editions all on cheap fly-blotted paper, their cardboard casings bent and flapping.

Here a half-dozen copies of *The Utility of Flagellation as Regards the Pleasures of the Marriage Bed and as a Medical Remedy*; here a parcel of Robert Owen's *A New View of Society*. Over there on the shelf closest to the window numerous copies of *Julia: or I Have Saved my Rose*, alongside a bundle of Hone's *The Political House that Jack Built*; and up there on the shelf behind the clerk's desk, stowed safely, a row or two of *Onanism Unveiled, or the Private Practices of the Youths of Both Sexes, showing its prevalence among schools, particularly female, pointing out the fatality that invariably attends its victims; developing the symptoms, the cause of the disease, the means of cure, as regards simple gonorrhoea &c.*

It was necessary to keep this last volume out of the reach of those casual types who came into the shop to browse with little or no intention of making a purchase. Mr. Nicholson liked to speculate that they came on recommendation of the Society for the Suppression of Vice, that venerable body of venereal bodies, which laboured ceaselessly and tirelessly to check the spread of open immorality and preserve the minds of the young from contamination by – well, my good fellow – by exposure to the likes of Old Peeping Tom himself and his disgusting shop. He smiled at the thought of all that corruption and hypocrisy, and how nothing so vile could be found in this place. He chuckled to himself. O, chums, he thought, how very good it was for business!

But his good humour did not last long.

The ancient shop bell wearily signalled an arrival. It was too early for customers, and Mr. Nicholson was not expecting company. He quickly ran through his stock of common pleadings, reasonably assuming it must be the peelers, or one of the legion to whom he owed money come to break his nose and hurdle him to Newgate. It was neither.

He had not spied the slinking toss-pot waiting for him in the alley, but he must have been there all the same; and by the frozen set of his pasty grimace, he must have been waiting through a good portion of the dawn.

"Ah! Is it muffin and crumpet time already?" chirruped Mr. Nicholson. "And what have you brought for Old Peeping Tom? A song? A riddle? Japes, jokes…?"

Carlo, the plainclothes spy from the Democratic Chapel, scowled and spat a brown plug of tobacco onto the threshold by way of a greeting. "I've been keepin' a look out for youse," the bully said, pulling down the brim of his hat even further and sinking his chin into the collar of his coat. It was a very dusty old police great-coat: several sizes too big.

"Why, I'm flattered, of course," said Peeping Tom. "But I don't believe that we have been introduced." He was hoping most sincerely that the plainclothesman had not recognised him from the prisoner's lodgings on Sunday afternoon.

Carlo snarled disdainfully. He picked up a print of Marie Taglioni at her most diaphanous, balanced on one long silk-clad leg with t'other lifted up behind her in an *attitude* of surprising elegance, and regarded it with idle interest, turning it this way and that, but with nothing approaching the correct regard or appreciation which the ballet-dancer's skill so evidently deserved.

"Ah've bin waitin' fer youse," he grunted. "The old Jew telt me youse generally dandered along o' a Wednesday."

A great palsy had laid hold of Mr. Nicholson's knees, but he nevertheless affected an air of affronted indignation. "Kindly do not handle the merchandise," he said, regarding the grubby fingers that were rubbing the edges of the print, "unless you intend to make a purchase."

Carlo's other hand darted out quicker than an adder and seized Mr. Nicholson by the tatterdemalion kerchief he had tied at a jaunty angle around his throat. He demonstrated a surprising strength for such a small man.

"Whatever it is you think I've done," gasped the print-seller, struggling for breath, "I swear it, I ain't done it. I'm a rate-payer in good standing, I am. A respectable tradesman. Well, respectable enough..."

The bully tightened his grip, squeezing the air out of Mr. Nicholson's fat neck. "Did youse tell the peelers about me?"

Mr. Nicholson spluttered. "The peelers! Stow it! I ain't no Judas. I ain't never sneaked to the bobbies in me life. Perhaps it was that busted snyde FIAT JUSTITIA!"

Carlo sneered contemptuously and let go the kerchief. He turned away and started rolling up the print of La Taglioni. Mr. Nicholson took the opportunity to remove his neckwear as a precaution against its further abuse.

"My part in the kimbau is done noo," the plainclothesman snarled, "an' ah'm vamoosin' tae Amerikay as soon as the last jig's bin jigged. To be nabbed noo, after all ah've been through, would be a tragedy." He stuffed the ballet-girl print inside the pocket of his oversized coat. "If youse want tae live youse'll keep your nose oot o' ma business. D'youse ken whit ah'm efter sayin'?"

"I ken that you are an aficionado of the Terpsichorean Art," quipped Mr. Nicholson, indicating the print. "That'll be one and ninepence half-penny."

The Scotch bully was hitching up his loose shabby trowsers, a hand to each leg, and laughing in a low rumble which grew louder and louder, his head thrown back, his mouth open wide to the ceiling. When the Wellingtons were completely revealed the laughter stopped abruptly.

For a moment it looked as though he might crack there and then.

"I – I don't understand..." whisperered Mr. Nicholson. "For pity's sake..." He felt like a fellow who had woken up in someone else's bad dream.

Carlo seemed to gather his wits. He raised a contemplative finger to his red neckerchief.

"Youse said when we met on Sunday afternoon that youse could put the kybosh on the whole gammon if youse're wantin' tae."

"O, I say a lot of things. Most of it nonsense," said Mr. Nicholson steadily.

"Drummond is dead."

Nicholson clapped his hand over a bead of cold sweat that was crawling down the back of his neck. "That's not good," he said.

"Aye, it's no'."

"They'll hang the Scotchman for sure..."

"Aye mebbe. But Daniel McNaughten dinnae kill 'im. Tak' it frae me."

"What did you say?"

"That's as much as I can telt youse wi'oot puttin' ma ain neck in the noose."

"Did your pal Inspector Tierney send you to tell me this?"said Mr. Nicholson.

"They cunts think they can buy an' sell a man's soul for a pair o' Wellingtons, or a regulation-issue overcoat. But youse see, the way ah'm lookin' at it, they still owe me... Ach, the system's all to do wi' keepin' the working man doon and gettin' cheap everythin'. It disnae matter whit ye dae, how far youse dander alang wi' 'em, daein' their biddin'. Man, if we could live on a shillin' a day, they'd see tae it we got ninepence."

"Well, I ain't gonna weep for you," said Mr. Nicholson. "It seems to me you've made a profession of tossing people in the shit, so why should I believe a thing you say – a worthless spy – or do a thing you ask of me? How am I to know this ain't all a part of some busted plot?"

Carlo sighed heavily. "Ah'm all but through wi' Tierney. Ah provided a guid service, ah should be paid. Simple as that."

"He's given you a pair of boots, ain't he? And a good coat. People are selling their children for less."

"Ah sold my soul."

"Yes, well, the market for souls is very slow, just now."

"Ah'm tellin' ye. Ah dinnae gie a cuss fer naeb'dy, but ah know that McNaughten's nay a murderer. He's a guid mony things, but he's no' that. Ah jist thought ye'd like to know. O, an' by the way," he was drawing his index finger across his throat, making a grinding sound through his clenched back teeth as he did so, "ah was never here."

"I ain't never seen you in me life before, old man," replied Mr. Nicholson in a tone of the utmost gravity.

But Carlo had already slunk back into the reeking, unpaved yard at the rear of the shop. After a moment or two, Mr. Nicholson followed him outside. He looked up and down the crooked lane until he was quite sure that the bully was nowhere to be seen.

"Zay say it vill snow again," the Jew old-clothes-man was saying sadly.

He did not follow the old man's gaze heavenwards – he rarely looked up for fear of missing something here on the earth below – but Mr. Nicholson nodded respectfully all the same.

"Yes, yes," he said, "there's always weather of one sort or another."

And this greeting exchanged, Mr. Nicholson returned to the relative safety of the little print-shop. He had been thinking about stepping off the treadmill, but now he knew that he never could. For after all, to step and step and step and not fall off is all there is in this life.

Evening edition

DEATH OF MR. DRUMMOND

SAD NEWS CONVEYED TO HER MAJESTY

It has now become our very painful duty to announce that Mr. Edward Drummond died this morning at about twenty minutes to eleven o'clock. Our readers will no doubt be fully prepared, from the account we were compelled to give yesterday of the hopeless state in which he was left by his medical attendants, to hear the melancholy intelligence.

The deceased, who throughout his short but severe illness bore his sufferings with great fortitude and resignation, remained perfectly sensible till the time of his death.

The unfortunate gentleman, who, we understand, was in his 59th year, bore a most estimable character, and was beloved by all who had the pleasure of his acquaintance; and it is almost impossible to describe the gloom which the melancholy event has cast over the circle in which he moved.

At a very early hour this morning a messenger from the Queen called to make inquiries, and returned with the intelligence of the dismal situation in which the deceased then was to Windsor. Immediately after the unfortunate gentleman breathed his last another messenger was despatched to convey the sad tidings to Her Majesty. A messenger from Her Majesty the Queen Dowager also called a few minutes after the deceased expired.

Mr. Drummond's death is the occasion of great and bitter sorrow not just to his family but to those outside his immediate family with whom he was acquainted, for he was a man universally beloved; an amiable and kindly man, of whom it was impossible to think that he should have a single enemy, and, moreover, a highly competent civil servant who had spent the greater part of his life in the dedicated service of his country. He was, it was said by many, courteous and obliging to everyone who had occasion to apply to him on business of a public nature, however trifling.

The melancholy report of his death was immediately conveyed to Sir Robert Peel by Sir James Graham, H.M. Secretary of State for the Home Office, who, in company with several other cabinet ministers, went in person to the Premier's private residence. Upon receiving the information, we are led to understand that Sir Robert was greatly affected, and immediately directed that his condolences should be forwarded to the afflicted relatives of the late amiable gentleman, who had so faithfully and diligently acted as his private secretary. Never, perhaps, was there an instance where the life of an individual has been sacrificed by the hands of a murderer that has created so painful an interest amongst all classes of the community.

In which McNaughten learns of the fate of Mr. Drummond.

The task of conveying to the prisoner the news of Mr. Drummond's demise fell to Inspector Hughes. Upon receiving the shocking intelligence McNaughten's face became flushed and red; then he broke out into a stream of incoherent exclamations as to the destruction of his mental faculties by means of Tory persecution.

"Things are very serious, son," said the Inspector, when the prisoner was done raving. "Very serious indeed. You know, you must know, what'll be made of this. Now, to my mind it's better by far to speak up now, before it all runs amok. A solicitor might be fetched, if you wish it. Do you have a friend in the metropolis, someone who might be able to help you in that regard – for I'm afraid the money you was taken with is being held over as evidences."

McNaughten turned his eyes upon the floor. He appeared absorbed in melancholy reflections. "I have nothing further to say," he said, quietly. He was tired and lean and broken.

The Inspector turned his soft brown gaze upon the boy. "This Carlo," he said, "what can you tell me about him? I have learned that he is an insurrectionist who has been induced to turn police-informer and is at present in the pay of the plainclothesmen – and that lot will do everything they can to protect their blessed business."

McNaughten sighed.

"And I also know," continued the Inspector, "that you was an associate of Abram Duncan – known as the Gray Goose. Now, what will be made of them associations is all too plain to see. But what perplexes me is this: see, if one of the Active Duty was sharing lodgings with you, and knew you to be – as will be made out – a trouble-maker, a socialist, a freethinker, a Chartist, a fanatic for Free Trade, or whatever it is you are supposed to be – then why didn't he go straightway to his commanding officer and tell him as much? Why didn't he keep a weather-eye on you and stop you shooting Mr. Drummond? Why didn't he come forward on Friday?"

He thought that he discerned a faint flicker, a stirring in the prisoner's countenance. He paused for a few moments in expectation of a response, but none came.

"Something about it just don't make sense to my mind," he resumed. "And to tell you the truth, it worries me what might be afoot here – and how implicated the plainclothesmen might be in some plot or other. Do you see how it might?" The Inspector gazed upon the prisoner's now lambent features. "That is always the problem with paid informers, you see," he sighed. "A man that can be bought once, can be bought again. You can never be sure you has their complete loyalty."

But none of this had a thing to do with the prisoner.

"You know, it might still be possible to save your neck, son," he confided to the impassive spectre before him, "but you has to offer me some explanations. You has to help me to help you, 'cos I'll tell you straight – I – I can't do it on me own."

The prisoner was staring dead ahead, mute as a wax-work.

Inspector Hughes tipped himself forward over the cracks in the pavement of the cell floor. "I just know that something has gone on here, something rotten... O, for the love of the mother what bore you, tell me what happened! Why'd you fire them pistols at Mr. Drummond?" It was the question all policemen longed to hear an answer to: as if explanation could expiate; as if to know was all that is required to understand and make whole again the shattered world.

The prisoner shuffled a little. He turned away. He looked up at the grate set high in the cell wall.

"I know what I'm about," he said at last. "I know what I'm about."

THE LION AND GOAT TAVERN, GROSVENOR-STREET
FOUR O'CLOCK P.M.

Wherein Mr. Nicholson considers guilt and innocence.

Mr. Nicholson narrowed his eyes as he regarded the respectable and well-respected company that was gathering in the long, low-beamed upstairs room of the Lion and Goat, in expectation of witnessing the inquest on the late Mr. Edward Drummond. Larks first and last was always his motto, and where, he wondered, looking about him, was the fun in this grim matter?

The coroner for the city and liberties of Westminster, and the nineteen jurors (drawn from the parish of St. George's Hanover-square and all rate-payers in good standing) would be joining them shortly. They were at present to be found a short distance across the carriage-way, where they were having a good look at the unfortunate corpse laid out upon its death-bed. The fat-bellied *casus bellum*.

The publican was spreading clean sawdust upon the floor in anticipation of the coroner's arrival, and had set full tobacco pipes and tankards of steaming hot water and brandy upon a table in readiness. Mr. Nicholson helped himself to a couple of the pipes and prepared to make the acquaintance of some of the assembly.

In keeping with the gravity of the occasion, he was out of his queer nabs and into a pair of sturdy tweed unmentionables, a plain cloth frac and (chiefly for the memorable impression it was guaranteed to leave) an old-fashioned full-skirted coat, such as a coachman might wear. He had wrapped the long mustard-coloured muffler twice about the lower-portion of his clean-shaven face, but not before daubing his cheeks with the ruddy hue off a stick of theatrical carmine. A luxuriant black wig protruded from beneath his wide-awake hat, a pair of matching eyebrows nudging its brim; and pince-nez, perched on the end of a nose more carbuncled than usual, completed the disguise. The look he was after was that of a moderately successful West End merchant; a man of modest, old-fashioned tastes, with nothing of the flash about him. It was his intention that should any in that place care to inquire, he would learn that Mr. Nicholson was the unfortunate deceased's cheesemonger.

And as the room filled up, he occupied his time in approaching complete strangers, shaking them firmly by the hand using the bear grip. He was not at all surprised when several responded in the appropriate manner, one or two even whispering some Masonic nonsense or other in his ever-cocked ear. Mr. Nicholson (need it be said) was not a Brother. Membership of any sort of society did not agree with him – there was too much to be lost, and nowhere near enough to be gained, by the compromises which mutuality of interest imposed upon a man – but he had found it useful before now to ascribe to himself the credible impression of Masonic-ness. He was adept at reading the nods and winks, and it did not take long for him to deduce that a good many in the room were of the medical persuasion.

It was plain to him that the guinea quacks were guilty as hell. But then, you see my merry Andrews, doctors killed people every day: nobody ever expected that the guilty ones would hang. There was a free-masonry to medicine, and the uninitiated could not possibly hope to appreciate all of its subtlety and awful mystery; nor unpick the bonds of its brotherhood.

Which was a great pity: for it seemed more than likely that the bottle-headed Scotch youth, who doubtless was as innocent of the death of Mr. Drummond as Old Peeping Tom was innocent of soap and water, would hang for firing paper pellets at a fat Tory who had had the misfortune to have been attended by one of the worst surgeons in London.

And even Old Peeping Tom couldn't make a jest out of that.

As a matter of act, he was feeling the injustice of the situation far more keenly than he ordinarily might have done. The visit of the plain-clothesman, Carlo, to his print-shop the morning before had troubled him mightily, and try as he might he could not put out of his head the villain's avowal that McNaughten was no murderer. Carlo was an informer: *ergo* he would never blab without first obtaining for himself the promise of a meat-pie topped off with gravy, a night in a dry police cell, or, at the very least, a jug or two of black-strap. So why had he come to Mr. Nicholson with such a choice tidbit and not asked for a thing in return – not counting the lithographic enticements of La Taglioni, which last he heard definitely weren't the going rate for informations? There had to be some reward in it, something that made it worth the while of the gag-low maggot. Someone must have sent him: the question was, *who* – and *why*? It never once occurred to Old Peeping Tom that a pestiferous, cheating, contaminating, noisome obscenity, such as was a plainclothesman, might be capable of nothing so nefarious as helping out a chum...

Mr. Nicholson mopped his forehead with a dirty bit of muslin and took another of the free brandies.

"Why are there no sandwiches?" he grumbled. "You'd've thought the publican would've supplied sandwiches – if only to soak up the drink. It ain't good for the gout to take so much brandy on an empty stomach."

"O, they'll bring the sandwiches when the coroner has concluded the business," opined one of the freemasons sympathetically. "They always do."

"Then what the devil is keeping him? To my mind," Mr. Nicholson averred to nobody in particular, "it oughter be a straightforward enough matter. The Scotchman was taken *in flagrante*, and I should say that the quacks have more than a little to answer to..."

A few of the freemasons took a backward step, their mouths hanging open at an angle of astonishment.

"Do you really think so?" said a clerical-looking gent with a tuppenny twist of hair that looked exactly as if a sparrow had alighted on his head.

"O, I do, sir," said Old Peeping Tom. "Why, Mr. Drummond could have lived quite long enough with a small piece of lead shot in his behind. An uncle of mine was at Trafalgar and he died just before Christmas, aged ninety-two, with a piece of French cannon lodged in his chest the size of a Dublin oyster." The freemasons had detached somewhat from the rest of the crowd, and were letting loose a volley of nods and winks. "I tell you, gentlemen, the only body that's safe in the hands of a guinea quack is a dead'un. I'd wager that if Mr. Drummond had been left alone, that gentleman would at this very moment be tucking into a large dish of calf's-foot jelly."

"I must say I had thought as much myself," mused the tuppenny twist.

Mr. Nicholson would have made more of all this were it not for the timely arrival of Mr. Gell, the coroner for the city and liberties of Westminster, and the jurors. The gentleman took his seat at the centre of the table and laid a few papers out upon it, as in a veritable hornpipe of expectation, throats were cleared, arms folded and unfolded, knees clasped, chins stroked and whiskers tugged. The hour come, the dead invoked and the mysteries put to fright, the coroner dipped his pen in the inkpot, appended his name to some official order and conferred briefly with his underlings. The long, low-beamed upstairs room fell to a hush as Mr. Gell called the inquest to order.

Mr. Warren had arrived with the coroner. He positioned himself in the front row with his leather notebook and pencil at the ready, and seeing him, Mr. Nicholson deftly removed the eyebrows, the wig, the pince-nez and the carbuncle, and went to stand very close by the gentleman's elbow – the better to steal a glimmer at his crooked pennings. He followed Mr. Warren's interested gaze to the opposite side of the crowded room, where a tall, lugubrious character, dressed very stiff and formal, was standing.

"As I live and breathe," said Mr. Nicholson. "It's Mr. Maule." Mr. Maule was the Attorney-General and Solicitor to the Treasury, and the very same to whom the peelers would be applying for the requisite funds in order that they might prosecute the case – should the coroner and jury find against the prisoner, that is. "But who's that flash cove skulking at his side?

Mr. Warren squinted. "I believe that gentleman to be an Inspector of the 'A' Division."

"Well, and I'll be blowed! Black Jack Tierney of the plainclothesmen, as I live and breathe! A devilish pairing, an' no mistake!"

Mr. Warren pursed his lips in a judicial manner.

"O! We live in dangerous times, Mr. Justitia," observed Mr. Nicholson. "Seems we are dependent upon spies and nipperkin detectivisits to save our souls from destructivism."

Mr. Warren nodded slightly.

"They shall hang McNaughten by his scrawny neck at the earliest convenience, you mark me: just like they did with Bellingham who shot Spencer Perceval. Get it done quick before the Mob is upon him," continued Old Peeping Tom. "Did you know, the Mob tried to pull Bellingham from the 'ackney that was taking him off to Newgate? Very popular he was. Or rather Mr. Perceval was very hated."

"O, do be quiet," snapped Mr. Warren. "They are about to begin."

The coroner adjusted his spectacles. "Before we proceed," he said, "might I ask if it is the intention of any party to appear on behalf of any person who might be accused?" Not a soul came forward. After an uncomfortable hiatus, Mr. Maule stepped forward and bowed at the coroner.

"I attend on behalf of the Crown," he said.

"Well, well, well," said Mr. Nicholson. "And don't they have it all nice and sorted..." He flashed a menacing look at Inspector Tierney: the screwbado was certainly looking pleased with himself.

Mr. Gell raised his eyebrows, mumbled something, and then turned to the jury. "Well, in that case," he said, "it will in all probability not be necessary for us to bestow a vast deal of time on deliberation on this melancholy occurrence. I am not aware that it is the intention of anyone to appear before us on behalf of any person who might hereafter be accused of the crime by which the deceased lost his life; but even if any person were to appear, I doubt it would be for the purpose of disproving the fact."

"Then for what purpose might such a person appear?" ventured one of the jurors, with a puzzled expression.

Mr. Gell removed his spectacles and took a chagrined look about him.

"Well," he said, "it might be for the purpose of proving that the person, whoever he might be, was not of sound mind, with a view to inducing the jury to give a different verdict from that which they might otherwise return."

The coroner replaced his spectacles on the end of his nose and consulted a paper on the table before him.

"Your task today," he instructed the jury, "is to return such a verdict as would send the party to another tribunal to be tried, where a proper opportunity would be afforded for making such an attempt in his defence. All you have to do is consider whether the evidence brought before you today is sufficient to induce you to send the person in question to his trial."

The same juror raised his hand.

"I can't help wondering," he said, "whether the person accused of having caused the death of the deceased ought not to be present."

There was a murmuring of approval in the crowd.

Mr. Gell once again took off his spectacles and put on a very pained expression. "Not very long ago a jury said they would rather adjourn than proceed without the presence of the accused person," he said, "and so I sent a messenger to Bridewell to desire the keeper to send the prisoner before the jury. The answer of the keeper was that he had no authority to do so; and the jury adjourned in order that a communication be sent to the Secretary of State, whose answer to that application was that the gaoler had done quite right in refusing to send the prisoner."

Mr. Warren was scribbling furiously in his notebook, but when Mr. Nicholson tried to make it out, it was all just pothooks and hangers.

"They could end it all there, if the coroner was so minded," he said, "and then we could have our sandwiches and baccy."

"You know you really ought to show more respect," said Mr. Warren.

Old Peeping Tom frowned. "Why should I? It's as plain as a pikestaff they've already decided the outcome..."

Mr. Gell had replaced his spectacles on the end of his nose and now he was calling a witness.

"Now then, see there," grumbled Old Peeping Tom as Police Constable James Silver, A63, took the stand, "if this ain't a sham, then I'm the King of Bohemia. What more can the blessed peelers tell us that we don't already know?"

"Will you be quiet?" snapped Mr. Warren. "It may be that some new evidences have come to light."

Mr. Nicholson squinted, very sceptically, at the young constable who had made the arrest, as he began his tale of derring-do: how last Friday afternoon he had been patrolling along Charing-cross, and was just by Groves's the fishmonger's when he had heard the report of a pistol on the other side of the road; how he had raced across to find a gentleman reeling with his left hand on his back and his coat-tails on fire; how he had seen a man returning a pistol to his left breast and drawing another from his right with his left hand, which he had then placed in his right hand and proceeded to aim at the same gentleman.

"You must have been very quick in crossing the road," observed Mr. Gell, "for you said it was the report of the first pistol that attracted your attention."

The peeler pulled his shoulders back, and stood up very straight.

"I crossed the road immediately, sir," he said, looking as true and honest as he might. "I had my eye on him from the first moment."

"On who?" called out Old Peeping Tom. "You know you haven't told us who the man was yet!"

Young Silver twisted his stove-pipe hat in his hands, and looked about him as if expectant of seeing the prisoner standing there in the crowd. Having failed to spy out the felon, his eyes came to rest fleetingly on the brooding stone-cut features of Inspector Tierney. "He's called Daniel McNaughten," said the Constable at last, in the forlorn tone of a man who had just been pigeoned and plucked at a game of cards. "And he's a wood-turner – from Glasgow."

Mr. Nicholson harrumphed a little, but permitted Constable Silver to recount the prisoner's rum statement, the troubling contents of his pockets and the subsequent search of his lodgings. It all tumbled from young Silver in much the same detail (at least to Mr. Nicholson's recollection) as it had on Saturday morning; but, whereas at Bow-street the bluebottle had been all puffed up pride and beaming, now the shine was quite gone from his brass buttons. As a matter of fact, the poor nibbling seemed worn down and there was something miserable in the looks he kept casting at Black Jack, something not at all befitting one of the "A" Division's finest.

"At the lodgings," said the Constable, "I found two caps which fitted the pistols."

"Where did you find them?"

"I found them in the pocket of a pair of trowsers."

"Was that all that was found?"

Silver mumbled something.

"Was that all that was found?" repeated the coroner.

The constable stepped up to the table and placed a flask, bullets and caps before the coroner.

"And where did you find the flask?" asked one of the jury.

"It was found in a table drawer," replied Silver.

"And what about the second pistol?" asked another, who was looking down the barrel of the very weapon. "Do we know if it was charged?"

Silver shrugged. "It was fired on the pavement in the struggle," he said. "It required all my strength to wrest the pistols from the assailant and prevent his escape and that was when he discharged it."

"And was there any trace of the firing?" asked Mr. Gell.

Silver glanced quickly at Inspector Tierney before responding. "I searched that patch of pavement more than a dozen times, sir," he said, "but I never found a thing."

Mr. Maule, who had all this while kept a non-committal, thoroughly legal eye on the bobby, now frowned darkly, and turned to murmur something to Inspector Tierney. The Active Duty man cupped his schin in his hand and nodded curtly at the coroner, and with no further ado Silver was being thanked for his evidences, and told, to his plain relief, that no further divulgements were required of him *for the time being*.

"Did you see that?" exclaimed Mr. Nicholson, "Did you see that? Who's in charge here? I say – who's in charge here?"

"Be quiet," hissed Mr. Warren, "or they shall remove you."

"Yes," hissed Mr. Nicholson back, "and where were your new evidences? It's a sham, I tell you; a sham! They ought to get out the sandwiches and have done with it."

"Sshh. Here comes Mr. Guthrie junior. I should like to hear what he has to say, if you don't mind."

"Ah yes," said Mr. Nicholson, "the doctors..."

The junior Guthrie commenced by reading out the report of a postmortem examination conducted at one o'clock that very day on the deceased in the presence of Mr. Guthrie senior, Mr. Bransby Cooper and three other medical gentlemen. After a few words of not very edifying chirurgical mish-mash, he related that they had all concluded that the wound Mr. Drummond had received in the back had been *inevitably fatal*.

"Yes, well," observed Mr. Nicholson, "I dare say that is so, as soon as the quacks were called out."

"But what was the matter with Mr. Drummond?" asked one of the jurors.

The junior Guthrie looked about him with a superior air. "Why, he died of a wound," he said.

There was a deal of laughter from the assembly.

"You mean the wound in his back?" persisted the juror.

Guthrie *fils* cast an irritated look towards the coroner.

"Was there another?" asked Mr. Gell.

Mr. Guthrie junior cleared his throat. He displayed all the showmanship of the proprietor of a Hall of Wonders: he waited until the fullest extent of tension had been achieved before drawing back the curtain. "The patient," he said at last, "received a small wound in the back, at the foot of the spine. He also received one small wound at the front of the abdomen, which consisted of an incision made for the purposes of extracting a bullet."

"Ah, now then," said Mr. Nicholson, "finally, the truth is extracted out of all this jalap and rhubarb."

Mr. Gell, who had been listening to all of this with the intensest interest, leaned forward. "Tell me," he inquired, "did you ever speak with Mr. Drummond about the wound which caused his death?"

The surgeon considered his response for a moment or two. "No, he never did speak to me on that subject. We did not permit him to speak much. He was very weak, you see."

Mr. Gell put his spectacles on top of his head, and leaned forward even more earnestly.

"And you are quite certain, are you," he said, "that Mr. Drummond's death could not have been caused by the manner in which the bullet was extracted?"

The junior Guthrie's mouth might have twitched ever so slightly. "The extraction was performed by my father," he said.

The coroner regarded him for a moment, then, satisfied, he replaced his spectacles.

"Of course," said the first juror, "when a surgeon of Mr. Guthrie senior's eminence extracts a bullet, it is unnecessary for anyone to ask whether it has been done skilfully; but in ordinary cases it is usual to inquire whether the death was caused by the first wound inflicted, or by the unskilful treatment of the surgeon. We are therefore bound to ask you, what it was that caused the death of Mr. Drummond."

Guthrie junior spoke very carefully and deliberately. "There can be no doubt," he said, "that the death was caused by a wound which had been inflicted on him by a pistol bullet."

"Quite so," persisted the juror, "and do we have assurances that it was indeed Mr. Guthrie senior who performed the operation?"

"I think," said Mr. Gell, "that we have spent long enough on this and have heard more than enough to move to a verdict."

"At last!" cried Mr. Nicholson. He glanced at Mr. Warren, who was stroking his chin, with a thoughtful aspect.

The jurors were unanimously pronouncing a verdict of "Wilful Murder" against Daniel McNaughten. They were shaking one another by the hand and waiting patiently for the sandwiches to come.

"Well, Mr. Justitia, sir, it seems that you and I shall see each other in court, I dare say," said Mr. Nicholson. "I say, is something troubling you? Only you don't look at all satisfied to my mind. Was it something the quack said? You know my opinion on *that*... It would be a terrible day for Justice, wouldn't it, if McNaughten was to hang because of the fumblings of a society doctor?"

Mr. Warren had drawn his lips very tight across his teeth.

"McNaughten fired a pistol at Mr. Drummond," he said, "and when all is said and done, that is *that*."

"Ho ho! But there's a world of difference between firing a pistol and committing murder," said Mr. Nicholson. He was still unattached to any particular notion of McNaughten's innocence, but he could not let slip his understanding that others were guilty.

"McNaughten," said Mr. Warren, "is a dangerous political Radical."

A gaunt and wizened fellow, who gave off the impression of being a very distinguished minister come to offer consolation at a hanging, had stopped stooped over his cane right in front of them. He turned now, fixing Mr. Warren with a gray and glittering look that was full of thought and understanding.

"An' where d'ye come by the understandin' that the plaintiff is a Radical?" he said in a disconcertingly mild voice. He was dressed in a dusty cloth frac, quite shiny with age; black knee breeches, *ditto*; overdarned and sagging plain worsted stockings; and a pair of antique buckled shoes. He wore the remnants of a cockade upon his breast, and his iron gray hair stuck out from beneath the brim of his broad hat like cornstalks poking from the head of a scarecrow. He could have been very old: he could have been no age at all. And despite all of this odd-ness of appearance, Mr. Nicholson found himself drawn to the fellow, who, the more he regarded him, seemed in some strange way to be the very repository of noble confidences and wisdom.

"It said so in *The Times*," replied FIAT JUSTITIA, a sight too defen-sively.

The wizened gent smiled a slow, considered smile. "It said no such thing," he said, simply, coolly.

Mr. Warren pursed his lips in a most supercilious fashion. "I should think that, after considering all of the available information," he said, "it seems more than likely that some political motivation is doubtless behind this dreadful calamity."

"O, aye," said the wizened gent in tones so low that the pair of them were obliged to draw ever closer, "I dinnae doubt that politics lie at the heart o' it..."

"Precisely!" said Mr. Warren. "Consider: we have an independent tradesman, quite successful by all accounts, yet, nevertheless, one of a dying breed, coming from a place that is at present suffering the most appalling conditions of depravity and privation. One who fancies him-self persecuted by the government – well, and ask yourself, who of his sort does not? A young man who blames Sir Robert Peel for all of soci-ety's ills – for having resiled from those expectations which he aroused in respect of the Corn Laws, not to mention the increase in duties and the iniquities of the Income Tax..."

"A young man, proud, genteel, self-reliant, industrious, abstemi-ous," continued the wizened gent. "O, youse'll recognise the type, I'm sure – wi' a small fortune in the bank, raised by the efforts of his own hands; tired of monopolies; tired of injustice; *fearful* o' revolution!"

Mr. Warren frowned.

"Indeed," he said, though he was sounding less certain. "He wishes the people of this country to have bread at its so-called natural price; he wishes supply to be freely opened – why, perhaps he even wishes for cheap labour..."

"Mebbe, mebbe," said the gentleman, resting his chin on his cane. "An' havin' a deal tae lose he sees how the nation is on the eve of great changes."

"Yes," said Mr. Warren, "and he sees an opportunity to gather honour and fame to himself – no matter what the cost to justice... The Anti-Corn Law League is a vile and reprehensible organisation, comprising unscrupulous men who will stop at nothing in order to safeguard their profits. They seek to destroy this country, and will do so, too!"

"He fears those changes," countered the old man, "as much as you dae yerse'en, sir."

"He – he – well, really!" said Mr. Warren, whose colour had got up. "I – I don't believe I ever heard such nonsense!"

"The government," the wizened gent was saying, every bit as steadily as before, "has laid tae rest, wi' violence and injustice, the just plaints o' the poor, whiles the middle classes – men like Daniel McNaughten – men such as yourse'en, sir – did nothin'. Well, an' noo it is your turn tae be put down by the tyrant government – an' who will come tae your assistance?"

Mr. Warren opened and then closed his mouth. The old gent's glittering eye and pulpit resonance were sufficient to silence a whole army of FIAT JUSTITIAS.

Questions were teeming and tumbling in Mr. Nicholson's fascinated mind as the fellow turned his gray, serious eyes upon him. It was as though he was surmising, reckoning, *judging* Old Peeping Tom – just like St. Peter himself would doubtless do one day at the gates of Heaven.

"And as fer youse," said the wizened gent when he had done weighing Old Peeping Tom's conscience, "ah should say that youse ought to know better." He shook that antient head in a slow emblem of disappointment, then, without another word, he leaned painfully upon his stick and hobbled towards the door.

A CURIOUS INCIDENT IN EDINBURGH

It has come to light that during Her Majesty's trip to Scotland last September, during which several riotous scenes took place, the deceased Mr. Drummond had been in the habit of riding about in Sir Robert Peel's carriage, whilst the Prime Minister rode with the royal party. On one occasion the Prime Minister's carriage was the object of a violent attack in the course of which its occupant was overthrown and no doubt would have suffered serious injury but for the intercession of several bystanders.

"A" Division
Report
26th inst. 6.00p.m.

Police Sergeant George Shew, A10, reports that in reference to the man as described by Inspector Tierney as having been seen about White-hall. P.S. perfectly recollects having seen (about a year ago) such a person standing about Whitehall Gardens, Whitehall Chapel, the corner of Downing-street, and on the steps of the Privy Council Office. P.S. should know him again if he was to see him at any time.

Signed, *Samuel Hughes, Inspector ("A" Division)*

En route to Newgate,
six o'clock p.m.

Wherein Inspector Hughes escorts the prisoner to Newgate, and considers the rights and wrongs of the matter.

The Inspector was in the back of the cab, jolting to Newgate, the prisoner beside him groaning piteously, grinding his fists into his temples – not at all inhibited by being handcuffed to his keeper. The prisoner had nobody but himself to blame for his predicament, but it was always a hard thing to witness so close the suffering of a fellow human being, and it was out of pity that Inspector Hughes allowed his arm to be kept at an awkward angle as the grinding intensified. He told himself that they should soon arrive at Newgate, and that only one of them would be at liberty to return home again. Of course, he would have to walk back to the station-house, for he had not been supplied with the return cab fare, and that remarkable woman Mrs. Hughes had stuck to her resolve concerning his allowance.

The boy was weeping hard; his thin chest heaving with sobs.

"Now then, now then," said the Inspector, "don't take on so. You shall need to have your senses about you and your head screwed on tight where you're going." It came to him that the invisible part of a man's life became more unfathomable the longer you examined it, until all you could say for sure was that there was a great mystery at the heart of existence. He reached across to rub his wrist as beyond the carriage the steamy gas-lit gleamings and shimmering of Strand slipped by.

Inspector Tierney had been very quick to justify the actions of his monkey, the informer, Carlo, who had failed to come forward the moment McNaughten shot at Mr. Drummond, despite knowing all too well who he was, on account of their long association in Glasgow, and the fact that until last Friday they had been sharing lodgings. Inspector Tierney was of the opinion that Carlo was a good agent and very close to leading the Active Duty to Abram Duncan, the Gray Goose – who, it was claimed, did not reside at Mrs. Dutton's lodging-house and Democratic Chapel down on Poplar-row, Newington Butts, after all, but would soon be drawn there by means of an ingenious scheme that was to drive together all the Scotch incendiaries currently residing in London.

Inspector Hughes turned down the corners of his mouth. Inspector Tierney had set himself well beyond the bounds of the proper procedures, but it was also the case that the prisoner had not helped himself in presenting as an emblem of innocence. In his last missive from Scotland, the Detective Sergeant had uncovered various troublous evidences. McNaughten had attended a meeting of the Glasgow Socialist Society, where Abram Duncan was a speaker; according to the principal of the Glasgow Mechanics' Institute he was one of a number of students who had clamoured for lectures on theology to be added to the curriculum, along with something called "Political Economy" – which certainly sounded most suspicious; and he had also requested that certain periodicals and newspapers be made available in the Reading Room. What was more, and most damning, two or three copies of the *Reformers Gazette* – which was on the Office of Home Affairs's list of prohibited republican and seditious materials – had been discovered in the prisoner's Glasgow lodgings.

Inspector Hughes had confiscated a good many numbers of the *Gazette* in the past few months, and was of the opinion that, despite its inflammatory title, it was no more likely to promote physical force than was the *Fashionable Guide*. It was a Temperance journal, in point of fact, and comprised items such as would suit a tradesman eager to improve his mind. But it could not be denied that the discovery did not sit well with the evidence of the book he had himself found in the prisoner's lodgings at Poplar-row. Possession of a copy of Cooper's *The Holy Scriptures Analysed, or, Extracts from the Bible: shewing its contradictions, absurdities and immoralities*, certainly strengthened the impression of the prisoner as a confounded Freethinker: the type to be found preaching sedition in a Democratic Chapel. And when all of this was taken together, it really didn't matter a jot that the Detective Sergeant had heard from plenty of other witnesses that the prisoner was a "mild and inoffensive person, who would sometimes speak roughly" but did not seem "especially remarkable in any way". Not when Inspector Tierney and Sergeant Shew had both testified to having seen the prisoner behaving suspiciously in the area of Whitehall.

Secluded in the deep shadows of the van, the prisoner, the poor mad ghost, groaned. The cab was drawing to a halt outside Newgate and the Inspector could sense something gray and dispiriting hovering above them, preparing to cloak their senses.

"O Christ!" lamented the prisoner.

"Don't worry, son," he said. "Newgate ain't so bad, and they hardly ever convict at the first hearing. There'll be time. There'll be time."

He helped the prisoner down from the cab (the manacles made climbing rather difficult), and unlocked the darbies, slipping the cuff off his own and onto the prisoner's right wrist and snapping the catch shut. The warder scraped open the gate, and Inspector Hughes took the boy by the arm and tried to march him forward; but McNaughten was stopped dead upon the pavement, paralysed, as if in an awful dream; and all of a sudden he was turning those pale almost not there eyes upon the Inspector, and looking at him for the first time.

"Are youse gonnae ask if I've somethin' tae say," he said, a curious smile playing about his lips.

"Save it for the hearing."

"But don't youse want tae know?"

Inspector Hughes ran a hand down his chin. "I'm tired," he said, "tired of being lied to."

The warder had seized the prisoner by the arm, and was urging him into the depths of the gaol. The Inspector caught his last look before he disappeared into the despondent brick forever: a milky smudge of anguish.

"I am guilty," McNaughten was saying, "I am guilty of firing..."

He was almost disappeared, but his voice hung in the air like an icicle; and its thaw scutched the pure whiteness of everything else that was pushed hard against the black, black of the prison walls, chilling the Inspector with every breath he took.

THE JUDGE AND JURY SOCIETY,
GARRICK'S HEAD HOTEL, BOW-STREET,
TEN O'CLOCK P.M.

In which Mr. Cockburn is dropped by his Party; learns something instructive about the plea of insanity, and how he might improve the Law; and devises with Mr. Nicholson a scheme to lay hold of the fee.

In the dim and roisterous cellar Cockie pulled nervously at his primrose gloves and informed the door-keeper that, having come at the invitation of the Lord Chief Baron himself, he did not believe that he would be required to pay the half a crown entrance – never mind the one shilling and sixpence for dormio, i.e. siesta (alias *bed*). Then he waited for M'Lud to come and claim him, good-naturedly returning the nods and beamings of all the other legal gents of the Tom and Jerry stamp who had come for a little larkery after darkery, and *something very delicate to suit the late palate*.

Unable to secure the cabriolet except on payment of five shillings – which, regrettably, he had been unable to lay his hands upon – he had braved the streets: a journey fraught with numerous hazards. Once or twice he believed he had had glimpses of the handsome, carroty boy who appeared to be dogging his steps; and, crossing Berkeley-square, he was almost certain that he had caught the hard-hatted profile of a bailiff waiting for him on the corner. His heart had quickened and dread mounted in his throat, yet he had ventured on, and now here he was. He had certain expectations of the evening. The Lord Chief Baron had impeccable sporting connexions and an inexhaustible appetite for gammon, and Sandy, who had rather left off the practice of facetiae just of late, was in sore need of both.

The past few days spent in getting up his mania, monomania, melancholia, delusion, hypochondria, hysteria, partial insanity, and all types of moral insanity, had left the gentleman quite depleted in positive thoughts. There had been a further letter, discarded unopened this time, in the same instantly recognised hand as before; and the daily visits to his chambers from the good-looking, carrot-haired youth. And then had come the dismal news that Mr. Drummond had expired. Sleep was a jagged ordeal; wakefulness an endless parade of failure and defeat. It seemed as if the entire metropolis was buzzing against him.

Certainly, the demise of Mr. Drummond had seen to it that there was not a single man of any standing, from Lord John Russell down, who would now wish to see Good Old Cockie pursue the matter that had been laid so indelicately before him, alongside the cutlets and the salmon, less than a week ago. It appeared that *murder* had not been part of whatever understanding might have been arrived at on that occasion. The Chief Whipper-in had not responded to any of the notes left for him. Mr. Johnston, the Liberal Member for Kilmarnock, Dumbarton,

Renfrew, Rutherglen, Port Glasgow, &c., District of Burghs was apparently *out of town*. And an attempt to impose himself upon the prisoner's parliamentary representative – Mr. Oswald, the Liberal Member for Glasgow – at the club had almost provoked an unpleasant scene, which was narrowly averted only by Sandy's having feigned an instance of mistaken identity.

As a consequence of all of this, *there was no sign, whatever, of the fee*.

Cockie was weary at the vicissitudes of this life, of having his fate juggled as if it were nothing more than a coin in a conjurer's trick. He had been thinking of abandoning the Scotchman to his fate, and, seeking to put the troublous matter out of mind, had attended a soirée the night before at the Mayfair home of the Steam Railway King – who owed a goodly portion of his considerable fortune to Sandy's deft arguments on his behalf in the Railway Committees of halcyon days. It made good sense to renew the acquaintance. He had given himself over to a full-throated rendition of *"La ci darem la mano"*. His Zerlina on this occasion was Princess Steam herself, and Cockie was delighted to find himself encouraged in the seduction by the winks and nods of her illustrious papa. A wealthy wife on the brink of middle age, stout and plain enough to feel only gratitude towards her handsome spouse, presented an appealing solution to Cockie. But as the duet had progressed, all of his thoughts had turned to the lady's Apollo Knot. It was such an *unfortunate* choice of hair-styling for one so amply endowed with chins, and ensured that the gleam was gone from Sandy's eye long before the coda. Like so many men whose lives had become a lie, he yearned for truth and beauty, and the desultory fact was that a railway bride offered him neither. His spirits had vaporised like so much steam as he kissed the extended gloved hand, put on a false smile and prepared his mind for talk of the points of horses; of last season, and the one before that.

He had scarce had an opportunity, however, to acknowledge his applause, when a Chancery judge of his acquaintance had taken him by the arm, and, under cover of talk of the prospect of Cerrito dancing next season at Her Majesty's, steered him towards a secluded corner of the room.

"The game's gone cold, old man," said the Judge, as soon as they were out of earshot. Cockie had raised one querulous eyebrow. "It's time to leave the table."

"I take it that you come as the emissary of a coterie," said Cockie.

"My dear old bean, I come as a *friend*," said the wretched poltroon – with whom Sandy had scarce exchanged more than a dozen words before that night. "Continue with the matter, and you will find yourself without a single ally."

Cockie brought his lips together in a thin smile. "I was privately, though expensively educated," he said. "Being French and highly indulgent, *ma chère maman* could not bear to think of her *petit fils* being sent away to school. And so, you see, I was denied the buggery and beatings that habitually bind men of our class together, *my dear old bean*."

The Chancery Judge had goggled at him.

"If I am to be relieved of an onerous burden," Sandy continued, "then that is all to the well and good; but what of the fee, sir? Why, I am a good few guineas out at pocket, as it stands, and already a blighted being."

"I have not the authority to barter with you, Mr. Cockburn," replied the Chancery Judge. "Suffice to say that when a gentleman is shot dead in cold blood, it is surely to be expected that the defence of his murderer will be left to the lowest Pump-court advocate."

Sandy brought a ruminative forefinger to his lips. "My client," he said, "has not been found guilty of anything yet."

A scowl settled upon the Chancery Judge's features. "Nobody will support you. You will be the consort of conspirators and rabble-rousers. You will be laughed to scorn. Besides, you know nothing of defending in a murder case at the Bailey. And you know even less of insanity."

Sandy tugged on the primrose gloves. "I think," he said, "you will find that I know enough."

"I hear cases every day, the outcome of which hang upon the state of mind of the plaintiff, and I tell you, sir, there is no case to answer here. None whatever."

"Ah, then you have examined my client?"

"No, sir, not *exactly*..."

"Then you have heard the opinion of qualified men who have had the opportunity to examine my client?"

"You will struggle to find deponents," said the Chancery Judge. "You will require a score of mad-doctors, all prepared to swear to it that the assassin is a monomaniac."

"A score, eh?" said Cockie. "Hum. Tell me, how many mad-doctors came forth last year in the case of the Begum's son whose wife declared him insane in order that she might lay claim to his fortune?"

"*That* was an entirely different matter."

"Why so?"

"The Begum's son was no murderer."

"May I remind you that nothing has been proved in respect of my client?"

"The Begum's son was a wealthy and very well-connected gentleman."

"Ha! Do I understand you? Are you saying that a poor deluded fellow, friendless and abandoned to his fate, is not entitled to a fair and just hearing as much as is anyone?"

The Chancery Judge had reddened to his gills in anger. "You, sir," he expostulated, "are either a fool or a madman, or both!"

Sandy stuck his tongue in his cheek. "Ours is an age of derangement," he said. "I certainly do not consider myself to be any less prey to sickness of mind, no more than I am impervious to bodily weakness. You may tell whomever it was who sent you that I intend to proceed – and that I intend to *win*."

He bowed gracefully and, smiling to himself, left the Chancery Judge fuming in the secluded corner. He helped himself to a glass of champagne and went and joined a party who were singing around the piano. He felt the kindling of something in his breast: a spark of his own divine flame. The Tories were in a funk. The Whigs were in a funk. False friends had turned into common enemies – and *vice versa*. The ramparts were manned. It would be difficult to move through the close ranks, he thought, yet there would be gaps. He felt quite heady... The warning clarion had blown shrilly in his ear, yet he was calm, and for the first time in a long while, utterly devoid of the cynic whim. Ambition stirs the mind in different ways, but for Cockie at that moment it was enough to know that he still had ambition. And there was something altogether blessed in realising that one had nothing whatever to lose.

The Chief Whipper-in might have dropped him like a hot codling, but he had been quite correct in one respect, Sandy thought, as he prepared to sing the bass part of *"Pretty warbler, cease to hover"*: seven hundred and fifty pounds was more than enough for a perfectly good defence. Let the prisoner take him on himself as his counsel, and damn them all!

But it had not been long before he had realised that matters were not going to be as straightforward as he had hitherto concluded. To begin with, the peelers had appealed to Mr. Maule, the Treasury Solicitor, asking that the prisoner's deposit receipt – wherein was contained all Cockie's hopes of payment – be retained as evidences; and Mr. Maule was inclined to agree with them. And as for the preparation of the case: it seemed that when it came to a murder trial, the insanity plea was not such a simple business after all. The great Erskine might admirably have laid out the ground for diminished responsibility, but his client, Hadfield, had only levelled a horse-pistol at the King: he had not *killed* anyone. If McNaughten was to be spared the gallows, Cockie was going to have to find a chasm in the law; and he did not yet have the requisite knowledge so to do. He did, however, know of a young man who might.

Earlier that day he had received in his rooms Mr. Forbes Winslow, a young surgeon and author of a slim volume entitled *The Anatomy of Suicide*, whose somewhat advanced opinions on the plea of insanity had been recommended to him by several associates. The son of an eminent mad-house doctor, Forbes Winslow had grown up in numerous asylums; an experience which had given him a degree of insight and understanding denied to most men of his class.

"Our knowledge of disorders of the mind," the young surgeon had told Cockie, "has advanced considerably during the last fifty years – yet the *law* remains fixed in the opinions of our grandfathers. A man may fancy himself the King of England, a tub of butter, or a pane of glass, yet it is possible for him to be viewed responsible for his conduct. And if he be guilty of a capital crime whilst labouring under any of these delusions, he is liable to undergo the extreme penalty of the law."

Cockie had lightly stroked his chin. "Even where it may be shown that the fellow was driven by an irresistible impulse to destroy – against which he may have struggled for some time?"

"The crucial distinction in law is that if it can be shown that the felon has no moral understanding of the act he has committed, then he may be found insane. If, however, he is found to be perfectly conscious that what he felt impelled to do was *wrong*, both in the sight of God and man, then he has no chance of escaping should the legal test be applied to him."

"So a man would need to be a dribbling imbecile to escape the gallows?"

Forbes Winslow smiled. "Not quite. But if a murderer admits to knowing that his act was both illegal and morally wrong, then he is liable to punishment – even though he committed the crime when under the influence of an implusive insanity. Think of Bellingham, who shot Spencer Perceval thirty years ago. He was clearly raving, yet he was hanged within eight days because he did not deny that what he had done was in any sense wrong."

"Cruel and inhumane in the extreme..."

"Yes, sir, I believe that it was. But you see, the law has never made subtle distinctions between sanity and insanity. It has merely allowed, on occasion, for extenuating circumstances to modify its rigid course. Few judges, to my mind, wish to have the blood of a poor suffering madman on their hands."

"You have seen my client?"

"I have not, sir, but I have followed the case with interest through the newspapers, and it seems to me to present several factors of immense interest with regard to the plea of insanity."

"It does? I had thought so, but after hearing your considered opinion I had begun to doubt that there was any case to answer. To my mind, McNaughten does not appear at all mad. I had wondered whether it would be possible to argue some form of partial insanity – monomania – Monsieur Marc in his excellent and most interesting work –"

Forbes Winslow pulled a little face. "Most people are entirely

[347]

ignorant of the subject of insanity," he said, "but almost all have an opinion."

"Indeed," said Cockie, suitably chastened.

"I do not believe, Mr. Cockburn, that there is a single lunatic in the land – whether idiotic, imbecilic, maniacal, monomaniacal or melancholic, to whatever degree – who does not retain some mental power. In short, sir, every case of insanity is *partial*. A man may be truly insane and irresponsible – suffering from a delusion so strong that nothing but a physical impediment could have prevented him from committing the worst atrocity – yet still be deemed capable of appreciating the fact that an act of assassination is quite contrary to the rule of law. This is the conundrum your client presents – the very nub of the issue upon which the law must be challenged."

"You really believe so?" said Cockie.

Mr. Forbes Winslow had smiled reassuringly. "McNaughten is a Monomaniac," he said. "I have no doubt of it."

"I am very relieved and gratified to hear you say so, sir."

"In the assumption of a conspiracy against him, on the part of the Glasgow Tory party, as evinced in his curious statement to the magistrate, he demonstrated a powerful delusion – and thereby undeniable insanity and irresponsibility. That is the loophole about which you must construct your defence, sir."

"I am assured that we will need to bring forth a dozen mad-house doctors prepared to argue in defence of my client."

Mr. Forbes Winslow had smiled again. "I can help you straightway to five or six," he had said.

Cockie was satisfied that that ought to do to begin with, and now, as he greeted Mr. Nicholson (in the guise of Lord Chief Baron, *alias* M'Lud) in the steamy, roiling glow of the Judge and Jury Society, it was all too easy to allow himself to think of possible glory; of making of himself a modern Erskine. He was relieved to see that he had a case; but more than this, he had a *cause*.

There was only one obstacle in his path.

"You know, Mr. Cockburn," said M'Lud as the two men secluded themselves in a dimly lit corner away from the roisterers, "if I were you I'd be asking meself about the pistols and the peelers and the doctors.

Them villains are sworn to stick together like the bundle of rods in Aesop's fable!"

"It's up to the prosecution to *prove* the charge, M'Lud," said Cockie.

"*Grounds*, sir?"

"Insanity."

The Lord Chief Baron stroked the ends of his judge's wig. "Well now," he said, "you would know best, of course, sir, but I ought to let you know that I have it on very good authority that the Scotch laddie is no murderer."

Mr. Cockburn nodded wearily. He was almost as tired of being brought well-meaning theories of McNaughten's innocence as he was of the wild and vindictive baying for the boy's blood he encountered wherever he went.

"That is all the more reason," he said, in as serious a voice as Old Peeping Tom had ever heard him use, "why we had better not let him hang."

The carroty-haired little silk must have been in deadly earnest, for he showed not a flicker of interest in the legs of the girl engaged to play the part of Salomé as they passed him by on their way to the tableaux. He was by turns contemplative and taciturn, brooding over matters deep and complex. Mr. Nicholson adjusted his wig and folded his hands over his rotundity. There was a good deal at stake: truth, justice, a life, a reputation. He studied Cockie for several moments until he was satisfied that he had deduced the source of the petit Q.C.'s contemplation: *to whit*, the only obstacle standing in the way of the carriage of justice, truth, liberty and all the rest of that gallimaufry.

"And what about the fee, Mr. Cockburn, sir?" he asked.

Cockie sighed again, more deeply then before. "Ah," he said, "now, therein lays the rub, M'Lud. I must say I had rather expected McNaughten's father to put in an appearance by now."

"Glasgow is a distance away," said Mr. Nicholson, "and it ain't always possible to shut up shop."

"If it were my son..." Cockie began, though he did not finish the thought.

"Perhaps the pa is duds cheer – gone to pot."

"By all accounts he has a very good business and is well connected."

"Well then – but what about the pile of rag and the deposit note the peelers found on the boy? There was plenty there to pay for his defence..."

Cockie laughed bitterly. "You must tell that to Mr. Maule. It appears that the damned peelers are insisting that the bank receipt is *evidences*, and that he is inclined to agree with 'em."

"Crikey! That ain't good."

"No," said the little fellow, "it *ain't*."

"Nil desperandum!" exclaimed Mr. Nicholson after a moment's deliberation. He reached across and tapped Cockie on the knee. "There is a fellow I know, right here in the metropolis, who is very skilled at extracting bank receipts from the clutches of the law."

"There is?"

"Ah yes, sir: William Clarkson – the Behemoth of the Bar." Mr. Nicholson beamed broadly beneath his long powdered wig. "Why, his name alone is sufficient to strike terror in the hearts of judges and opposing counsels alike. Ho ho! He'll get your deposit for you, Mr. Cockburn – if it can be got, that is."

"He shall need a brief," said Cockie, looking a little more hopeful.

"Well, that's easily arranged," said the Lord Chief Baron. "You must know an agent who'll oblige. What about William Cornes Humphries?"

"Yes, I know him of course. His practice promotes a good many Private and Railway bills – but won't anyone query the likelihood of such a fellow being engaged by anonymous friends of the plaintiff in a *murder* trial?"

The Lord Chief Baron was touched by Mr. Cockburn's innocence.

"O, bless you, Mr. Cockburn, sir," he said, drying his eyes with the end of his wig, "Mr. Humphries is very skilled in drawing up briefs for all manner of prisoners who find 'emselves with few friends, few relations and limited funds. You have him draw up a brief with the name of a drunk and obscure attorney of his acquaintance upon it – merely to satisfy the etiquette of the Bar – and then bid him take it to Newgate-street and engage Mr. Clarkson."

Cockie brought the tips of his gloved fingers up to his nose and contemplated for a moment or two. "But won't Mr. Humphries require something for his trouble? Not to mention the drunk and obscure attorney? And I dare say that Mr. Clarkson wouldn't put on his wig and collar bands if his own ma was about to be topped without the guinea fee in his back pocket."

"Larks!" declared Mr. Nicholson. It was time for the Lord Chief Baron to call to order this session of the Judge and Jury Society. He pulled Cockie into the centre of the room, clambered onto his judge's bench, beat his gavel, and bid the company – lawyers all, in staggering degrees of drunkenness – to gather about him. It was then that something wondrous happened – something entirely in contradiction of one of the most firmly held principles of the Bar. Having had a brief outline of the rouse put to them, several of the frolicsome inebriates stumped up, *out of their own pockets,* mind, almost enough to defray Mr. Humphries' costs, a trifle for the drunk and obscure attorney, and, most importantly, a good portion of the guinea retainer for Mr. Clarkson. And the most amazing part of all was that only a few of them did so as a wager. It would appear that Mr. Cockburn had indeed stumbled upon a cause that was dear to a good many legal hearts.

And so overcome was Mr. Nicholson at having witnessed this miraculous event that before the end of the remarkable evening, he reached beneath his judicial robes and – o my pippins, just fancy! – *made up the shortfall himself.*

The Fifth Meeting

He did not blame Abram Duncan for his predicament. He was always careful to express how Abram had guided him towards a higher estimation of himself and his abilities, giving nothing but good guidance and encouragement. And nor did he once in my hearing ever blame his father for having failed to secure that bond of affection which ought rightly to exist between a father and son. It would seem that he alone bore the responsibility for his numerous failures and inadequacies.

"There was the life before and there was the life after," he told me at our fifth meeting. "It was as though one day I awakened to the under-standing that my life was not worth a candle. There was nothing but the sense of oppression, heavy and hard, weighing down upon me."

"And what was the cause of this *oppression*?"

He smiled the curious half-smile that habitually comes over his features.

"The cause," he said, "was everything I was and everything I ever would be. It came from within me, and so I could not easily vanquish it without destroying myself."

It would seem that for some time following the attack upon him even his beloved patterns wore him down with their spiralling promises. His pride, he said, was "nothing but a great charred lump". Since the assault on his person, he had developed a cough, on occasion so troublesome that he had to beat his head against the door-jamb for pure relief. Sometimes there would be blood. He spent his days alone and did not go out much; whenever he did he sensed that people were staring at him as if he was a "plague thing, worm-low and worthless". Lassies would hold their shawls over their faces when he passed them in the street, laughing behind his back; laddies would glower and grimace at him, flashing imagined or half-imagined blades.

For much of this time there was no Carlo to protect him. He began to wonder if there ever had been.

At night he dreamed little, and when sleep did come he was tormented by the image of himself dangling from a corner of the earth with nothing but space above him and beneath. No Heaven, no Hell, just aeons and aeons of black, black chaos.

Abram would come by the shop from time to time, but he did not let him in. When he called through the shutter, McNaughten would work the treadle harder and harder, drowning him out. And yes, he was afraid that there were others who would come for him in the night, softly whistling down dark wynds. But as time went by and they did not come, his fear gradually assumed a less defined focus until it became an essential part of him: like breathing.

"Why did you not, in all this time, seek the help of others: your father, Abram Duncan, the Captain of Police?" I asked.

"I should have plucked the fear writhing from my bosom," he said, "and flung it into the river. But it was too late, too late. After a time my fear of what would be discovered if I did tell was greater than my fear of being found out as an informer."

The hearth was growing cold, the candle wearing down.

He drew a great sigh, settling back in his chair. "I have said enough," he whispered. "Perhaps – perhaps too much..."

Saturday 28th January, 1843

Early edition

PRISONER McNAUGHTEN

FINAL EXAMINATION AT BOW-STREET

Colonel Rowan (Commissioner of the Metropolitan Police), Mr. Hall (Chief Magistrate of Bow-street, police office), and Mr. Maule (Solicitor to the Treasury) had a long interview with Sir J. Graham at the Home Office yesterday morning; after which, we understand, orders were given to bring up the miscreant McNaughten for final examination at Bow-street today at 12 o'clock. It is not supposed that the inquiry will be a long one, as the facts attending to the dreadful murder are so clear, and not disputed by the prisoner himself. With respect to his state of mind, that will form a question for the jury to decide on his trial, and must depend upon the evidence then produced.

Bow-street Magistrates' Court
HALF PAST ELEVEN A.M.

Wherein Mr. Warren and numerous others visit the prisoner in his cell, and note his calm demeanour, his thoughtful mood, and his remarkable fortitude in the face of so much peril.

In consequence of the melancholy death of Mr. Drummond, it was decided that the prisoner should be finally examined at the earliest convenience, in order that he might take his trial as soon as possible at the Central Criminal Court sessions. The chief turnkey at Newgate had explained the procedure to McNaughten as best he could, as he closed the manacles about his ankles and wrists, and led him through the little covered alley to find the hackney carriage. They arrived at Bow-street a

[354]

good hour earlier than they needed, but the neighbourhood was already crowded with persons anxious to catch a sight of the assassin. To avoid a riot, it was necessary to take him in through a back cellar door. They locked him in one of the small cells attached to the court, where he waited perfectly still and unflinching upon the board bed.

Mr. Warren had all of this from the turnkey, noting it with great care in his notebook. He was among a profusion of gentlemen, all of whom had occasion to observe the prisoner in his cell on production of a card countersigned by an officer of the court (or coinage of reasonable value). He disapproved vehemently of a system that permitted so many idlers to peer and gawp, though he agreed with the opinion of the majority that the prisoner's powers of concentration and focus were exceptional; certainly, he seemed utterly unaffected by the great crush surrounding him.

An envoy of Mr. Beard at the Regent-street Polytechnic requested that the prisoner's likeness be recorded in a daguerrotype for the benefit of numerous physiognomists. Three gentlemen expressed an interest in reading his bumps. An artist who undertook commissions for the larger potteries made detailed sketches of the prisoner – though his oft-repeated request that the wretched man stand in the attitude of one firing a pistol went entirely unheeded. And it was often expressed in Mr. Warren's hearing that Mr. Deville the plaster-cast man on the Strand should take a death-mask when they came to cut McNaughten down from the gibbet.

Mr. Warren's own expression was one of more or less permanent disapproval: he loathed it that a murderer should have acquired for himself a celebrity as great as that of the Duke of Wellington – or any other great man one cared to name – and far in excess of that enjoyed by his unfortunate victim, whose name one hardly heard at all any more. But he had to own that it was indeed remarkable how all of this attention provoked not the slightest emotion on the part of the prisoner. How different from the vain posturing of that vile miscreant Oxford was the mild-mannered, modest, even gentlemanly demeanour of the Scotchman.

The presence in the narrow corridor of so many visitors made the Bow-street cell seem unendurably small and he overheard the prisoner remark to the the guard that it was much simpler than those he had lately occupied in Tothill-fields and Newgate, there being no furniture apart from a hard wooden bench. Mr. Warren's ears pricked, fully expectant at witnessing the ingratitude of an evil idler. But McNaughten was saying how he approved the sparseness of it: how he preferred the blank monotony of the walls, the dry-rubbed, soundless floor.

The Bow-street turnkey, a very jolly fellow, remembered the prisoner from the week before; he asked after him in a very kindly and familiar manner.

"So 'tis better here than at Newgate, then," he said.

"Och, it was not so bad as I had feared," murmured the prisoner.

"Lonely though, I'll wager."

The prisoner said something to the effect that he was used to spending long hours in his own company. "Though it is very hard to be prevented the use o' a knife and fork," he averred, "and they dinnae permit one tae have a candle alight after eight o'clock o' a night. Ye've just tae sling your hammock and try tae sleep. It is frustratin' not to be permitted tae read so much o' the Bible and the Prayer book, which had so thoughtfully been provided for my instruction, as I would've liked."

"Must you pick oakum?" asked the turnkey. "Gar, 'tis filthy work that: an hour alone leaves the 'ands very torn and dirty."

"I was spared that particular task."

"Coo, you was lucky! They say a fortnight pickin' oakum an' the 'ands ain't easily put to any other occupation for a good long while."

"Whit a pity it is that so many in the workhouses must spend so long in the task," said the prisoner with a sigh. "Och, 'twill be a great day, will it not, when it is no longer necessary tae punish the poor?"

And the turnkey agreed that it would.

"Might I have some water?" the prisoner asked after a few minutes in which he had sat with his hands upon his knees, staring at the wall. "For it is not agreeable tae go a day wi'out washin' the face, hands an' nether parts, an' the turnkey at Newgate woke me too late for ablutions. I am aye clean in my habits. They checked my head for chats at Newgate, but found not one." He ran a hand through his hair. "So they dinnae see the need to shorn me."

"O, they shan't do that 'till you receives yer sentence," said the turnkey. "They shall take yer clo'es from you an' all. You shall have to wear the uniform."

The prisoner's features clouded a little. "And how much further will the matter be pursued?" he said mournfully, "tae the very End?"

"Yes, well," said the turnkey, "that is how it usually goes with these matters."

The prisoner then asked if he would be redeemed. The turnkey said that it was not for him to say.

Bow-street Magistrates' Court,
A SHORT WHILE LATER

Wherein Inspector Hughes has yet more occasion for appallment.

Inspector Tierney gripped the rail of the dock tightly; it weren't in the nature of such a close man to stand in a dock and make himself the object of public knowledge and interest. The scranning cove was more accustomed to sitting at the clerk's table proclaiming silence, ordering some poor beggar-child to hold his head up when the magistrate was addressing him, or having some apple-woman and her baby removed whenever the gravity of justice was disturbed by the mewlings of a starveling. He was more used, by far, to stroking his close-shaven chin incriminatingly as some poor tailor was arraigned for seditious assembly.

Well, now it was his turn to be inquisited: the watcher, watched.

Mr. Maule, the Treasury Solicitor, was sat beside Mr. Hall, the Magistrate, and without paying any of the regard due to that gentleman – whose court this was – it was he who turned to Inspector Tierney and commenced questioning.

"Tell the court about your first encounter with the prisoner," he said.

Inspector Hughes was standing in a cramped corner beside the dais, close by the entrance to the cells. He didn't care for such flagrant disregard of the proper procedures, and he wondered why Mr. Hall didn't do more to stand up for the magistracy.

"I saw the prisoner the evening he was apprehended at the station-house in Gardiner's-lane." The plainclothesman made his reply in a more modulated tone than the one he ordinarily used in that place. "I first saw him between four and five o'clock, as the charge was being entered on the police-sheet. He was then standing in an ante-room." It was a lie, of course. Inspector Tierney had never clapped eyes on the prisoner until the wretch was already down in the cells, which was when he had taken it upon himself to *interrogate*... He was drumming upon the railing: twice or thrice he glanced over at the crowd with a telling concern.

He need not have worried, for the room was filled with Active Duty, in various guises and ready to spring to arms should McNaughten's associates make 'emselves known by crying out "*spy!*" or heaving a brickbat at the witness. Inspector Hughes's steady gaze roved about the massing room, picking out each and every one; the corners of his mouth turning down and down.

"Had you any conversation with the prisoner before then?" Mr. Maule asked, looking very grave.

"Not at that time," said the spy. He released his hold on the rail a little, assuming a more gallant stance. "I spoke with him three or four times afterwards, when he was in the cell."

A beefy-jawed fellow, standing at the very front of the crowd, stuck in with a cavilling tone, his hands tucked behind him under the skirts of a voluminous cabman's coat.

"You oughter ask him if he thought to caution the plaintiff," he cried. He peered theatrically at Inspector Tierney.

"Silence in court!" said Inspector Hughes, though inwardly he approved the substance of the interlocution.

The fellow in the coat nudged the writing elbow of the gentleman standing beside him. "Pay no heed to what that master of tergiversation has to say, Mr. Justitia," he croaked, "that devil is a police spy, a *police spy*, I tell you!"

And Tierney, upon hearing this, turned a little pale.

"Quiet there!" commanded Inspector Hughes. "Silence in court!"

"State what passed between you," Mr. Maule addressed Inspector

Tierney, "but first let me ask you whether anything was said to induce him to make any communication?"

"Do you mark that?" squawked the beefy man incredulously. "Such flagrant floutings of the rules! O, 'tis a perfect disgrace, I tell you! Whatever next: the suspension of habeas corpus?"

Inspector Hughes tipped himself forward onto the toes of his boots. "Silence in court," he said, somewhat restively.

The scranning cove snapped his fingers in the direction of the beefy fellow, as if to say the hazard was nothing to him. "When I first entered the cell," he said, "I gave him strict caution not to say anything to me which might criminate himself." He had turned quite deliberately towards the prisoner, as if defying him to argue against, or qualify the statement with his own recollection. But McNaughten did neither. Instead, he returned the look steadily.

"Now state what passed," said Mr. Maule, and the plainclothesman dropped his voice to a confidential tone.

"I asked him where he came from, and he said from Glasgow, that he had been from there about three months. He said he had been in business in Glasgow, on his own account, as a turner; that he gave up that business, and was going into another line, but was prevented. I said, 'You have a good share of money', to which he replied that he had, but he had wrought hard at it; that he had tried to do the work of three ordinary men daily. We talked about the Paisley weavers, and he expressed great sympathy for their plight. Then I asked him about the railway that now passes between Glasgow and Edinburgh, and the steamers passing between Glasgow and Liverpool. I think he said he had come on the *British Queen*. I asked him whether he would take any food, and he expressed a wish to have some tea or coffee. While the sergeant went to fetch it, I asked him whether Drummond was a Scotch name. He said it was: that it was the family name of the Earl of Perth, but the title had died away. Nothing further passed that evening."

"We only have your word for that," said the square-rigged fellow in the front, prompting another request for silence from Inspector Hughes.

"And when did you see him again?" asked Mr. Maule.

"About nine o'clock of the following morning. I asked him whether he had taken his breakfast, and he said he had. He also asked what o'clock it was, and I told him a quarter past nine had just gone. He then asked if I would allow him to have some water to wash with, to which I consented, and sent the sergeant who had been confined with him during the night to get some. When the sergeant had left I said to the prisoner, 'I suppose you will assign some reason to the magistrates this morning for the act you have committed?' He said he would – a short one."

Mr. Hall coughed and, with a look of irritation, Mr. Maule gave way to him. "Do you hear what is being said?" the Magistrate asked the prisoner.

McNaughten nodded his head very slightly and slowly.

"Please answer yes or no."

"Yes, sir," he said, the faint smile playing about his lips.

Tierney brought a finger up to his face, stroking his top lip as he regarded the prisoner thoughtfully for a moment or two. Then he replaced his hand upon the rail before him, and drummed lightly. "I said," he continued, "'I suppose you are aware of the gentleman you shot at?' He said, 'It is Sir Robert Peel, isn't it?' I said at first, 'No', but instantly recalled the word. I said, 'We are not aware exactly who it is yet; but recollect the caution I gave you last night, for anything you say might be used against you.' The prisoner who was sitting down at the time looked up at me and said, 'But you won't use this or these words against me?' I said, 'I don't know; I gave you a proper caution.' I said nothing more, but immediately left him."

Inspector Tierney's testimony was proof of the supernatural power of insinuation, as insubstantial as the Cock-lane ghost: it ought never to have been admitted in a court of law, but it did the job very well. The prisoner intended to kill the Prime Minister: a police inspector of the "A" Division had just said as much. It tied in so neatly with what had been expected; it was plausible; it seemed to be the truth. Inspector Hughes had exhausted all his powers of listening and watching to the utmost: he was done with the matter. He waited a further moment, but there came not one word of protest, not one dissenting murmur.

The fat cove whistled softly. The gentleman with the leather notebook who was stood beside him had stopped writing things down and was gazing at the prisoner, who was smiling faintly.

McNaughten had not taken his eyes from the plainclothesman throughout the whole process and he did not do so now. But Inspector Tierney did not return the look. He was studying his nails and breathing freely. After a short while he closed his eyes in a little gesture of assent towards a sign from Mr. Maule that all was done, just as the old clock on the wall heaved its minute hand to the XII, striking one.

"You have heard what the witness has said," said Mr. Hall to the prisoner. "Do you wish to put any questions to him?"

"No, sir."

And if the prisoner ain't prepared to speak up for himself, the Inspector wondered, then why should I worry myself on his account?

"And have you told us everything that passed?" inquired the magistrate of the plainclothesman.

Inspector Tierney bowed. "I have," he said, "to the best of my recollection."

Mr. Maule smiled slightly. "That is the case on behalf of the prosecution, sir," he said.

The magistrate turned to the prisoner. "When you were last brought before me," he said kindly, as one might to a child, "I told you that you might make any statement you thought proper, having previously given you a caution that whatever you said would be taken down in writing and used against you. You must consider that caution now repeated. Do you wish to say anything more?"

"No, sir."

"You have already made a statement, which was taken down in writing, do you wish to have that read over to you?"

"No, thank you."

"Prisoner, for your information, I must tell you that you will not be brought up again before me. I shall commit you today to take your trial; the sessions at which you will be tried will commence on Monday next, but I cannot say what day may be fixed for your trial. You are entitled to have, if you please, a copy of the depositions given to you; if you wish to have them, say so."

"Yes. I should like to have them."

"Prisoner, you stand committed to Newgate to take your trial for wilful murder."

The prisoner bowed respectfully to the Court, and in another moment was removed from the bar.

"No man's life here is worth purchase," said the beefy-jawed cove.

The gentleman beside him was putting away his notebook. "Nothing can save McNaughten now," he said.

GREEN PARK,
THREE O'CLOCK P.M.

In which Mr. Cockburn considers the boulders and potholes strewn along his chosen path.

Not trusting the newspapers, Cockie had sent his clerk, Mr. Frayling, to Bow-street that morning in order to obtain a faithful and trustworthy record of the proceedings. He had already guessed how it would go. He had not been disappointed. He took a post-prandial walk in the park, and smoked a cigar against the cold air.

It seemed that the prisoner still looked extremely well; indeed, according to Frayling, his incarceration did not appear to have had the slightest effect upon his health. He had given the tolerable appearance of education and intelligence, and throughout the whole of the examination had seemed to pay extreme attention to what was going forward. None of which augured well for the plea of insanity that Cockie was hoping to argue for. The amusing *aperçu* that Mr. Guthrie senior, having apparently decided to withdraw all association (on the part of either himself or his son and heir) with the death of Mr. Drummond, had sent Mr. Bransby Cooper to testify, roused him a little. As did Frayling's rendering of the Magistrate's considerable surprise that there had been no shock or alarm evinced on the part of the victim, despite the ball having apparently traversed round the left half of the body. The worst surgeon in London was adamant that this was so.

Cockie was by now more aware than ever before of events chugging along like a great engine – one that would neither be slowed, nor diverted. He knew that this was a device that could destroy him; but he was too mindful of the opportunity which it presented to allow himself to be down for too long. It was quite true that he no longer cared a jot for the nonsense of doctors and bullets; peelers and pistols; the numerous sightings of skulking figures on the steps of government buildings. None of this troubled him – not even in some indeterminate part of his conscience. He was persuaded to let others be exercised by these trifles, and determined that his reason not be obfuscated by *irrelevancies*.

His task was the refinement of argument, the chimera of rhetoric; and insanity was, as Mr. Forbes Winslow told him often as he inducted Cockie into the deepest learning on the topic, a *complicated,* twisted matter. And the question of deciding whether one could readily assume that all murderous acts were either wilful or the results of madness was a fraught and tangled puzzle for one trained in the infallibles of law to have to deal with.

He sent up a wisp of cigar smoke to conceal the bare branches hanging over him. This time there was to be no hedge or tack, he thought. *Right or wrong*.

He wished only to come out of this alive; he hoped that his only sin was in trying to be too clever and that his only failing would be an inadvertent smutching of a scintilla of his integrity – the integrity he would in ordinary circumstances have counted as so essential to his sense of self. Trusting that this was not a vain hope, he drew again on the cigar, holding the warm smoke against his lungs and the cold, cold air for as long as he could. When he let it go he was no longer thinking of himself, but of the plaintiff: the poor, mad scapegoat who had been betrayed by everyone. It helped to think of McNaughten like that: to see him as an unfortunate victim of circumstance who could find no succour, no support. It helped to blame the father, the oft-quoted "friends and associates", the ominous shadow of *the system*.

Such thinking fired him. Before long he was damning and blasting to Hell the Treasury Solicitor, the Office of Home Affairs, and the whole of Scotland-yard. The peelers had had a detectivist gathering depositions in Glasgow for several days by now – the likely source of most of the nonsense that was daily served up in the newspapers. It would be difficult to catch them at the next stage, and the cost and difficulty of deponing witnesses residing in Scotland likely to be high. The newspapers come from Glasgow that very morning had carried a report that the Lord Provost of Glasgow, Sir James Campbell, had been visited by the prisoner the previous May. The Member for Kilmarnock had already invoked Campbell as a possible friendly witness on account of some association with the prisoner's father, even though the gentleman had been an unsuccessful Tory candidate for one of the Glasgow seats in '41. It appeared that he was prepared to state that the plaintiff had visited him, requesting his aid in vanquishing "certain parties" who "incessantly dogged him". Campbell had found McNaughten to be a "jolly-looking man, speaking very coolly although evidently labouring under some hallucination of mind".

It was all most helpful. Cockie had shared the observation with Mr. Forbes Winslow, as they considered a list of mad-house doctors who might be called upon for the defence.

"What greater *proof* of insanity can there be," he had said, "and what greater proof that politics was not the motive, but rather the folly of his own notions – the force of a powerful delusion – than that the plaintiff should have turned to the highest representative within his orbit of those whom it was alleged – as he had himself suggested in his Bow-street statement – were his professed enemy?"

Mr. Forbes Winslow had agreed that it was certainly most compelling. Neither of them mooted the possibility that, always assuming the version of the encounter carried in the *Herald* to be a true account, McNaughten might have been voicing a genuine concern, and was indeed the victim of unscrupulous Tory agents who had urged him on with vile and dread threats until he saw no alternative but to take his heinous action. The fact that McNaughten might be no more demented than were Mr. Cockburn and Mr. Forbes Winslow was no longer to be admitted: it was an awkward and inconvenient possibility that lay far beyond the scope of the Argument.

Cockie released a stream of blue-gray smoke that swiftly wrapped itself about him like a shroud. For a moment or two he was dead, dead even to the charm of a little redwing hopping and scratching in the snow, oblivious to its puny seeping song. When he gradually felt his senses return, he was vaguely alive to the little stripe of flame on the bird's flank: the only thing of any colour all about him.

The state may be rotten – and it was – an entire nation turned mono-maniac by weak and corrupt governance – but this was all the more reason why, he told himself, he must stick to the course he had set. It would, he reasoned, be better for society. And better for the client too. Mr. Forbes Winslow was encouraging in his descriptions of the many advances made in the modern Bethlem. And there was the possibility that McNaughten might be permitted to live out the rest of his life in the Glasgow asylum, close to his friends and family. Then again, perhaps it did not matter where one lived out one's days: perhaps all that mattered was that one did not hang.

Cockie was watching the bird; smoking, lost in thought. It was only at the third bidding that he heard the voice at his back.

"Excuse me – Mr. Cockburn, sir – Mr. *Alexander* Cockburn – I pray you, excuse me, sir!"

He made a weary half-turn towards Constitution Hill – the apparent source of the interlocution – coming face to face with a handsome, well-built young man dressed in a country smock, breeches and worn, heavy boots.

The boy was smiling at him, his bright blue eyes dancing. He snatched off his cap at once, revealing an unruly shock of carroty curls.

"Father? It is I – Alexander Dalton – your son! O, you are just as mother described you! I knew you at once!"

"I'm sorry, do I know you?" said Sandy, feeling his heart freeze.

The smile disappeared in an instant; the broad shoulders dropped. The boy reached up uncertainly, running his hand through his hair. It was a fine hand, delicate, long-fingered; entirely at odds with the rest of him.

"I'm sorry," he mumbled, shuffling awkwardly, "I – I meant no harm or intrusion."

Cockie threw the end of his cigar onto the snow. The earth hissed at him.

"I'm afraid you have been mistaken," he said. "I am not who you think I am."

He buried his chin in his overcoat and began to hurry away, his breath coming hard and heavy. He headed towards the Queen's palace, feeling affronted, ambushed, guilty, and cruel.

"I only wanted," the boy was crying at his back, "I only wanted to take you by the hand and thank you for my life. That is all. That is all..."

When Cockie was at the track-way he turned back briefly, catching his breath. The boy was still standing where he had left him, cap in hand. He was a good distance away, but Cockie knew that he was looking at him, and he was sure that he was looking at him with understanding – and what was worse, much worse, with *acceptance*.

For he knew that look, you see; he knew those eyes. He had never forgotten either. And now he knew that he never would.

PEEPING TOM OF LONDON TOWN

I SAW wee Cockburn leaving after a huddle at the Garrick's Head with a wry smile on his face and a loose note tucked inside his kid glove. It appears that friends of McNaughten have engaged a "highly respectable and intelligent" agent here in London to prepare his defence, and hopes are high that the fee will soon be in hand. THINKS I TO MYSELF THINKS I, Cockie, you are hoping to make your name with a great trial: let us hope that the wink ain't been winkt on this one.

Morning edition

PARTICULARS OF
THE FUNERAL OF MR. DRUMMOND

The scenes of grief openly expressed at Mr. Drummond's funeral, which took place at Charlton, near Woolwich, Kent, yesterday morning, amply demonstrate how very close are the family of the unfortunate gentleman, of which three brothers and a sister are yet living.

In accordance with the wishes of the deceased's relatives, the funeral was conducted in the most private manner; the mourners consisting solely of members of the Drummond family. The mournful cavalcade left Grosvenor-street at the early hour of eight o'clock on its way to Charlton, the procession following the order:

MUTES
Page, bearing the plume of feathers,
The Hearse,
Drawn by four horses, containing the body of the deceased,
and supported by eight hearse pages as bearers.

Mourning coach,
Drawn by four horses, containing the following members of
the deceased's family –
Col. Berkeley Drummond,   Rev. Arthur Drummond,
Mr. Charles Drummond,   Mr. C. Drummond, jun.
The private carriage of the deceased.

The route taken was over Vauxhall-bridge, by Kennington
and Camberwell to New Cross, thence to Deptford, and over
Blackheath to Charlton, at which place the procession arrived
about ten minutes past eleven. On reaching the churchyard the
body was met by the Hon. and Rev. Mr. Boscawen, a close friend
of the deceased's family, vicar of Wotton nr. Dorking, Surrey,
who commenced reading the service for the burial of the dead.
At the conclusion of the service, the mournful cavalcade moved
towards the vault prepared for the reception of the body, and
the scene was of the most painful character. The three brothers
of the deceased were very much affected, and, when the coffin
was lowered into the vault, the feelings of Colonel Drummond in
particular were completely overcome.

The vault in which the deceased is interred is a very ancient
one, having been erected more than 200 years since. It had fallen
into decay and was advertised; no persons coming forward to
claim it, the vicar, Rev. Arthur Drummond, younger brother of
the deceased, appropriated for his own family.

It is most curious that close by lie the remains of Spencer
Perceval, who was shot by the lunatic Bellingham, on Monday,
11th May, 1812, as he passed through the passage connecting
Westminster Hall to St. Stephens Hall in the old Palace of Westminster.

There is no small number of persons impressed by the irony
of this observation. It will be recollected that Bellingham was executed within the week at Newgate.

Inspector Hughes makes a painful discovery.

Over the course of the day, a shrill east wind had got up which gradually blew the snow out over the sea; and following in its wake vapours poured off the Essex marshes. Hugging close the curving line of the river, the vapours had arrived in London an hour before, clogged with the soot and smuts from how many thousand chimneys, and coating the whole of the metropolis with a clammy, stinging, greasy layer that filled the noses and mouths of all those who were foolish or desperate enough to be out of doors. Inspector Hughes was one of the unfortunates: he was stood in the station-yard, greeting the yellow confusion with a small sigh.

He had come outside to escape the pandemonium of the front-office, where the scranning cove, Inspector Tierney, was issuing the command to "close up!" In a clatter of heavy boots, a small contingent of plainclothesmen was preparing to depart for Poplar-row and the End of the World. The easeful fog provided a cloak to the Inspector's feelings and respite from the unstinting demands of the busiest day he could ever remember in thirteen years of policing the metropolis. For, as all policemen knew, you can't do a thing about a fog.

There was but a few hours left before Mr. Clarkson commenced battle for the prisoner McNaughten's defence, and so the Inspector had gone through the contents of the buff boxes with Mr. Maule, the Treasury Solicitor, and had brought forward the police witnesses to be sworn in before the Grand Jury at the Bailey. And with but a few hours before the regalia set off at the trot (with Her Majesty in the gold carriage at the walk), the shining of bull's eye lanterns up alleyways, along gutters, and into doorways – every inch of the distance between Gardiner's-lane and Trafalgar-square – was become imperative. The Inspector had lost count of the numbers he had moved on in the various patrols he had undertaken with his constables. Every doorway from Buckingham Palace to Westminster Abbey and back again was now free from itinerant dangers; and the station-house cells filled to bursting with the Desperate Poor. Her Majesty could ride to Westminster without fear of attack, and make her speech. The brave tars and soldiers would be praised; taxes raised or lowered; the distress deplored; tuppennies would be increased to quarterns; the Lords and Gentlemen would murmur their assent; Her Majesty would beseech them to be wise; and all would be set square.

As the fog wrapped itself tenderly around him and the gas-stars glowed above, Inspector Hughes found his thoughts straying to the mournful little procession he had witnessed the previous morning. Mr. Drummond's funeral cortège had been a very private affair – none of the Quality who wished to pay their respects had been permitted to do so by the family, not even Sir Robert Peel – and quiet as a Man o' War stealing across the ocean, it had made its morose progress through Mayfair, Piccadilly, Belgravia, creeping past the fashionable squares and the back of the Queen's palace, before descending into Pimlico and Tothill, slipping over the Vauxhall-bridge, and on to the Surrey-side. The Inspector had stood stoical in the river chill for above an hour with two constables from the "B" Division. It being such a modest affair, there had been no practical necessity to halt the traffic streaming into Westminster; but he had put up his hand in any case. He was glad that he had seen off Mr. Drummond on his last journey. It was the decent thing to do.

His reverie was broken by the sound of the back door creaking open and slamming shut. Peering across the smothered yard, he could just make out Constable Silver lumbering into the mustard smoke; little drops of moisture, illuminated by the gas, clung to the vapour that had wrapped itself around the young man's head, like a streamer of spangled gauze, making him seem other-worldly, distant.

"You oughter be in your stow in the station-house barrack by now, getting some snooze," said the Inspector. "You has to be at the Bailey tomorrow morning, and Mr. Clarkson can be very hard in the matter of questioning police witnesses: very hard indeed. You shall need to be on your mettle."

"I ain't going," Silver said.

The Inspector tipped himself forward onto his toes and considered for a moment. "I see. And why's that, then?" he said. He was thinking how flat he sounded; how resigned.

"I ain't got the stomach for it."

"Ho! That's just jumpy nerves, that is."

"It ain't nerves." Silver sighed in the fog.

"The Superintendent tells me you could make sergeant before the year is out. That'd be five bob more a week. You and your cook could set up home on that."

The boy's voice was cracking in the damp air. "You was always kind to me, Inspector Hughes. I feel very bad knowing that I has let you down. But I can't go on with it no more, sir."

"I see..."

"I don't care for it one bit..."

"No, well, I don't give a jack for it neither, son," said the Inspector. "But that's how it is, see. It ain't for us to question. Our task in the 'A' Division is to defend Parliament and the business of government; and if the Commissioners, the Home Secretary and the Prime Minister all think that it's in the interest of the country that a case be wrung out in one way rather than another, well, we has an obligation to support 'em as best we can – no matter what we think of the rights and wrongs."

"There never was any shot in McNaughten's gun," said Silver, in a cold, flat tone.

"Yes," said the Inspector after he had considered for a few moments, "that seems most likely."

"Which means he didn't murder Mr. Drummond."

"He bought a pair of pistols and a flask and caps and a pile of shot, and he fired at a gentleman. And now that gentleman's dead. That's all we know, and I dare say that's all we shall ever know."

"He never bought the shot."

"Well, he never bought it off the Jew pawn-broker – we know that."

Silver drew in a long breath which he released slowly into the chill, moist air. "Do you remember how it was that first night, sir? How anxious everyone was? How we was all concerned lest the police be made to look like a bunch of fools?"

"Yes, well, Mr. Drummond was shot a few yards across the carriage-way from Scotland-yard in broad day on a crowded thoroughfare... It don't look good, Silver, no matter how you paints it."

"The Superintendent said he didn't want there to be any doubt. He kept saying how there'd been five assassination attempts in the past three years – three of 'em against Her Majesty – and all of 'em let off with a rap across the knuckles."

"Francis was transported for life to Van Diemen's Land – I don't consider that a rap across the knuckles. And if Prince Albert hadn't intervened when he did, that simple boy might have been hanged drawn and quartered – an' all for a flash in the pan..."

"The Superintendent kept saying how the public was blaming the police for it – that the streets were full of bad people and any one of 'em could say he was a lunatic and get away with murder. He said the law had lost all of its power and that the streets of the metropolis would soon be as ungovernable as those of Manchester or Glasgow. He was most anxious that there be no doubt whatever with McNaughten. He said the force couldn't afford another blunder."

"We done everything in accordance with the proper procedures. It's Inspector Tierney and the Active Duty the Superintendent oughter be reading the Riot Act: not the likes of us."

"He said if we never found nothing at McNaughten's lodgings, then I was to make sure that we found the pile of shot and the powder flask."

Inspector Hughes pushed his toes hard up against his boots and winced.

"I told you," the boy was crying accusingly, "I told you that all I saw with me own eyes at the shooting was what looked like a burning piece of paper on the ground at Mr. Drummond's feet – and you know how hard I looked for that second ball. The Superintendant told me to keep cank about it, so I did – but, sir, there's a world of difference between keeping cank and *lying in a court of law*! When I thought McNaughten would get a punishment he deserved for being a fanatic for corn and all of that, I didn't mind so much. But now that Mr. Drummond's dead, and the coroner says it's murder – I tell you, Inspector, I can't live with meself."

The Inspector had closed his eyes as if to keep out the insinuating truth.

Silver sniffed loudly. "I'm on me way to Scotland-yard," he said in a broken voice. "I'm giving me notice. I've come to say goodbye to you, and to thank you for all you've tried to teach me. And sorry..."

The gas-lamp gave to the fog a dismal yellow tinge, the colour of rotting leaves, which coiled about Silver so dense he seemed to quiver and flicker indeterminate, insubstantial. "You can run if you wants, boy," the Inspector said, his words creeping into the thick, damp air. "I won't try and stop you. But I will tell you this: it won't change a thing. Not for the prisoner; not for nobody. If you run off, they shall just find another constable to buff himself. It's gone too far, now, you see... too far. And the best that you can do, son – if it ain't the *right* – is go to the Bailey tomorrow and answer as truthfully as you can without mentioning the very bad thing that you was told to do. Let 'em make you sergeant. Pocket your five bob. Marry your girl. Make a life. You've earned it. Ho! You might even say you deserve it. Yes, well, we all deserve a little bit of happiness, don't we?"

Silver seized at the fog, crying in rage. "But I done wrong!"

"We've all done wrong, son."

"You ain't – you ain't never done wrong!"

Inspector Hughes ran his hand wearily over his chin. "You ain't the first peeler to find yourself on the wrong side of the law, and you won't be the last. How do you think I learned to stick doggedly to the proper procedures and never ever waiver from them – no matter how difficult that might be? O, some policemen never learn, I grant you. Some shall always try and make the evidences fit round their inklings, and the devil take the consequences. And a good many will turn out to have been mistaken, and shall have to see it all the way to the gallows...."

"O, so, it don't matter...!"

"O no, son; it matters. It matters a very great deal. But the thing is this – you shall never forget how you feel now – *never*: I know I never did. And in the end it's that understanding what'll make of you an' 'alf-decent peeler."

"But if they turns the prisoner off I shan't be able to live with meself."

"O, you'd be surprised what you can live with." When Silver groaned, it was as if something clutched at the Inspector's heart. He felt his shoulders drop, for the first time in a long while. "Now, now – don't take on so," he said. "I never likes to hazard a guess at an outcome, Constable, but the prisoner has Mr. Cockburn defending him, and *he's* got Mr. Clarkson arguing for him tomorrow – and Mr. Clarkson is very good at arguing."

The boy was broken, but he was coming back together again. "I 'as turned it over and over in me mind the past week or more, sir: I tell you I've driven meself half-mad with it..."

"Constable Silver, the fact is you apprehended a fellow who was in the act of firing a pistol at a gentleman on a crowded street. You acted with no thought for your own safety. You done everything what was expected of a man fit to wear that uniform, and more. Don't, for pity's sake, don't let them take that away from you, son. Go to the Bailey tomorrow and, if you are called, you tell Mr. Clarkson as much as you dare, and trust in justice to do the rest."

They stood in the fog for a while longer without saying another word, contemplating all the little wrongs of this life; all the great. Then they bid each other goodnight, and the Inspector watched Silver go; he watched until he was satisfied that the constable had passed out of the thick unblest vapour, out of the raw and unforgiving chill.

No.7, Poplar-row, Newington Butts,
Five minutes earlier

In which Mr. Nicholson witnesses the End of the World.

It was pitch dark and freezing cold in the House of the Everlasting Covenant, and yet the room was already entirely full when Mr. Nicholson arrived. Only the light from the street-lamp, softened by the incipient fog, enabled him to grope his way through the immense throng of people crushed into there, their breath rising in steamy clouds of expectation. It was by a happy accident that he arrived in front of the makeshift altar, beside a small-waisted acolyte with high, round breasts.

"Good evening, Miss," he said, doffing his hat, "allow me to introduce myself: Renton Nicholson, book-seller." The girl turned her oval face upon him, pale in the gloom, her eyes large and searching. He took her to be an impoverished milliner, or some such sylphide of *chapeaux* and band-boxes. "Might I ask, what brings such a pretty creature to this dismal place?"

"Time will soon come to an end, sir, and we are going to leave the earth," she said in a pleasing voice, soft and sweet, and not at all raving. "The Lord is coming to relieve the good of all their suffering."

Mr. Nicholson was smitten. "I could relieve you of all your suffering, if you would but let me," he said gallantly. He reached into his pocket for a card, pressing it into the satin-stitcher's small, icy, cold hand. "Might I call on you tomorrow?"

"But the world is about to be destroyed," she said, frowning slightly.

"O yes – so it is. But if it turns out that it ain't destroyed, then, I wonder, might I –?"

A look of appallment had come over the creature's face, and when he saw that the large enticing eyes were shining with tears, Mr. Nicholson felt a great shame. He quickly mumbled an apology and turned to look upon the altar.

It was just at that moment that there came the blare of a tin trumpet from the back of the room, followed by a great sough. A familiar stunted figure in a slouch hat was making his way through the crowd, half-heartedly waving a little calico flag. The orange tip of his short clay-pipe protruded from beneath the brim of his hat, glowing devilish in the dark. Mr. Nicholson watched with ill-disguised disparagement as Carlo, without removing his pipe, tootled tunelessly a couple more times upon the bugle. And then with a collective gasp of suppressed ecstasy or strangled agony– for the two are very much alike – the crowd broke apart as a second figure processed through, on his way to the makeshift altar. Carlo struck a Lucifer on the wall and lit two candles standing in tins, illuminating the determined features of none other than the wizened gentleman from the Inquest, who straightway began to recite from memory the last chapter of Revelation.

He certainly spoke very well. He was powerful, dignified, and without a trace of affectation; and he was able to invest all the nonsense about crystal streams, and trees of life, and the healing of nations, and there being no need for candles where they were all going, and prophecy and angels, with a plausibility that was entirely lacking in the original text. When he came to the part about "my reward is with me, to give every man according as his work shall be", a few of the boldest in the room cried out "Hallelujah!" – but for the most part the congregation was enrapt, training all of its attention upon the messenger, if not the message.

"I am the root and the offspring of David, and the bright and Morning Star!" said the wizened gent.

The effect was positively galvanic. Nobody cheered, applauded, or in any way whatever expressly relieved their feelings; but on all sides Mr. Nicholson found himself assailed by a kind of hard breathing that gradually gathered momentum. It was the unmistakeable sound of suppressed emotion, not very different from that which could be heard any night of the week seeping from the recesses of Waterloo Bridge, or from the shadows of any gropecunt-alley in the land. And hearing it Mr. Nicholson was astonished and then alarmed to experience, quite in spite of himself, a definite stirring in the pit of his groin. The lovely *réligieuse* next to him was panting – though whether in fear, panic, anticipation, or from some other motive he could not rightly tell; all he knew was the pounding of his own blood as people on all sides of him joined in the groaning and gasping.

"O! O! O! O!"

"Bend me," the girl was murmuring. "Bend me…"

"O! I am coming Lord!" a few cried out in voices tremulous. "I am coming! O, o, o, I am coming!"

And hearing them, Mr. Nicholson felt his own thrill subside and another, entirely different instinct take its place: revulsion.

He stroked his chin, and peered hard at the wizened gent.

"The People cannae understand why ah have done nothin'," he was saying in a compelling undertone. "But ah huvnae been idle. I'd tae move swiftly and under cover of darkness, but my soul is a tabernacle. What will now come tae pass is the slaughterin' of the troublesome, the thankless, the filthy, the unrighteous. He forgetteth not the cry o' the humble! The needy shall not be overlooked; the expectation o' the poor shall not perish for ever. We are ready to receive you, Lord Jesus! Even so! Come, come, Lord Jesus!"

From behind Mr. Nicholson came a brilliant flash of light, and a sound so loud that, he would happily have wagered, it must have been heard on the opposite bank of the river. It was not a scream or a shriek; it was a yell, a yell so prolonged that it filled the parlour entirely.

Afterwards he was astonished that it had taken him so long to turn around in order to determine the source of the noise, but time had seemed to run slower, somehow, and such a thrill had surged through the crowd all about him: people were more agitated than before, swaying, rocking their bodies to and fro where they stood, moaning, sighing, weeping – all of which was very curious, to be sure, and so contrary to Mr. Nicholson's own sense of balance, sanity, that he could not help but be o'ertaken with wonder.

And, my merry Andrews, it was also the case that, for the longest time, he did not *dare* to look, afraid of what he might see. When he did, with mounting dread, turn around he was astonished by the sight of the prisoner's landlady, Mrs. Dutton, bathed in an eerie veil of light, and floating like the Air Brahmin of Cuddapah towards the altar.

Mr. Nicholson had seen enough of the world, of gulls and rum lays and jigs and blabs, of peep shows and penny gaffs to know a deception when he saw one. He wanted to run to the makeshift altar and denounce the whole jape; but when he looked about him, at the scarred and battered faces bathed and softened in the glow that was emanating from the landlady, the calm, the *hope* that was settled there, chums, Old Peeping Tom did not have the heart to break the spell.

Mrs. Dutton was now speaking in more articulated words, various Scriptures of an exhortative kind. She spoke the first word of each text three times over, each one louder than the last.

"Kiss! Kiss!! Kiss!!! the Son," she cried, "lest he be angry, and ye perish from the way!"

A great groan passed through the throng and streaks of light burst upon the room; "Glory! Glory!" went up the cry. People were falling to their knees; crying, laughing; laughing, crying. Only Mr. Nicholson and one or two others remained upright. He struggled to keep his eyes trained upon the landlady all the while, who, he could see in each bolt of light that swept across the room, was floating a few inches clear of the ground, spinning around and around like a demented ballet-girl, her head tilted back and a great agonised scream issuing from her gaping mouth.

It was a good line she'd got into, he was thinking; and then the really extraordinary thing happened and even Mr. Nicholson's obdurate counfoundment was shaken to its very basis.

AT ABOUT THE SAME TIME

In which Mr. Warren witnesses the End of the World.

There was not one person of Quality to be espied among the great crowd, at least so far as he was able to tell in the dark. The lingering stench of unwashed linen and rag-shop bonnets was proof enough of the lamentable condition in which the greater portion of the congregation found itself. But there was certainly something very *charismatic* about the place. Mr. Warren had heard a good many dissenting preachers in his day, including his own father, and though he was not, in general, all that well disposed towards messianism, he would have had to say that very few, if any, could rival this fellow for oratory, drama and zeal.

By some stroke of good fortune, Mr. Warren had found a position at the back of the assembly, by the doorway, and being by a good head taller than just about everyone else there, had a decent view of everything in the room. His attention had immediately been drawn to the stunted fellow who had introduced the proceedings by blowing on a trumpet. His features quite obscured by a slouch hat, a pipe dangling insolently, there was to Mr. Warren's mind something familiar about the fellow. It was not long before he remembered him as the plainclothesman who had purported to be the prisoner's bedmate, and who had used the landlady so cruelly. This was not of itself, he supposed, all that surprising. The fellow conducted himself with an air of detachment, Mr. Warren observed; indeed, there was something *proprietorial* about him that brought to mind the manner of a stage-manager at the pantomime.

As Mr. Warren watched, the fellow attended to a small woman who was standing at his side in the shadows. He draped a gauze veil over her and handed her a small lamp, and then struck a Lucifer on his boot heel. The effect was immediate – a strong odour of sulphur ensuing a brilliant, sustained flare. Mr. Warren immediately deduced that the lamp must have held a small piece of lime – such as Macready used at Covent-garden. In the lamp glare, diffused by the copious amounts of gauze, the woman appeared *ghostly* – although there was no obscuring the plain fact that she was none other than the prisoner's landlady: the unfortunate lunatic Mrs. Dutton.

Mr. Warren thought it an act of the supremest folly to hand to a madwoman draped in gauze a piece of flaming lime in such a crowded place. He feared for the safety of everyone in the room, and was very thankful that he had had the good fortune to take up a position so close to the door. However, not everyone in the room was as sensible as was he. The spectacle of the landlady bathed in a spectral light and looking very wild was more than most people around him could bear. Consider too that she appeared to be floating, as it were, through their midst, an hysterical shriek issuing forth all the while, and you will imagine something, a little, of the consternation the extraordinary image provoked. A good many people fell to their knees; a good many more were groaning and gasping in a manner that made Mr. Warren (who, needless to say, remained quite aloof and utterly unmoved by the ludicrous spectacle) feel distinctly *uncomfortable*. So much so, that he was on the cusp of leaving, when he became aware of an unsteady beam of light cutting a swath across the room. For an instant Mr. Warren, much to his subsequent shame, was seized with a wholly irrational notion; but quickly laying hold of his reason, he followed the beam's trajectory and saw that it was coming from the street. In another moment there was an almighty commotion: a great deal of bashing and battering and shouting; of pushing and shoving.

Mr. Warren was forced against the wall, a brilliant light shining straight in his eyes. By squinting hard he was able to make out the chimney-hatted shape of a peeler, and realised that he was looking straight along the beam of a bull's eye lantern.

"Keep your places!" came a voice of undeniable authority, "I am Inspector Tierney of the 'A' Division, and I have with me two sergeants and four constables. Thanks to the efforts of an informer who has served his government well, we have learned of an audacious plot to disrupt Queen's Speech Day! I have to tell you that the plotters are here, right now, in this very house!"

The plainclothesman had assumed an heroic stance in the doorway, legs astride, one hand on his hip, his finger extended accusingly towards the wizened gent standing behind the makeshift altar.

"Abram Duncan!" declared the plainclothesman, "you are hereby charged with sedition, conspiracy, tumult and riot. Anything you say will be used in evidence..."

He was prevented from going any further in reading out the charge. The sergeants had been ordering the crowd to remain calm, but as people began to surmise that the End had indeed come, they began to cry upon Jesus and St. Peter and the Cherubims and Seraphims, and to fling themselves upon their knees, tearing at hair and clothes, and beating their breasts. A great press of bodies charged at the narrow doorway, against which the peelers there stationed were utterly powerless.

Inspector Tierney attempted to push against the crowd as he made his way towards the altar, but the more he pushed forward the more he was pushed back.

"I order you to seize that man!" he cried, indicating the wizened gent. "Stop him! Stop in the name of the law!"

Mr. Warren lay himself flat against the wall as the congregation rushed past. He stole a final glimpse of the preacher, who was still standing at the makeshift altar, his eyes fixed on some invisible object; his features utterly resolute.

"Hae mercy, Lord, on Thy dear servant," he was saying in a perfectly calm and steady voice, "who has come up to tell us that he has been deceived, that his word has nivver been frae above but frae beneath, and that it is all a lie."

It was at that very moment that the room was suddenly plunged into pitchy darkness, and an even greater confusion ensued. There were screams and shouts, there was the smell of burning, of sulphur. Then there was another flash of light, a piercing shriek, and a great burst of flame illuminating all the chaos.

The gauze that had been wrapped around the landlady was on fire and the poor madwoman was running in circles, beating at the flames with her hands and shrieking piteously. Mr. Warren watched in horror as the unmistakable beefy shape of the Legal Correspondent stepped forward. He had a double-caped Benjamin over his arm which he closed about the woman, throwing her to the floor and holding her down until the flames were quite smothered. In all the frenzy the portmanteau that had been serving as an altar had been overturned, and had sprung open, spilling its contents on to the floor. As the madwoman's screams subsided into shocked whimperings, Mr. Warren's horrified gaze fell upon the desiccated corpse of a small infant wrapped in plaid that had rolled across the floor and come to a stop at his feet.

"The wean! The wean!"

Mrs. Dutton was crawling towards the tiny corpse; she snatched it up from the edge of Mr. Warren's boot, cradling it, crooning over it. And all the while the flames were beginning to leap about the room.

"Come on," Mr. Nicholson was urging her. "You have to get out of here."

But the woman just sat there rocking to and fro.

"Wisht, wean," she was crooning, "wisht now; dinnae greet!"

"You can't stay here. You and your – your baby – you must leave now!"

"I'll tak' care o' her."

And the last thing Mr. Warren saw as, with kerchiefs clamped to their faces, he and the Legal Correspondent ran from the blazing room, was the stunted stage-manager in the slouch hat crouched beside the little madwoman and her dead child in the middle of the inferno.

Neither he nor Mr. Nicholson noticed the little family run from the burning building into the clutches of the lurking fog. And by then the plainclothes inspector was too intent on shouting at the "L" Division men, who were running about with buckets of water from the street pump, waving their rattles and crying for the engine, to pay them any heed. The last Mr. Warren saw of Inspector Tierney, he was shaking his fist at the swirling clouds, and, with a face like death, cursing Abram Duncan who had, of course, vanished into thin air.

The Sixth Meeting

He was quite clear on this one point: *he had no explanation*. All he could say was that the river had an awful look to it that night, and as he crossed the deserted bridge into Westminster, the pistols already in his pocket, he had yet to arrive at a decision.

"But you considered what you were about to do? You planned it? You mused upon your motivation?"

He smiled.

"And you were aware that what you were contemplating was wrong!"

"I was," he said, "resigned to my fate."

"But you have had *opportunities*; you acquired a sum of money that is beyond the dreams of most men of your class; you had intelligence, a skill; you were thrifty and presentable. You *must* have known that it is illegal, not to say morally reprehensible, to shoot a gentleman in the back. Are you denying culpability? For if you are, I must say I do not believe you!"

"That is your opinion."

"It is not just my opinion – it is the opinion of a good many right-minded gentlemen. You see, the difficulty I have with this notion of irresistible impulse is that it can so easily be confounded with *unresistible* impulse. It is never wise to assume that a murderous act is not at all wilful. Even where it may be proved that it is the result of insanity, it cannot be denied that a degree of wickedness might also reside therein. Do you understand what I am saying? You have amply demonstrated to me that you had a conscience, that you knew the difference between right and wrong. And yet you did it – you took another life!"

He had leaned back in his chair, his arms folded across his chest, and was considering me with a somewhat sardonic expression.

"Whit is it you want me tae say?" he asked. "Ah've told you that I have long been afflicted with a deep melancholy; pains in the head and lungs; what I considered to be all the usual dark fears an' sensations. Let that explanation suffice, for it is the best I can offer."

"But none of that accounts for the utter dejectedness, the lack of fidelity, the *amorality* of your position..."

He smiled in that vague fluttering manner. "I have studied physiognomy and surgery, including dissection," he said.

"So have I."

"Well, then you will understand me when I say that it is entirely possible for such symptoms as I have long suffered to be the phantasmagoric products of a malady afflictin' the chemicals o' the brain. Perhaps stimulated by too much readin'; or the effects o' self-mesmerism, and infusions of Indian hemp – practices in which I regularly indulged in order to counter other troublesome aspects o' my affliction." He laughed abruptly at the irony of his situation. "I would also say that I never could stop myself frae thinkin': from a young age I dwelt too long upon the dark apprehension that the world is empty of any meaning, beyond that paltry stock o' purpose wi' which we embellish the void o' our existence."

"That is very shocking," I said. "It is the sort of profane and dangerous nonsense one expects of a Continental philosopher."

"An' for a long time," he continued, closing his eyes against my objections, "for a certain portion o' every day I no longer cared if I should live or die." He brought a hand up to cover his face. "And yet, and yet," he cried, "though I loathed the pain and uncertainty of this world, I couldnae surrender tae the nothing."

The night before the incident, he walked to Westminster pier and stood for a long while in the cold beside the ruins of the Old Palace, contemplating the river, and the role he was to perform. No, he could not say with any degree of honesty that he was troubled by his conscience at that time; though he did have thoughts of running away. He recollected considering the procurement of a passage to Canada – of which he had thought many, many times before, but without taking the necessary steps. The pistols were heavy; but he endowed them with none of the

[383]

foreboding one might imagine. He trusted that all would go in accordance with the plan and that no harm would befall him.

It was very dark by the river, and there was an icy blast coming off the water, which left a trail of sharp peaks in its wake: like teeth, he fancied. He wondered how it would be to be eaten by the river. He often thought of drowning. His mother had drowned, so he had been told, when he was a little child.

Such melancholy thoughts came to him out of nowhere, as they always did. He was never aware of them until they had overtaken him. No, he would not say that he was any more disposed to such considerations than customarily: that is to say, he experienced no particular dread on account of the task to which he had been appointed. He supposes that he believed it to be important, else he would not have agreed to it; but he considered it to be a rather small matter. If he thought about it at all, he would have hoped that, after its commission, he would feel, perhaps, a little lighter, a relief...

He might also have hoped for sanctuary.

Yes, that is precisely it.

Sanctuary.

Until that moment he believed that he might have been thinking of the future in a somewhat positive light. That very morning, as he broke his fast with a penny roll and dish of coffee, he had seen a placement in the advertising half of *The Times*.

WANTED, a TRAVELLER, for the sale of English cutlery. NO-ONE need apply who does not possess a GOOD connexion, and EXCELLENT references, &c., &c.

A year or so before he had read Mander's *Regulations for a Traveller*, and was gratified to discover how many of the recommendations therein – Temperance, Assiduity, Early Rising, Punctuality – were qualities he possessed in abundance. He thought he might learn to ride and keep a horse. He should have liked that.

But as he stood looking at the river, it came to him that it was his destiny to stand at a freezing pier head for ever: that he would never do more in his life than dream of drowning, or of running away.

It was as though the very longing itself was a terrible affliction. He felt it very keenly at that moment.

He had made the necessary calculations.

And that night, the night before the occurrence, as he stood beside the skeleton of the Old Palace, a watchman's lamp was caught suddenly in the sway of the wind. It swung from the post to which it was fixed, and in brief puddles of light it showed to him piles of bricks topped with snow; a shovel sunk into a mound of frosty sand; the frozen ditches with planks slung across them; the pulleys and the ropes; an upturned bucket, sparkling. And there above it all arose the sketchy tracery of burnt ruins against the night sky. He observed how everything was halted at the precise point between ascent and decline: between death and another beginning. And at that instant came a persistent tugging on his sleeve, and a small chapped palm opened up between him and the indifferent chill.

"Cigar-light, sir? Fusee for your cigar?"

He handed over a sixpence, and watched the child wrap the coin in his raggit sleeve; how wearily, like an ancient being, the wretched mite climbed back beneath the duck-boards.

"The life of the poor," he said, "is a curse upon the heart."

But no – that is not an explanation. There is no explanation.

Everything is as mysterious to him as ever it was.

THE OLD BAILEY,
TEN O'CLOCK A.M.

In which Mr. Clarkson, the Behemoth of the Bar,
badgers for the fee.

My pippins, the world did not end. The old cock-chafer kept on turning,
as Mr. Nicholson had known all along it would, being of the opinion
that, when the time did come to shut up shop for ever, it would not
be such a noisy affair, with trumpets, yelling, lime-light, fire, heaving
bosoms, &c., &c.; but something a deal more commonplace. Bathos
being the defining characteristic of our little fretting hour, when the
End did finally come, as it surely would, it was bound to be a matter of
no great consequence: the product of some oversight or clerical misad-
ministration; an accident most likely. O, yes: and none of us would be
any the wiser.

Such were the contents of Mr. Nicholson's thoughts as he moved
towards his place in the Bailey's press box – a vantage point for which
he had just parted with his last shilling. He had come as himself for
once: a poor hungry fellow, who would doubtless starve unless something turned up.

That something was the prisoner McNaughten's deposit receipt – or
rather that portion against which might be defrayed the expenses that
had already been paid out for the Scotchman's defence. Mr. Nicholson was very pleased to see that Mr. Clarkson was already in position, and that he seemed as testy, rude and implacable as ever – a man
so thoroughly unlikable that even his own mother would have been
hard-pressed to find any circumstance of any aspect of that fellow's
life worth recording to his advantage. Excellent man! Mr. Nicholson
returned the Behemoth's gruff nod, and told himself that Clarkson's
presence there today was a sign that marvellous forces were at work,
and that all would be well.

Inspector Hughes had put himself on duty at the entrance to the bar and, spying him there, Mr. Nicholson felt a stirring of something like affection for the stalwart cove, who, he thought, was looking exceptionally down in the mouth even by the Inspector's own standard of lugubriousness. However, the peeler pulled himself up even straighter than usual, if such a thing were possible, and saluted very smartly towards the judge's chair as an imposing figure of rubicund countenance entered. Lord Abinger, Chief Baron of the Court of Exchequer. Mr. Nicholson felt a glimmer of satisfaction: the Judge was a very steady and conscientious *Whig*. An augur, he thought to himself, a sign that all will be well.

Mr. Clarkson apparently shared his pleasure, for the counsel's fierce eyebrows, which had been clashed together in ready bellicosity, softened into an expression of ordinary pugilism as soon as the judge entered. Doubtless he had been expecting to be brow-beaten and over-ruled on every application, and was ready to employ his entire repertoire of testiness, bluntness and oratorical corrosiveness – for it didn't matter a whit if a point of law is as plain as A B C to everyone else, not if the judge was determined to be D E F to it. But Lord Abinger, as well as not being a Tory, or in any sense a friend of the present administration, was also not a combative man: merely an irritable one.

Mr. Nicholson noted all of this in good heart. He found that he was smiling as the prisoner was brought forward.

McNaughten looked even thinner and paler than on previous occasions and, looking at him, it was almost impossible to dispel the clicking sound of a trap springing open.

"How say you, prisoner," said the clerk once the charge had been read, "are you guilty or not guilty?"

McNaughten kept his gaze level to the bench, preserving an external composure of manner, but made no effort to reply.

"Prisoner, you must answer the question," repeated the clerk, "whether you are guilty or not?"

There was another long hesitation before the flat, emotionless avowal.

"I was driven to desperation by persecution."

Lord Abinger, who had been regarding McNaughten closely all

this while, interposed with his customary irritation of tone. "Will you answer the question," he snapped. "You must say either guilty or not guilty."

In the pause that ensued, Mr. Clarkson leaned forward so hard on his fists that you could hear his knuckles crack. Inspector Hughes rubbed his decent chin musingly. McNaughten turned his face upon the ceiling.

"I am guilty of firing," he said at last. A gasp of astonishment swept across the court, and Mr. Clarkson muttered something to himself: something not fit for publication.

"By that do you mean to say," said the Judge, with a great deliberation of emphasis that belied his considerable annoyance, "that you are *not* guilty of the remainder of the charge; that is, of intending to murder Mr. Drummond?"

He was looking hard at the prisoner, who looked straight back as only a man of either firm nerves, or shallow feelings could.

"Yes," came the reply.

The Judge and the prisoner held each other's look for several moments together: the one with a most intent and searching gaze, the other almost business-like in the intransigence that met it. It was the intense gaze that travelled away first.

"Enter a plea of Not Guilty," said Abinger, and Mr. Clarkson swung into action.

"Owing to the date for this arraignment having been brought forward, due to the demise of Mr. Drummond," he declaimed, speaking that word *demise* as if the gentleman's death constituted nothing more than the most unspeakable inconvenience, "it is UTTERLY IMPOSSIBLE to defend the prisoner if he is to be tried at the present session. Mr. Humphries – the agent instructed to defend – was consulted NO MORE THAN THREE DAYS AGO. I therefore URGE," and he said the word *urge* with such force that nobody could be in any denial that he would far rather have used a much less polite word if the etiquette of the Bar permitted, "that the trial be POSTPONED until the NEXT SESSION."

Lord Abinger shot a disapproving look at the counsel, but said and did nothing more, which strategy momentarily disarmed Mr. Clarkson.

"It appears from the matter contained in the voluminous depositions taken at Bow-street as well as others taken at GLASGOW," the barrister continued, as soon as he had recovered his equilibrium, "that it will be necessary to make inquiries in Scotland which may be most important to the interest of the prisoner and THE PUBLIC. These inquiries, however, will require both time AND FUNDS!"

The counsel engaged for the prosecution, who had been listening to all of this with a pained expression, now half rose and waved a palsied hand as if in surrender. He informed the judge that, having read all of the depositions, it was true that they did indeed contain matters which it would be very proper to lay before the jury. Mr. Clarkson cast a look of blazing hatred in his direction, and brought his fist down hard upon the table in front of him, like a man cheated out of his winnings.

"Hah!" he exclaimed. He cast a look of pure defiance about the room. "But what about THE FUNDS!"

The prosecuting counsel made another indeterminate gesture.

"I have here an affidavit," blazed Clarkson, "sworn by Mr. William Cornes Humphries of 119 Newgate-street – the agent engaged by the prisoner – stating that he has seen depositions from the arresting officer, copies of which had been furnished to my client at Bow-street police court, that he had taken from the prisoner all his money – including an accountable receipt for seven hundred and fifty pounds that had been deposited by him in one of the banks at Glasgow. This action has left the prisoner BEREFT OF FUNDS by which to procure for himself LEGAL REPRESENTATION!"

The prosecuting counsel half rose once again. "We would request that the accountable receipt referred to is *not* delivered," he said wanly. "It has the potential to become a *very* important document on behalf of the case for the prosecution. The defence has been given every opportunity to inspect it."

Mr. Clarkson's nostrils flared and his whiskers seemed to proliferate. At last! A challenge!

"AND we shall need time to CASH the ORDER!" he bellowed.

The opposing counsel made another mute appeal to the bench, and after further moments of whispering beneath his wig, the Judge turned back from his co-arbiter and, settling an authoritative eye upon Mr.

Clarkson, announced that he would agree to allow the trial to stand over until Friday the third of March.

"Four weeks", muttered Mr Nicholson. It was not a good deal of time in which to prepare a case of such momentum.

"And I hereby order," the Judge continued, "that sufficient funds should be supplied to the prisoner for the purposes of preparing his defence – upon the accountable receipt found upon him at the time of his arrest."

Mr. Clarkson was momentarily lost for words. He shrugged expansively at the court and exchanged a look of purest astonishment with his compadre, Mr. Nicholson. The latter was thinking how the matter had gone off quicker than the Knutsford tailor; but it was an excellent result: the best possible. Mr. Nicholson's suspicions were immediately aroused. Whig jobbery, he thought at once; but then if it had been anything of the sort, why was Cockie skulking about town with the air of one who has been trebly gammoned? Not Whig jobbery then, he concluded; but even so, Mr. Nicholson divined a measure of skill in what he had just witnessed – a sleight of hand as deft as that in any street game of three-cup shuffle.

Sir,

You have brought it all about yourself. You have acted just as a person situated as you are might be expected to act. I had not expected other, and I know that my mother did not. I do not blame you – or her. I blame my own poor judgement. You were given a choice between position and favour on the one side, and the love and support of a worthless fellow on the other – your own flesh and blood. The choice was not difficult and certainly you did not take the difficult portion.

But I do not blame you in that. I blame you for the time that you held me on your knee and whispered that you loved me – for so I have been told and I have no reason to believe this an untruth, or that you never meant it. All I can say is it would have been better by far had I never received the memory of your love.

I have wished only to repay your affection with my own. It is a sorrow to me that I have been denied this. When somebody who is precious to you dies it is not unusual to dream that you are with them still, and when you wake it is hard to live upon this earth knowing you are alone. My mother, the good man who raised me and my little sister are now all departed from the earth and I am quite alone. This sorrows me, but it sorrows me far, far more to know that my dream of you was nothing.

But the world about me is no less good. Your love would not make me a better man – though it might make me a happier one. This disappointment will make me wiser and more sensible, and so you may be said to have done your duty as a father.

You would not let me speak to you, but I only wanted to tell you that I love you as well as you deserve. Even as you deserve. Sir, I love you.

Your son,
Alexander Dalton Cockburn

In which Mr. Cockburn prepares to meet the prisoner.

Black, black, black: Newgate's walls bore down hard upon the Sunday
School Union across the street from where sat Mr. Cockburn, in one of
those too smoky, too greasy coffee-shops, pitying the children of the
poor. He had still the letter in his breast pocket, lacking the heart to destroy it; and when his thoughts roamed to consideration of its contents,
as they did frequently, he experienced first a queasiness of conscience,
then a rush of powerful feeling: he had a son, and his son loved him, no
matter what he had done. The thought left him smiling gently to himself like a simpleton before the ill-feeling returned once more to burrow
in his heart, causing him to wish, like how many countless others, that
fate had brought him anywhere but here.

He waved a hand against the greasy air then sunk his brow upon it
as the woman brought him another jug of coffee.

He would brazen it out, as he had brazened out so much of his life;
but he could not shake himself of the vision of the boy, the boy with his
own hands and Polly's eyes, who was out there somewhere, wandering
those bleak and friendless streets, comfortless, alone, flat broke.

Sandy was waiting for the agent Mr. Humphries to come and take
him to the prisoner. He had been waiting for three-quarters of an hour
and long since given over to looking out of the steamy window, to
brooding. He had almost given up hope of the solicitor ever appearing,
when the very same stepped in at the door with the tell-tale pink rib-
bons trailing from the brief he clutched in his hand.

"Exciting, ain't it, Mr. Cockburn?" Mr. Humphries was saying; although there was not a tinge of excitement in his voice. He was round
like an owl, with an owl's air of detached curiosity, and very hard to
read. "Yes, indeed. Four weeks. Four weeks." He said it in the flat, af-
fectless, *professional* tone in which he delivered every pronouncement:
a tone which never gave a thing away.

"Four weeks to put together a defence from scratch!" Sandy laughed somewhat edgily, and gave everything away at once. "I can't help but think that Abinger has done it on purpose." No doubt, he was thinking, at the connivance of the Whig Chief Whipper-in. "Still, we have made a good start with the depositions." He tried to match the solicitor's aridity of tone, but it was not in his tenor. "We have the material sent by the Scotland-yard Detective from Glasgow, and some other evidences which the Treasury Solicitor surrendered to us – eventually."

Mr. Humphries turned his owlish gaze upon the barrister. "You will have seen the sworn testimony of the policeman," he said, glancing at the brief. "Inspector Tierney..."

"Indeed I have. It contains the only reference to Sir Robert Peel to be found anywhere outside of the newspapers, and is as specious a piece of evidence as ever I set my eyes upon."

"I couldn't agree more, sir," said Mr. Humphries. "And have you seen the opinions of the two doctors sent by the government to give their opinion of the prisoner's mind?"

"I have been informed that we shall need a dozen mad-doctors to testify that the prisoner is labouring under a delusion. Thanks to an association with Mr. Forbes Winslow, I have secured the interest of nine."

Mr. Humphries gave no indication as to whether he considered this a good thing or a bad. Instead, he sat down opposite Sandy and helped himself to some of the coffee. "And tell me," he asked as he poured, "what did you make of the father's testimony to the police detective?"

It had been a scant, reluctant estimation of a son by his father. Daniel McNaughten senior could not account for his son having given up his business a year ago; and neither could he assert any knowledge of a political proclivity on the part of the prisoner – although when urged, said he believed him to be for the Whigs (he himself was a Conservative). The prisoner had called upon him several months ago and sought his help in obtaining a situation in a West India House.

Sandy leafed through his notes. "The prisoner is then alleged to have said to his father: 'Do you know there is such a thing as a spy system going on in the land for there is and I am persecuted by them. Go where I would so will they watch me about and see me home to my lodging and watch for me out again.'

"Interesting, ain't it?" observed Mr. Humphries, blowing on his coffee.

"To which the father replied," Sandy sought out the exact phrasing, "why would spies watch an obscure person like you?" His eyes grazed over the rest of the testimony, mostly comprising the description of how McNaughten had called again numerous times, in increasing desperation, to beg for his father's help.

Mr. Humphries sipped his coffee. "Some parents seem to make it the whole business of their life to prepare their children for that day when they must quit this world altogether," he said dispassionately. "This they hope to accomplish by behaving, while they are yet alive, with an abominable lack of kindliness and all that due support which ought properly to exist between a father and a child." He made Mr. Cockburn the object of his acute scrutiny. "I suppose," he continued, "they must be cruel to be kind, as the Bard has it."

Sandy reddened a little. "The pater and I," he said, "have often found ourselves playing on a yielding surface after rain; but I have always known that the old fellow would bowl through the entire innings."

"Well then, I should say you're very lucky, sir," said the solicitor. "Very lucky indeed."

Yes, thought Sandy, I am a spoilt, selfish man who does not know the meaning of true love; who bought solace with the same *insouciance* with which he bought everything else, whether he could afford it or not and whether he had earned it or not.

"The pa – a respectable and well-to-do tradesman, by all accounts – ought to make a very good impression to the jury," Mr. Humphries was saying. "And he will certainly speak to the boy's state of mind with a sight more eloquence than can a hundred mad-house doctors. Your ordinary jurist has little time for mad-house doctors." Sandy was sensing that Mr. Humphries did not have a deal of confidence in the defence. "And scant pity for lunatics who fire pistols. More coffee, sir?" inquired the solicitor, peering at him.

"Damn it all, Mr. Humphries. Speak with candour, why don't you!"

The agent looked at Sandy intently for a few moments. "We must try and think of the case," he said at last, "as a way of *making amends*."

"*Amends?*"

"Yes. As one of those briefs taken on for the benefit of society. Whatever the outcome, there will be people who shall praise you for the gesture; you'll see."

"Faugh! People will throw mud at me in the streets – you know damn well they will! Everyone wants this wretched boy to hang. Why, even his own father is indifferent to his fate."

"You shall have to harden your instincts, sir," said Mr. Humphries. "No barrister can ever care so much what is to be said about him."

"Yes, well, there you have it. I am afraid, you see, that I am quite out of my element. I am not an Old Bailey man..."

Mr. Humphries chuckled. "Ah! The Bailey!" he said, and for an instant his features lit up with a certain fondness.

"I really don't know how you fellows do it, day after day," said Sandy, dragging his hands through his hair. "What if the client hangs because I have the argument wrong? There is none of this – this anxiety in the dry certitude of the Parliamentary hearings, I can tell you that, sir."

Mr. Humphries fixed him with his most implacable expression. "Your argument is certainly a very tricky one," he said. "That the prisoner's moral perceptions have been impaired by a mental disease; that no rational or logical motive lies behind his peculiar action; that the shooting of Mr. Drummond was the product of a temporary delusion, and nothing else..."

Sandy sighed, exasperated. "Yes, yes – but the argument is only a part of it." He looked about him. "What if," he said, dropping his voice to a confidential tone, "what if it's already been decided to make an example of McNaughten? What if this entire case is nothing more than a farce to which we have been applied in order to lend a credible impression? What if nothing is what it seems to be? What then? Forgive me, but I must raise these concerns with somebody..."

Mr. Humphries shared out the last of the coffee, but offered no opinion one way or the other.

Sandy sighed deeply, feeling foolish.

"You have a *plausible* argument," said the solicitor, turning his owl's

eyes upon him. "Your anxiety on the point of the prisoner's moral inca-
pacity is not misplaced. You are demonstrating a very sensible degree
of caution; that is all. To my mind, proof of delusion may not be enough
in itself to protect the client from the gallows – but never forget that
ain't down to you, sir: that's down to the workings of the Law, plain and
simple. And you shall have to trust the jury on that – which is not to say
that you can't help 'em along. But if they don't want to swallow it, well
then there ain't a thing that you or anyone else can do." Mr. Humphries
was smiling at him. "Now then, we have a great deal of work to do if
you are to stand up in the Bailey four weeks from now," he said, "and
make the best speech in defence of a poor suffering lunatic as has ever
been heard."

A LOW TAVERN CLOSE BY COVENT-GARDEN
AT ABOUT THE SAME TIME

In which a footman's loyalty to his mistress is tested.

It had taken him two days of close inquiry, but Mr. Warren had
succeeded in discovering the Black who had served as Mr. Drummond's
footman until the day after that gentleman's untimely demise. He had
found him working in the chorus of a newly opened negro burletta – *Jim
Crow in His New Place*; a slight woolly-haired figure dressed in a heavily
patched Ethiopian costume, a corn-sack slung across his shoulder, and
his dark face smeared all over with burnt cork. Having determined that
this was one and the same Jas. Parrott, Mr. Warren had left his card at the
stage door requesting that the fellow meet with him in a tavern he knew,
situated in a dank alley close by the produce market. The air outside was
redolent with the stench of rotten vegetables, the brown snow under-
foot slushed with decaying cabbage leaves.

He was very pleased, and in no small measure surprised, when Parrott entered at the appointed hour. Seeing him in his very curious costume, a pair of market-porters who were lurched against the bar, burst
out a cheerless chorus, much to the footman's evident discomfiture:

"Wheel about and turn about,
And do jes so;
Ebery time I turn about,
I jump Jim Crow..."

This done, the porters returned to their previous occupation: that of staring disconsolately at their glasses. The rest of the tavern's customers were too drunk, too intent upon their gin bitters to care much who came and went about them, which was just how Mr. Warren wanted it. He had no desire to share with other interested parties the intelligences that he hoped to coax from the manservant, who took a seat at the table, an altogether humane expression of concern upon his features.

Ever since Mr. Drummond's death, Mr. Warren had been feeling somewhat cast adrift. It had been unsettling to find himself undirected and abandoned, and with only the slightest understanding of what was expected of him. There were certain concerns that he would have liked to have explained to him; but Mr. Drummond was gone, and all attempts to enter the late Secretary's house in order to speak to his relatives vigorously rebuffed. He had walked to Charlton in hopes of spying out the funeral, but not even Sir Robert Peel had been welcome inside the church. As far as employees at Drummond's bank were concerned, it appeared they had all been instructed not to speak to the newspapers on pain of dismissal. And, of course, not one of the surgeons would suffer him to come within one hundred yards of them. So, when he had learned from the Grosvenor-street milkman that the Drummond's footman had been dismissed in *mysterious and unexplained circumstances*, Mr. Warren had spied out at once an opportunity.

And Parrott was now before him: an aspect of the utmost dejection.

"It must be hard for you, of course," said Mr. Warren, covertly laying a half-crown upon the table. "I don't suppose there is a good deal of money in minstrelsy..."

"I receive one and threepence a performance," replied the nigger, apparently affecting not to notice the half-crown.

"Really!" exclaimed Mr. Warren, "one and threepence for jumping around pretending to play the banjo?" The footman was evidently more cunning than he seemed. Mr. Warren slipped another sixpence on to the table, and wondered by how much higher he ought to go.

"It is a living, I suppose," the footman sighed. "I consider myself fortunate to have any sort of occupation at the present time – and the more particularly since Miss Drummond has refused to supply me with any sort of a reference. Certainly, I am unlikely to find another valeting position."

"But why did Miss Drummond dismiss you?" asked Mr. Warren.

Parrott's smooth face was marred by an intemperate frown. "Because she is a very cruel and irrational lady," he said. "Do you know, sir, she sat there day after day and permitted the doctors to use her poor brother so ill, and never said a word against them – nor a word of kindness to Mr. Drummond?"

Mr. Warren was not going to pay for the tittle-tattle of the servants' hall. "You were close to your master in his last days, were you?" he inquired in an airy tone, as if it was all the same to him.

The Negro appeared very moved. "As close as a master and his servant can be, sir," he said. "He was a good man, and I loved him very much."

"And did Mr. Drummond ever speak to you of the circumstances in which he met his *tragic* end?"

The footman had begun to weep. "The doctors did not permit him to speak much, sir."

"I see. Well that is very disappointing to hear, I must say."

Parrott wiped his face upon his coat-sleeve, removing a portion of the burnt cork. "They hardly ever left his side – not for a minute."

"So it was difficult for Mr. Drummond to say even one word in explanation as to why he had been shot?" Mr. Warren pushed the little pile of coins towards Parrott. "You are quite sure of that?"

"I never heard him say one word – though when his family learned it was a Scotchman who was responsible, there was speculation that it might have had something to do with religion – or with Mr. Drummond's visit to Edinburgh with the Queen last October."

Mr. Warren slipped another sixpence onto the top of the pile. "Hum. That is most interesting... I wonder, did your late lamented master ever speak of *Corn* or the *Anti-Corn Law League*?"

Parrott considered for a moment or two. "He used to argue with his brother, Master George, about the bread tax, and the Income Tax, too."

"Really?"

"O, yes. My master was of the opinion that we must make this a cheap country in which to live."

"He said that?"

"Many times. His thoughts were always of the poor, you see. He was a very good man."

"He wanted to make this a cheap country in which to live...? What the deuce did he mean by that?"

But if Parrott knew the answer to Mr. Warren's question, he was not in the mood for explaining. His face had creased with grief, as a great wash of lamentation overtook him. "He was so good – such a Christian gentleman," ran the general current of his outpourings. "And the doctors, O, sir, they treated him so very cruelly. And him so brave, he never once complained. They laid him on his back to remove the shot, and the burn that was there festered – ah, terrible it was, the way he suffered..."

"Yes, yes," snapped Mr. Warren, "I am quite sure that it was." He had little doubt of the doctors' share of culpability in the demise of the Secretary; what Mr. Warren sought was an understanding of McNaughten's role in the same – beyond the fact that he had fired a pistol at the gentleman.

"And it was all so needless," blubbed the footman.

"Yes, yes, it is all very sad."

"The bullet had been there for years – certainly all the time I attended Mr. Drummond, and had never caused him any trouble – until the surgeons decided to dig it out of him, that is..."

Mr. Warren pricked his ears. "Are you telling me," he said, seizing upon the footman's words, "that the shot that the surgeons removed from your master was not the same that was fired into him by McNaughten?"

"O, no, sir. That wound was quite slight and on his hip. If the doctors hadn't bored into it with their fingers and implements and then laid my master upon his back so that it became irritated and inflamed, it might have healed within a week or so. I was speaking of the piece of shot that was in my master's *front*."

"And where did *that* come from?"

It appeared that Parrott was recollecting, perhaps too late, the obligations of a servant – even a dismissed one – to maintain discretion in respect of the private lives of his employers: in which case, thought Mr. Warren, the footman was to be admired. But then again, his hesitancy might have been nothing more than a ploy to extract yet more money from his interrogator: in which case the footman was going to be disappointed. Mr. Warren sat back and waited patiently for the Black fellow to either quit or continue.

Parrott sighed heavily. "I have worried over this for a long time," he said. "You see, a servant overhears certain confidences..."

"Go on," said Mr. Warren.

"...things of which he is not supposed to take any note. Sometimes it is as though you are invisible to all the others in a room."

"Yes, yes, but what did you hear?"

Parrott leaned in towards Mr. Warren. "It will be a great relief to unburden myself to you, sir," he said. "I believe that Mr. Drummond received the wound in his front from a *duel*."

"A duel! Surely not!" Mr. Warren was trying to reconcile his memory of the mild-mannered Secretary with this fresh-sprung notion of an assiduous and hot-headed demander of satisfaction.

"O, yes, sir, I heard it whispered several times as Mr. Drummond lay dying. It was a duel with the Duke of Wellington. Indeed, I heard His Grace with my own ears thank Miss Drummond for keeping it a secret all these years."

Mr. Warren was very astonished, though he pretended to carry it off very well.

The footman had begun to weep again. "I cannot tell you what a relief it is, sir, to have unburdened myself to you," he sobbed. "O, they were so very cruel. And my poor dear master such a good kind man. He ought to be avenged. Now you see why I removed the shot from Miss Drummond's pocket."

"You stole the shot?"

"O no, sir, I have never stolen a thing in my life before. I took it as evidence."

[400]

Mr. Warren felt a quickening in his breast. To think that he might be but another sixpence away from beholding the only piece of hard evidence in the whole matter... "You – you have the shot that was removed from Mr. Drummond?"

"O, no, sir," said Parrott. He seemed insulted by the notion. "I took it to the station-house yesterday evening."

"'od's teeth!" cried Mr. Warren. "You have given it to the peelers? Well then, we shall never know..." He reached across and withdrew the pile of coins from the table and placed them in his pocket. "I'm afraid," he said, very piqued, "that you have told me nothing that is of any interest to me."

Great gouges were being formed in the burnt cork by the tears that were coursing down Parrott's face. "He was so very good. The best of men. Do you know, sir, what were his dying words – after all that he had suffered? 'Forgive him', he said, '*forgive him...*'"

"Forgive him?" said Mr.Warren. "Forgive whom? The Duke of Wellington?"

Parrott was looking at him uncomprehendingly. "I believe he meant his assassin," he said, "the poor mad Scotchman."

Mr. Warren's gaze passed over the smooth, honest features of the Negro. He was thinking that he did not know *what* Mr. Drummond had meant by his dying words – but he was certain that the gentleman must have meant *something*.

NEWGATE GAOL,
A LITTLE WHILE AFTER

In which Mr. Cockburn meets the prisoner.

The prison was dank and sunless, a great winding passage yearning into the distance. Mr. Humphries led Mr. Cockburn along it to the meeting-room set with high windows along one side that looked out through two rows of iron bars onto a line of prisoners who were standing close together in a freezing yard and separated from their visitors by a trelliswork fence. Beyond that was an impossibly high wall that blocked out the sky, and with it all hope of freedom.

"How perfectly dreadful," Mr. Cockburn said.

The solicitor was stout, implacable, brusque. "If you wish, I can show you the bread-room. It is an education."

"The bread-room?"

"It's where the prisoners' bread is cut and weighed; but when they aren't using the table for that, it's where they lay down the condemned so's they can shackle 'em. They lead 'em through the kitchen, you see, to the gallows across the way, there."

The prisoner was standing in the doorway with his gaoler. Sandy looked straight at him. The prisoner turned away, his eyes drifting to some indeterminate foci.

"This is Mr. Cockburn," said Mr. Humphries. "He is Queen's Counsel and a very distinguished gentleman. And he is going to try and save your neck."

Cockie held out his hand, but the prisoner did not take it. "Good afternoon, Mr. McNaughten," he said. The prisoner shuffled awkwardly. He was staring hard at the floor, and made no attempt to answer.

"And tell me, how do you find it here? I trust that you are treated well? You must let us know if you require anything – anything at all – and we shall try and accommodate your wishes."

The prisoner made no response. Mr. Cockburn looked across at Mr. Humphries, with one raised eyebrow.

"Why don't you begin by telling Mr. Cockburn how you – a decent working man such as yourself – come to be at such a pretty pass?"

"The Tories in ma native city compelled me," said the prisoner quietly and without looking up. "They huve entirely destroyed my peace o' mind. The've driven me intae a consumption. They've accused me o' crimes o' which I am not guilty; they wish to murder me. It can be proved by evidence."

"And who do you mean by *they*?" persisted the solicitor. "Do you mean Mr. Lamond, the Tory agent in Glasgow, or Sir James Campbell? Do you mean *your father*?" Mr. Humphries asked all of this in the firm yet disinterested tones of the professional interrogator. "Very well then: perhaps you can tell us why this situation caused you to shoot at a gentleman with nothing more than a passing acquaintance of the Glasgow Tories?"

There was a slight smile, but no answer.

Mr. Humphries turned his owl-like gaze upon the yard below the windows. His hands, clasped behind his back, fluttered a little.

Sandy made a delicate gesture towards the prisoner.

"You know," he said, "I should like to help you, Mr. McNaughten. I should like to help you very much, but I need to know *everything*. I need to understand how you came to be there at Charing-cross, with pistols on your person, and why you acted as you did... If there is anything at all in the circumstance that can help your defence, then you must let me know; you must help me in order that I can help you."

The prisoner made a soft groan and rocked himself gently to and fro.

"I understand. It is distressing for you; of course it is."

Mr. Humphries turned from the window and came to stand at the prisoner's shoulder. "Mr. Cockburn needs to hear from you," he said, "and in your own words, why you shot at that gentleman. Was the gentleman responsible for the torments you were suffering? Was it he who pursued you and harassed you in the manner you described at Bow-street?"

"You said at the time of your arrest," said Cockie, "'*Now he shall not trouble my peace of mind any longer*.' To whom were you referring? Was it Mr. Drummond?"

"What did you mean by that?" rejoindered Mr. Humphries.

The prisoner permitted each silence to stretch into a vast nothing.

Mr. Humphries crossed once more to the window, sighing a little. But Cockie kept his eye upon McNaughten all the while: he intended to watch until he thought that he might understand; until he could see what the prisoner wanted him to see.

"Tell me, Mr. McNaughten," he said gently and at length, "how do you feel? Do you have that longed-for peace of mind?"

"It is not necessary," said the prisoner, "that, whilst I live, I live happily. But it is necessary that so long as I live I should live honourably."

They looked at each other for a long time. It was as though, Cockie thought, each was searching for the understanding that might make a fractured soul complete.

"You've read Kant," he said at last in a cracked voice, as though it was a thing of great consequence.

"O, I have read many things, sir."

And then, in another moment, he was being summoned. He shambled to the door on the guard's command. He did not look back. Like all the greatest philosophers, he went on in silence: as if aware that there are times when it is more truthful to say nothing, nothing at all.

Sandy waited while Mr. Humphries exchanged a few civilities with the turnkey. He did not care to follow McNaughten's disappearance back into the enveloping darkness. The turnkey led them to the porch, where they stepped through a low door into another world of light and cool air, into the privilege of the sleet and snow.

"We will plead insanity," directed Mr. Cockburn, turning to the solicitor.

"Insanity it is, then," said Mr. Humphries, placing his hat upon his head. He was dry, very dry.

"That is – *partial* insanity – the product of monomania. We will demonstrate that the commission of the fatal act occurred at a time when the client was suffering from a powerful delusion that caused him to assume there was a conspiracy against him on the part of the Tories, which delusion he was unable to resist, and which, if true, would undoubtedly *justify* the shooting of Mr. Drummond."

The pair of them stood on the step for a moment, waiting for the worst of the sleet to pass overhead. They were watching the multitude momentarily illuminated in the last dying light of the day.

"Give me an hour, sir," said Mr. Humphries, "one hour – and I could find you five hundred in this very place willing to swear that the crime to which they were driven was entirely accountable to a powerful delusion, which, if proven to be the stuff of reality, would justify all manner of atrocity..."

Sandy sighed and prepared to step onto the pavement.

"It may well be," he said, "as my enemies would have it, that I am about to gammon the public to the utmost of my skill, and urge Justice to forfeit her obligations towards the safety of the citizenry, in finding for a dangerous man. But it is my sincere belief, sir, that insanity – of which we are seeing a great increase, at the present time – deserves supervision. And irrespective of the rights and wrongs of this particular case, I am of the opinion that it will, at the very least, urge a proper and thorough legislative investigation of this great social malady." He tugged peremptorily upon the primrose gloves.

"That's the ticket, Mr. Cockburn, sir," said the solicitor in a tone that might almost be taken for encouragement.

As he hailed a cab, Sandy had no longer any doubt what it was he must do. And what was more, for the first time in his life, he was determined to see it through to the end. It was as much as any man could ask of him – or he of himself.

MR. NICHOLSON'S PRINT-SHOP, HOLYWELL-STREET
SOMETIME IN THE NIGHT JUST PAST

In which the plainclothesman holds Mr. Nicholson to account.

"Now that fuckin' cunt Tierney is tellin' me ah shall never huv ma reward," Carlo was saying, "an' ah'm mad as hell aboot that, ah can tell youse."

The plainclothesman was pausing for a wee rest in between the savage beatings he was dealing Mr. Nicholson – the kickings to the bollocks, the poundings to the smeller and peepers – pausing merely to moisten a little stick of white clay, to strike his Lucifer casually against the wall, to scratch his chin.

"They fuckin' peelers still owe me," he kept saying. "Duncan's vamoosed, right enough, but no' through ony fault o' mine. Ah played ma part – it's no' down tae me if the peelers cannae dae their job. O, aye, an' that wee shite, Dan, didnae help. The whole plot would a worked like an engine if he'd kept tae his books and turnin'. If he hadnae shot the Tory cunt Poplar-row would never hae come intae the newspapers, an' the likes o' youse wouldnae huv come sniffin' aboot. Ah thought ah did youse a favour, by the way – aye, an' Dan too – but seems the likes o' youse cannae leave onything alane."

He did not appear to mind the blood-smear coming off the rags bound about his fists, his fists like cannon balls.

"Why'd youse huv tae come to the chapel, and bring your pal wit' ye? Ah'd huv bin able to keep ma mind oan Duncan an' the prize, if ah hadnae bin keepin' an eye on youse two troublemakers. Ahm owed more 'n a few bawbies, ah can tell youse. Ah've bin workin' oan that chapel rouse for weeks – keepin' that mad old bitch frae squawkin', not tae say Duncan himself. Fuckin' bampot he is."

The words floated to his poor victim as if on a breeze. They came to him as he came to them: vague, uncertain of meaning or place or time, drifting, drifting on a sea of pain.

"Aye, well an' ahm a vengeful fucker, see, an' ah huv tae tak' it oot on somebody. Youse'll dae jist fine, ye fat cunt. Aye. Youse'll dae." The devil pulled on his red kerchief. "Ah saw youse sniggerin' at the chapel. Ah've watched the way youse daunder aboot lookin' like ye own the place," he was saying. "Youse can scupper the whole jig, can ye? Aye, well pally, not now ye cannae. O, youse wanted the truth and youse shall have it!"

He kicked Mr. Nicholson in the trowsers.

"O, aye! It'll be the last thing you hear on this god-forsaken earth, mind, but youse'll hear it – by Christ – youse'll be told. Ye slorty fat bastard. Ye cunt, ye."

Blood was filling Old Peeping Tom's eyes; blood from the cosh wound on his temple. A stocking filled with marbles. Never turn your back on a busted cheat. He had broken his own golden rule and now he was being punished for it.

"Youse'll dae well tae keep your nose out o'that which disnae concern ye. Ahm a fuckin' professional, see. This is whit ah dae fer a livin'." He kicked Mr. Nicholson in the head. "Youse're nocht but a fuckin' punch and judy man..."

The blood, the blood was filling his eyes, dim-darkening; closing down his senses altogether. And soon Mr. Nicholson was aware of nothing, nothing at all, beyond the gulping pangs of life. And when he came to, the devil was taking a rest to spit on the floor, moisten again the clay tip, press another pinch of tobacco in the bowl.

"Now youse knows as much as ony ane," he was saying, "and it shall die wit' ye – ye nosy interfering slorty crimmerin' bastard, ye; ye cunt, ye; ye fuck, fuck fuck. Try an' find me oot, will ye! Try an' slammer ma best hopes! Ye wee shite. Aye, well ahm owed, ah should say. Ahm owed! They bastards..."

The poor victim rocked against his bonds and succeeded in moving a few inches across the floor towards the door, as the plainclothesman watched him with an idle amusement, drawing on his pipe all the while. It was as if he had all the time in the world, and he was well practised in the art of watching another man's last desperate hopes: the studied, expert air; the casual adjustments to the bloody strips of rag about his fists – fists like cannon balls – using his teeth to pull them tight.

After a few moments Carlo prepared to strike another light. Mr. Nicholson could see what was coming. He grunted against the filthy rag in his tater trap, groaned with the effort of taking breath, but he refused to beg for mercy, my pippins. Who ever would've thought he had such courage? He instinctively shut his eyes against a few more indolent kicks.

Cunt cunt cunt. Fuck fuck fuck. And then came the sulphurous burning, the crackle of a Lucifer struck and tossed fizzing into the motey depths.

It was the last thing he remembered before, exhausted by the effort of so much surviving, his poor head dropped and welcome extinction descended, like an angel come to preserve him from any more harm from this cruel world.

In which Mr. Nicholson is rescued and shares a confidence with
Inspector Hughes.

The Jew old-clothes-man it was who had saved his bacon. He had heard the disturbance, the cracking, the groaning and the grunting. He may also have heard the truth, but as to that he could not say. He was alone and old, and Holywell-street was not a kind place. And so he had been afraid to intervene, thinking it better to watch and wait and then offer what assistance he might as soon as the villain had skulked back along the pissy alley into the snowy murk. But it was just as well he had, for he had been able to put out the fire before it took much hold, and with great effort drag Mr. Nicholson onto the street to be revived by what passed for fresh air in that part of Strand.

As Inspector Hughes said, a print-shop and fire didn't go together too well; Mr. Nicholson owed everything to the old Jew – not for the first time in his sorry life, he mused.

"It's a strange thing, but I had been considering having a word with you, Mr. Nicholson," the Inspector said, helping him to some brandy. "You or the other newspaperman – the one you hangs with. I has a mat-ter – a certain – yes, yes, well, it was as well I came now, I dare say..."

Mr. Nicholson took the brandy in both hands and raised it in salute. He was saying once again how he had never been so glad in all his life to see the dirty street, them broken paves, that filthy busted sky, and then he knocked the draft back in one quick glug.

"I 'as often thought it meself, Inspector – I mean to say, you need informations, and I, well, I make it me business to find out what's go-ing on in the Metropolis, don't I – there has to be some mutual – some bargain to be struck. And you has always seemed a very rum cove to me. Very rum indeed."

Inspector Hughes stayed him with a raised palm.

"Now, now. I ain't come here to play games, Mr. Nicholson. I come here tonight to end all the games once and for all. I know what you're about. And I know that while there's a lot of bad in what you do, there's a lot worse out there. No, no. I had it in mind to share out the gammon with you, in good meaty slices, and see where that might get us. Now how does that sound to you?"

Mr. Nicholson heaved a huge, painful sigh of relief, and bid the Inspector take the weight off his feet. Then he poured two crocks each of the Old Tom he kept at the base of the high desk, and sinking his share with great difficulty, began to tell all, all he knew, every scrap.

"This Carlo," said Inspector Hughes, with a deep sigh when Mr. Nicholson was done, "has been a friend of the prisoner since their youth. I've turned up a few references to him in past copies of the *Gazette*, where he was apparently passing himself off as a Chartist, but I dare say he's been informing for some time. Anyway, he was taken last year in the Staffordshire riots by Inspector Tierney and it seems it didn't take long for the two of them to strike a bargain. Carlo knew Abram Duncan, you see. And the Gray Goose was worth more'n a pair of wellington boots to Tierney, by anybody's reckoning."

"Ah yes – Abram Duncan, the Gray Goose," said Mr. Nicholson. "He's the poor fool who thought he was leading souls to the Land of Milk and Honey, when all the time he was being duped by government agents, and made out to be a dangerous insurrectionist with a price on his head bigger than the government debt."

"Though it seems that Carlo had the better of the Active Duty an' all," said the Inspector. "I reckon that, having lured them to Poplar-row on Wednesday night, it was him who helped the Gray Goose to fly the coop at the Crack of Doom."

"I'm not sure the jape ran quite that way," said Mr. Nicholson. "Carlo wanted his reward. He'd have handed over his own mother – always supposing he had one – if he thought there was a bob or two in it. He didn't care tuppence for the Gray Goose."

The Inspector sighed, long, slow. "Maybe, maybe; but whatever his part in the kimbau was or is, Carlo ain't the principal. You pick up any clew you choose in this tangle, Mr. Nicholson, and it's the Active Duty and the Office of Home Affairs what'll be found holding the other end," he said. "Yes, and most of the time they'll be standing in Scotland-yard at the side of a great big ball o' yarn."

He was vaguely surprised to discover that this admission didn't seem to pain him as much as it might once have done.

Mr. Nicholson nodded. "I cannot be sure whether it be Whigs or Tories," he said. "Suffice to say they are each endeavouring to blame the other – not to say the Anti-Corn Law League, the one party I am quite certain had not a thing to do with it. And you know when all is said and done, Inspector, it really don't matter a jot. For they have all the same interest, you see, when it comes down to it."

Inspector Hughes turned down the corners of his mouth. "'Ere you don't look too good if I might say so," he said. "I reckon you wants to buy yourself a bit of beefsteak for that eye."

But Mr. Nicholson wasn't listening to this good advice. A new sweat was breaking on his old face and his mouth was filling up with fresh blood. He clamped the kerchief to his lip, and sighed. It was hard to read his swollen busted features, but something about that sigh moved the Inspector to pity.

"A great host of agents has gone forth," Mr. Nicholson was saying, slowly, carefully, for it hurt a good deal to speak, "selected from the most ruthless, the most worthless, damnable breed of men – men who have nothing left to lose – bought for the price of a hot dinner in a tavern and then set loose like blood-hounds from the slip to find their victims amongst those every bit as famished and despairing as they are." He looked up at the Inspector. "That ain't right, now, is it?"

"No, no," said the Inspector, "it ain't." He reached inside his pocket and dropped a small object in Mr. Nicholson's palm.

"I have always believed," he said, "that it is the task of a policeman to gather as many of the evidences and informations as he might, and ponder 'em until he can see how they all joins up. For it is all in the connexions, if you will: what may be made of them. O, yes, what'll be made of 'em. It's a little like writing a story, save you must only put down what you knows to be true. See there's plots, and then there's plots. And this whole matter is cobbled and twisted to a degree that I can't ever see it being laid straight again. Truth and justice – that's what it is all about, Mr. Nicholson. Without them we ain't got a hope. Now, I don't know the truth of this particular matter; in fact I has decided I most likely will never know. Yes, well and life, as they say, is a mystery – but there's *that*, Mr. Nicholson." He pointed at the object he had just handed over. "That is material evidence."

Mr. Nicholson was looking down at a piece of shot.

"And I tell you what," continued the Inspector, "before it come out of poor Mr. Drummond, it come out of a dueller – a busted *rifled* dueller – not some sorry mismatched fowling smooth-bore bought off a Jew ferret down in Whitechapel for a few shillings. It may not be much, Mr. Nicholson, but that is as much as I know for sure."

"Can I keep it?" asked Mr. Nicholson, clutching the piece of shot tight in his hand.

"Keep it," said the peeler. "You might as well. The truth it contains will be safer here than anywhere else in the metropolis." And then with another sigh he lifted his long, thin body up into the tiny space, his chimney-stove hat scraping the jagged lines of scorched invocations and entreaties.

"O, must you – so soon, Inspector," whispered Old Peeping Tom. "I feel we are only just begun here."

"I 'as a home to go to, and Mrs. Hughes is very close to her time. But I shall leave the bull's eye, if you like." He unpegged the lantern from his belt and handed it to Mr. Nicholson.

"You're very kind. Let me give you something in return – a small token of my gratitude." His puffy peepers moved slowly about the shop, lighting upon a fourpenny edition of *The Connubial Guide, or Married People's Best Friend*.

"O, no, no – I couldn't possibly, Mr. Nicholson – it ain't allowed – perquisites, see."

"It contains a new and effectual means of regulating the number of a family," said Mr. Nicholson, pressing the book into the hand of the Inspector.

Inspector Hughes stroked his chin as he turned a few of the pages, thoughtful. "Well, I suppose – if you insist," he said at last, tucking the volume away out of sight in his pocket. "Mind you take care now." And then he was gone, pulling the door shut behind him, the little cracked bell all forlorn.

Now that he was quite alone, the old disease of heart and conscience took hold of Mr. Nicholson. He carefully lowered himself to the floor beside the cashier's desk, his secret supply of gin to hand, the bull's eye trained upon the door. And there he sat in silence and waited for the sun to spread her rays along the filthy lane, to lope acoss the broken shop, stirring the ashes and the dust. He sat quite tranquil through the remainder of the night, gratefully enumerating every painful breath, the soft cooing of the pigeons, the first stirrings of life on the streets beyond. He waited for understanding, and, yes, my pippins, for Carlo's lumbering adumbration to appear at the door: for when it did, by gum, when it did, Old Peeping Tom would be ready for him! O, yes, o yes, he'd be ready alright!

No. 19, LOWER GROSVENOR-STREET, MAYFAIR,
FIVE O'CLOCK P.M.

In which Mr. Warren finally gains admission to the late Mr. Drummond's residence.

Miss Drummond was sitting sewing in the gilt-edged and tasselled parlour, the front parlour of the Mayfair house in which she had been born, and which she had scarcely left in the past dozen or more years; settled before the fire roaring up the chimney, soft in the warm rosy glow of the Argand lamp; her small, black velvet-slippered feet set up before her on the plump velvet footstool, the thick velvet curtains secured fast behind her against the gusty, rain-gashed night.

This was her favourite time of the day, especially in the winter. O, she was entirely familiar with that sinking feeling which caused the Duchess of Bedford to take to her boudoir each day at four with a pot of tea and a toasted muffin, but for her the time when the lamp was set, the fire stoked up, and no more was expected of her than to surrender to the draining away of her energies, was a rare moment of *contentment*.

She was aware of the newspaperman creeping into the room, to stand before her. Through her half-opened lashes she watched him for several minutes altogether, nervously twisting the brim of his beaverskin hat in his fingers. She cursed the girl for letting him in: Parrott would *never* have permitted such an intrusion. But Parrott was gone now; long gone. She watched as the newspaperman plucked a damp, dark curl from off his brow. He was murmuring to himself that it was very warm in the parlour: *very warm indeed*. There was a row of tremulous sweat-beads on the edge of his upper lip.

No bottom, she thought. Where were all the gentlemen gone?

The newspaperman coughed. "Forgive me, madam," he said, as she opened her eyes to peer at him. "Samuel Warren, barrister-at-law. Your maidservant let me in. I sent my card ahead. Forgive my intruding at such a time as this..." He stooped solicitously in imitation of a bow, and tried his best to look grave and well-mannered: *which was simply not good enough*.

"O, pooh pooh. Such a time as this? Why, whatever can you mean?" She placed one soft, round hand to the side of her soft, round head and inspected him keenly. Rather Large Self-esteem, she deduced, denoting arrogance, self-conceit and pride. In combination with superior sentiments and intellect, the faculty could contribute to true greatness of mind; but Miss Drummond could see no evidence of that in this instance.

"I have always taken especial pleasure in this time of day," she said. "Though I loved it best when I was a girl and the light would suddenly drop a shade before asserting itself once more as each of the candles was lit in order. It is not the same now that we have the Argand, although it has a very steady beam, which certainly makes sewing much easier in the evenings, and I do find the faint tang of oil to be pleasantly warming on the chest. Even so, I confess to missing the *romance* of the candles. Do you agree?"

"Indeed, madam," said the newspaperman, "but I was not so much referring to the time of day, as to the unfortunate and very sad loss of your brother."

"I understood your meaning. And I was agreeing with you, after a fashion. I was considering the lassitude which invariably visits one at this time of day, especially in the winter; how conducive it is to the formation of phantasmata and mesmeric encounters with the *other side*. My dear brother is not lost to us. He is among us. He sees and hears all, just as he always did." She paused to take a sip of Rowland's Aqua d'Oro and warm water, the better to effortlessly submit to that perfect balancing of wakefulness and sleep, which she always found to be the very essence of that hour. "I am very sensitive to that pervasive sadness which emanates from contemplation of the past and leads to gloomy anticipations in respect of the future. I believe it is necessary to abandon the mind to afternoon apparitions. Don't you agree? Please say that you do."

Mr. Warren turned the brim of his hat and pursed his lips. He made a somewhat grudging inclination of his head by way of answer.

"Listen!" Miss Drummond's chin dimpled as her little mouth formed into a tight, expectant smile. "Do you hear it?"

Mr. Warren obligingly cocked his ear, although he was clearly at a loss.

"There it comes, the *pibrochead*," she trilled. "Ah! The Duke of Perth's Lament is coming to me down the chimney!" She closed her eyes, humming to herself and moving her index finger back and forth as though in time to music.

Mr. Warren sighed a little invocation, and she opened her sharp eyes at once. "I am afraid that I must pooh-pooh the tempered understanding that these encounters are no more than an *indulgence* of mine," she said. "To me they are tangible proof that everything is knowable, and that love and hope will triumph in the end – even over death, which is in every other respect so very *final*. Don't you agree? You do not think me foolish?" she coaxed, coquettish. "Not even a little?"

"No, not at all, Miss Drummond, I think you very charming."

She delicately raised a tiny arched eyebrow.

"You think me fanciful!"

"No, madam, I protest! Not at all. What you have just said has a great deal of – of sense to it. Now, if I might just prevail..."

But Miss Drummond was neither to be condescended to nor interrogated in her own parlour.

"My, my, but what am I thinking? Where are my manners! Come, come, we must have tea! Would you oblige?" With a dainty gesture she indicated the tasselled bell-pull dangling down one side of the hearth. Mr. Warren very properly went across and gave it a little tug.

"You must understand that I am not at all a fanciful person," she imparted as the bell tinkled in the distance. "I have nursed two aged parents, you know – not to mention a beloved elder sister – in this very house: sacrificing my youth and all of my dreams of happiness in order so to do. No-one who has not performed that sad duty of a loving daughter at the death-beds of her dam and sire can ever know how thoroughly it depletes the good humours. Don't you agree?"

"Indeed, I do, Madam," said Mr. Warren, with immense condescension. "I was wondering – pray, do not think me impertinent – but there is an immense public interest in the circumstances of your brother's calamitous passing, and one or two issues arising upon which I should like to set my mind to rest..." She was smiling at him, but there was a sardonic cast to her pin-sharp eyes. "To begin with," he continued, "there has been a certain amount of speculation regarding the treatment Mr. Drummond received from the doctors. Several witnesses – including a member of your own family – have testified to the fact that he seemed perfectly well within a few moments of being fired at – and yet..."

"*Seemed* so," said the little round lady. "There is a realm of difference between how things might appear and how they, in fact, might be found to be. My late sister, for example, continued in her activities until two weeks before she died. Dear Charlotte Matilda! She was always far more interested in the world outside than am I, which was how she came to escape the sensations, the pervasive odours, the rattles, sighs and moans that accompanied the long and drawn-out deaths of our dear parents – not to say the burden of responsibility – which had so cloaked my own youth – until, alas, it was her turn to suffer all of them for herself. She had liked the opera, very much, you know, and Swan and Edgar, and dancing; whereas I have never seen the point of such frivolities. Indeed, I avoid them: for they mostly entail leaving the house, and the streets are filled with all the hazards of encounter. And I do not care to have encounters – save those which are invited."

"O forgive me, dear Miss Drummond," said Mr. Warren. He attempted a gallant bow, merely succeeding in dropping his hat, which rolled across the floor towards the fireplace. "I fear that you feel I am intruding," he stammered. "Allow me – please – I give my assurances – that is not my intention – it is just that – well – there has been so much interest – so many inconsistencies. I have a few questions, concerning your late brother's visit to Scotland with Her Majesty, and some threatening letters he once showed to me, and – and the question of the *bullet* which was removed from him in the days before his passing."

The little lady had been watching him amusedly all the while, but now she turned her attention to the arrival of the under-housemaid, who was carrying a tray of Spode tea-things. She watched their rattling progress across the room with a critical expression, as Lizzie, the girl, bobbed her way towards an occasional table, upon which she set down the tray.

"Lizzie," said Miss Drummond curtly. Her mouth had become a tight line of disapproval. "You are to inform Mrs. Gaff that I will be taking nothing more than a pot of chocolate and some Welsh Rabbit for my supper; and seeing as even you are quite capable of preparing such a repast without even a modicum of bother, she is not to *trouble* herself any further."

Lizzie bobbed up and down, then up again. "Yes, ma'am," she squeaked. "Beg pardon, ma'am, will that be all, ma'am?" She bobbed once again, a hand darting out to catch a stray curl that had escaped the confines of her cap. But Miss Drummond's eyes had already latched onto it, and were hardening into two little black beads.

"Lizzie! It is a condition of your employment here that you remain neat and tidy at all times!" She rapped out the words with her knuckles upon her flat palm, "Neat – and – tidy!"

Mr. Warren had gone in pursuit of his hat. He was standing rather disconsolately by the fireplace, and appeared aghast as the dainty termagent turned her beady eyes upon him.

"A girl who has reached the age of twelve years ought to be able to take care of a good deal more than an unruly bush of hair, don't you agree? And as her employer, I have a sacred duty to ensure that she does not slide from slovenliness into idleness before descending into sinfulness! Now, is that not right, Mr. Warren?"

He shot a hapless look in Lizzie's direction. The child was on the brink of tears. The little lady, so serene in her wing-backed chair, with her little feet pendulating carelessly, twinkled assiduously and dismissed the wretched girl by bidding her to go and instruct Mrs. Gaff to box her ears.

"How I hate any sort of a spectacle!" said Miss Drummond when Lizzie had fled from the room. Her pudgy hands were folded across her bosom, her sharp little eyes fixed on Mr. Warren. "I have such a dread here now," she said, indicating her full, soft *embonpoint*, "a pressure on my heart, a cramp if I lean forward too abruptly. It puts me in mind of how dear Matty used to complain of an obstruction just beneath the ribs. The canker growing there had quite filled the cavity. Her incessant moaning filled the middle landing of the house for two weeks. I will require a liberal dose of Holloway's Pills and some beef-tea later on. Do pour; you may partake of a small piece of cake, if you so desire it."

Mr. Warren handed Miss Drummond a cup of tea. She took the Aqua d'Oro from her pocket and added a few drops. "I am restored," she announced, sipping delicately, "calm in the presence of death. Matty often comes in visitation at this time, to glide through the rooms she loved so much – with a grace she rarely knew in mortal form."

She took up her sewing and made a few tiny stitches, as though she had entirely forgotten that Mr. Warren was there. He wiped his forehead with his hand, and wondered if he had been dismissed.

"Might – might I ask," he said, after a few uncomfortable minutes had passed in silence, "what it is that you are making?"

"It is a crewel-work cover for the footstool."

"It is charming – utterly charming. And tell me, is – is that a Scotch pattern of some sort?

"It is a sprig of heathers tied about with a riband of Clan Drummond of Perth plaid."

"It's quite, quite – I – I have seen the Prince Consort in tartan dress."

"Really! But he has not a drop of Scotch blood in him!"

"I believe it to be very fashionable at the moment."

"*Fashion*?"

"Your brother, I believe, had the privilege of accompanying Her Majesty on her visit to Scotland last year?"

"Yes, of course. He is Groom-in-Waiting."

"O, forgive me, I did not mean Colonel Drummond – I – I meant your *late* brother."

The eyes had lost some of their pin-sharpness. Miss Drummond leaned back against the chair and half closed them.

"Berkeley had to wear his dress uniform, of course, but Neddie considered wearing the tartan – he even made inquiries at Gieves and Hawkes, but he was very affronted by their careless manner."

"Really! I'm very surprised to hear that."

"They jested as they took the measure of him. They said that the poor weavers of Paisley would have a slice of bacon with their potatoes with such a great supply of Clan Drummond tartan to be got in. Neddie did not think that a very sensible remark for a royal warrant-holder to make. He rejected the idea of the kilt quite early on, though he vacillated over the wearing of the trews for several weeks more."

"Really – that's – that's most interesting... I – I wonder – did – did he ever talk about the incident in Edinburgh, madam? The time he rode in the Prime Minister's carriage and was the object of a vile assault? He told me something of it himself, and it has occurred to me – I wonder – did, did he ever entertain any suspicion that his assassin might have been among that dreadful throng – the mob which overturned Sir Robert Peel's carriage in the Edinburgh street?"

When she turned her eyes upon him, they were still acute, although the effect of the drops was beginning to be apparent. "The Mob had no love of Neddie," she said, "although he would often essay a broad opinion of the Mob..."

Mr. Warren ran a finger around the inside of his collar. "I recollect," he said, "how at the time a great deal was made of the notion that the Scotch had taken Mr. Drummond for Sir Robert Peel."

Her dainty eyebrows rose imperious at the mention of the Prime Minister. "True nobility is a faculty like any other," she said, "and I dare say may be present in a footman – as Neddie often claimed – and yet be entirely lacking in a Prince; but rest assured, it is distinctly absent from Sir Robert Peel."

"Indeed."

"Having to defer to Sir Robert's judgement and opinion on everything, from the steam engine to the Corn Laws, put my dear brother in a very ill temper. And as for the Income Tax..."

"O, quite so: the dreadful imposition..."

"Neddie would never say as much, of course. Loyalty to office is a mark of Full Adhesiveness: a family trait, you know."

"Ah, yes – loyalty... an admirable quality in a civil servant. Was Mr. Drummond more satisfied with the Duke of Wellington? I had heard that there may have been some – forgive the impropriety, but I must know – these are grave matters – affecting the wheels of justice no less – I had heard that Mr. Drummond and the Duke of Wellington – what I mean is – was there ever any *disagreeableness* between them?"

Miss Drummond was smiling dreamily. "The Duke of Wellington is every bit as charming as he was thirty years ago. His organ of

Firmness predominates, you know."

"So I have heard. But what did your late brother think of him? Did they ever quarrel?"

"Neddie found it hard to justify the Duke of Wellington's pronounced understanding of the great necessity to put down the will of the People by the bayonet. He seemed to think that that would be a great *pity*." Mr. Warren moved to speak, but she raised her little hand to halt him. "There it is again," she whispered, her eyes roving about the room, "the *pibrochead*."

She closed her eyes and a dreamy expression settled upon her features.

"The absence of any shock or alarm was remarkable," she was saying, "and he suffered so little pain that when Mr. Bransby Cooper pressed him on the point he replied, 'What you call pain – what do you mean by it?' He was laughing. He said that he felt the pain of oppression, merely. Of course, by Saturday he could no longer speak, let alone laugh."

"Remarkable," murmured Mr. Warren. "So, there were to be no last words?"

Her eyes opened again slowly. "At nine o'clock on Wednesday morning he pressed Mr. Guthrie's hand and, with a smile on his countenance, asked if all hope was past. When Mr. Guthrie told him that it was, he said that he had endeavoured to live honestly, doing as much good as he could, and he placed his hope in God's mercy for his redemption."

"So he *could* still speak?" said Mr. Warren.

"I was crying by his side," said Miss Drummond, "and he turned to me and said, 'We have lived long and happily together, and my only regret is in parting with you'." There was a small tear shining in the corner of her hard, bright eye.

"That is very moving," said Mr. Warren, "but madam, I must know... on the day that he was fired at, Mr. Drummond spoke to me of certain matters. He showed me threatening letters, vile, impugning, and suggestive of the disaster which overtook him – letters contained in a secret volume..."

But she did not answer. She was listening to the silence with her eyes closed, waving her fat little hand in the air. She seemed to have forgotten all about him. Mr. Warren coughed; he muttered under his breath; he sighed; but it was all to no avail.

After some little while the clock on the mantel-shelf whirred and chimed. "Only half past five?" she observed at length. "My, time moves so slowly."

Mr. Warren wiped his dripping brow with the sleeve of his coat. "The letters...?" he entreated. "The threatening letters? I must know, you see. I have to know... A blemish has been left upon the nation's character by this horrid murder. There are soft-headed men who ought to know better, but who are attempting to twist and torture the truth so that your brother's murderer will be excused. I am one of those who believe that those laws are the most merciful which deter men from atrocious crimes..."

"It is all taken care of," she said.

"Madam, it may be the case that a grave injustice has been perpetrated..."

She placed her head on one side, focusing upon him with immense curiosity.

"There are too many secrets," she said, "too many secrets. The weight of them! Poor dear Neddie – not Over Large, you see, his Secretiveness – a tendency to repress, at least until the judgement had approved of giving utterance. In him it was simply the propensity to conceal, driven by prudence; but he was not *really* cunning. Indeed, he baulked at too much deceit – the burden of it, carried within him – it was too much, too, too much. No, no, 'twere better it were ended! Better, better by far." She sipped at the Rowland's Aqua d'Oro, slipping in and out of the space between the fading light of the afternoon and the humming flicker of the Argand. "Tabula rasa," she murmured, "a new beginning. A new beginning for us all."

In which Mr. Cockburn prepares for war, and finds
his loyalty sorely tested.

The Buff and Blue of the eating room: faded, scuffed, knocked back.
The Whig party at dinner: winded, drunk, acescent. The food at
Brooks's was substantial, but not at all *good*. Sandy bolted half a doz-
en *huitres*, sipped at a dull *consommé tortue clair*; picked over greasy
filets de sole meunière; left the dry fowl in its glutinous oyster sauce for
the servant; waved aside *petit soufflé* and a watery cherry ice. He was
bored with nodding at the dyspeptic opinions of portly country Members; weary with the acid comments of spindly lip-chewers. He could
not imagine why he had come. Mr. Johnston, the Liberal Member for
Kilmarnock &c., was not there, and neither was Mr. Oswald: which
was a *shame*. Sandy had entertained such hopes of quizzing the former
on the provenance of the witnesses he had supplied – some associates
of McNaughten's from Glasgow: a parcel of surly working men who
had known him for many years and would attest to his state of mind. He
told himself that it was probably just as well that the two Members had
not deigned to come. He reached for the claret. Too much knowledge
was not always a good thing when one was concocting an argument.

On the other side of the table the Chief Whipper-in was apparently
in the receipt of some nabob's secret disclosure. His heavy-lidded gaze
turned towards Sandy, who nodded an elegant greeting and waited until
the heavy-lidded gaze slid off him and the Whipper-in turned smilingly
towards the cadaverous leader, Lord John Russell, who was seated at
the top of the table making slender utterances.

Perhaps, Sandy mused, indigestion was at the root of everything.
Still, it was the case that the wine was good. He poured himself another
glass. He had already drunk a good deal, but not quite so much that he
did not yet care what impression he gave.

"I had heard," said the Member for East Cumberland, the Hon.

somebody-or-other, as he reached for the port that Sandy had neglected to pass, "that Lord Brougham has changed his opinion and is now going about town accusing the Anti-Corn Law League of inciting to assassination the wretch who murdered Mr. Drummond."

Sandy sniffed. "It is my understanding that Lord Brougham – whom I greatly admire – has never been much in favour of the League. It is his opinion, often stated, that a country that has elected representation and a free press has no need of association for political purposes. He may be wrong in some of that, to my mind at least, but nevertheless, there is nothing so extraordinary in your disclosure – and not one iota of truth."

"You are in no doubt as to the error of Brougham's opinion? You are certain, are you, that McNaughten is a madman? Surely, the manner in which he carried out this wretched deed – the determination and acumen he has demonstrated – harks more of the devil than want of wit? If your argument is that we ought not to make martyrs of these rascals," persisted the Member for East Cumberland, "then I agree with you: the dignity of martyrdom has something of a fascination to fanatics. There ought to be a bad and very degrading punishment – but not so bad that it will never be inflicted. That, I am sure, is the best way to see off these mountebank attempts against the Queen and other people of high station."

"Hear hear hear," mumbled the nabob who had lost the attention of the Chief Whipper-in.

Sandy nodded blandly, turning the stem of his claret glass in his hand.

"After all, there are worse fates than death," the Member continued.

"Worse fates than death, you say?" said Cockie against the rising tide of hear hears. "What can possibly be worse than death?" He looked up from beneath his pale lashes towards the Whipper-in, who was swirling his brandy extravagantly around the glass, lifting it to his nose, savouring: all very slow and deliberate, and watching Sandy all the while.

It was not necessary for the Member for East Cumberland to exhaust his imagination or Sandy's patience any longer in conjuring up

[423]

an especially cruel and unusual punishment, for the table was visited by one of those mysterious silences that settle periodically upon gatherings where lesser men attend the great, flattering them by laying down their knives and forks and glasses and conversations as soon as it becomes apparent that the great have something of importance which they wish to impart.

Lord John Russell had made the appropriate signal to those nearest him.

"I am not alone," he was saying, in his rickety voice, his bony hands dancing before him as if plucking at a harp, "I am sure, in having my recollection of the dreadful circumstances under which Bellingham murdered Perceval restored to me in light of Mr. Drummond's unfortunate demise. The times we find ourselves in today are not unlike those in which we lived twenty years ago. The preservation of the Constitution must always be uppermost before us, but we must too ensure that we have the support of *all* degrees of society in whatever course we are conduced to take – lest the whisper of a faction may prevail against the nation!"

As the applause died down, Sandy found himself thinking that Russell had all his best years behind him. His prime would have been '31-'32 – when he held the House rapt for three hours at a time with that tiny indistinct voice, as he talked of Liberty like a real giant of statesmanship. Power had worn him down to nothing. It galled Sandy to think that he was still there at the helm of the Whig party, talking of the People!

"Lord John Russell knows something of the People," Sandy muttered to the fellow on his right. "Why, when he was Home Secretary back in '39 he offered arms to the magistracy of Birmingham so that they might put down the People and their petition!"

"When the French authorites desisted from responding to those ghastly attempts on Louis Philippe by visiting a bloody death upon the perpetrator," Lord John Russell was saying, "and instead took the more benign measure of consigning one of the offenders to an asylum, I believe it was true to say that the epidemic of regicide was all but brought to an end."

The Hon. somebody-or-other raised an eyebrow in Sandy's direction. "Now then," he rejoindered, "if that is to be your strategy, Cockie, old man, then I must applaud you! Put into Bethlem all the lunatics who would disrupt our way of living! Ha! Excellent!"

Sandy brought a hand up to his mouth and pinched his lips. It would do no good to speak another word. One did not come to a dinner like this to hear the truth spoken – or to speak it oneself, come to that. He watched bitterly the pious fraud at the top of the table accepting the plaudits lobbed at him, like an opera dancer picking up the roses thrown to her from the gallery: the dissemblance of gratitude, the despising.

"Lord John Russell thinks you a very clever man, Cockie." The Chief Whipper-in had materialised at the back of Sandy's chair. "He has agreed to afford you a measure of support in your endeavour – so long as you do nothing to damage the Party, of course."

Sandy smiled. "You know, I was just thinking," he said, "how correct in every respect is Tom Paine's avowal that government is at best a necessary evil, at worst an intolerable one."

"You think so, do you? But where would we be without it, Cockie, old man? Or do you suppose that we might leave the governance of the country to the lawyers?"

"I believe we could do worse than entrust the constitution to the operation of the Law."

The Chief Whipper-in yawned. "Ah, the constitution," he said. He was looking along the table towards the leader. "Yes. Justice is sufficient to maintain and support us all..."

"It ought to be – if unalloyed – its due process uncontaminated by interest."

"Come now, Cockie! You are sounding more and more like the oak in the story who berated the reed for being weak. Do you recall – what was the oak's fate?"

"It was torn up by the roots in a hurricane."

"Whereas the slender reed, weak as it was, knew how it is necessary to bend a little with the wind, if one wishes to survive."

"There is a point, sir, when resistance becomes the highest virtue and the greatest duty."

The Chief Whipper-in thrust his tongue in his cheek. Sandy watched it work its way across the mouth, probing each of the teeth in turn; digging out little particles of decay.

"A few of us are withdrawing to the Subscription Room," said the Chief Whipper-in after a few moments. "I trust you will join us? I believe there is a betting book open on the table: who killed poor Mr. Drummond? Last time I inquired, the odds on your client were reassuringly long. As a matter of fact, the Duke of Wellington appears now to be favourite..."

Sandy laughed to hear it; he laughed, though he was not at all amused.

MR. WARREN'S PRIVATE STUDY, BEDFORD-SQUARE,
LATE AT NIGHT

---

*Wherein Mr. Warren is brought to a costly realisation
of his own fallibility.*

Mr. Warren had decided to carry the matter over just a little further, and then no more. Over the past few weeks, he had repeatedly expressed, in print and in person, his utter incredulity that anyone could possibly pretend that McNaughten, sane or insane, had *not* drawn his incentive from the wholly incendiary insinuations of the Anti-Corn LawLeague; and he had been prepared to battle any objections that were raised – particularly in the absence of any *proofs* of such a motivation on the part of the prisoner. Indeed, he was somewhat surprised (if not disappointed) by the rapidity with which the shrewd and sagacious people of England appeared to adopt most of the foregoing as a matter of *fact*.

Of course, he could not claim to have achieved all of this on his own: the police, the Office of Home Affairs and numerous other commentators had all done their bit. FIAT JUSTITIA was merely among the most prominent, and having played his part to the best of his ability, he was done with all of that.

He waited in vain for a sign that he had done well; but no promise having been made to him, apart from the carefully phrased suggestion of a dead man, there was no need of any acknowledgement of the service he had performed – and, consequently, no gratitude and no guerdon. After a little while, he had begun to appreciate that the lack of official recognition in the matter was perhaps a *blessing*. For he was by then beginning to move towards a profounder understanding of the circumstances in which Mr. Drummond had met his death than he had hitherto enjoyed.

A week ago, Sir Robert Peel had burst out in session, accusing Cobden of having made an assault upon his integrity, by holding him individually responsible for the nation's suffering and distress, and of having brought everything upon himself – even of having promoted assassination as a remedy. Then there had been a half-hearted rousing in the Lords, where an attempt had been made to identify Mr. Cobden and the League with dark and smazy dealings, with pistols upon bright and hard snowy streets and with intrigue, culminating in that odious, most horrible transaction – the shooting of Mr. Drummond. But that outburst had come from a Whig. In all of this Mr. Warren saw nothing more significant than the ebullition of ill-regulated intellects. He told himself that if either the Whigs or Tories had had a shred of evidence – one way or t'other – then he, nay, the entire nation would have been told of it. All he saw was a closing of ranks, and the restoration of the status quo.

And that, he supposed, was all that mattered.

He did not, however, give up on the task that he had set himself, that of discovering the actual motivation that had led to McNaughten's firing a pistol at the Prime Minister's private secretary. And as time went on he became more assiduous in directing his attention towards the establishment of McNaughten's sanity: partly because he wished to determine whether or not mental intoxication might result from the *passive* imbibing of the doctrines of socialism and infidelity to the rule of law; and partly because he wished to do all he might to prevent that impossible swank Cockburn from a great victory that might well remove from the Law its deterrent. It was, he believed, bad enough that Cockie stood to pocket a substantial sum in fees for the defence of the Scotchman. It nauseated him to consider the affected sentimentality of the barrister's argument which seemed determined to persuade us to give our sympathy to the murderer and not to the murdered. He had seen written in several places how the prisoner was "unfortunate"; was in "an unhappy situation", and all of us must therefore "regret his fate". Such was the dainty language in vogue which tended to foster the false morality of the morbid humanitarians of the day.

One especially dank and squalid night he had found himself in an alley close by Gardiner's-lane station-house, and looking in to the pock-dashed face and red-rimmed piggy eyes of a brass buttoned and collar-badged "A" Division sergeant. He knew that there was every chance of being sold a mog as he palmed the sov on to Sergeant Shew, but it was the only method by which he might finally glimpse the contents of the buff boxes and the depositions made to the Treasury Solicitor. It did not take him long to realise that the peelers knew almost as little as did he.

A few copies of the *Reformer's Gazette*, a ticket to see the steam gun, a strange token, and a book of blasphemous sayings were not the most staggering indication of a man's politics that Mr. Warren had ever beheld. It was doubtless true, as Sergeant Shew pointed out, that a book which set out to prove that the Bible was bunkum wouldn't go down at all well with a jury; but this did not satisfy Mr. Warren's longing for certitude. Indeed, the prospect of knowing for sure receded with every piece of information he received from the peeler.

"There's this plainclothesman, see," the peeler had told him, "who bought the prisoner's business off him for a song, and the two of 'em knew the Gray Goose when they was all hugger-mugger in Glasgow."

"And was the prisoner a Chartist, as far as you know?"

"No, he weren't," said Shew.

"So what is the significance of the information?"

Shew had frowned. "Hurry up, why don't yer?" he snapped. "I could spend a good while in quod for doin' business with the likes of you. Inspector Hughes can be ever so batey..."

Mr. Warren riffled through the pages. He read the worthless recollections of a man from whom the prisoner had once rented a workshop and who had "never noticed anything strange in his manner". A clerk in the Glasgow and Ship Bank had sworn on oath that last summer McNaughten had withdrawn five pounds "of his own money". The principal of the Mechanics' Institute in Glasgow was of the opinion that the boy had "always spoke tolerably fair and made as respectable an appearance as any of the other students". A surgeon who had taught the prisoner anatomy said "he seemed to understand the subject well enough, although he had not troubled to attend the examination."

Mr. Warren threw the papers back at Shew with disgust. "Is that it?" he demanded. "Is that the entire case for the crown?"

"There's a convict they've taken off the hulks."

"A convict, eh?" remarked Mr. Warren tartly. "Well, his testimony will be worth listening to."

His sarcasm was wasted on Shew. "He says McNaughten and him

was walking past Sir Robert Peel's house just before Christmas," said the bacon-faced peeler, "when the prisoner said 'damn him' or 'sink him', or something like that. And then when they passed the Treasury he said, 'Look across the street, there is where all the wealth of the world is,' or something like that."

"Really?" said Mr. Warren with a yawn.

"O, but that ain't all; when they got to the Abbey, McNaughten said, 'You see how time has affected that massive building,' or something like that..." Shew stood there nodding and raising his eyebrows in a suggestive manner.

"Why do the police believe that McNaughten intended to kill the Prime Minister?" said Mr. Warren. "Just tell me that."

"O, well sir, a good many folk want to kill Sir Robert Peel..."

"Yes, yes, I dare say – but upon what understanding of the matter do the police found their belief in this case?"

Shew thought for a moment. "Inspector Tierney told them."

"Inspector Tierney?"

"He said the prisoner confessed to him." Shew shrugged off another gust of London street stink. "But he never."

"He did not?"

"I was there, weren't I? O, Tierney sent me off to get some coffee, but I sent someone else instead and lurked in the hallway outside the cell. I heard every word of McNaughten's confession."

"Did you, now..."

"It'll cost yer." The peeler held out his hand. "Two sovs," he said.

Mr. Warren thought for a moment, before handing over the money.

"Inspector Tierney," began Sergeant Shew, "can be very *persuasive*. I have seen him, with me own eyes, many times, *persuadin'*. Why, I dare say he could persuade your own good self to swear to being Spring-heel'd Jack, if he had a mind to."

"I very much doubt it," said Mr. Warren. "If you're going to tell me merely that this fellow Tierney persuaded the prisoner McNaughten to confess to seeking the life of Sir Robert Peel, then I am afraid I shall want back some of the money I just gave to you. Two sovs is not pro rata for informations I could just as easily have arrived at myself."

"O, no, Mr. Warren, sir. That's just it. He wouldn't be persuaded. He wouldn't say a word on that. No matter what Inspector Tierney said, did or threatened would be done to him. O, no. He would not be shifted."

"So he said nothing of interest...?"

"They spoke about the steamers."

"Steamers?"

"Yes. Inspector Tierney said he'd been to Glasgow a few weeks earlier, returning a Scotch rebel taken in the Staffordshire riots. McNaughten asked him what steamer he had taken from Liverpool, and Inspector Tierney said he had forgotten, but he thought it was the *British Queen*. And McNaughten said he must have been mistaken, since the *British Queen* didn't sail at that time of the year, and that it must have been the *Princess Royal*."

"And was it?"

"Inspector Tierney seemed to think it might have been. He asked McNaughten if that was the steamer he had come over in. But it weren't."

"You surprise me."

"He said he'd come over in the *Fire King*. I belive he said it was a seven hundred-tonner, and was at one time the fastest vessel afloat..."

"Good heavens," groaned Mr. Warren.

"Then they started talking about the railway between Edinburgh and Glasgow," continued Shew. "McNaughten said there were four trains a day, and the journey took two hours and a half – though the forenoon train was a little quicker on account of it not stopping at all the stations. I believe he said you could travel third class for half a crown."

"This is all very fascinating," snapped Mr. Warren, "but I must ask you to proceed to the point." The alley was not the most salubrious. It was freezing cold and dark.

Shew narrowed his little eyes so that they resembled nothing more than two crooked slits in a pitted wall. "Alright, alright," he said. "Coo! I'm only telling you what they said. Now then, let me see, where was I? Steamers, trains.... Ah yes! Paisley!"

"At last," muttered Mr. Warren, "something of interest."

"Inspector Tierney asked McNaughten if he had ever been to Paisley."

"And..."

"And he said that he had. Inspector Tierney said that it was a great place for shawls, and McNaughten agreed that it was, most of the inhabitants being weavers. He said they could make on a loom patterns of greater intricacy than any Hindoo could effect with a crewel and wool. And it was a great pity that so many of them were out of employ." Shew folded his arms and nodded.

"That's it?" said Mr. Warren.

"That's it," said the peeler.

"Nothing about the Prime Minister?"

"Not one word."

"Nothing about Mr. Drummond?"

"Ah, now then, as to that he was most particular that he would not be drawn."

Recollecting now the less than satisfactory encounter with the police sergeant, Mr. Warren poured himself another glass of claret assuagements. These past few days he had been doing a good deal of drinking, and an even greater amount of contemplating, and it seemed to him that the more he pursued his convictions respecting the shooting of Mr. Drummond, the more he strove to banish all doubt, the closer he brought himself to challenging everything that he had hitherto accepted as the truth about the way in which the world operates. Wherever he went, he always found himself in the same cheerless place at the end of every day: a place where he was left alone with nothing but his conscience. He had come to terms with so much, yet the incessant mazings continued to perplex him in the depths of night, in the unsteady frowze of claret, and even in the soothing steam of liver and bacon as he sat mulling deep in maundering and greasy corners.

He tried now, once again, to tease it out for himself, this time reaching as far into the argument as a spirited assault upon the legitimacy of petit barristers raking up musty precedents, quoting the opinions of men who lived more than a century ago and knew no more of madness than they did of electro-magnetism. But he knew that he could not win this argument with himself simply by knocking down Cockie. It is the Law, he thought, it is the Law that is wrong: it is wrong to assume that just because a man is mad he ought to be excused punishment.

But this was not the nub of his vexation. It was a trifling point, merely; a means of distracting himself from the gnawing apprehension that things were not at all how he had once believed them to be; that the world was suddenly and by so much a far darker place than he had ever perceived, so riddled with hopelessness and emptiness: so devoid of order and truth and justice...

"It is the Law," he said to his glass. "It has all to do with the Law."

He drank the claret down in one draught, and waited for all to be made clear and quiet and knowable once more. He waited, and he waited, but although understanding beckoned to him, he did not dare follow in her footsteps: he was afraid, you see, afraid of what he might discover about himself and what he had suffered to be done.

THE JUDGE AND JURY SOCIETY,
AT ABOUT THE SAME TIME

In which Mr. Nicholson is finally rewarded for all of his hard work.

The Lord Chief Baron was jolly pleased to see Good Old Cockie in the rich and intoxicating steam-griddled air of the J. & J., plucking his primrose gloves and dropping a little secret smile. It had been a good fortnight since their last meeting: the girls had missed him so, and as for Mr. Nicholson himself, well, he had begun to feel quite forsaken.

"Good news, M'Lud," said Cockie.

"Aha!"

"Indeed!"

"The fee!"

"The fee."

"When?"

"Yesterday."

"How much?"

"Two hundred pounds – drawn on the accountable receipt found on the client at the time of his arrest. I have come to repay the debt owed you."

"Gammon! I thought the day might never come!"

"We must celebrate! This is my first fee," said Cockie, "since the close of the last session – and that was a meagre one. Why, I don't believe I've felt such a thrill since I put a hundred guineas on Priam to win the Goodwood Cup in '31!"

They passed together into the reeking glare and then on to a shallow corner away from the most conspicuous part of the stage.

"And as to the rest – ?" inquired Mr. Nicholson when they were out of ear-shot.

"– progressing satisfactorily."

"I heard the Lord Provost of Glasgow visited your chambers, sir."

"He has come to testify on our behalf as to the prisoner's state of mind."

"How very sporting of him! And him a Tory gentleman, too! I must say it's too bad you can't persuade the Glasgow Whig to join the game."

"Mr. Oswald is most insistent that he has never clept eyes on McNaughten," said Cockie, as they drank a little jolt of champagne.

"Which all goes to show," said the Lord Chief Baron, shifting his judge's wig, "how a working man'll always have more luck in trusting a Tory than he ever will a Whig. For a Tory don't care if you have nothing, sir, but then he won't ask you for a penny neither; whereas a Whig'll take all you have and use it to build a poorhouse, and then, when you try and cadge a brown off him, he'll point it out to you and say, there you go, my good man, that's all there is for the likes of you."

Mr. Cockburn smiled wanly and raised his glass to a spangled creature on the far side of the room.

"I cannot make excuses for my party," he said. "Besides, the Whigs have not entirely abandoned us: Mr. Johnston, the Liberal Member for Kilmarnock, Dumbarton, Renfrew, Rutherglen, Port Glasgow, &c., District of Burghs, has been most helpful in bringing forth a clutch of respectable tradesmen prepared to testify to the prisoner's deludedness."

The Lord Chief Baron sighed. "Which reminds me," he said, "what news of the pa?"

"Ah! The pa! The pa has agreed to take the stand. I depose him tomorrow. He shall testify as to McNaughten's deluded state of mind."

"What more can a father do?"

"Quite."

"You shall have a great victory, sir – one way or another."

"I certainly intend to discharge my sacred function to the best of my ability..."

"Capital! Capital!"

"But I must confess, M'Lud, to feeling an anxiety so intense – a great burden..."

"Qualms, sir? At this late stage!"

"It is just that there is so much right and wrong to the matter."

"Lor'! Not them clapped-out old bawds!"

"Life and death, M'Lud. Life and death... It was never thus in the committee rooms. I wonder, can there be a duty more painful or more paralysing to the energies or the mind of an advocate – a man's life hanging in the balance?"

"O, but surely, Mr. C., 'tis all life and death to someone – whether it be bullets or ballots, testimonials or taxes, railroads or ramrods."

"Yes, but then, you see, *interest* always mollifies the dilemma in those cases where somebody is set to win something..."

"Someone always has to lose, sir."

"There are degrees of loss..."

"Not if you is the loser, sir." Cockie sighed, and so Mr. Nicholson reached across and placed a great beefy paw upon the slender shoulder draped in a frock-coat of most decided cut. "But enough of this gloomy talk!" he said with great equanimity. "Save it for the trial! Tonight only one thing matters, and that is the fact that you has the *fee*!"

And then, with a great roar and a wink and a chummy nudge, the pair of them went forth together into the helter-skelter, nine-times-round-the-stage combat: into the veil of the mystery; down, down the trap.

In which Mr. Cockburn is urged to consider a father's love for his son.

Mr. McNaughten senior was much smaller than Sandy had imagined him to be. He had had for so long in his mind the picture of a brute, utterly indifferent to the fate of his son, that the clean linen, the good quality beaver-skin hat, the well-cut coat, the taciturnity and self-containment took him a little by surprise. In short, Mr. McNaughten senior seemed to him to be the very model of respectability. He would, as Mr. Humphries had remarked, make a very good impression upon the jury.

Only his hands, work-roughened, though not at all clumsy, stroking the smooth nap of his hat, told of the manner in which Mr. McNaughten senior had made his elevation through Glasgow society. Here was a man who had worked hard for all he had. He regarded Cockie with a sort of doubtful eye, and nodded a brusque greeting as he was invited to sit and helped to a cup of tea: he eschewed the offer of something a wee bit stronger.

"Dan's a *natural* son o' mine," he said. "He cam' tae me on the death o' his mother, and I apprenticed him tae me fer about four years and a half, after which he became my journeyman. He's a hard worker, and a very steady, industrious young man. He's exceedingly temperate in his habits, an' very skilful on the lathe. He's a harmless lad, inoffensive; a wee bit quiet, perhaps an' gi'en to dreamin' and ideas ayont his degree – but there's no' an idle bone in his body."

"I do not doubt it," said Cockie.

"I taught him everything I know, an' when he left me he went into business as a turner on his own account – ornamental – and did well enough by it, too."

"He certainly seems to have put by a good store of money."

"Aye. He's been earning his own way since he was about seven years o' age, an' he never spent a penny more 'n he had tae. Half the time he never even kept lodgings."

"In the time he was in business on his own account – a period of how long –?"

"About five years, I should say."

"How often did you see him after he left your employ?"

"I dinnae see him all that often, to tell the truth – although before then we was in each other's comp'ny every day. I s'pose he seemed taeme tae be more distant than he had been before."

"Do you know why that might have been?"

"As to that I cannae say. He'd often pass me in the street and no' speak a word or even notice me."

"And this began to occur when, exactly?"

"About four or five years ago, I would say."

"In about '37 or '38?"

"Aye, then abouts... I suppose if I thought about it I might've thought maybe he was a wee bit ashamed at havin' set up his business in opposition tae my own, and but a few doors away."

"Was he correct in that feeling?"

"Aye, mebbe – no – not really. He was in the ornamental line. I never got intae that part o' the trade."

"I see. So, it seems that apart from the distance that developed between you, at this time, let us say by the year 1838, you had little concern about Dan."

"Aye, he seemed to be getting on wi' it. He'd a guid business. He never wanted fer anything. An' I knew him to be steady an' carefu' an' hard-workin'. That's how he was raised tae be."

"When did you start to be concerned for him?"

"About two year ago he cam' to my house, saying he wished tae talk in private. My wife disnae care for Dan: she minds the old wives calling me fornicator behind my back. I've telt her, dinnae gie 'em ony fash; that boy has never cost the Kirk a penny since he was in my care. But you know how women are. She worries what's said. So, I told him to go away, an' come by the shop in the mornin'."

"And how did he appear to you?"

"Och, he was very agitated, I should say. He'd a wild look tae his eyes, an' he was a wee bit dishevelled – like he'd been out o' doors fer a guid long while, in all weathers."

"And yet you sent him away."

"Aye – just till the next day, mind."

"And when you saw him the next day what did he tell you?"

"He told me that various prosecutions had been raised agin him – he wouldnae say what they were, but he begged me tae speak tae the authorities and put a stop tae 'em. He said I'd tae speak tae the Sheriff – who I know quite well, as a matter o' fact."

"And did you?"

"No, I did not. I told Dan he was a barmpot. Why would any one want to persecute the likes o' him fer? I tried to turn the conversation, an' we spoke about this and that for a wee while, an' he seemed to be his old self again. Then he said he'd tae leave Glesga' and would I help him tae find a situation in a West India House, or a counting-house, or some such. I said he'd better get along to a respectable teacher and learn writing and arithmetic and mebbe then I'd consider it."

"Did you see him again?"

"Aye, he cam' by the shop a week after and asked me if I'd seen the Sheriff. I told him that after our last conversation I'd have thought he'd have gone tae school and put all that clishmaclaver out o' his head. He said he was bein' followed night and day, and his life was in danger. I said who's daft enough to follow youse about? He said he couldnae tell me their names since he was bound by oaths and the crew would kill him if they found out he'd spoken to anyone else about the matter. I then asked him if he'd joined a combination. He knows my strong feelings agin Radicalism. At times party politics run very high in Glesga', an' we've had arguments before."

"What did Dan say when you asked him about the combination?"

"He asked me if I was aware that there was a spy system in Glesga'."

"And what did you say to that?"

"I thought afterwards maybe I should have told him to see a doctor. But I put it down to some prank or delusion. I thought it would pass, an' would dae the lad nae guid tae have that particular slur against his character. He's never shown any signs of disease before, but his mother

[438]

wasnae all there. She was a bad lot, though I only came to that opinion after I'd lain wi' the dirty bitch. She was a *suicide*. I dare say she might have passed something to the lad – an impairment o' some sort... Or maybe he brought it on himself by workin' too hard, or readin' too much. It even came to my mind that it had to do wi' the disappointment over me not lettin' him have a wee share o' ma business. I wonder now if perhaps he was a wee bit angry about that, an' that was why he stopped calling at the shop. He used tae pass me in the street wi'out the slightest bit o' notice."

"How long did you say he worked for you?"

"From the age of about seven until he was seventeen or eighteen, I should say."

"I dare say that must have seemed most unfair to him, to be edged out like that."

"I have a growing family I maun provide fer. I coulda left that boy tae the Kirk, an' he'd have fared a sight worse. Instead o' which I raised him myself as best I could, taught him a trade, fed an' claithed him, kept him oot o' trouble. I done my best by him – as he would tell youse himself, if he's able tae."

"Does it ever trouble you to think that if you had listened to him then perhaps he might not have shot Mr. Drummond in the back?"

"Tell me, Mr. Cockburn, do you have a son?"

Cockie waved the query aside.

"No? Well, let me tell youse – they dinnae raise 'emselves; but when you huv done all ye can by 'em, as I believe I have done by Dan, then there's no' a soul on earth wha can cast up to youse the race they run."

"Do you really believe that to be so?" said Cockie, dropping his voice almost to a whisper.

But Mr. McNaughten senior did not appear to mark him. He was contemplating the crown of his hat, running his calloused thumb over it in slow concentric arcs. "Och, he was a guid wee lad," he said at last. "He used to stand by that lathe watchin' everything I done and never say a word. It was all goin' in: everything; every single thing. Aye, I tell ye what: I never saw a lad take tae the trade so well as Dan."

THE QUEEN AGAINST DANIEL McNAUGHTEN, 1843
Central Criminal Court, Old Bailey

The Queen *against* Daniel McNaughten, for the wilful murder
of Mr. Drummond
Before Chief Justice TINDAL, Justice WILLIAMS,
and Justice COLERIDGE

Mr Warren prepared to take down the whole in his stenographic sound-hand, as the Recorder of London opened the indictment.

"On the 20th of January, at the parish of St. Martin in the Fields, Daniel McNaughten did feloniously assault Mr. Edward Drummond with a certain pistol, which he then and there held in his right hand, loaded with gunpowder and a leaden bullet, and which he, of his malice aforethought, discharged at and against the said Edward Drummond, thereby giving him a certain mortal wound…&c., &c."

It was to be the last time the piece of shot was referred to so directly by the prosecution. Sergeant Shew, it was, who would later testify to having discovered the powder flask and five bullets when he (Constable Silver, it seemed, was no longer taking the glory to himself) searched the prisoner's lodgings on the evening of the crime; and Mr. Guthrie senior, when it was his turn to be called, spoke of how the bullet had first struck Mr. Drummond on the behind and then curved upward, thereby injuring the diaphragm. This was, he said, a wound which never heals under any circumstances, for it invariably gives rise to inflammation. The inflammation, he concluded, had killed the gentleman. The bullet may have played its part in that, one way or another, but it was never mentioned again.

All this was to come, however. For now, as Sir William Webb Follett, the Solicitor General, rose to his feet, nothing was further from his mind than the bullet and the pistols: they had become an irrelevance, and at that moment he wished only to satisfy the court – by the facts of the case, by the threats used by the prisoner before he committed his crime, and by his declarations afterwards – that it was not the life of *Mr. Drummond* that McNaughten had sought, but that of Sir Robert Peel.

The Solicitor General said, in the clearest terms, that this would be proven, before proceeding to prove nothing of the sort.

Mr. Warren sighed over his leather notebook and looked about him, as best he was able, through the cloud of breath, the buzz.

Across the way His Royal Highness Prince Albert supported his brow on an elegant hand and frowned in concentration. Mr. Charles Dickens's eyes were shining with the intensest interest, but the penny-a-liner had a bemused smile upon his lips all the while, which spoke volumes as to how little he grasped the importance of the case. The Legal Correspondent of *Old Peeping Tom* was winking from the press box, and seemed much better in the face than he had upon the last few occasions on which Mr. Warren had made his acquaintance. And Good Old Cockie was sprawled across the defence bench in an attitude of elegant insouciance, the silk gown spread out about him, his wig on straight, plucking from time to time at the primrose gloves as he attended to the Solicitor General. Mr. Clarkson was next to him on the defence counsel benches, his permanently infuriated eyebrows clashing together; and behind him their co-counsels, Mr. Bodkin and Mr. Monteith, passed notes to and fro, smirked at the prosecution, and raised their eyebrows in false surprise. They were mocking, sceptical, and above all *confident*, no matter what was said and done: a really big case, thought Mr. Warren, on a really important matter must have made a most welcome change from all those shabby guinea fees earned in ten minutes.

Mr. Warren regarded them all with a small pang of envy. All of those, it occurred to him, who had pursued this case were assured of some benefit or other; only he, who had surely proved the most assiduous pursuer of the matter, stood to leave the Bailey a loser.

He glanced peremptorily at the prisoner. McNaughten was pale but seemed quite aloof from it all, his long tapering hands lightly gripping the rail; his eyes fixed upon the object, not giving a thing away.

The poor suffering monomaniac *pro tempore*, thought Mr. Warren, with an unbecoming sneer. Faugh! Perhaps if he was to be spared, McNaughten might combine with Oxford, and the pair of them could occupy their time at Bethlem in conducting an academy for the instruction of criminal youth in the art of insanity.

He felt sour. He grudgingly acknowledged the Solicitor General's observation that it was difficult for well-regulated minds to understand the motives by which persons labouring under such morbid influences were actuated. He was a little more gratified when the gentleman observed that there had been several attempts made upon the life of the monarch of the French people – crimes for which it was difficult to assign any motive, but that of an ill-regulated mind, worked upon by political feeling. Just because there was an absence of any adequate and assignable motive, the Solicitor General informed the jury, that, in itself, cannot be taken as a proof of want of reason in the perpetrator.

No, thought Mr. Warren, want of reason is not even the stub-end of it. It is about Terror, and Terror is omnipresent and heartless, exacting and *certain*. There are too many who cannot bear the chaos of this life another moment, who look for answers in the reasonable-seeming resolution of powder, steam guns, petards. He supposed that, in the end, it would be the overwhelming desire for coherence, for things to *make sense*, rather than the irrational and compulsive that would prove mankind's undoing.

The Solicitor General limned the enigma of the prisoner: hard-working, sober, prudent; a simple working man of acquisitive habits, who had saved a considerable sum by the time he retired from wood-turning in 1840, at the age of five-and-twenty. It was an expertly dashed-off sketch of McNaughten by the man sent to hang him. It was not necessary to fill in the details, merely to imply, to suggest. A young man who studied *natural philosophy* at the *Mechanics' Institute in Glasgow*, and who took an active part in various alterations which were made to the rules of that place, and who was in the habit of getting books from the library; one who, moreover, attended lectures in anatomy. A young man who had visited the Strangers' Gallery and expressed an opinion of the gentleman he heard debating there, who had walked by the house of Sir Robert Peel. The ten-pound householders in the jury box would have known his sort: he was the shop-boy let go after they caught him with his hand in the cash-box; the boot-boy who spat on the floor behind them when their backs were turned; the madman raving on the corner who frightened one's wife on her way to church.

And, before he sat down, the Solicitor General was good enough to remind the jury of their very painful duty, a duty which must, nevertheless be discharged; expressing his perfect satisfaction that when they had heard the witnesses, when they had maturely deliberated upon and considered the evidence, their verdict would be one of justice – justice between the public and the prisoner.

Yes, thought Mr. Warren looking up from his notebook: justice.

COURTYARD, OLD BAILEY,
A SHORT WHILE LATER

In which Inspector Hughes and Constable Silver try to put the past behind them.

Inspector Hughes was waiting in the yard for Constable Silver to give his testimony as to the manner in which he had apprehended Mc-Naughten in the act of firing pistols at Mr. Drummond. He had not troubled to enter the court. He knew how it would go – if not how it would end. He had hung about just so's he could give the boy a little reassurance that all would be well.

They nodded at one other, then set off towards Whitehall, wordless, thoughtful.

"It's all behind us now, boy," said the Inspector at last, as they prepared to cross the Strand by the rheumatic belt depot.

Silver nodded, but he did not smile and nor did he seem to be in the least part reassured.

They strolled past King Charles's statue, past Drummonds counting-house, past Scotland-yard, past the Salopian coffee-house, past Downing-street, not minding the puddles washing over their boots.

"Yes, yes, it's all over and done with now," said the Inspector as they rounded the corner of Gardiner's-lane.

CENTRAL CRIMINAL COURT, OLD BAILEY,
AT ABOUT THE SAME TIME

In which the prosecution continues to put its case, and witnesses are summoned to tell their version of events.

First the pot-boy, then the surgeon – and now it was the turn of Inspector Tierney to subpoena his conscience. Mr. Nicholson appraised the plainclothesman as he listened to his faithful rendition of the conversation with the prisoner on the night of the incident. It had not been an interrogation, merely a conversation, insisted the scranning cove, conducted in the interest of getting at the truth and spurred on by a natural curiosity. That was all.

"I said, 'I suppose you are aware of who the gentleman is you shot at?'" he told the Prosecuting Counsel, "and the prisoner said, 'It is Sir Robert Peel, is it not?' I at first said, 'no,' but in a moment recollecting myself, said, 'We do not exactly know who the gentleman is yet.' Then turning round, I said, 'Recollect the caution I gave you just now, not to say anything to incriminate yourself, as it may be used in evidence against you,' to which he immediately replied, 'But you will not use this against me?' I said, 'I make you no promise; I gave you the caution.' I then left the cell."

Cockie looked across at Mr. Clarkson, who bent his head, giving way. It was Cockie's moment, and he was ready. His blue eyes sharp, clear, focused. He snapped the primrose gloves, and with a slight sardonic smile, rose, the silk billowing behind him, then falling.

"Why did you visit the prisoner in his cell?"

"It is my duty to visit all the cells in the course of the night."

"Is it your duty to put questions to the prisoners?"

"As long as I do not interfere with the case in point I do not see any harm in putting questions to prisoners."

"Did anyone direct you to put such questions?"

"Certainly not."

"Was not your object in this interview to induce the prisoner

[444]

to make a confession of some sort?"

"I did it for the purpose of letting him know that I was ready to receive any communication he thought it proper to make."

"Do you mean to swear that you had no motive lurking in your mind when you asked him the question?"

"I had no particular motive – other than the anxiety of human nature, under such revolting circumstances, to know who and what he was."

"Did you mention the conversation to anyone else?"

"Yes, I mentioned it to the Commissioners of Police in a private report."

"Now, perhaps you will tell me upon your solemn oath whether, when you made that observation to the prisoner, you did not do so with the intention of extorting a confession from him?"

"The remark was thoughtlessly made," said the spy, the words all but sticking in his throat. He inspected his nails and tried to look as though he didn't care a fig; but Mr. Cockburn was the more skilful at nonchalance. He scooped up the silk behind him, his hands upon his hips, then he leaned forward in an attitude of great anticipation, with a mock quizzical expression on his face, and waited.

"I tried to turn the conversation as soon as I thought he was going to make a full confession," said the spy at last, when the anticipation had become unbearable. "I did not wish to hear it."

Cockie raised one eyebrow. "No further questions," he said. He sat down, and Mr. Clarkson reached across and patted him on the shoulder.

Then it was the turn of Mr. Howe of the Board of Trade, who had taken a lurker for a police officer in plainclothes, and Sergeant Shew who had seen a lurker standing near Lady Dover's eating a piece of bread, and the recruiting officer who had indicated a lurker to a plainclothesman on the day of the shooting. These dubious rogues were not worthy of the effort it would take to cross-examine 'em; and so Mr. Cockburn gave way to Mr. Clarkson, who shrugged at Mr. Bodkin, who turned to Mr. Monteith with a sigh and a rueful shake of the head.

Mr. Stephenson of the Treasury was next up – Mr. Drummond's erstwhile deputy and worthy successor, and the only person ostensibly to benefit from the calamity. Indeed, the betting book at Brooks's now had has his odds shortened considerably; and Mr. Monteith conveyed to Mr. Bodkin a little note which made them both laugh. Inquiring of its contents afterwards, Mr. Nicholson was shown the scrap: *Cui bono?* it read: *to whose benefit?*

They were still laughing as the convict, Gordon, took the stand with his description of a desultory walk along a wintry Whitehall, in the course of which, he claimed, the prisoner had made some coarse utterance in respect of the Prime Minister. Mr. Nicholson didn't ever care to see a fellow blab on a chum, but when he looked at McNaughten, he could not discern the least condemnation in his expression, and so he grudgingly hoped that the fellow spared Van Diemens Land would now go home and live a long and comfortable life: though seeing as Gordon's home was Glasgow, that seemed unlikely. The convict was followed by two fellows from whom McNaughten had once rented a workshop, and who deposed that they had not noticed anything strange in his manner; then came a lecturer from the Mechanics' Institute who stated that the prisoner always spoke tolerably fair and made as respectable an appearance as he might; and finally a surgeon from whom McNaughten had once had anatomy lessons. He told of a young man of little eduation, who had a want of polish about him, but who seemed capable of understanding what was said to him.

"Now, sir," asked Mr. Cockburn when it was his turn to cross-examine the anatomist, "do you mean to say you had an opportunity of forming a judgement as to the man's sanity or insanity?"

Cockie had his chin cupped in his hand and one ear cocked towards the doctor, as he watched the jury with a studied air of perturbation.

"No," said the anatomist. "I merely came to say that he appeared to understand what he heard of my lectures."

Cockie stretched his eyes in dismay and tut-tutted under his breath. Several of the jurors accordingly cast disapproving looks towards the surgeon for wasting their time. The witness thus discredited, Cockie took his seat with a peremptory nod at Mr. Clarkson, who, much delighted, turned and shook his head at Mr. Bodkin in mock disapproval, who whispered something to Mr. Monteith, who laughed, as he reached across and tapped Mr. Cockburn on the shoulder, passing him a note which he had just had of a court clerk.

Mr. Nicholson watched as Cockie read the missive. He marked how the ironical light in the barrister's eye clouded suddenly as he crumpled the note and thrust it in his pocket.

But within an instance, all eyes were upon the next witness. For she had come – not gliding, not babbling; no lime-light, no gauze; she had come as what she was: a tired woman past her prime, broken and defeated, in distress; her widow's weeds waxy and spotted here and there with rust; the thick black hair threaded with silver; the delicate face worn and bearing no trace of what once held a thousand people enrapt – that is, not until the Bible was held up before her and her eyes met it shining. She clasped it to her and recited the oath as if it were the music of the angels.

The Solicitor General had risen and was fixing her with a stern, admonishing look. But Mrs. Dutton did not mark him: she knew better than anyone there that this was the only place where a woman like her might be heard – unless, that is, they were clever, or foolish, enough to found their own church. But she also knew that, unless she wanted to spend the rest of her days locked away with all the other pauper lunatics (and let us not forget the troubling matter of the dead baby), she was to say what she had been told to say, and nothing more.

O aye, she might have been mad, but Lizzie Dutton wasnae daft.

She pulled her shawl about her shoulders and in her low, meliflu-ous tone told them all about the movement of Daniel McNaughton's hours; how she never knew what he did all day; how he always paid for his rent and laundry punctually; how he had no friends and no con-versation; how he rarely looked you in the eye; and how she saw the constable find the powder and the shot in the table drawer. She needed a prompt to recollect how he had told her he had been in Scotland at the time of the Queen's visit there; and she looked down at the Bible as she added how she did not believe he had been in the same part as Her Majesty.

She never looked at the prisoner – though he never took his eyes from her. Not one trace of accusation was there, however. McNaughten was just as he always was: benign, mild and accepting.

The Solicitor General yielded to Mr. Clarkson, and Mrs. Dutton's small threadbare-gloved hand gripped the rail, as the Behemoth approached her. Beneath his pertinacious coaxing, she elicited a man of very sober habits who once lived in her attic; reserved, penurious, with his one change of linen and no fire in his grate, a shy, depressive man out of a situation with very small means. And Mr. Clarkson, though he was careful not to expend all the fury of the eyebrows upon the frail creature before him – bullying a widow would not play at all well with the jurors – persisted in asking her, three, four, five times, if she had ever observed anything, anything *peculiar* about the prisoner.

"Ah've heard him get out o' his bed at night and moan repeatedly," she said at last, "but ah never thought it peculiar. It's the times, sir, I should say: the times. I should say there's nothing peculiar about that, tae my mind."

And satisfied, Mr. Clarkson nodded gruffly and waved his hand at the Judge.

The Solicitor General rose to re-examine the landlady, to steer her back to the shiftiness implicit in a man who went out all day and never returned until the evening, who did not take his meals in his room, who kept a powder flask and bullets in his table drawer. How strange it is; how strange, he said; how very *peculiar*. He asked her about the prisoner's possessions, which were very meagre – suspiciously so, it seemed, beneath the scrutiny of the prosecution.

She seemed tired now, looking about her wearily. "Well, there was a book," she said, "but the police took it away."

The Judge interposed himself. "A book?" he queried, "pray, what sort of book?"

The Solicitor General stroked his top lip, smiling lightly, and nodded conspiratorily at his co-counsel. Cockie frowned, mouthing an oath, as Mr. Clarkson half-rose from the defence benches behind him ready to bluster that he knew nothing of any *book*.

But the Judge was giving all of his attention to the glittering eyes of Mrs. Dutton. "You can tell us," he said, kindly, "it's quite alright. Was it a very bad sort of book?"

Mr. Clarkson snorted in his most bullish manner, as the landlady half-closed her eyes as if lost in remembrance of something from long ago, something pleasant, for with remembrance came a faint smile and a slight inclination of the head, sweet, coquettish, sad.

"O no, sir, not at all," she was saying. Now it was the turn of the Solicitor General to frown, and for Mr. Clarkson and Mr. Cockburn to smile at one another. "The policeman said it was blasphemy, but it wasnae," and for the first time since she had taken the stand she looked at Dan, and smiled. "It was a very religious book. *Extracts from the Bible*."

The Solicitor General rose to object, but the Judge would not permit him to say a word.

"And how do you know it was a good book?" he asked the little lady.

"Ah, now your honour – I knew that because it was *my* book," she said, "I gave it to him – and I am a verra religious person."

The Solicitor General darted a furious look to his co-counsel, as the Judge thanked Mrs. Dutton and dismissed her from the witness box.

And when Mr. Nicholson looked at the prisoner, he saw that he was smiling, and keeping his sad pale eyes upon the tiny lady as she stepped down from the witness box and crossed the court-room to the door, a little of the faded grace restored, moving effortlessly: almost *gliding*.

DOWNING-STREET,
ABOUT HALF PAST SIX O'CLOCK P.M.

In which Mr. Cockburn is summoned to Downing-street, before he can make his Argument.

Mr. Clarkson had been outraged. He had turned to Mr. Bodkin, who had harrumphed to Mr. Monteith, who had shaken his head disgustedly. One day on a big case was larks enough, they all protested. They had a score of guinea fees lined up for the morrow. And Cockie had only paid them for today. The case-hardened knaves had tried to reason with him, as Cockie had thrown off his wig and stalked from the court-room as soon as Justice Tindal acceded to his astonishing request that the

[449]

case for the defence be entered upon the following morning. He was, he claimed, labouring under a severe indisposition, his voice was very hoarse, and he could speak only with great pain. He did not feel that in his present state he could do justice to the prisoner; and this taken together with the length to which the evidence on behalf of the prisoner was likely to run, it would be quite impossible to close the proceedings that night in any case.

Frayling was shaking down the wig before he placed it in the box, and avowing total innocence of what the deuce was going on as Clarkson, Bodkin and Monteith badgered him all at once. "Mr. Cockburn never said a word to me," Cockie heard him protest as he left the court. "There was a note, is all I know... But don't worry – the guvnor's good for the rest of the fee: he's definitely good for it!"

When he arrived, a carriage ride later, at Downing-street, Cockie was taken straightway to the Prime Minister's private office. Sir Robert Peel had a large sheet of drawing paper spread out before him on a mahogany table, and was indicating something upon it to his new Private Secretary, Mr. Stephenson.

Cockie, still in his gown, stood in the doorway and waited to be announced.

"Ah! Mr. Cockburn! Coom, do, and take a look at this."

Sandy peered bemusedly over Sir Robert Peel's shoulder at a page of pencil sketches of filigree fineness: trefoils, griffins, adumbrations of towers and robing-rooms; the tracery of an arched window here, a turreted guard-room there; all faint and spidery. The Hon. Bart. withdrew another sheet from the pile that was before him, and brought his finger to his lips in contemplation of a further abundance of crenellations, Tudor roses, kings, and ape heads engaged in the act of either swallowing or disgorging ivy-clad poles.

"Now then," said the Prime Minister, "have you ever seen sooch fine sketching? Mr. Pugin has done a fine job on the designs for the new parliament building..."

Sandy turned away with a hard, disapproving laugh. "Perhaps, sir," he said, "you would be so good as to bowl out to me the precise nature of the hoax to which I appear to have been subjected."

Sir Robert Peel did not turn to regard him. How large his head is, Sandy thought; how like a lion's, with thick curls the colour of sand coiling all about it.

"I find it hard to troost artists, Mr. Cockburn," Sir Robert Peel was saying. "Being a mathematician, I am drawn to the plain and straight-forward in life. To certainties. In politics, as I dare say in law too, one moost learn to penetrate the surface – to eschew artifice, if you will; whereas it seems to me that artists employ artifice in order to reveal the truth. An altogether oontrustworthy occupation, don't you agree?"

"That's all very well – but what happened in court today was a trav-esty," Sandy said. "I never expected it to be a straightforward matter, but I went along in the full expectation of a fair fight. I thought at least I was to have that."

"Ah, then it would seem that you prefer things plain too," said the Prime Minister.

"If I didn't know better, I'd say that someone had paid the Solicitor General to – to... Damn it all! I've seen better arguments put by student barristers after a night of drunken debauchery!"

Sir Robert Peel was still contemplating the drawings. "It will be nothing short of miraculous to see these sketches rendered into stoon," he said, tracing the disarticulated skeleton of parliament with a firm, thick finger: a shambles of wainscotting and old-fashioned heads. "How would you like to walk through this doorway on your way into St. Stephen's porch – perhaps as a Member, eh Mr. Cockburn?" Then with a slight wave of his hand he signalled that it was time for Mr. Ste-phenson, who had just poured them both some claret, to leave.

"I am to give my recommendations to the Commissioners for Woods and Forests tomorrow in respect of contract number 4," said the Prime Minister, "that's the work in the New Palace Yard that was delayed on account of the quicksand. What do you think I ought to say, Mr. Cock-burn? Yes or no?"

"I am not at all knowledgeable about architecture, sir," replied San-dy. He thrust his hands into his pockets and took a turn about the office, anathematising under his breath. "If pressed I would have to say that it is a little too *Lady of Shalott* for my taste."

"Hum. Best nod it through, eh? The Prince Consort, you see, is rather set on it. *Fait accompli.*"

Sandy drank the claret in one draught and set down the cup hard upon the desk. Sir Robert Peel was regarding him closely. "Stephenson," he said to his Secretary, "before you go, perhaps you would be so kind..."

The Secretary crossed to a large desk that was standing in the opposite corner and unlocked a drawer from which he retrieved a copy of the Reverend Thomas Malthus's essay on population.

He handed it to the Prime Minister.

"Will that be all, sir?"

"Thank you, yes."

The Prime Minister was leafing through the volume. He waited until the Secretary's footsteps had died away in the hall outside before speaking. "Thirty years ago when I was Chief Secretary of Ireland," he said, stroking the page before him with his thumb, "a murder was committed on the road between Carrick and Clonmel. A man had employed four others and paid them two guineas each to kill his enemy. It was a dastardly plot; they made it quite impossible for the poor victim to escape, and sooch was the public horror that a heinous thing like this could coom to pass, that the government offered a reward for the discoovery of the murderers. Well, if you can believe it, Mr. Cockburn, the very same miscreant who had hired the murderers came forward himself and informed against them! They were hanged, of course, and he claimed the reward. With these very hands, sir, in my office in Dooblin Castle, I paid over the sum of two thousand pounds to a monster in human shape." He had turned up one of the hands, laying it flat upon the open page. He looked at it for a few moments, before folding it slowly into a soft fist.

"I have had a horror of informers ever since. Parasites that dwell in the entrails of society, feeding on the desperation and misery of oothers." He took the book by the spine, shaking it gently so that the uncut pages fanned out, revealing a series of pockets. "I dare say he thought nobody would ever think of looking here – certainly not the Duke of Wellington... But I knew Ned better than he knew himself. Did you know we entered politics within a year of each other?" He broke off, suddenly looking very grave indeed. "We lived too long in the dark, and that is all the matter."

Sandy took the proffered volume.

"The statement I have removed there will best explain certain aspects," said Sir Robert Peel, "though you may read them all, if you wish. Joostice must follow its own course – undirected – no matter what our fears might be. It's joost that – well – I promised Ned that I would not let the fellow hang."

"He will not hang, sir," said Sandy. "The argument is unassailable. There is no case to answer."

The Prime Minister looked away. "It is joost the truth after all," he said. "And as I told Ned many times in this very room, good men have nothing to fear from the truth."

Honoured Sir –

I wish to advise you that I do not seek any remuneration for the task. I have more than enough money, and have no desire for any more. If you wish you may make a donation into the funds for the relief of the poor of Paisley, but I shall not insist that you do. I have the pistols, and I will be waiting for you outside the counting-house from half past three o'clock. I pray you, do not be late. The constable generally reaches that end of Charing-cross by four, and makes his turn shortly after. I trust that you will make all the arrangements in respect of the aftermath. All I ask is that you do not abandon me. Apart from that I believe, sincerely, that all my reward shall be in knowing that I have played my part in preserving the rule of law in this land.

These are dark and terrible times, sir, and too many have nothing to lose by rising up with pikestaffs, muskets, vitriol and fire – whereas I, sir, wish only to preserve.

I remain, sir, your humble servant,

Daniel McNaughten.

And Sandy, not venturing to say another word, mutely replaced the letter inside the uncut page from whence it came and set the volume down upon the table.

"You have no doubt as to the veracity of this communication," he asked. He had grown very pale.

"O, no, no, none whatever," replied the Prime Minister. "These *occurrences* – they are not ooncommon in the business of goovernment. When times are difficult, and one moost hold with a joost hand the balance between a small indiscretion and the value of any noomber of human lives... No, no. I do not condone what is done, but I have come to accept the need for certain practices – committed in the name of *order*."

With an unuttered oath and imprecation, Cockie turned his face towards the ceiling and stood in silence.

After a time Sir Robert Peel's Secretary returned, holding open the door for him.

Sir Robert Peel offered his hand. "You know how it is, Mr. Cockburn," he said. And he patted Cockie on the shoulder.

A distant clock chimed the hour as, like one who walks in his sleep without any sense of fear, Sandy left the Prime Minister sitting in the gloom of the half-light of the evening, alone.

THE QUEEN AGAINST DANIEL McNAUGHTEN, 1843
Central Criminal Court, Old Bailey

Mr. Cockburn looked like a man who had nothing left to lose, save for an argument. He stood up to address the court at nine o'clock in the morning and did not sit down again until ten minutes to one in the afternoon. He spoke of an anxiety so intense; he spoke of a responsibility so overwhelming; he spoke of a mind so agitated; he spoke of a matter of life and death; he spoke of love and cherishing; he spoke of the impenetrable depth of a man's soul; he spoke of the love between a father and his son; he spoke of strong political feelings; he spoke of despotical governments and spies; he spoke of apprehension and of trembling.

It was a daring, thrilling, passionate and eloquent address; it was pure Cockie. It was still not yet half past ten.

He moved on to express his regret that alas! there would be not one member of the jury who had not brought to the judgement-seat a mind imbued with preconceived notions on the case, which in all corners of this vast metropolis, from end to end, even to the remotest climes of this extensive empire, had been entirely canvassed, discussed and determined. He decried the insatiate desire for vengeance that had arisen in men's minds, the wild and merciless cry for blood that had gone forth.

Then he turned his attention to the vexed question of insanity, as it was perceived in the Law, and gave assurances that he would present evidence as to the mental condition of the prisoner at the time he had fired the pistols; evidence that would not be of that naked, vague and uncertain character (and here he looked across to the Solicitor General), but testimony positive and precise, that would demonstrate how the prisoner had become a victim of a powerful, a fierce and fearful delusion – a moment of madness.

He followed through with a forensic dissection of the precedent in the case, coupled to a quite brilliant deconstruction of the Solicitor General's own enervated attempt to do the same from the day before;

and all the while he remained the very model of decorum and good manners. Then he drew a vivid portrait of the prisoner at the bar, in softly muted tones. A natural son, who had not always met with that full measure of kindness which was usually shown to legitimate offspring (and here he paused for a moment, before continuing); a man of gloomy, reserved and unsocial habits; a man of singular sensitivity of mind, who spent his days in incessant labour and toil, and at nights gave himself up to the study of abstruse and difficult matters; a man whose mind was tinctured with refinement; a man who became firmly persuaded of the substantiality of persecuting creatures, the product of his own fevered brain; a man who, as the poet had it, could not escape from himself; a man who, in increasing desperation, sought help from his own father, from the police in his native town; from the Lord Provost of Glasgow, from a Member of Parliament, only to find that in every case that help which he most needed was not forthcoming (would to God that it had been!); a man in whom there existed not a single trace of political enthusiasm, nor the sentiments of an assassin.

A man who acted as a sane man would have done, and who nevertheless manifested beyond all doubt the continued existence of his delusions. A man, moreover, of whom there was not one tittle of evidence that he had attended political meetings, or sought to end the life of the Prime Minister. And here Cockie paused, studying the faces of the jury intently, before he set about destroying in a clutch of words the career of the scranning cove.

"I hardly know," he said with heavy sarcasm, "whether I am throwing away time in devoting a single observation to the evidence of a man whose own statement justifies me in saying that he was acting a thoroughly treacherous part; a man who now shows himself in his true colours: an inquisitor and a spy; but who, in the garb of fairness and honesty, sought to worm himself into the secrets of the unhappy man at the bar. The statement of that witness may be consistent with truth or may be a fabrication; I know not, care not. Sure I am of this, no British Jury will hesitate to admit any one single fact which is an essential ingredient in the proof of the case, on the unsupported testimony of an individual who has manifested such black perfidy, which will remain indelibly stamped upon his character."

Only Inspector Hughes and the Legal Correspondent noticed Jack Tierney rise and creep from the court-room. They nodded at one another, and for the first time in the span of their acquaintance, Mr. Nicholson thought that he saw the glimmer of a satisfied smile on the peeler's physog.

Finally, shortly before one o'clock, having taken the better part of two hours to rake painstakingly through the nebulae of jurisprudence in respect of the insanity defence – including a number of erudite definitions of monomania for good measure – Sandy threw himself upon the mercy of the jury.

"Gentlemen," he said, as if addressing each of them in turn. The yeomen smiled to themselves to be thus hailed by one who was undoubtedly the finest and truest gentleman any of them had ever seen. "Gentlemen, the life of the prisoner is in our hands. It is for you to say whether you will visit one on whom God has been pleased to bring the heaviest of all human calamities – insanity – the most painful, the most appalling of all mortal ills – with the consequences of an act which most undoubtedly never would have been committed, but for this calamity. It is for you to say whether you will consign a fellow being under such circumstances to a painful and ignominious death. May God protect both you and him from the consequences of erring reason and mistaken judgement! I trust the case in your hands, with the full conviction that justice will be upheld in the verdict to which you shall come."

Then he sat down, exhausted; his co-counsels, appeased with enhanced fees, reaching across to pat him warmly on the back.

There was still a parade of witnesses to come, of course, the examination and cross-examination to endure, the verdict; but he knew that it was over. He had said his piece, and he had not been cheated out of his moment.

The Seventh Meeting

"Your case," I told him, "cannot be approached without a shudder. And I was not alone in being scandalised by the startling action of the Judge in stopping the trial before the jury had been given a proper summation or opportunity to deliberate upon the arguments set before them. It shocks me, still, to think of it. And yet... what say you? Within days of your acquittal another madman openly threatened the lives of Her Majesty and Sir Robert Peel, and that of Mr. Goulburn was menaced by a person for whom, had he put his threats in execution, the plea of insanity would probably have been put up."

McNaughten smiled in that wholly irritating way of his, but made no reply.

"*Homicidal monomania*! Pah! What was Cockburn thinking of when he concocted that meaningless phrase? Come, you are an intelligent man – you must have an opinion on all of this? The testimony of Dr. Monro of Bethlem, in particular, was in every way, monstrous! If such a course were to be allowed again in a court of justice, what security have any of us for life, liberty or property? Well, what say you?"

McNaughten lowered his lids and sighed.

"You must see," I said, "the difficulty of my situation. I need to have explained to me – I need to know – to understand – and you are the only means I have of discovering for myself the absolute truth of the matter – its rights and wrongs. I must have peace of mind. Have pity on me, McNaughten, I beg of you."

He turned up his face to the ceiling, contemplating the cracks and cobwebs for a few weighty moments.

"Be careful of judging," he said at last, "lest you be judged yourself."

"Do not prevaricate. Do not toy with me. If I judge, that is because I must make some sense of all of this, and you have refused to supply me with the information I need in order that I may quieten my reason and my conscience."

"I wish," he said, "tae return tae my native place. I'll be safe there. I'll be comfortable. I've a shop, a guid business. I have money in the bank on a deposit receipt. I've friends, guid friends, and a family – a lovin' father. *That* is my life, not this, this torment."

"It is gone," I told him. "It can never be restored to you. You have destroyed it – all of it – by your actions."

He looked at me for a long time. There was no grief in his expression. There was no anger or accusation. I looked away before he did. I could no longer bear the understanding that I read in his features: the pity I saw there. Pity for *me*.

"We are not so different, sir, you and I," he said at length. "We've both believed in the possibility of a better world. And the hope of it has degraded us."

Then he closed his eyes, and with a great sigh, began.

Politics did, after all, *have* something *to do with it*. It was in about '38 or '39 that Abram Duncan began to pursue the cause of universal suffrage with a vigour that few men evince. It was very surprising when Carlo followed him in the Great Struggle. When challenged, his reply was always that it was not necessary to *believe*, only to *live*. The Charter, it seemed, was a good living. Abram and Carlo certainly got about the country. The Gray Goose's fame spread far and wide. It was dangerous work, but there were few men who would dare to challenge Carlo; and it is to be supposed that it was for this reason that Abram, who would never raise a hand against another living thing, tolerated him.

Few of those who attended the assemblies and rallies were unaware that provocateurs in the pay of the government moved freely amongst them. It was Carlo's preferred method to build upon these fears by warning the crowd to take great care concerning what they said and to whom they said it. He would then denounce at random some innocent fellow as a plainclothesman, who would invariably be beaten half to death by his brothers. Perhaps it was in this manner that he came to the attention of the government agents who saw much to admire in his cunning and nerve: or most likely he was already known to them for some time past as a man who could be *relied upon*. Carlo became a police spy. Duncan, of course, had not the least awareness of this. He believed Carlo to be as sincere in his support of the Charter as he was himself. He was a trusting man, with no real understanding of the extent of the spy system; and Carlo was very clever in the way in which he won the trust of Duncan. He flattered him, by declaring that it was Abram who had saved him from a life of desperation by showing him a purpose. Indeed, Abram would often declare in the latter portion of their life together that the salvation of Carlo was one of the proudest achievements of his life.

As for Dan, at this time he was living in lodgings in that part of Glasgow known as Anderston, and doing well enough in his business. The pains in the head and all the other symptoms of a great oppressiveness still beset him, but having read a great deal on the subject, he had formed the opinion that he was suffering from some disease of the brain or spine, for which he resorted to many remedies: infusions of Indian hemp and the immersion of his body in cold water being the most efficacious.

His lodging was very comfortable: the walls of the room thick and oil-painted; the floor a deal one, covered with two small pieces of carpet – for ornament as well as use; it being, in one sense, intended to prevent the feet coming into contact with the cold floor, it not being agreeable to do so when one jumps newly out of bed. On the mantelshelf were a variety of dishes – all china. Close to the door stood an old-fashioned eight-day clock with a fir case painted in imitation of mahogany; at its side an old fir chest of the same colour, and next to it several band-boxes.

There was an old chair set before the bed upon which he would sit to read whenever he needed to focus his thoughts against the buzzing in his head. Sitting there, he would often feel the gray descend upon him particle by particle, and with it came the oblivion of thought, of reason. On that particular occasion, the one that he wished to impart, it was dark outside when he opened his eyes. The bed lay on the left hand and was of considerable length and breadth, sufficient to hold two persons with ease, three at a pinch. It was an excellent feather bed, with good blankets with a capital thick mat.

At first he could not believe what he saw, but there upon the bed was Carlo. His greasy hat was pulled down over his face, and his legs were stretched out before him, crossed at the ankles. He had one arm folded behind his head, and with the other he struck a Lucifer upon the wall and proceeded to light his pipe, the noxious smell of which quickly filled up the room, making the head swim.

He had slowly raised his hand and pointed his index finger at McNaughten, miming the action of cocking a pistol with his thumb. Then he had laughed. He was thin and dirty-looking and seemed far older than when last they had met. His whiskers had a silver tinge to them, and his eyes were lost in two red bloated sacs of skin – as if he'd been drinking or crying. He began to speak in slurred and abandoned tones of how men's love for one another had grown cold, how the system was *flippit*. How the enemy must be shaken over the mouth of Hell, and he did not care how many fell in. How it had all to do with what part you played in the Great Struggle.

After that, Carlo would come again and again to his lodgings, to his workplace, seeking him out in the town wherever he might be. As the pair of them sat together, Carlo drinking steadily from an old crock of whisky, Dan would find himself pulled into plots, hearing things that he did not wish to know. The fears and terrors which were never far from his mind began to surface again, and it was not long before Dan had taken to fleeing in the dead of night whenever he heard that Carlo was returned – sometimes taking refuge in the forest rather than being woken in this fearsome manner. Many times he had met morning in the cold and damp and been forced to beg a portion of bread and milk from strangers.

For a brief period he had succeeded in pursuing the study of anatomy at the house of a doctor in Cambusneathan, but he was obliged to return to Glasgow in order to take the examination. He had not understood, however, that it was necessary to study Latin as a requirement for entry to the exam, and seeing as he had never done so, there was little hope of attaining the required standard in the time remaining. When he returned to his lodging that night, he felt dispirited and quite broken. Carlo was once again waiting for him. It was upon that very night that Dan arrived at an understanding of the precise way in which Carlo was deceiving Abram.

Following this, Dan gave over much of his days to consideration of the manner in which he might warn Abram Duncan of the danger he was in, but fear of the consequences for himself always prevented him from taking action. It is true to say that at this time his mind was a torture-chamber, and any feelings of fellowship he might once have held for Carlo were now replaced in his heart with cold fear.

Carlo had bragged to him of the sums of money he took for denouncing men, and how Abram was the greatest prize of all, whom he would relinquish to the authorities as soon as the right price was offered. He hoped that at the next election he might extract a good deal from the Whig click, who were concerned that if Abram stood he might well win a seat in parliament – so favoured was he by the electorate. Carlo had the beginnings of a plan, he said, to denounce Abram as a dangerous incendiarist, bringing him into the hands of the police, in exchange for a handsome reward. However, in the end Abram and the other Radical candidates withdrew before the hustings, because they had not enough money to stand.

When Sir Robert Peel won the country in '41, Dan hoped that the end of Lord John Russell's Whig ministry would also entail the end of the spy system. However, he was dismayed to discover that Carlo had expectation of maintaining his practice under the new government. It was this discovery that prompted him to report his concerns to his father and to Sir James Campbell – the Lord Provost of Glasgow and a Conservative gentleman – on the grounds that it was well known how Sir Robert Peel abhorred the practice of paid informers, and would have preferred the whole country to establish modern police procedures, following the model of his Metropolitan force. However, the Lord Provost told Dan that there were certain individuals at large who sought to undermine our system of government and indeed our way of life, and they could not be permitted to succeed. He would not listen when Dan tried to tell him that it was the actions of the government agents that posed the worst portion of the threat, and that the spy system rather encouraged such behaviour by the rewards and status it offered to the worst sort of person. Instead, Sir James Campbell gave assurances that, upon assuming charge of the Treasury, Sir Robert Peel had insisted that, through the agency of the Commissioners at Scotland-yard and the Office of Home Affairs, the rewards accruing to informing were to be not at all great – and consequently the current pro rata was so miserable it could not possibly provide any sort of an incentive.

The Lord Provost did not seem to appreciate that there were a good many men who existed on the edge of starvation who would sell their own souls for a few pence.

Dan first visited London a month or so after the election: he came with the intention of finding Abram and warning him against any further association with Carlo – although the mechanism of his sojourn there is vague to him now, like a dream. His enterprise was fraught with danger, for he did not care to think what the consequences to himself would be if Carlo had realised what he was about. Duncan, however, would not listen to him. Carlo had, he argued, seen the light of God's glory and was determined to live by it evermore. He had redeemed himself utterly by working tirelessly for a year or so in the cause of suffragism; whereas McNaughten had never done a thing to change society for the better: indeed, he had gone about the place boasting of how he gave not a fig for politics, and had wasted that most sacred possession –the vote – all for the sake of saving himself a few shillings. He had acted only in his own selfish interests, despite being blessed with a good mind and a capacity for principled reasoning and hard-work. There was, Duncan told him, no room for him in the Great Struggle to which he and Carlo were enjoined. Perhaps he would be better suited to the Anti-Corn Law League, which sought only to preserve the interests of men like him.

For several months after, Dan remained in the most abject condition. Oppressiveness overtook him, and the pains in his head and occlusion of sense rarely abated even for a few minutes together. He gradually fell out of sorts, rarely troubling to keep himself clean or to eat sufficient. It was at this time that he gave up his shop to Carlo, having sold previously some of the better machines and tools. His thoughts were twisted and fractured. He did it almost on a whim one day, having reasoned that in this way he might draw Carlo away from Duncan and the spy network, and perhaps Duncan would come to learn of the act and he would be restored once more in his favour. Carlo gave his word that he would settle to the trade, but within a few weeks he had returned to his more lucrative line. There were many opportunities for rewards now that the Charter was being taken all over the nation, and millions were appending their name to it.

When the Charter failed in '42 Dan began to fear very much for the future of society. He wrote to the Whig Member for Glasgow expressing his anxiety that there was a spy system run by men who had every interest in provoking violence and dissent; but he received no reply. The summer riots were anathema to him – the fruition of all of his worst anxieties. And everywhere he read daily of Abram Duncan denounced in increasingly declamatory tones – a good deal of which he knew to be the work of Carlo, who had seized upon the opportunity and was trying once again to place Duncan in as bad a light as possible so that he might eventually sell him for a rich reward. Dan again and again attempted to alert the authorities, but was repeatedly turned away. He would recount all of his suspicions, and explain how he went in terror of what would be done to him if it were ever discovered that he had spoken out. Yet not one shred of hope was offered him.

When he heard that the Queen was to visit Edinburgh, and that Sir Robert Peel was to accompany her, it occurred to him that he might take advantage of the occasion to alert either of them or their attendants to the situation. This was his express purpose in travelling to the city. The riot that occurred in Edinburgh at the same time had nothing whatever to do with him; nor, as far as he could deduce, had it a thing to do with Carlo. He believed it to be one of those great ground-swells of popular opinion that occur from time to time: a genuine outpouring of discontent.

He saw Her Majesty ride past at such a dash, as if Francis, Oxford and Bean themselves were all in hot pursuit, and then he saw the Prime Minister's carriage coming up close behind. He heard a sort of thrumming, marked out by angry taunts, and then in an instant the crowd surged forward. Sir Robert Peel's driver used his whip well, lashing out in all directions; the nags reared, kicking a few of the rebels out of the way. But the crowd was quite large and began to throw flower-pots, stones, anything they could lay their hands on.

There was, of course, no protection since the guard had all raced on ahead with the royal party.

Dan stood there like a dummy. He saw Sir Robert Peel's crest upon the door of the carriage as it was lifted atop the great sway of bodies. He saw the driver, gashed and bloody. He was aware of the panic of the horses, the desperate scrabbling of their hooves upon the cobbles. His first thought was to flee, but the crowd took him up in a great heave, pushing him forward until he feared he might be crushed in the press of bodies; and it was at this moment that he came face to face with a gentleman who was squashed against the glass of the carriage window:

his mouth a perfect O of astonishment, his hands up before him as if in supplication.

Someone broke the window, or stoved the door in, or ripped it off its hinge – he did not see precisely what happened – and the mob began to pull the gentleman out, tossing him like a barrel and jeering all the while. Then one of them saw the wee cockade of tartan he was wearing at his breast, and began to tear at him, screeching, "A Drummond! A Drummond!"

They spat on the gentleman as he rolled into the gutter.

The whole spectacle made Dan vomit. He was trying to leave the scene, when one of the carriage horses succeeded in getting to its feet and, terrified, began to rear up, dashing what remained of the carriage to pieces. People were pulling one another out of the way of the flailing hooves, scattering in all directions, and for some reason, Dan seized the opportunity to do something that was quite contrary to his instinct. He dashed forward and, dodging the thrashings of the terrified animal, he pulled the gentleman to his feet. They ran into the back-streets, panting like hounds, hot and dusty, until the gentleman, who was rather large, signalled that he could go no further. They took shelter in a cellar and waited for the hooting of the crowd to fade, gradually replaced by the sound of the guard marching past and a volley of shots.

"Thank you," said the gentleman.

They bided in the cellar a while longer, discussing the terrible scene they had just witnessed, and lamenting the precarious state of the country. After a while had passed in this manner, Dan disclosed all of his fears.

It was the first time that anyone had listened to what he had to say. The gentleman did not laugh at him, nor did he try to dissuade him of his opinions and account. He nodded in agreement; he said that it was indeed a great shame that it was necessary to resort to the use of paid informers – especially when so much of what they reported was inaccurate, on account of there being every incentive to them to be the means of provoking much of the unrest that they then informed against.

The land, he said, was in chaos. But in chaos there was opportunity. All that was required was one event – a precipitous occurrence that would unite all the right-thinking people of the land against those who sought to destroy our way of life and constitution.

He spoke so well, with such reason and knowledge, Dan found himself transfixed.

At length they heard the guard return along the street, and the gentleman sent Dan out to hail them. It did not occur to him until it was too late what would be made of his appearance: hatless, the shabby apparel, much dishevelled; the bruises and cuts to his face.

The guard surrounded him immediately.

"Put your hands on your head, you dog," the officer command.

To them he was another lousy rebel to be shot dead in the streets. There was not even a thing on his person to tell who he was. In every direction he turned he was looking down the muzzle of a cocked musket, and he almost filled his breeks for fear.

It was at that very moment the gentleman emerged from the cellar.

"I am Mr. Drummond, Sir Robert Peel's Private Secretary," he said, "and this young man has just saved my life."

"It was," Dan said, having reached the conclusion of this part of his curious narrative, "a very decent thing to dae: it was perhaps the grandest thing that any man ever did for me in my whole life. It was even, you might say, sir, the principal reason fer everything that has happened. It is why I am here now."

He had suddenly the look of a man who sees before him the vision of a shining citadel built on the cinders of the old. He was saying that as soon as the matter was laid before him, he knew that he was the eccentric chuck, and that his purpose was to draw the line that connects us one to the other: the unfathomable architecture of belonging.

"You mean that you and Mr. Drummond," I said, very astonished, "you made the plot between you?"

He was smiling.

"It is the firmest proof I ever had," he said, "that our lives are determined by unseen forces, spirals emanating from the pericentre: the incessant motion o' the planets, the waves, of light, of air, of breath. One imbalance; one slight adjustment: that is all that is required. You see, sir, it is not enough to be: one must also *do*."

"You must be mad," I said. "Or think me so to believe such a thing." But I knew. A precipitous occurrence, some incident that would confirm the rule of law, uphold the constitution, allow the workings of fear to do their ameliatory business. "Mr. Drummond could be a very persuasive gentleman," I resumed. "I dare say we should be grateful that it is only the two perpetrators who appear to have paid the price for this, this *plot*." And for a moment it seemed to me that it might be possible to set the world in balance after all.

"The surface is crooked and rank an' buckled an' broken," said Mc-Naughten, "but if youse ever once believe that you could trace upon it the possibility of somethin' beautiful: a new beginnin' for one poor man, for all –" He halted. "Ah, now, *that* is true madness, sir, is it no'?"

It was as though at that moment he almost believed; and, reader, so did I.

We sat together for a few more moments, each contemplating his understanding of the strange pattern of this life. After a little while he looked up to the ceiling.

"I forgot tae say," he said, "that in ma lodgings there were two umbrellas suspended by their handles frae the top o' the clock-case."

CHAMBERS OF MR. ALEXANDER COCKBURN, Q.C.
PEAR TREE-COURT, TEMPLE,
A FEW DAYS LATER

Wherein Mr. Cockburn is congratulated and receives the finest reward of all.

And Cockie – whose reputation was assured, no matter what might be said, not only by virtue of having made a very brilliant speech, and having won the argument to boot, but by the full publicity of a very long report in the *Morning Chronicle* on the Monday morning following – was quite happy to meet with Lord Brougham at his chambers in order to discuss the wider implications of the celebrated trial. He would have liked to meet the gentleman at the House of Lords, but regretted that he was now so busy, with such a great quantity of cases, it was not possible for him, alas, at the present time, to leave the Temple.

The case had, he agreed, contained so many improprieties, so many evidences that ought never to have been given, so many statements drawn from witnesses that served as evidence but which, strictly speaking, by law were not admissable. He too shared Lord Brougham's intense discontent that the trial had been so abruptly terminated – as soon as the Judge had heard Mr. Forbes Winslow testify to the prisoner's delusion, it seemed he had decided to end the matter there and then. It was infinitely to have been preferred that the prosecution had brought forth medical witnesses of their own, but they had not. And of course the Solicitor General ought to have been asked to rebut the arguments of the defence; for as Sandy had previously told the Prime Minister, no one was more desirous of a fair fight then was he.

And yes, he too had found it particularly irksome that the Chief Justice had not stated explicitly the basis for his instructions to the Jury, though doubtless there was some degree of need in his action.

Lord Brougham twitched a little. "Her Majesty has written to the Prime Minister," he said. "She wishes to know why Judge Tindal advised the jury to pronounce the verdict of Not Guilty on account of Insanity whilst everybody was morally convinced that McNaughten was perfectly conscious and aware of what he did. And neither did Tindal state explicitly the basis for his instructions to the jury."

"I suppose we shall never know why he did that," said Sandy, the glimmer of a smile playing on his lips. "But these *occurrences* are not uncommon. When times are difficult, in particular, one must hold with a just hand the balance between a small indiscretion and the value of any number of human lives &c., &c."

"Her Majesty is concerned that the judges have too much power."

"Ah!" said Cockie.

"And I feel," said the gentleman looking very grave, "that it is my bounden duty to call to the attention of their Lordships the state of the law relating to the crimes of persons alleged to be labouring under partial insanity."

"It is certainly a very fashionable topic just now," said Cockie.

"Of course, I do so with the more reluctance, because any such proposition should come from either of my noble and learned friends. It is only the present emergency of the case that induces me to take it up."

Cockie stifled a yawn. "The Lord Chancellor has already approached me," he said, "seeking my opinion on what may be done, as he put it, *to remedy the evil*. He assured me that he intends to take an early opportunity of again adverting to the subject"

"I am very glad to hear it," said Lord Brougham.

"And now, if you'll excuse me, my Lord, I must conclude this interview; although I remain, of course, most anxious to render both you and the Lord Chancellor the best assistance in my power."

He had heard the approaching steps upon the stair, and Mr. Frayling in conversation at the door with Hatchett, and soon, in another moment, there they were – all three of them – in the front office. The boy looked tired and dishevelled and hungry, none of which was at all to be wondered at. But as Sandy came towards him with his arms open wide, he was rewarded with a slight shy smile.

"My Lord," said Cockie, without taking his eyes off the boy, "have you met my son? Mr. Alexander Dalton Cockburn, Lord Brougham. Lord Brougham, my boy, my own dear boy."

WHITEHALL,
A FEW WEEKS LATER.

The last in the book...

Inspector Hughes had to say that he was satisfied with the way it had all turned out. Well, and things always seemed a little easier to bear when the recollection of snow and ice and bleak winds had thawed so completely from the memory, and the days were a proper length, with the sunshine sparkling off the pavings and the buildings, in that interval of sweetness before the effluvia starts to take a hold in the full-blown heat of the summer. Leastways, he was pleased that the prisoner hadn't got turned off: first of all because, as he had often said to Silver (who had decided after all to stay in the force, though he did not make sergeant), it didn't do no good to make martyrs, see; and then again, because he had never been entirely settled in his own mind as to what it was, exactly, that did for Mr. Drummond.

O, it was quite clear that the bit o' lead shot fired into the Secretary's rump wouldn't have helped matters one jot – 'specially once them sawbones got their hands on the poor gentleman; but it was also the case that the law was very clear on the matter of murder, in that it required evidence of *intent*, and the Inspector had never believed that the Scotchman had intended to *kill* Mr. Drummond.

There were clever gentlemen, far cleverer than he was, who would say that, given the way it had all turned out, it'd be a sight more difficult from now on for insurrectionists to conceal their true intent behind the veil o' madness – Mr. Warren, for one (whom the Inspector permitted to follow him about from time to time on his night inspections of the Acre, in the interest of some book or other that the gentleman hoped to write). But they both knew that it wasn't the insurrectionists you had to watch, since them buggers were plainly not right in the head – the majority of 'em, anyway – no more than were the ranters and the ravers. And as Silver liked to say, there weren't a person in the whole metropolis who weren't mad on account of something or other. It was the disease of the times, you might say.

"There are more things in Heaven and Earth, Inspector, than are dreamt of in our philosophy," as Mr. Warren once said in the course of their perambulations, prior to having a bucket of slops poured over him in Duck-lane. And, yes, Inspector Hughes had to agree with him that there were.

He was pleased that the case had done so much for Mr. Cockburn's reputation, since Inspector Hughes had always thought that Mr. Cockburn was a very decent cove – and Lord knows, one needed all the decent coves one could find in this world. He saw him on occasion alighting from the steamer at Westminster Pier, and they always exchanged a nod or two. It had been a stroke of luck his valet coming in to the station-house that day and inquiring after a young country lad, for Inspector Hughes had only seen a boy matching the description the day before, very cold and hungry, and had pointed him towards a tuppenny rope over in St. Giles – which was just where the valet had found the lad.

And he was most gratified to see that Mr. Nicholson appeared to have learned some of his lessons, an' all. Well, things were difficult enough on the gleaming strip with all its ranters and sledge-beggars, and poor old apple-women and spies and ancient secrets and important gentlemen and serious business of state, without jesters hobbling about on crutches, in ludicrous trowsers and fanciful whiskers, waving loaves of bread about on pikes and foretelling the End o' the World for a spree or a jape.

"You know, you has a very good business here, Mr. Nicholson," he had observed one time not so long ago when he had accepted the fellow's invitation to partake of a glass of ale at the Garrick's Head. He didn't care to stay long enough to see the young ladies parading in next to nothing, for he didn't approve of that sort of thing, and besides, Mrs. Hughes had a plate of veal and gravy waiting for him at home; but he had been very impressed with the decorations of the place, not to say the calibre of the clientele, all the same. "Ho! Yes, indeed," he had affirmed, looking approvingly all about him, "you has a very good business indeed. And put it together with all your other interests, the newspapers and the print-shop, I wonder that you have time to frolic about the place causing mischief."

Mr. Nicholson had sighed and shrugged his shoulders.

"Ah, but you see, Inspector," he said, "the thing of it is I always seem to owe a lot of people."

"What do you mean, owe? What d'you owe 'em?"

"Money, favours, informations – O! I owes 'em a great deal. The demands made upon my worthless person are ceaseless. I should like to have a simple life, Inspector, with a pretty, slim-waisted little wife waiting for me at home, and a brood of handsome kiddies, and every once in a while a plate of beef skirt with some nice boiled potatoes tucked underneath it; but for some reason, I can't seem to shake off me creditors long enough to partake of any of that." Then he had smiled sadly. "I just can't seem to help meself."

"Well, if that really is the case, Mr. Nicholson," the Inspector had advised, "mind you confine your activities to those occasions when me own back is turned." And on that they had knocked glasses together.

It was the Superintendant who had told Inspector Hughes that Abram Duncan was earning a living as an itinerant preacher in Arbroath, and that Mrs. Dutton was keeping a new lodging-house over in Newington, thanks to the kind intervention of some gentleman who had seen her at the Bailey and been moved by her plight. As for that devilish blighter, Carlo, it was rumoured that he'd hot-footed it to America with a ballet-girl, where the pair of them was on the boards: a levitation and ventrilo-quism affair, as it happened. Some people just seemed to be able to get away with murder, didn't they?

Still, most days when he took his stroll up from the Devil's Acre to see King Charles and back again, the Inspector was satisfied that the gleaming strip had been restored to the semblance of order. Cer-tainly, things were a little more reliable now that Jack Tierney weren't permitted to do much spying in the metropolis. The Commissioners had informed the Under-Secretary at the Home Office that they would be running down their Active Duty force once O'Connor and all the Chartists were convicted by Judge Abinger at Staffordshire, and so the scranning cove was kept busy out of town these days. He was going to Wales soon, to investigate some toll-gate smashing that had been going on there for a while. Yes, and the Welchies were welcome to him and his bullies, poor little buggers.

And so it was all in the past now, and life went on.

He hadn't thought about the token for a good long while; it had quite slipped from his mind. But one Sunday, a couple of weeks ago, he and the boy had taken a stroll up to Charing-cross and into the Adelaide Gallery. That blessed boy had a great passion on him for the steam gun, and had been asking for a while if they might go and see it, and well, Inspector Hughes had never been in the scientific galleries before – al-though he had read a great deal about them in the *Reformers Gazette*.

The boy and he particularly enjoyed the American native hut; and the electro-magnets; and the voltaic light, which was indeed very bright; and a galvanic watch which had not needed winding in twenty years; and the microscopic images silhouetted on the wall, which the boy had later said was his favourite part. They had a look, too, at the

Jacquard loom – which was all very clever though the silk it made weren't a patch on that his old pa had used to turn out by hand in Bethnal-green. Inspector Hughes had tried to explain how it worked, but the boy weren't too good at listening.

And as for the steam gun, well, Inspector Hughes didn't think it would do in a war; and the noise it made as it fired off its bullets into the target! Lor'! It was enough to wake the dead. He had been glad to leave the boy with its marvellous rat-a-tat-tatting, and take a little stroll about the other exhibits.

He came across a cabinet, standing all forlorn in a corner of the gallery. He had no idea what it did, and it required a ha'penny to find out; but he was in a munificent mood, not to say curious, so he thought he'd give it a go. He had dropped his coin in a slot at the top of the cabinet, and a great huffing and a puffing ensued as two pistons began to move up and down either side of a great brass chimney, out of the top of which poured billows of pure white smoke, and a great whirring and chugging filled the corner of the gallery, so loud that several people had stopped to stare. He had begun to wish he hadn't been so curious when, shortly after it had started, the machine slowed down and then stopped altogether, much to the Inspector's relief.

He had moved off smartly to find the boy, who'd been calling to him to go and see the 'gyptians, when an elderly gentleman had tapped him on the shoulder.

"Excuse me, Constable," he said, indicating the machine, "but I believe that you have forgotten to collect your coin."

He had returned to the confounded machine, and sure enough, there had been a little aperture at the bottom of the cabinet. He'd had to bend down to reach inside it and retrieve his ha'penny.

"Well, I never," he had said, much amused.

He had been about to put it back in his pocket, when the arc of the rainbow had caught his eye; then he'd seen the cloud sitting beneath it, and, when he had turned it over, there on the other side was inscribed as clear as day: GENESIS IX xiii.

The Final Meeting

After a little while I went to take my leave of him. I had fallen into an interesting and convivial conversation over a plate of cold beef and some cheese with the master and one or two other gentlemen who had an interest in the subject of lunacy; but now it was growing late. I found him in the yard knitting, which is, apparently, the chief occupation of the men in that place. It was that hour or so before sunset, and the gray surrounds were burnished and lifted a little. Our endeavour was at an end, and there was nothing more that he could tell me. Our recent meetings had become more and more sporadically placed, and often declined all too quickly into that somewhat maudlin philosophising to which the untrained mind is all too prey. However, there remained one piece of information I wished to impart to him; one more attempt at eliciting a reaction.

"You know," I told him carefully "that Sir Robert Peel is dead? He fell from his horse while riding on Constitution Hill a fortnight ago. He died in great pain a few days later."

He betrayed no emotion, nor exhibited the slightest concern. He wrapped the yarn around his forefinger, concentrating all his efforts upon the agitation of needles.

"One should have thought," I continued, "that, considering what has happened, you would have felt some interest in that gentleman."

He looked at me, a quick sidelong glance, the slight suggestive smile playing about his lips. It was an admonitory look, the like of which I had seen often enough in our communication to understand that it meant he had never spoken on *that* subject, and now never would.

"And how are you, McNaughten?" I asked.

"Ach," he said, quoting those pathetic words of Horace, albeit in the vernacular, "'*what exile from his country can from himself escape?*'"

For this was the continual burthen of his complaint: that he is ill-used in that place and ought by now to be allowed to return to his native Glasgow; then all would be well with him, &c., &c. Naturally, his complaints were altogether unfounded, for he was treated with the utmost

[474]

kindness consistent with his situation; and as he had exhibited neither violence, nor ill-behaviour of any sort, it had never been necessary to resort to any measure of physical coercion, apart from a brief period two or three years ago when he refused to eat and had to be forcibly fed with the stomach pump, for his own good.

Shortly afterwards, I left him there. As I crossed the yard, the sun was setting and a narrow filament of blue-gray lambency streaking across the horizon like a distant sea. When I was out of his sight, I took one final look back and saw him put away his knitting. Then he placed his hands in his jacket pockets, and as the light dropped from the sky, walked very rapidly to and fro, his face intent on the ground as if he were tracing there the lineaments of some intricate pattern that only he could see.

S. W. 30th July, 1850.

[THE END]

Daniel McNaughten was committed to the Bethlem Royal Hospital on March 15th, 1843, under an order from Sir James Graham, Her Majesty's Secretary of State for the Home Department. He died at Broadmoor Asylum for the Criminally Insane on May 3rd, 1865, having been transferred there soon after its opening a year before. The last entry on his case-sheet reads: Gradually sank and died at 1.10a.m. The cause of death was given as anaemia, brain disease and gradual failure of the heart's action.

THE M'NAUGHTEN RULES

The verdict, and the question of the nature and extent of the unsoundness of mind which would excuse the commission of a felony of this sort, having been made the subject of debate in the House of Lords, it was determined to take the opinion of the Judges on the law governing such cases. Accordingly, on the 26th May, all the Judges attended their Lordships, but no questions were then put.

On the 19th June, the Judges again attended the House of Lords; when (no argument having been had) the following questions of law were propounded to them:

1st. What is the law respecting alleged crimes committed by persons afflicted with insane delusion, in respect of one or more particular subjects or persons: as, for instance, where at the time of the commission of the alleged crime, the accused knew he was acting contrary to law, but did the act complained of with a view, under the influence of insane delusion, of redressing or revenging some supposed grievance or injury, or of producing some supposed public benefit?

2nd. What are the proper questions to be submitted to the jury, when a person alleged to be afflicted with insane delusion respecting one or more particular subjects or persons, is charged with the commission of a crime (murder, for example), and insanity is set up as a defence?

3rd. In what terms ought the question to be left to the jury, as to the prisoner's state of mind at the time when the act was committed?

4th. If a person under an insane delusion as to existing facts, commits an offence in consequence thereof, is he thereby excused?

5th. Can a medical man conversant with the disease of insanity, who never saw the prisoner previously to the trial, but who was present during the whole trial and the examination of all the witnesses, be asked his opinion as to the state of the prisoner's mind at the time of the commission of the alleged crime, or his opinion whether the prisoner was conscious at the time of doing the act, that he was acting contrary to law, or whether he was labouring under any and what delusion at the time?

The fifteen Judges answered each of the questions in turn, and all but one of them were of accord with the conclusion that in order to establish a defence on the grounds of insanity, it must clearly be proven that, at the time of committing the act, the party accused was labouring under such a defect of reason, from disease of the mind, as not to know the nature and quality of the act he was doing; or, if he did know it, that he did not know he was doing what was wrong.

A person committing a criminal act under the influence of an insane delusion is therefore punishable if he knew that what he did was wrong. A person labouring under a partial delusion only, who is not in other respects insane, must be considered in the same relationship to responsibility as if the grounding facts of the delusion were real. And a doctor who has never examined the accused cannot ever be asked his opinion of the defendant's state of mind at the time he committed the offence. Such a question, it was agreed, involves a judgement on the truth of the facts, which is the province of the jury.

Only one of the judges dissented, vigorously objecting to having been asked to supply answers to abstract questions without having heard the argument of counsel, and fearing that the answers to such questions might embarrass the administration of justice when they are cited in criminal trials. As to the rest, nobody appeared to mind very much at all that their findings almost certainly went against the finding of Justice Tindal (who did not dissent) in the inciting case; and if the rules were to be applied post judice, M'Naughten would almost certainly have been found guilty, and hanged.

And nobody, apart from the one dissenter, appeared to fear that the form and manner in which the Judges had been required to give the matter their consideration gave it such a vaunted authority that any subsequent modification was an impossibility.

When they were done the Lords expressed their grateful thanks to the Judges; the Lord Chancellor summing up the opinion of them all when he affirmed the right of his noble and learned friends to have the opinions of judges on abstract questions of existing law. He thanked them for the attention and learning with which they had answered those questions.

And it would be more than a hundred years before anyone could ever again in a court of law submit successfully as Cockie had done, that an accused person was not responsible if his unlawful act was the product of mental disease or defect, whether he knew or not that what he did was wrong.

The Rules were known thereafter as the M'Naughten Rules.

ACKNOWLEDGEMENTS

A number of individuals and institutions are owed thanks for the help and support they have given to me during the research and development of this book. In no particular order, I would like to acknowledge the staff of the British Library and the British Library Newspaper Collections at Colindale; the National Archives, Kew; the Wellcome Institute; the National Library of Wales; the General Register Office of England and Wales; the General Register Office of Scotland; the Mitchell Library, Glasgow; the Parlimentary Archives, Westminster; and the Metropolitan Archives, London. Thanks are also due to Lesley Whitelaw of the Middle Temple Archives; Guy Holborn of the Lincoln's Inn Library; Rosemary Moodie and Seonaid McDonald of the HBOS Bank Archives; and the Glasgow and West of Scotland Family History Society. Andrew Roberts's excellent website on the Lunacy Commission (http://www.mdx.ac.uk/WWW/STUDY/1.HTM) was invaluable in tracking down primary sources and giving a context to this dense terrain; as was Mark Crail's Chartist Ancestors site (http://www.chartists.net). Both sites are the worthy results of passion and erudition, and give internet research a good name.

On a personal note, I would like to thank my husband and two sons for living with this story as long as I have, and to say sorry for all the burnt suppers. Sincere thanks are also due to Aurea Carpenter and Rebecca Nicolson at Short Books for their patience, endurance and trust that a book would materialise out of the miasma of research and dithering. My agent, Kate Jones, was there at the conception, and I wish every day that she could be here still to see the outcome. And finally, although this story does not have much that is good to say about doctors, I would like to express my heartfelt gratititude to four: Dr Robin Howard, Mr. Neil Kitchen, Mr. George Ladas and Dr. Sanjay Popat.

Siân Busby,
London, December 2008

Siân Busby is an award-winning writer, broadcaster and film maker. She is married to the BBC Business Editor, Robert Peston, and has two children. She lives in North London.